Looking Landwards

Stories Commemorating the 75th Anniversary of
The Institution of Agricultural Engineers

IAgrE

**INSTITUTION OF
AGRICULTURAL
ENGINEERS**

75 Years of promoting
professionalism
1938 – 2013

Looking Landwards

Edited by Ian Whates

NewCon Press
England

First edition, published in the UK October 2013
by NewCon Press
in association with The Institution of Agricultural Engineers

NCP 061 (hardback)
NCP 062 (softback)

10 9 8 7 6 5 4 3 2 1

Contents

Looking Landwards

An Introduction

Andy Newbold & Chris Whetnall

The Institution of Agricultural Engineers (IAgrE) was set up seventy-five years ago by a group of far seeing engineers who saw the need to establish agricultural engineering as a profession in its own right.

UK agriculture has always been quick to take up new technologies and, in one way or another, agricultural engineers have to be involved in this. With their unique combination of engineering knowledge and skill sets, ag-engineers are true multi-disciplinary engineers. It is this multidisciplinary aspect that is, and will be, needed to solve the problems of global food security.

Who would have imagined seventy-five years ago that the profession would have seen changes such as the ability for the manufacturers of a combine harvester to control a machine in real time in the field thousands of miles from the factory where it was produced? Or that a cow could choose when and how often it is milked and that the complete milking process would be controlled, again in real time, by robotics with the farmer monitoring things remotely on his smart phone. So what would have been science fiction only twenty years ago is now a reality.

Long before the advent of computer control of machines, science fiction writers were visualising such things. Indeed, it is now probably only a preoccupation with health and safety issues that holds back the wholesale introduction of such technologies. The technology exists for autonomous driverless tractors but a major leap in faith will be required before we see them in the fields as a matter of course.

And so it seemed a good idea that, in its 75th anniversary year, rather than update the history of IAgrE, we should promote a forward looking event. Members of IAgrE are sometimes asked to outline their vision for the future and, indeed, any company wishing to remain in business must take a view as to where their sector will be in say five, ten and twenty years' time. So rather than extend the notion of IAgrE members articulating their vision based on their understanding of reality, the decision was made to open this vision to the public in the form of a science fiction competition.

The response has been tremendous. What you read here is just a proportion of the submissions. Who knows, in amongst the authors may be those whose vision, as outlined in their story, becomes reality. Just like Isaac Asimov, who first used the word *robotics* in print back in 1942. It is now commonplace, as is their use in so many areas of engineering. Of course there is the possibility that in twenty years' time, the authors of some of these stories may look back on their efforts with embarrassment... "How could I have got is so wrong?" may be the cry.

We must thank those whose efforts have brought this anthology to life. The authors of course, Ian Whates of NewCon Press, who has worked so hard to get this anthology in to print, a loyal IAgrE member whose bright idea this originally was (we will not embarrass him for fear that his employer may not be aware of the time spent in reading submissions) and to those members and Trustees of IAgrE who supported the idea from the outset.

We hope you enjoy this read.

Andy Newbold – IAgrE President 2012 – 2014
Chris Whetnall – IAgrE CEO 1999 – 2013
August 2013

The Blossom Project

M Frost

Isa had never seen a real cow before. Through the portal into the next cubicle, she made out the creamy shape of what looked to be a large dog with feet like a horse and ears that stuck out to the side. *It's bigger than I expected from the pictures,* she thought.

She watched her mother call up the program and step onto the photometric pad. Beams of light emerging from the floor and ceiling connected in front of her. She focused on her mother's olive-skinned hands as they interrupted the beams of light in a specified, three-dimensional sequence. Isa would have used BCI to control the program, but she knew her mother hated the way the neural interface left her skin itching for days.

Isa gasped as the normal photometrics suddenly swirled and coalesced into a highly-resolved structure, with much more advanced imaging than anything Isa had experienced with her Xvid games. Inside a cocoon of red latticework, something was moving. *What is that?*

Her mother seemed to read her thoughts. "Isa, this is the calf I told you about. Once she's born, this girl will save the world…" She trailed off, squinting, then spun her hands. Now, the projection was between the two of them. Isa couldn't see the command her mother used, but she did see her mother grab the cloven nib of one of the calf's feet.

Isa jumped off the air cushion. She was adept at interactive games, but this was beyond anything she had ever seen. *Mother's actually touching the baby!* She watched, fascinated, as her mother initiated a remote interface and translinked a program directly into the calf's brain. After an additional moment of study, Isa's mother logged out of the photometrics.

Isa glanced at the cow. Her bright coat had turned orange with sweat, but any discomfort she had felt during the procedure appeared to have passed.

"Isn't she pretty? I call her Blossom, after the cow who saved the world from smallpox." Her mother joined Isa. "To be fair, Blossom had help from a little boy, James, who was just a few years younger than you are now when Jenner gave him the cowpox vaccine."

Isa knew about Entpox, the virus that caused the Outbreak, and she knew that her mother was working on a vaccine, but she had never heard of smallpox.

"It's gone now, eradicated," the older woman explained when Isa asked. "But over a hundred years ago it killed a lot of people, just like *Entomopoxvirinae –*" She corrected herself, "Entpox does today."

She treats me like a baby sometimes. "I know the Latin name," Isa said, annoyed. The hurt look on her mother's face made her regret the words almost immediately. *Mother rarely talks about her work, and this is the first time I've even seen the animal lab.* As a peace offering, Isa asked, "Did any cows survive naturally, I mean, outside of places like this?"

Her mother's reply was interrupted as a lithe, younger man walked in. "Did any cows survive naturally?" he repeated in a thick accent that Isa could not place, then scoffed. "You mean in Auzealand, where they banned Ent-Crops from the start. Not like we'll ever see *those* cows. Or sheep. Auzea bordermen are as likely to shoot first as ask questions." He squatted down to consider Isa. "Have you ever met an Auzealander?"

Isa caught the flutter of concern on her mother's face. She stared at the man. *His skin is darker than mine, but only a little,* she noticed. "No," she told the man, knowing enough to lie.

"Ah, too bad," he said, shrugging his narrow shoulders. "I have hundreds of questions for them. It's been a while since we raised cows on any kind of scale." He turned to Isa's mother. "Genene, how did the surgery go?"

"Fine, Chatresh" Isa's mother replied. "I integrated the improved *entX* gene cassette and then performed the downlink. The neurobehavioral macro executed properly."

Isa only understood the software side of the conversation. "What's the macro for?" She blurted, angry at the man for interrupting her time with her mother.

With a look that Isa took for a smirk, Chatresh replied, pointing to Blossom. "The macro is to help us tell the calf what to do and where to go remotely. We don't want to touch it too much, you see, part of the quarantine. But we need it to do what we ask because this special little cow shares a gene with you and your mother."

"You mean, the reason we survived the Outbreak."

"Indeed. And the reason you live here with all of us mad scientists instead of in a school compound." Chatresh reached to tweak her nose, but Isa squirmed out of his reach. "We've just improved our odds a bit. A dollop of epigenetics, a dash of genetic engineering. If we're successful, the calf will grow up to produce milk – lots and lots of milk – that contains a protein to protect people from Entpox. Then, we'll clone her and be well on our way to not only eradicating Entpox but also rebuilding the dairy industry."

"Farm cities again?" Isa frowned, remembering a conversation her mother once had with her father, the one time she had actually seen Jack through a video Net hack. She had understood that the old farm cities were responsible for vast wastelands in which no human could live.

The look of alarm on her mother's face told her Isa had made a mistake.

"Farm cities?" Chatresh repeated slowly, then continued in a too-boisterous voice. "No, little Isa, beautiful farm pods in farm TOWERS! Come, let me show you."

He held out his hand, and Isa knew enough to play along, to try to cover the damage she had done. She put her hand in his.

Genene watched the botanist show off his ecopods. Isa seemed genuinely delighted to look through the portals at the mini-ecosystems Chatresh and his team had designed for each of the expected calf clones, keeping them isolated to prevent potential disease spread while optimising the nutrient balance to grow Entpox-resistant forage alongside the hoped-for Guernseys. For the moment, only crops grew in the pods, supplemented with synthetic fertilizers instead of organic manure.

She tried to calculate the impact of Isa's slip of the tongue. *Farm cities – she must have picked that up from Jack. Isa doesn't know how charged that term is.* Genene wasn't sure which would be worse: Chatresh thinking that she herself was the source, or that Isa had contact with an Auzealander. *Is he going to blackmail me with this?* Her concern deepened. *If he figures out that Jack and I have been communicating, I could face treason. Jail would hardly be worse than the isolation we have at the lab, but I can't bear the thought of being cut off from my work.*

Or Isa, Genene thought with a pang. As they took a transparent tube up through the glittering tower of ecopods, which spiralled off the lift like nucleotide spokes on a genetic helix, she twisted her hair anxiously. *Why did I bring Isa today? Because she's so starved for my company these days, since there are no other children here? Because I wanted her to see why we are quarantined on an island so we don't accidentally do as much harm with our genetic tinkering as the Ent-Crops did?*

She pondered the more realistic reason. *So she understands later why I didn't try to join Jack? Maybe I'm afraid she's going to hate me once she finds out what we could have had. A little farm near Jack's family on North Island with some cows and a herd of sheep and lush grazing lands as far as the eye can see.* Genene recognized that, since she had never visited New Zealand before, this was a fantasy. But it was the image she had nurtured since surviving the first days of the Outbreak, when she realized that she was pregnant by a man who, through fate, had been visiting the Maori side of his family when the Outbreak began. The political unrest that followed – which included the unlikely union of Australia and New Zealand to protect themselves and their agriculture from the rest of the infected world – had separated her from Jack.

Several years ago, on one of their illegal Net hacks, Jack had first broached the possibility that she and Isa might join him in Auzealand. Genene had demurred, feeling guilty. She knew Jack had worked his contacts in the government to obtain a formal offer for political asylum for her and Isa, made possible only because they were immune to Entpox and at a quarantined facility to boot. *And because my knowledge would be invaluable to Auzealand's government, I have to admit.* However, her research team had just made their first breakthrough, successfully growing ruminant embryos in an artificial womb, since no surrogate cows existed anymore. She felt she had to stay, since – *what line had she sold the funders?* – her research 'held the promise of a new era of health and prosperity for the world'.

Except in Auzealand, the joint WHO-OIE's global eradication program to contain Entpox had wiped out all but the most isolated herds. The disease was equally infectious to people and ruminants, and since the medical community had no reliable tests at the time to determine who carried the disease, people without symptoms spread

Entpox into even carefully quarantined collections.

The only ruminants to survive were the thousands of embryos frozen for research or genetic preservation. She recalled her relief at finding many of the laboratories intact, including private banks like Swiss Village Farm that she had expected to be plundered in the riots that accompanied the early years of the Outbreak. *How many people died from Entpox? Probably fewer than those who died of starvation after we killed all the cows and burned most of the crops.*

"What do you think, Genene?" Chatresh interrupted her train of thought.

"Excuse me?" She was flustered. *I should have been paying more attention to what he was telling Isa.*

"Do these look like farm cities to you?" He asked, his tone guarded.

"No," she replied, her heart thudding in her chest.

Isa woke with a start. She could hear her mother's voice, low but tense, in the next room. *Why is she up so late?* Suddenly, she bolted up in her bed, recognizing a second voice, also low, also tense. *That's Dad!*

Trying not to make a sound, Isa crept from her bunk to the door. She crouched low, just in case they had video on, but when she peeked into the main room, the photometric pad was dark. *We only ever did video that one time. Too dangerous, Dad said.*

Isa heard her father say, "Do you think they mean to harm her?" He sounded concerned.

Her mother replied, "I don't – I don't know. I think Chatresh was warning me."

"Warning you?"

"As a… I wouldn't say friend. As a colleague who recognises that such views might not be politic at this time and who might use this information to his advantage. The corporations and the global economy are only just now beginning to recover. Considering how much blame the ag sector has taken…" Her mother absently twisted thin locks of hair until they were wound as tight as a string, a gesture Isa only saw when she was troubled.

She's been doing that a lot since she took me to the lab. With a pang, Isa recognized the cause. *Farm cities. This is my fault.*

"Rightly or wrongly," her father replied, then paused for a long

13

time. "I can be there in five days."

Her mother dropped the lock of hair, and it unwound with a flip. "I'm still not sure. The calf –"

Isa heard her father sigh, a deep, accepting sound. "You always did put animals first. It's one of the things I love about you."

"Isa –"

Isa was startled, afraid at first that her mother had seen her.

"Yes?" Jack prompted.

"For Isa." Her mother relented. "Five days?"

"Perhaps sooner."

Isa realized that they were talking about her. *Are we leaving?* She was not supposed to know that her father wanted them to join him in Auzealand, but this was not the first time she had spied on one of their conversations.

"Send me the hacks." Genene said, then added, "Only you, Jack. You're the only person I know in the world who could pull this off. You know what the defences are like here. We're more secure than the military."

Isa could imagine her father shrugging, humble. "It's a gift."

"Isa shares your gift," her mother said softly, then ended the transmission. Into the darkness, Genene added, "She should be with you."

Anxious, Isa snuck back to her bunk, crawling between the covers. *What changed? Is she worried that something is going to happen to me because of what I said about the farm cities? Or is it something else?*

Isa thought of the shiny room where the doctors performed tests on her every week, and shuddered.

Genene watched her daughter swallow a cup of LyteWater and felt guilty. *Drugging my own daughter? I think this is a new low for me.* She thought she had reached the bottom when she first came to this facility in the first years of the Outbreak, agreeing to let the project study her and Isa in return for, not just their safety in the decaying political climate, but the scientific opportunities the project offered.

As Isa's eyes started to droop, Genene ran her fingers across her daughter's cool brow. *Forgive me, my darling. I've made a lot of mistakes.* Thinking of what she was about to do, Genene sat down beside her daughter, fighting panic. *Jack's right. Isa's in danger here. The tests are getting more invasive, and what I'm about to do is no worse than what her doctors already have done. If she stays, she'll be a research pincushion for the rest of her life.*

Once she was certain Isa would not wake, Genene lifted her unresisting body and carried her to the tube. As they descended the thirty storeys to the animal research suite, Isa's body seemed to get heavier. Genene shifted to bear more of her daughter's weight on her shoulder. *I have to trust that Jack's code turned the surveillance cameras off.*

She cued the door, not to the photometrics room, but to Blossom's cubicle. Blossom wasn't there, since the cow spent most of her time in an ecopod when they weren't running diagnostics. The room still had a faint, bovine aroma to it, not entirely masked by the odor of disinfectant. Genene found it comforting, since the smell reminded her of her large animal rotations in veterinary school, before the Outbreak.

She set Isa on the floor, then hurried to the photometrics lab. After booting the system, she initiated Jack's second hack. This one let her operate the genetics core, which normally was date-time restricted to prevent access outside of designated experiments. Her fingers flashing in the beams of light, Genene accessed the *entX* cassette, then activated the surgical program. *Just a few changes, that's all I need to keep it stable in primate cells instead of bovine ones.* Careful not to leave a trace of her work in the genetics core, Genene isolated the code to the workspace, then swapped the insertion sequence with the new one.

As the sequences aligned properly, she breathed thanks to each of her comparative genetics professors, ending with the man who had been her mentor and more. Earl Davidson had never been her lover, but Genene knew that was only because *he* could not get past the impropriety. She had long since admitted to herself that she had initially taken up with Jack to make Earl jealous.

Holding the modified *entX* code in one hand, she reached for her daughter's ankle with the other.

Unethical. Genene heard Earl's voice echo in her head.

Unethical? That moral code was for a different time. Besides, Earl, you broke my heart when you died of the pox. You have no right to trouble me now.

She inserted the gene into the thin marrow of her daughter's tiny fibula, and saw, through the portal, her daughter's calf twitch. Then Genene used Jack's hack to scrub any trace of what she had done.

Genene felt the dampness of tears on her cheeks. *I hope this can help you and your people create a vaccine, Jack. This – and Isa – are all I can give.*

Isa opened her eyes, uncertain why the world seemed so fuzzy and distant. Her left ankle stung, and she automatically moved to rub it. Her mother's slap on her wrist stopped her, and woke her further.

"Why did you do that?" Isa asked, hurt.

"Don't touch it." Her mother hissed. "Be quiet."

Isa had never seen her mother look so unsettled, with a thick lock of her black hair loose across her forehead.

"I don't understand."

"You don't need to understand." Genene's tone was sharp, but not angry. "Can you stand?"

To her surprise, although her ankle tingled when she moved, Isa could walk. In the dark, they left their quarters and took one tube to a corridor Isa had never seen, then took another, down. Then sideways. When the door opened, she smelled salt and heard the roar of the ocean. Her apprehension warred with excitement. Since her mother was so busy and access to the aquaponics lab was restricted, Isa rarely got to see the ocean.

As her mother helped her into an airboat, Isa realized with another thrill that she might meet her father in person for the first time. The craft rose smoothly, with only the slightest hum. Genene directed it away from the research facility and towards the great dark shadows that Isa knew to be the aquaponics tanks. *They hold the ocean back,* she thought, remembering her lessons. *Dyke against the rising sea, and source of food.*

"Is the project letting us go?" Isa asked.

In reply, her mother shook her head no. Suddenly queasy, Isa hunched lower in the boat as it skimmed past the last tank and over a ceaseless blackness that she knew to be the sea.

Isa saw a flash that she thought at first was lightning. Her mother saw it too, and revved the engine. The airboat bobbled, but increased speed.

When another flash illuminated her mother's face, Isa realized it was a rotating beacon from the island. *They'll see us!*

Her mother seemed to have the same concern, and angled the boat lower, fighting the anti-grav system. They lost speed, but continued course closer to the waves.

A siren sounded, distant but unmistakable.

Isa felt as if she had been expecting it. She glanced at her mother, but couldn't make out her features in the darkness.

The tinny noise of the siren repeated, driving out the kernel of hope that had been growing in Isa for the past two days and replacing it with a knot of anxiety.

Her mother had to shout over the now constant sound of the siren as she crossed the boat. "I need you to trust me. Can you do that?"

"Yes," Isa replied, trying to sound brave.

"Get in this pod."

Isa found the lips of the escape pod with her fingers. When she hesitated, her mother lifted her roughly and shut her in. Sounds muffled as her mother closed the lid against her.

"No!" Isa yelled, realizing with a jolt that the pod was meant only for one.

She can't hear me. Isa fumbled for the comm button, hit it. "Mother, no!" At first, she thought that her mother meant to serve as a diversion for the guards, leading them away from the rendezvous.

"Darling, turn off the comm. Do not activate the lights. Now listen – no, just listen to me and do exactly what I tell you to do. Don't tell anyone about your ankle except your father. *Just* your father, do you hear me?"

"Yes," Isa replied, choked, as she recognized instead that her mother had never intended to come with her.

"Don't trust anyone except him and his family. Tell *no one else* about Blossom, are we clear?" Isa heard tears break the calm in her mother's voice.

Before Isa could muster the strength to say *I love you* despite her feeling of betrayal, the pod was flung overboard. Isa bit off a scream as the shell hit the water. Buffeted at first by the waves, the pod quickly descended. As her ears began to pop, Isa remembered to cut the comm, and after that, the descent was silent and dark.

When the pod bumped against the silt floor of the ocean, Isa wondered if she was going to die, but then reasoned that her mother would never do that to her.

But she would leave me. The thought ate a hole in her stomach.

An hour passed. Isa's ankle itched. Unable to scratch it, all she could do was focus on the itching, which was maddening. Then, because she remembered that the comm was off, she screamed for a while.

When her voice failed, she curled into a foetal position and waited. *For the guards or for father?*

When he did come, as a submarine cutting through the dark waters, Isa screamed again, out of surprise this time as light flooded her pod. Bright white spots clouded her vision as she felt the pod being secured. After a faint clank of metal, the lid was opened.

Large, calloused hands lifted her out of the pod. What she recognized was her father's voice. "Isa, you're safe."

"She didn't come," Isa accused him with her raspy, angry voice. "Why didn't you make her come?"

Jack replied softly, sounding resigned. "She stayed to deliver the calf."

With a sob, Isa launched herself into her father's arms.

In Genene's vision, green tongues of grass whisked Isa's heels as she chased a lamb, while Jack's herding dog barked in the distance. Two other children, her cousins, ran beside Isa. They were happy and healthy.

When Genene opened her eyes, the cold stares of the tribunal greeted her instead, as they had every morning for the past few weeks.

She had been found far from the rendezvous site, hours after Jack signalled to her that he had recovered Isa. She had already run a hack in her own quarters to destroy any trace of her communications with Auzealand. After Jack's signal, she had run the same hack on her portable pad, then fractured it with a metal hook and threw it in the ocean.

Destroying the pad hadn't made her feel better. *I have only Jack's word that Isa won't be as much a research subject in Auzealand as she was here.*

One of the judges spoke. "Tell us again what happened on the night of May 31, 2071."

Genene replied with her rehearsed story, careful never to deviate from the version of events she had constructed, a blend of fabrication and truth. She recognised that the tribunal was scrutinising every detail for signs of discrepancy. Still, her heart twisted, as it did every time she planted the blame on Isa. "I realised on May 20, when I heard Isa use that phrase…"

"Farm cities?" One of the funding representatives clarified.

"Yes," Genene acknowledged. "I had suspected for some time that she might be communicating with her father, and this confirmed it."

The admiral demanded, "Why should we believe that a girl could bypass our secure systems?"

"You've all seen her scores. She has her father's gift with computers, but I suspect that Jack initiated contact and taught her what to do. On May 31, I discovered her missing and went looking for her." Facing the possibility she might never see Isa again put a choke in Genene's voice as she lied to the tribunal. "I'm grateful to the project for helping me look for her that night."

She already had heard rumours that, in her absence, Blossom's pregnancy was not proceeding normally. *Survival, that's what this is about. Not mine, but the survival of the project.*

As if in answer to her concern, the hearing was interrupted. Chatresh, his normally swarthy face grey, hurried into the room and passed a note to their scientific supervisor.

Blossom? Genene tugged at a thin lock of hair, breaking several strands.

She could not hear most of the whispered discussion among the tribunal members that followed, but she could tell that the argument was heated. She did hear one thing Chatresh said, in response to a question. "She's the only veterinarian. I can't do it." At that, several members of the tribunal turned and stared at her.

They have to let me help, that's what I've been counting on.

The admiral finally addressed Genene. "It appears the precious calf is coming into this world improperly positioned and ahead of schedule."

Exactly twenty-seven days ahead of schedule. Genene fretted. *While trouble with Blossom gets me back to the lab, I'm not ready to make another sacrifice. Not so soon after giving up Isa.*

"Today's hearing is postponed." The admiral locked eyes with Genene before letting his gavel fall.

As if I need reminding that my future depends on the project's success.

An hour later, Genene zipped the biosuit and donned the close-fitting cap. The face shield molded to her face, and she had to fight the usual moment of alarm before her body accepted that she could breathe normally. When Chatresh expressed reservations, she replied, "Dystocia is best fixed the old fashioned way."

As she entered the cubicle, Blossom was sweating and pacing. With a grunt, the Guernsey went down, then stood again, kicking at her belly.

Genene remembered the old days of halters and leads as she activated the cow's neurobehavioral macro. Blossom quieted.

Now for May Rose. Genene had finally settled on the name she would call the calf, regardless of whatever alphanumeric code the project decided to assign. *After a prize Guernsey cow from the 19th century whose picture I found in our Net archives.*

For the first time in over a decade, Genene slid her arms into a cow's uterus, feeling the sharp point of Rose's right front hoof. *It's just like riding a bike,* Genene told herself, then grimaced at the irony. *I haven't touched a bike since the Outbreak either.*

She pushed the calf deeper into the womb to unpin her head and the leg that were trapped. Then, because she didn't want to damage the uterus, Genene let Blossom's contractions do most of the work. As Rose started to emerge, her pink lips moving soundlessly, Genene pulled.

After a long, desperate moment as Rose squeezed through Blossom's pelvis, Genene rocked back with the weight of the calf in her arms. They collapsed gracelessly onto an air cushion.

Blossom turned, her eyes wide.

"Surprised you, didn't she?" Genene asked the cow, giddy with relief. She activated the suit mechanics so she could lift the calf and let any remaining fluid drain from her lungs, then set her back down carefully. Blossom, driven not by the macro but by some deep bovine instinct, began to lick strings of placenta off Rose's ruby coat.

Genene thought again of Isa on her green island. *A fresh start – for both of us, I hope.*

Contraband

Terry Martin

"Drone incoming," Clements shouted from the bow of the seventy-two-foot barge.

Poised with her short pole, she could have been a Valkyrie from Valhalla. Raven, her pet crow, stamped on her shoulder then pecked at her unkempt wavy red locks as if wanting to hide there. "Back off, Raven!" she said, waving a hand, but the bird hopped around to her other shoulder and buried its head in her hair.

Even Dog searched the skies when the high-pitched noise of the drone's propeller and buzz of its engines reached the ears of the rest of the crew. It took Baxter a moment to find the craft through the thin mist that rose from the inland waters of The Wash. He was constantly amazed at how quickly Clements spotted anything out of the norm. It was why she was such a good pilot in the biofields. Dog snorted through his tusks and lumbered along the roof of the hold, morning dew still twinkling on his bristly grey fur.

Normally a drone didn't bother Baxter. But normally Baxter didn't break the law. Well... nothing more than the occasional motoring offence, and he'd been without a car for three years. Oh yes, there had been that spliff a girlfriend had shared with him, what, twelve years ago? But right now he was committing an offence that guaranteed a ten-year stretch, and possibly, depending on the judge, considerably longer. Until they sold-on their contraband Baxter couldn't relax.

This trip was make-or-break. The way their luck had gone over the past few weeks, Baxter wasn't at all confident that smuggling ninety-six bottles of premium French red in the empty engine compartment was such a wise decision, but they were desperate. Prohibition laws meant a bottle of good wine could fetch at least a hundred times more than when alcohol was legal. And red wine was a commodity the biotechs at the algae farms were crying out for, or so Baxter had been reliably informed.

Reliability was in short supply too; though, as highlighted by the fiasco with their seized diesel engine three months earlier. A new engine had been expensively out of reach of their haulage business, so Baxter had negotiated a reconditioned one. It never materialised and the suppliers, who'd insisted on payment up front, appeared never to have existed. He had borrowed with the barge as collateral and now the loan sharks wanted their money and, of course, their exorbitant interest.

The irony of where they now punted the barge wasn't lost on him. Around them, like a vast magic carpet, spread the bright green algae farms of East Anglia and the East Midlands supplying the UK's biofuels industry with ninety per cent of its raw material. Ironic also that the flooded fens were now the home of an algae industry that, begun fifty years earlier, might have helped reduce the effects of global warming, and minimised the rise of the world's oceans.

Baxter turned, gripped the twenty-five-foot quant firmly with his calloused hands and thrust it into the bed of the Welland Channel – a misnomer in itself. Having seen an old road atlas, he knew this had once been the A16. Larger boats still used the River Welland itself but a punted barge would flounder in such deep water. Once he had a solid purchase he leaned hard on the pole and started walking towards the back of the barge, his thighs burning with lactic acid and his calves twitching with the onset of cramp. Passing him casually on the port side, Rozinski, with his perpetual weathered grin firmly in place and pole balanced horizontally in his hands, made his way towards the prow in readiness for his next turn.

Baxter still wasn't sure about the Latvian. Clements had agreed on hiring another crewman after the engine seized. She was a tough woman who, despite a life spent on barges, looked nearer thirty-five than forty-five. But she wasn't up to punting a loaded barge, and Baxter sometimes wondered if he was. It was back breaking work. Rozinski had heard of their plight and needed a job. He had approached them as they sat in the Floating Coffin – a seedy pub in the port area of Boston Fort – where they were nursing two large black Americanos. A good Italian coffee was the next best thing to a pint of bitter in Baxter's eyes. Not quite the same buzz though. Rozinski was six-foot four and built like a Norse hero: shoulder length blond hair, slightly ginger stubble, and a jaw-line that would have done Judge Dredd proud. His cut-down sleeveless tee-shirt struggled to cover sculptured muscles. He'd accepted their first, and embarrassingly low, wage offer and had proved an asset in more than just his powerful frame. It was a month before they found out he had been the North of England cage fighting champion, losing the title only when he refused to take a fall. His retirement had been less about the ethics than his wondering if he was as good as he thought; how many of his opponents had thrown a fight? Having Rozinski at your side was often enough to stop an impending brawl.

It didn't take Baxter long to finish his stint at propulsion, the drone still keeping slow pace above them, bio tubes rippling across the 'fields' in the barge's wake. They'd built up some momentum, making pushing easier. Once the tide turned they'd have to moor up or drop anchor. Fighting against the tide, if it didn't kill you, was likely to undo all the hard work of the previous day.

Striding back to the bow, Baxter could see in the distance the towers of the reactors monopolising the horizon like a dead lichen-covered forest, dwarfing the occasional wind turbine that also fed power to the biogrid.

Baxter could hear Clements, from her position on the bow, mumbling "Shit" over and over, as if she were counting seconds. She had one hand raised in an attempt to block the low sun, glancing round to give Baxter a hopeless look as he approached. Drones didn't usually follow the barges; they just flew back and forth, sending their live feeds to the Water Guard main station at Lynn Fort. He clenched a defiant fist across his chest, mouthed, "Come on," and was relieved to see the hint of a smile before she flicked a glance to the back of the boat. Rozinski was just about reaching the end of his walk to the stern.

Baxter's mind wandered as he worked the pole, thoughts flitting here and there as he felt the barge moving beneath his feet. Maybe the Water Guard *were* changing the way they monitored waterway traffic, he told himself; cracking down on smuggling more like. Keep a clean sheet all your life and no questions asked. Yet as soon as you veer off the straight and narrow, bang, the law goes for the jugular.

They were making good time but would still have to moor up and catch the returning tide later. As Baxter headed back to the prow he noticed the reactors were getting closer, their pipework finally revealed, destroying the illusion they were bright green hydras; or Triffids, thought Baxter.

"Don't worry, Bozz," Rozinski called across the barge, a finger in the direction of the sky, "that's just routine." But they both knew it was a lie.

Baxter pushed his quant into the water, searching for a firm pivot, found it and began pushing even before Rozinski had removed his pole from the murky water at the stern, giving the Latvian a satisfied twist to his grin when they passed.

Baxter panicked a moment as his quant refused to budge from the sludge of the channel bed, but a practiced twist and heave sent him tottering on the edge of the stern with his right boot anchored on the low gun wale. Rozinski's grin became a loud laugh of light-hearted derision; the more meaningful as he'd been in the same position about half an hour earlier, only managing to recover by letting the pole travel vertically through his hands in a hundred-and-fifty-degree arc and then pulling the quant in reverse. Not the best way to avoid being dragged overboard. This slowed the barge but it was better than having to throw out the anchor and wait until your crewman swam back.

Engineering skills were limited to a few garage lathes these days, multinationals having drained the country of the most skilled engineers, and their old seized engine now sat on the bench of one of them. He shook his head again at his naïvety and how easily he'd been duped by the bastards who'd sold him the non-existent engine. Guilt still hung heavy in his thoughts and cut a deep red minus in their bank account. This trip was going to pay for the engine's rebuild and a make a nice profit to boot. Well, that was the plan. The constant buzz of the drone didn't bode well though.

Marsh gases bubbled up a stench of rotting vegetation that once covered the flat lands hereabouts, but Baxter's sense of smell had long ago learned to cope with the noxious odours. A bark from Rozinski set him back on his task. He was letting the drone get to him. Tiredness and boredom didn't help and neither, when he admitted it to himself, did the guilt trip, but once you had the barge moving at a decent pace it was in your best interests to keep it that way. The barge was a pig to get moving.

As they reached the rising green towers of the newer reactors, and quite beautiful they looked, in Baxter's eyes, Clements shouted a warning from the front of the barge, "Eh up! Water Guard!"

Baxter didn't stop pushing but, even as Clements shouted, he also heard the familiar whine of the Briggs and Stratton engine that powered the patrol's fluorescent green hovercraft. Taking supplies to the Spalding Bio Farm for the technicians and maintenance crews wasn't a crime, in fact their journey had been booked and logged back at Sutton Fort before they'd headed West along the Holbeach Channel, the route of the old A17, to the Welland Channel. It was far safer to stick to the marked routes than risk snagging on the roof of an old farmhouse or damaging the floating production tubing of the cheaper reactors.

At least the two officers from the Water Guard were thoughtful. Rather than hit the side with their magnetic winch and interrupt their pushing, they drew up at the stern, cut their engine, and began drawing in their craft. Carbines were slung across their backs, fluorescent green flak jackets over dark green uniforms. Expensive micro headsets were barely visible but it was obvious the WGs were in constant contact with their base. They were obviously intent on coming aboard to check credentials and, with all hands keeping the barge moving, they were unlikely to be offered a guided tour. Now that the hovercraft was silenced the ominous buzz from above reminded Baxter they were also on a monitor in a control room somewhere.

Dog snorted mucus menacingly in the face of the first officer, no older than his late teens, as he clambered on deck. He started to unclip his pistol.

"He'll not hurt you," Baxter called out. "A genetic softy. Just looks like a real wild boar, is all."

The young lad didn't look convinced but the automatic stayed in its holster. His backup, a man in his late forties and most likely the senior in rank, had slid his carbine around and up in an easy action that said *professional*. Chances *he* didn't take.

"Dog! Bed!" Baxter shouted. He wasn't convinced either, having seen what Dog's tusks could do to a man's thigh. It *was* true about Dog, though. His genes had been altered to make him more placid. Baxter doubted the officer would still have had a face if Dog were a normal boar. This was his barge though, as much as the rest of the crew, and he hadn't budged.

"Dog! Bed!"

Baxter hadn't heard Clements leave her post but she was halfway along the roof of the hold when he glanced round, Raven flapping in her locks like a trapped bat. Unruffled, Rozinski was nonchalantly finding a purchase with his quant at the front of the barge.

"Bed!" she repeated, as Dog turned his dripping snout in her direction. Reluctantly, and to Baxter's relief, Dog slowly lumbered to his pen, welded to the front of the cabin, giving Clements a look that unsettled even Baxter as he passed her.

"Come to the front," she called to the officer as she turned and hurried back to her position. "We can talk while I guide." The older man, carbine slung on his back once more, nodded to his junior and then accepted a hand to climb aboard.

"We've a consignment of electronic stuff for Curry's and the latest Marvel releases for Forbidden Planet." Baxter called over his shoulder as he led them forward. "Don't know why the biotechs love paper so much. Costs the Earth these days."

Despite the effort of pushing the barge, Rozinski was still able to smile at the officers as he passed them on the other side.

"He's always so blooming happy," Baxter said, mostly to himself.

"We've a tip off there's a haul of elicit wine coming through. Seen any strange vessels around?" asked the senior officer at the back. Baxter avoided stopping dead in his tracks. His arteries felt as if they'd been zapped by liquid nitrogen. Thankfully they weren't able to see his chin drop. Running alcohol wasn't just a smuggling offence. Prohibition laws were on a par with terrorism. But vineyards were suffering in the ever-changing weather patterns making wine a very lucrative commodity if you were willing to take the chance to make a quick buck.

Hoping his pause was taken for recollection Baxter finally said, "Saw a Dutch tug as we crossed the River Welland. Not seen her before. *Rood Tulp* I think she was called." He was pleased to see a look pass between them as he glanced around.

"I'll leave you with Clements. She has the cargo inventory."

As he pushed his pole into the muddy bed he overheard the older officer mention *Rood Tulp* into his microphone. Almost instantly the buzzing from above went up a notch in volume with a direction change that left them with just the lapping of water along the barge's length. Baxter was surprised at the relief he felt as the drone disappeared from view despite having two Water Guards on board.

Rozinski's smile was no longer one that Baxter felt easy with. There was a coldness in his eyes as they passed and a purposefulness in his stride that made Baxter look back quickly at the officers. The

Latvian had more to lose than any of them if their contraband was found packed tight with bubble wrap in the empty engine compartment. Feeding a family of six with another child on the way on benefits that wouldn't keep a cat alive led Rozinski to visit the back-street loan sharks more times than Baxter had fingers, or so the Latvian had told them.

"Don't do anything silly," he mouthed, but Rozinski didn't even look his way. If they played it cool they had a chance that their elicit haul of wine wouldn't be detected. The coldness in his blood returned, making his muscles protest even more.

"Fanzy a push, offizers," he heard Rozinski call, poking his quant in their direction. What was he up too?

He had to act before things got out of hand.

"Drop anchor!" he shouted, lifting his quant free of the bed and turning back to the front of the boat. Rozinski looked less surprised than Clements. "Offer the officers a cuppa. It's about time we had a break. My back's killing me."

Clements recovered quickly, knowing Baxter rarely made rash decisions, recon engine aside, and that he had a reason for his order. At the end of the day he was the senior partner owning fifty-one per cent of the barge. She used her pole to manoeuvre the barge alongside one of the mooring pylons that lined the channel at four-hundred-metre intervals. They all braced themselves and grabbed something secure as the barge bumped to a halt. Dog snorted in protest as its trotters skidded on the roof.

"I'll put the kettle on," Baxter called as he made his way aft again, and, "Apologies for our initial hospitality, officers. We'll not make Spalding before the tide turns anyway, so we might just as well moor up and head out again early tomorrow. Appreciate you boarding from the stern though. That was thoughtful." Giving them a bit of praise wasn't likely to change anything but doing the opposite most certainly would.

He reached the cabin and put the battered brown enamel kettle over the hob, lighting the jets beneath. The younger WG entered the cabin first with the barge's inventory under his arm and sat on one of the three high stools surrounding their circular wooden table, clean but stained with years of culinary misadventures. Rozinski leant, arms crossed, against the engine housing. Nothing like broadcasting the obvious, thought Baxter. The senior officer launched himself onto the kitchen top next to Clements, his legs dangling over the cupboards, giving him a commanding view over them all. He eyed the Latvian thoughtfully.

Baxter started to wonder if he'd made the correct decision. The guards might have glanced at their papers quickly and left. Now they were going to be on the barge for a good half an hour. Yet he still had the feeling that the Latvian might try something desperate.

"How's traffic been," he asked, in an attempt to break a tension that was slowly building and at the same time spotting the officer's name and rank on the left breast of his flak jacket: Johnson and Superintendent. What was such a senior officer doing on a patrol hovercraft?

"Busy," Johnson replied. "And lots of traders taking stupid risks. Caught three in the last week." He paused, cast his gaze slowly over the crew. "I blame it on the biotechs. They're the ones desperate for wine and meat. Our jurisdiction doesn't cover the algae towns though. We could stop all this if it did. The constables," layering his last word with disrespect, "could do more, but the techies earn too much money for their own good."

"You're telling me," Baxter agreed. "But it's good business for us."

"Good enough?"

"A struggle at times." Baxter nodded, feeling his convers-ational skills crumbling, his mouth wanting to babble on.

Clements passed the officers their teas, the younger one's eyes lingering on her tight royal blue sports top, where nipples dominated an otherwise nondescript bust, though Baxter knew, when unleashed, were, in his eyes, perfect.

"We couldn't help noticing you've a problem with your engine," Johnson said.

Baxter was pleased that his crew didn't react. Maybe he'd been wrong about Rozinski. It seemed likely that the failed engine was the main reason for the Water Guards' interest in the barge.

"Packed up three months ago. Got ripped off buying a recon." No reason to lie.

"We all make mizdakes." Rozinski took a sip of his black tea, still leaning against the housing, dominating the cabin with his bulk.

At the table the younger officer was flicking through the

paperwork, glancing across occasionally at Clements. She was old enough to be his mother but she was still a looker.

"Everyone seems to be out to get what they can these days," Johnson complained. "There's just not enough of us to make an impact. I've been on these waters for the last thirty years and smuggling's increased, yet my budget gets cut each year. The algae farms are great for the economy and keep the green campaigners happy – well mostly – but the majority of the biotechs get paid far more than a senior guard. Clasper here," he nodded to the lad, "Probably earns in a month what they earn over a couple of days. Didn't bother me once. It's eating at me now, though."

He was quiet for a while, allowing Baxter to reflect on his words. It wasn't often that guards discussed their opinions with the likes of the barge traders. Particularly not senior guard officers.

"Tea's good," he said to Clements. "Proper leaves?"

She looked at Baxter, who gave a slight nod. Owning up to a little thieving might make the guards less inclined to think them capable of bigger crimes was Baxter's logic. His decisions had been wrong in the past though, and he was constantly aware of that. "We delivered a consignment of tea to the Humber Fort last September. Seems we missed a box when we unloaded."

"Haven't had a decent cuppa for years," was all Johnson said. "Artificial tea's just not the same." He closed his eyes for a moment as if in bliss. Then he snapped them opened with a look of relief as Clasper turned at the same instant. "Looks like your tip paid off. Just come through." He touched the headset. "The *Rood Tulp was* carrying alcohol. They reckon a thousand bottles of red wine. That's some haul."

It was indeed. Their engine compartment held less than a hundred bottles. But at £200 a bottle, or thereabouts, it wasn't to be sniffed at. A thousand bottles was big business. If the Dutch ship had sold to the Spalding Farm their own consignment would have been worth far less in a flooded black market.

"That'll all be recorded on the drone. Can't board a vessel these days without it being monitored. The good thing about being the senior officer on patrol is I can order where the drones go. Now then, I think it's about time we left you to your business."

Johnson slipped off the top and put his mug there. Clasper

stamped their papers and squiggled a signature at the bottom before standing. Baxter noticed the relief flood into Rozinski's face. Clements even sighed.

"Oh," Johnson said, turning back, "Clasper here's a bit of a mechanic. He'll take a look at your engine for you before we go."

The colour drained from Clements face turning her tanned features grey. A wrench appeared in Rozinski's scarred right hand, but Johnson's automatic was already out of the holster and pointing at him.

"Put that down." It was said quietly and with a hint of regret, or so Baxter thought. But they were done for now. They'd taken a terrible risk and it hadn't paid off. It was his idea. He'd persuaded the others that the chance was worth taking. Once again his decision had been flawed.

"They're not in on this," he blurted. "It was my idea... To get us out of debt."

"Move over there together." Johnson gestured with his Glock, ignoring Baxter's plea. Clasper did likewise with his carbine as he edged around the cabin. Rozinski, like a cornered dog, followed suit until the crew members were all on the opposite side of the table to the engine compartment.

Clasper slung his carbine around to his back and opened the doors; looked at Johnson immediately. "'Bout eighteen cases."

"On another day that'd be a decent cop," the older guard said. "Today?" Baxter raised his eyebrows as Johnson put the automatic back in its holster. "We don't take bribes but in this case a half dozen bottles seems a reasonable gift under the circumstances. It'll be another half hour before the drone heads back this way."

They watched, dumbfounded, confused and relieved as the young guard extricated a case from the bubble wrap that protected their hoard.

"I know you're honest traders," Johnson said. "Just the climate's not conducive to honesty right now. There's them." He raised a hand high above his head. "And there's us." His hand moved to his thighs. "And never the twain shall meet. Except when there's a bit of profit to be had. And it's usually them," his hand shot up again, "that benefit."

He followed Clasper up and along the deck to the rear and helped him slip the case of mixed reds under some tarpaulin folded at the rear of their hovercraft. The crew had followed in stunned silence, Dog's trotters clipping a merry tune on the deck by their side, Raven cawing defiance as if she alone had sent the guards scurrying off.

Johnson shouted above the sound of the Briggs and Stratton as it burst into noisy life, "Needless to say you won't be bothered by the Water Guard on this trip again. But be assured, we will be keeping an eye on you in the future." With that they shut off the electromagnet, hauled in the winch, swung about and were soon travelling away at speed, Johnson standing with a hand on the cage to steady himself, looking back at Baxter and the crew.

Raven flew after them briefly then returned, landing lightly again on Clement's shoulder, wings flapping for balance.

"Hell," she whispered, as her legs buckled and she ended up sitting on the deck. She put a hand up as Rozinski and Baxter both went to assist her. "I'm okay. Just a tad shocked is all. Leave me be a minute. That was just too close."

Rozinski uncharacteristically hugged Baxter and Baxter surprised himself by hugging back. They pulled away, looked at each other, then at Clements, and burst into laughter.

"Maybe our luck's changing at last."

When Shepherds Dream of Electric Sheep

Sam Fleming

"Of all occupations from which gain is secured, there is none better than agriculture, nothing more productive, nothing sweeter, nothing more worthy of a free man"
— Cicero

Henry turned off the engine. The Ranger rocked forwards and stopped, held by the gearbox, just like the off-road instructor had taught him. In the field beyond the fence, Saoirse was working her two sheepdogs, Moss and Fly. Whistles pierced the air like arrows and Moss, the black and white one, bounded off to the left. Fly, who was red and white, jinked right but stayed low, stalking. A couple of the sheep jostled into the flock, and one with a collar stamped belligerently.

Henry tongued a tooth switch and started the E-sheep app. With a few blinks or facial movements he could open fences and move any or all of his flock to another field, bring the ram over for tupping without worrying about marking, and check that they were healthy. Neural implants took care of everything.

It hadn't been cheap, of course. But the Warburtons had always been early adopters. 'Innovate and diversify!' had been his Grandfather's rallying call, and it had stood them in good stead through water rationing and the fuel escalator. Biddable sheep were further proof of how right old Patrick had been.

"Hello there!"

Saoirse didn't turn round when he let himself into the field. "Henry," she said, and whistled again before barking, "Stand, Moss. Stand!"

"Bit of an awkward bunch you've got there."

"Aye."

"At least today's a good day for it, after the weather we've been having."

"Aye." She frowned, put the half disc of the whistle between her lips and blew a note so loud Henry thought his eardrums would burst. Both dogs dropped to the grass, their gazes not leaving the sheep.

"I'm having a dinner party on Friday night. I wondered if you might like to come," he said.

Saoirse's expression barely flickered. Henry told himself it was a perfectly reasonable invitation. They were neighbours, after all, and she was by herself since her father passed away from the last MERS variant. Henry's own father, William, had died in a boating accident two summers previously, and his mother spent so much time in the VR unit pretending William was still alive she might as well not be there at all. They were both alone, near enough. Saoirse had her dogs, of course, and Henry had his various enterprise partners. But neither of them had anyone special.

"Farrier's coming round Friday," she said, then blew four quick blasts. The dogs left the sheep and ran over, tongues lolling.

"The farrier?"

"For the horses." She glanced at him, eyes like rain-wet granite shining in her tanned, weather-lined face. Henry's heart skipped a beat. "You learned about farriers yet?"

"Er, no." His face stung as it reddened. He'd bought the farm when his father had told him it was his turn to diversify. The long days and hard labour had put previous generations off agriculture, despite the attraction of property, but technology had progressed. He'd been able to automate almost everything, and contract out what he couldn't, so he got to look out his bedroom window every morning and see animals and crops that he owned, as any proper gentleman farmer should.

"Farrier puts shoes on horses."

Saoirse was so old school it was practically barbaric. Where he had drones to manage the crops and fields, she kept bees and used horses. They weren't even modded. Samson and Delilah, she called them. They were Boulonnais, giant beasts that looked as if they had been carved from marble or compressed cloud.

"Why would you put shoes on a horse?"

"If you walked about on rough ground on your fingernails all day, you'd want protecting too. Didn't they teach you anything at that fancy school?"

"I wrote the software I use to manage the feed stocks," he said, hurt. He'd told her that before. The Quarter-Baaster app was getting good reviews and making a slow but steady trickle of income from similarly forward-thinking agronomists.

Saoirse smiled, like the sun coming out on a stormy day. "I know that, Henry, you idiot."

Coming from her, this was a term of endearment. She sighed and fondled her dogs. They gazed at her with unembarrassed adoration. Henry wished he were one of her dogs.

"Time was," she said, "when farming was good husbandry and looking after your crops, praying for a dry spell. These days it's all coding and meteorological models telling robots when to plough, when to plant, when to harvest, when to milk."

"Too many mouths," Henry said, trying to be sympathetic but not really understanding why she sounded as if she would replace all the robots with people. Nobody wanted to do that work. Eighteen hour days for hardly any return?

"If it were all about mouths, Henry, you'd be growing nothing but oilseed rape, soy and European rice. There'd be no sheep or cows or pigs or chickens. You'd have a locust farm like Bert Hackensack and algae pools instead of barley. You've got the best water supply for forty miles and you're growing crops that look pretty come harvest. Your trouble is you're a bloody romantic."

Henry spluttered, indignant. "You're the one with the dogs and the heavy horses, Saoirse. I don't think you can accuse *me* of being romantic."

"Nothing romantic about what I do. It's hard work and getting your hands dirty, not lording it about with your gadgets and your electric sheep, your fine house and your tweeds. When you have to worry about finding a new roof for the cow shed, or a new strain of dieback is getting into your coppices and doubling your fuel bill because you have to import pellets for the biomass plant on the dryer, then I'll stop thinking of you as a hobby farmer with more money than sense. Come on, dogs."

She brushed past him, Moss looking up with yellow eyes as he slithered past, his panting sounding like laughter.

Henry watched her climb into her battered red Toyota Hilux, the dogs leaping into the back and lying down without being told. The sharp pain of mockery made him spiteful, and he decided the dogs must be modded. They couldn't possibly be so obedient otherwise.

Only after she'd gone did it occur to him she hadn't given him a answer regarding Friday night.

He called past on his way to town the next morning, where he had an appointment with his accountant. He parked underneath the spinning vertical helix of Saoirse's wind turbine, which was one of her scant acknowledgements of living in the late twenty-first century. Cattle in the shed huffed and blew, lowing softly in the dim. He could smell them, that unmistakeable odour of manure, sharp but sweet cud and the malty scent of cow pellets. There were sugar beets in the trough, from the crop that had been ruined in the last flash freeze, rendered unusable for anything bar low quality ethanol feedstock or animal fodder. The guttering was loose on the roof, fat drops splattering metronomically from the morning's shower. Old tractor tyres, tinged green with moss, held down a tatty blue tarpaulin covering ancient engine parts. He could see rusting metal through holes gnawed by rats in the plastic. A sparrow darted across the yard from the apple tree in the farmhouse garden and disappeared under the roof of the cattle shed. A robin hopped along the wall, scolding him for trespassing, and a silver-grey farm fox watched him through lidded eyes from the top of a straw bale inside the open barn.

The Hilux was parked by the tack room, and when Henry stepped out onto the wet, muddy concrete, cold air biting his cheeks, a small dog shot out from underneath it, yapping non-stop, its legs a blur under its stout, white body.

"Hello, Snudge," Henry said.

Snudge pranced around, repeatedly darting in to nip at Henry's ankles before thinking better of it at the last minute. He seemed to want Henry's trousers but was nervous of his feet.

Henry tried not to kick him as he walked to the house.

At this time of day he wasn't expecting Saoirse to be in. She would be out on the farm somewhere, doing by hand one of the endless jobs his farm management system did for him automatically. She clearly thought she could anchor the world in the eighteenth century single-handed.

He rang the doorbell. No answer. Rather than give up, he went to the back door and knocked. A flurry of scrabbling claws and barking told him the dogs were there, and a few moments later Saoirse opened the door. Her ash-blonde, greying hair was pulled back into a braid almost as thick as her wrist and hung over her left shoulder. Her thin lips were pressed together and the lines on her face were more noticeable than usual. She wore a heavy plaid shirt, the sleeves rolled up to the elbows, fingerless gloves, faded green cords and thick, woollen socks.

"Is everything all right?" he asked, yesterday's slight forgotten in concern sparked by her expression.

"I'm trying to get the feed-in tariff sorted out for the micro-generation, but the stupid computer keeps losing my data and I can't find the section where you apply for a discount for set-aside carbon capture. They've changed everything since last year."

Saoirse's farm was barely making ends meet, and the loss of the beet had hit her hard. The difference made by her micro-generation and standing trees could be the difference that kept her in business.

"I'd be happy to take a look." He smiled. "I'm pretty good with computers."

She thought about it for a few moments, still as a hawk on a fence post, then stepped aside and ushered him in.

"Boots off there." She indicated the row of boots and shoes below the coats hanging from hooks on the wall. As he pulled off his wellingtons, he was surrounded by five wriggling dogs, tails wagging and cold, wet noses sniffing eagerly. "Come away, dogs," she said, and sent them into the kitchen. As well as Moss, Fly and Snudge, she had two black labs called Ben and Flo, gundogs she used for hunting rabbit and other game. "I'll put the kettle on. The office is just through here."

The house was cold. That was Henry's first impression. Cold and slightly stale. It smelled of dog, burning wood, wet waxed cotton and bacon. The floor in the outroom was tiled, and there was an adjoining small toilet room he identified by the strong scent of pine coming from behind the cracked-open door between the washing machine and the sack of dog biscuits.

The outroom led into the kitchen, dominated by an old Aga and a battered oak table. Everything was well-used but spotless. Saoirse filled the copper kettle from the tap and set it on the hotplate before taking him through to the office at the front of the house, between the living room and the dining room.

"You have a lovely house," Henry said. She grunted. "I mean it. You said I have a fine house, but this is beautiful. Has it been in the family long?"

"As long as the family remembers, anyway. It's ours, and that's what matters. It's not a manor house like yours, just a farmhouse. Room for the dogs. Room for me. Room for those that might want to visit."

"And do they?"

"What?"

"Visit?"

She didn't answer. "Computer's in here. I'll bring your tea."

Henry opened his mouth to say he'd prefer coffee then thought better of it.

Her computer was an antique. He was surprised the hardware was even capable of connecting. It had a manual user interface – the only time he ever typed anything anywhere was if there had been a system malfunction or a virus, and he was bringing it back in safe mode to stop his wetware being infected. He'd said he was good with computers, but he hadn't expected this obsolete horror.

Still, he couldn't let her know that.

At the side of the keyboard – keyboard! – was a sheet of paper – paper! – covered in careful, neat script detailing the various outputs and inputs from the microhydro up the hill, the turbine on the house and the biomass plant running the dryer. There was also a note of the acreage covered by woodland, the balance of harvest and plantation, and the resulting carbon reduction worked out by hand. Henry knew the theory, of course, but generally told his system what the numbers were and let it work everything out for him. It wasn't that he didn't know how to do it, he told himself, he just had better things to do. Why go to the effort when there was a system that would do everything much faster and with less fuss?

He set to work, forcing himself to be patient and not get frustrated. The hard part, after all, was merely figuring out how to make Saoirse's system do what he wanted it to do.

She brought him tea after about ten minutes and sat down in the other chair – an old, green, wing-backed thing with tattered upholstery and four grubby, unmatched cushions covered in dog hair. She was wearing a pair of half-moon glasses and had a pencil tucked behind one ear.

"Are you going to watch?" Henry asked, uncomfortable even though Saoirse wouldn't be able to tell he was struggling. She couldn't do it, either.

"You might need information I haven't written down."

"You've been very thorough. Thank you for the tea. I'll let you know when I'm done."

"And then you'll show me how to do it?"

Henry hesitated, harbouring fantasies of coming to Saoirse's rescue every time she had to use her computer. "If you like."

"I do."

"Then of course."

By the time Henry had worked out how to submit Saoirse's information accurately on her ancient system, and shown her how to do so – in the process increasing her subsidy by recalculating the accumulator – he'd missed his appointment. The accountant would probably charge him for the time, but he didn't care. For a blissful hour he'd sat close enough to her to touch her, with the two labs keeping their feet warm, and she'd listened attentively to every word he said without once disparaging him.

"So, could I talk you into dinner on Friday night?" he asked as he gathered his things to leave. His task manager had grown too insistent to ignore and he couldn't quite bring himself to turn it off.

"I don't do parties." She stood, as straight-backed as a grandfather clock, one hand in her pocket and the other resting lightly on the occasional table where dried flowers exuded a ghostly aroma of times long past.

"It's a dinner party. Just me and a few of my enterprise partners. I've got a chef coming in to do the catering and we're going to talk about business opportunities. Perhaps we could find some new outlets for your Blackface, save you a few trips to the farmer's market."

"Busy Friday," she said, without so much as a pause for thought.

Henry did his best to appear nonchalant. "Some other time, then. You might find it very useful to open up new sale opportunities.

Sam Fleming

Diversification is the foundation of a robust business."

"I'll bear that in mind." It was the same tone he'd heard from people who had accepted a business v-card with the intention of deleting it immediately. "Thanks for your help."

Halfway down the path, he looked back. She'd already closed the door.

Winter settled in a couple of weeks later. The Met Office said the Jet Stream had flipped again, and they could expect the cold spell to last. Henry did well out of it. With lucky timing, there had been a positive review of his Quarter-Baaster app in Farmer's Weekly. The summer of alternating floods and drought meant there was a shortage of fodder; a lot of farmers were keen to make the most of what stocks they had. He made an effort to upgrade the app with new features, and ported the code for other livestock. He was especially pleased to have cracked integration with the E-Sheep flock management system and the E-Cow equivalent.

Although his head was full of protein per kilogramme live weight and realtime wholesaler price comparison, not to mention branching out into automated drone delivery to rural pick-up points, his thoughts strayed more often than was constructive to Saoirse and how she was managing.

Even with snow chains, the Ranger slip-slid on tracks covered in sheet ice and bunded with snow as deep as he was tall. He found her in the small barn, after spotting the familiar red of the Hilux. It was warm and dim in the barn, and smelled of straw and dust.

"Close the door, man!" she snapped. "You're letting the heat out."

She had rigged a feed from the dryer to keep the place warm, and Henry saw why when he drew closer. There was a border collie in a nest of straw, lying on her side while seven squeaking pups wriggled and fought for a place to suckle.

"Is that Fly?"

"No. Fly's too young. This is Jet. She's a good dog, aren't you girl?"

"I didn't know you had three collies."

"Didn't until four weeks ago. Arranged it mid-October. Some young feller bought out Jim Morgan –"

"Did he own Meadowlea?"

40

"Aye. This young fellow – Burchfield, I think his name is – thought a farm should have a sheepdog. Bought Jet from a breeder down south, decided he wanted puppies. Farm folded three weeks after he had her serviced. I said I'd take her."

"What happened to Burchfield?"

"Don't know and couldn't care less."

"They're beautiful. What are you going to do with them all?"

"You're not getting one, Henry Warburton. No call for a working dog when you can type 'baa' against your palm and have the flock come to you. What would you do? Put wires in the dog's brain so he could message the sheep with a by-your-leave?" She laughed, snorting like a horse with a fly on his nose.

"There's no need to be unkind."

"Aye. Maybe so." She reached across and fondled Jet, who licked her arm. There was a softness in Saoirse's face Henry hadn't seen before.

"I came to see how you're getting on, what with the weather being so bad."

"You should have been here three years ago. That was proper weather then. Soon as we cleared the road it filled again. Moss and me, we rescued six of Helen Riley's prize cattle. Bert lost his entire stock and had to have crates of them shipped across from Germany come spring. There's a thing you don't see every day. Thousands of grasshoppers in big, wooden boxes."

"You've got plenty of supplies?"

"Don't you worry about me."

"Well let me know if you need anything. I can always get one of our supply drones to airlift some fodder across."

"Oh aye? And how much would that cost? I'll be all right. You see to your own. I can always put snow shoes on the horses and get the old sleigh out the back of the barn."

"Snow shoes?"

She grinned. "Special order with the farrier."

It was a minute or so before Henry realised she was pulling his leg.

"Why don't you come over to my place for dinner tomorrow night?" he asked. "There won't be anyone else. Well, there's Beryl, but she doesn't count. She's just the cook."

"She doesn't count? If that's the case why don't you get one of your robots to cook for you?"

"That's not what I meant."

"What *did* you mean?"

"Just that it would be you and me and no one else actually eating."

"Don't think I'd feel right, sitting there while Beryl slaved away in the kitchen. I went to school with her. Her mam used to do my pigtails for me after my mam died. No, Henry, thanks all the same. Maybe one of your business friends can come and keep you company."

Two weeks before Christmas he woke up to darkness. The house lights were programmed to come on gradually at seven, to simulate natural sunrise. He tongued his clock and the display faded into view in the top right of his vision. It was almost eight.

Perturbed, he got out of bed. The house was freezing. When he tongued the switch for the house operating system, his vision flashed an error message. The cold stabbed through his skin and sent icy fingers skittering up and down his nerves.

The entire system had gone down. His farm had crashed. It was impossible. There were satellites, fibre optics and wireless relay. Three levels of redundancy.

He didn't know what to do.

Dragging a thermal fleece over his head against the cold, he ran downstairs. It was pitch black, and without the majordomo he couldn't just tell his internal system to negotiate night vision with the house cameras. He had no idea how long the system had been down or what had caused the outage.

Panic drove him to the front door, fumbling by memory in the dark. He opened it, stepped into the glass-walled porch, gasped in the cold. Something about the quality of the darkness made him pause. Even on the blackest night in the middle of winter, there should have been some light coming from outside. There was nothing.

He ran back upstairs, looked out of the bedroom window, down into the valley where the town should be.

The sky was a torn blanket of grey over a billion light-filled jewels. Snow sparkled like diamonds as far as he could see. It had reached halfway up his house. His front porch was buried. His satellite dish was buried. Everything was smothered by snow. Winter was suffocating the world.

And his sheep. His sheep would be out there. Without the E-sheep system they wouldn't know what to do. His tongue fiddled with the switch on his lower left molar. He should have had it installed on his wisdom tooth. Maybe he'd have made better decisions.

Shivering, he did the only thing he could and climbed back into bed. It would be light in an hour or so. He could assess the damage then, and do what he could for his sheep.

He didn't sleep, but sat huddled under the covers until the sun had made it possible to see. He made his way back downstairs, which was still dark, and tried to make coffee, but with the power out he had no way to heat water, so went back upstairs.

The only way out was the window. The snow was about three metres deep. If he jumped it might well break his fall, but he would probably be buried and die.

He got back into bed, and this time it wasn't because he felt cold.

At mid-morning there was a shout outside and the buzz of an engine. He scrambled to the window and saw Saoirse sitting on a snowmobile, with Snudge, Moss, Fly, Ben and Flo riding in a trailer behind her, each of them wearing a warm jacket. He opened the window and stuck his head out.

"Word is you've dropped off the face of the world," she called. "You look all right to me."

"System's crashed in the snow," he replied, teeth chattering. "Can't get out."

"We'll soon see about that."

She unhitched a shovel from the back of the snowmobile and set about digging down to his front door, Snudge joining in with enthusiasm. Within half an hour she'd cleared a set of steps in the snow.

"Right then. You've got sheep out there need finding. Put some proper clothes on and let's go get them."

The impossibility of what she was saying couldn't stand up to his deep desire not to be found disappointing. He grabbed the warmest clothes he had, yanked them on and ran down to meet her.

The world outside was cold, crisp, clear and smelled preposterously clean. The quiet was unreal. He could hear a crow calling from the other side of the valley.

"I don't know where to look for them," he said, gratefully accepting a mug of hot tea from a battered tartan thermos. It was hot, black, sweet and pungent with alcohol.

"Where did you have them last?"

He gestured vaguely.

"Then we'll start over there. Do you have snowshoes?"

He shook his head.

"Good job I brought spares then, isn't it?" A deft tug and two objects that looked like the unholy union of a tennis racket and a banana fell to the ground. She showed him how to put them on and didn't laugh when his first few steps put him flat on his face.

"Come on, dogs," she said, and Henry noticed they had little boots on their feet.

They set out, Saoirse not giving him a chance to panic. The dogs trotted across the crusty snow, tongues lolling even in the cold. Henry noticed their breath formed the same clouds of vapour as his own and Saoirse's.

After half an hour of slow trudging past snow-laden trees and the occasional dead drone, the dogs began to bark and ran off ahead. Muffled bleating made his heart race.

"I think I'm going to visit the dentist in the spring," he said. "Would any of Jet's puppies be for sale?"

"Maybe," Saoirse said. "How about we talk about it when we've got your sheep safe?"

"Over dinner? I'm not much good at anything besides beans on toast, I'm afraid."

She turned to look at him, grey eyes sparkling, face split by a grin. "That sounds perfect."

Inversion Centre

Darren Goossens

"So with this realignment of the key national priorities and its feeding into the formulation of the funding guidelines that buttress the decision making process of the National Education and Research Development Agency, under the aegis of the Long-term Infrastructure Provision Program Initiative, we find that we are compelled to recommend that the DesertFarm project realign its funding model to take advantage of opportunities offered by tapping into non-traditional sources of support. We are so strongly behind the project in a principle-based sense that we have ensured that the legislation required to free your management team from the constraints of reliance on taxpayer funding is currently before the requisite senate committee and is expected to be passed by the end of the week."

Brandon blinked three times. He turned to look at me and blinked again, then turned back to the face hovering above the conference table.

Diplomatic to the last, he said: "So you're giving us the arse?"

The deputy secretary to the undersecretary to the chief adviser to the Minister assisting the Minister for Innovativity and Climate Change Mitigation said: "We're encouraging you to identify and pursue alternative funding."

"By cutting our budget by sixty per cent."

The secretary maintained a bland face. I wondered if he was a projection of a real person or entirely computer generated. Maybe the real secretary was having a coffee or an intern in his office.

"The project has had significant support at the Federal level from the Australian taxpayer, and at state level from the South Australian taxpayer. It is time for those funds to be redirected to enable us to meet other challenges. We understand you are hosting a visiting delegation this afternoon. From the United States Department of Food Security. Perhaps a dialogue with them is in order."

"They're just some sightseers from Texas," I said.

"Perhaps you need to think about selling your work more forcefully," said the image.

Brandon sagged for a moment, frowned, and sat up taller, as if making one last effort. "We're almost there. My model shows that –"

At the word 'almost' the secretary unsuccessfully suppressed a sneer. If AI were behind this it was a good one.

"As they say, professor Rekveldt, don't shoot the messenger. Good afternoon."

The space above the table went dark. The room's lights ramped up automatically.

I tried to think of something consoling. *Don't worry, I'm sure you'll find another life's work*, perhaps. Luckily, or so I thought at the time, I was saved from my impending inanity by Liza Platt, Deputy Director (Operations) knocking twice and coming in unasked.

"How'd your meeting with Brooke go? I thought it was supposed to last for another half hour," I said.

"I'll get to *that* in a minute. I want to know how it –" she looked at Brandon. "Oh, as well as that, huh? So no bulk carrier port yet."

I shook my head. "We don't even have operating funds, let alone anything to finish the port."

She looked aghast. "They're pulling the plug? But we're almost –"
"Don't say it."
"Well, I guess my news isn't so bad now."

Brandon looked at her with hollow eyes. "*More* bad news?" His voice creaked.

The last thirty minutes had given him a five o'clock shadow, a tic in his left eye and a haunted expression.

"Yes, Chief. Um, don't shoot –" She squinted at my frantic waving. "Anyway, AAGGMNEAKESMHR" – Australians Against Globalisation, Genetic Modification and Nuclear Energy of Any Kind Except the Sun and Maybe Hot Rocks (apparently their leader had had a long discussion with an Physics Nobel Laureate about the ultimate source of solar electricity and Earth's interior heat and, to his credit, had taken her words on board – "seem to be hacking into our system again. A robotic harvester is charging about madly through the wheat fields."

Brandon groaned. "Not crop circles again?"

"I don't think so... Too many straight lines for that. Maybe crop Sudoku?"

Our fearless leader slumped further down into his chair. "They're holding us down and shaving rude words into our hair. Hell. We're being bullied by a bunch of vegetarians and Luddites."

I said: "I don't think Luddites would be able to hack into our computer systems."

He glared at me. "Maybe the vegans run their IT department. The Luddites probably do Industrial Relations."

Still standing in the doorway, Liza said: "I think you should take a look, boss."

I stood up. Brandon gripped the edge of the oval oak table and dragged himself to his feet.

"Where's Alec?" he said. "Sorry, stupid question. He's in room 34 with AIlsa. Let's go."

As I reached room 34, I heard a softly spoken artificial voice: "There's no evidence."

Alec looked at the wall. His yearly planner showed nothing. Why write on it when every day was the same?

Corby's keyboard – he still used one – clattered from the other side of the partition. Corby made Alec seem gregarious. He typed as if he was driving nails, and you could always tell when he hit 'Enter' – his keyboard bounced against the desk. He had carefully arranged his desk so that he could not see whoever came into the office and they could not see him. Everybody preferred that arrangement.

Apparently to no one, Alec said: "There's got to be something. Maybe a modulation on top of our usual signals, something multiplexed in."

Again, the neutral but if anything female voice came from the air. "No. I am sending the shutdown signal on every band and at the same time analysing every band the harvesters are equipped to receive. Everything matches."

The IT engineer looked up as three of us wedged ourselves into his doorway. Brandon pushed through first.

"Oh, hi guys," Alec said in his quiet, sleepy voice. "I could swear nobody's got in. But there it is."

Without turning around he gestured to the monitor on the wall behind him. It showed a wide angle aerial view of the research farm. Golden wheat lay framed on two sides by scrubby desert and on one by shining sea, and on the fourth by a row of offices, laboratories, buildings, airfields and hangars. With a combination of solar energy, desalination technology and zero tillage, we were greening the desert. We hoped.

"That looks like an X," said Liza. "An X three hundred metres tall."

Alec yawned and smiled lop-sidedly. "Maybe they're playing noughts and crosses; next they'll do a big O, and then another X."

We turned back to Alec. "And AIlsa can't pick anything up?" I said.

"Nope," said Alec. "She'd know."

"Maybe –" Brandon said.

"– and the logs clearly show that no new program was downloaded into the machine earlier, either. Transmission monitoring logs go back to when the machines were commissioned. It's a very complete record."

"Damn right," grunted Corby from his hiding place.

"Corby designed it," said Alec. "We coded it right here."

"Damn right." Another grunt from Corby. "Must be problem with the *harvesters*."

He knew very well that I had done the detail design on them. I fumed silently.

Brandon pinched the bridge of his nose. "First crop circles, now malign elves reprogramming harvesters."

I heard Corby snort.

"Corby," I said, "do you need a box of tissues for that cough? Or a dose of cyanide?"

He laughed in a way I found insulting. As far as I was concerned his partition was not thick enough.

Liza was watching the monitor again. "Boss," she said thoughtfully.

Brandon grunted and turned around. His eyes widened.

"When were the Americans going to fly in?" said Liza. "What odds the next letter is a U on the front?"

On the monitor we saw that 'S SUX' was written in the wheat in letters three hundred metres on a side.

I looked at the time-stamp in the corner of the screen. "In a little under two hours," I said. "And we're hoping to convince them to save the project."

Liza pulled a doubtful face.

Brandon clenched his fists. "We've got to get rid of that or we'll look like amateurs with lousy security. They'll never deal with us."

"'Amateurs with lousy security' looks to be an accurate picture right now," said Alec.

Corby laughed.

Brandon waved a finger at us all. "Then make us look inaccurately competent! And that's an order. Now, since I hate micromanagement, I'll be in my quarters watching a replay of the 2021 Grand Final. Maybe this time St Kilda will win."

And he was gone.

I looked at Liza as we walked down the long grey corridor away from Alec's cave.

"There are no signals getting in to the machines. That only leaves one possibility – a physical device attached to the machines."

"Or the AI is missing something."

I guess it says a lot about my unthinking faith in machines that I had not thought of that. "I guess so. But she doesn't miss things unless she's told to." I thought through some of the implications of that. I bit my lip. "Hell."

We both stopped. Through the walls I could hear the roar of the liquid nitrogen truck filling our tanks. It seemed very loud.

"Either way this is an inside job." Her eyes were round, her voice hushed.

I waggled my finger and pointed in some irrelevant direction. "I'll get down to maintenance and see about parachuting someone onto that harvester. You – do what you can on the AI angle."

"Can I trust Alec, do you think?"

"I've no idea," I said over my shoulder as I hurried away. "Can I trust *you*?"

She said something, which may have been "Piss off", and then I rounded a corner and started running.

"Well, has to be you, doesn't it?" said Brooke Willows (terrible name) when I reached Maintenance. "You designed them, you helped build them, you're across the problem and you're also a bit of an IT guy."

"No, not that last thing," I shook my hands in front of me. "I program but I'm not an IT guy."

She rolled her eyes. "Anyway, you're the resident expert. You still get all funny when anybody proposes an upgrade or mod to them."

I ratcheted my indignation up a notch. "I do not, I just like to have... input into the... um –"

She rolled her eyes *and* raised her eyebrows. "Whatever. How good are you with a microcopter?"

I was sorely tempted to say "Not good enough," but I knew that she knew I flew them as a hobby, so all I said was, "I guess we'll find out."

I matched speeds with the whirring harvester, aiming to lower myself onto its upper walkway. Judging by my view from the air, the machine was writing a capital U and had rounded the curve, so it should be going straight for a few minutes yet. I edged closer. My feet brushed the handrail. Closer. Air whistled in my ears. I felt as if I was going a hundred kilometres an hour when it can't have been more than ten. Wheat stalks flickered past beneath me. I hovered above the deck for a second and dropped, coming down hard on my left ankle. I stood on the walkway and tried to get my balance. To my right was the top of the ladder, to my left the cabin containing the manual controls and several of the more important inspection points. I shrugged out of the microcopter and went inside, sliding into the big ergonomic seat. I tried some of the controls – no response. The HUD was working, flashing blue and red numbers onto the window; the real time map showed buildings, vehicles and recharging stations, with a circle like a gun sight showing me the harvester's progress. But nothing I did had any effect, even the reboot command. I was going to have to find the culprit if there was one (I had the sudden and uncomfortable realisation that any device might contain a self-destruct or a bomb), or give the harvester a hard reset. Maybe that would trigger an explosion? I had no idea.

I unclipped every inspection panel I could find, holding my breath each time. I figured if someone had plugged a box of some sort into the control system, the cabin was the most likely place – all the crucial systems converged there.

I found nothing.

"Liza – anything?" I said, shining my penlight into wiring looms and running the light over circuit boards.

Her voice came, oddly personal and close, in my ear. "I think maybe I have."

"Oww! Some idiot left a burr on this access panel!" I cursed.

"That would be me. What have you found?"

She sounded sheepish. "Uh, I found some log files that the IT guys seem to be unaware of. They show that some instructions *were* sent to the harvester, and –"

I looked skyward – why hadn't *I* thought of that? "I have a personal back up of the logs that I keep synced," I blurted, "and –"

Her silence seemed somehow *more* silent than it should have been.

"You're talking about my logs, aren't you?" I said.

"Brandon has full admin access when he wants it. So I went looking around in the system... and you sort of said trust nobody, and you do know a *lot* about the harvesters. So I..."

"Well," I said, sighing at my own stupidity. "It was a good idea. I should have thought. My copies sit on my computer, but *it* gets incrementally backed up to my file space, and that will have its own log, which will tell us about any retrospective changes made to the logs."

"And to think Brooke told me you denied being an IT guy."

That settled it. There was no alien device on board, bomb or otherwise. I reached into a small opening that had a red outline around it and then yellow-and-black diagonally striped tape around *that*.

I flipped up a hinged cover and pushed a big red button. The harvester lurched to a halt, throwing me against the windscreen.

I harrumphed and made myself comfortable in the harvester driver's seat, then unfolded my computer and spread it out, covering the dials and gauges of the control panel. I started hunting though my own files, and comparing time-stamps.

I had to blink. "According to my data, Brooke sent the harvester a fat packet just before it went haywire."

I could hear the incredulity in her voice. "Brooke?"

"Well, her terminal seems to be the origin of the instructions. I'll send you a snippet. . . She *is* head of Maintenance..." But it didn't sound right.

I was relieved when Liza said: "No, at the time your file shows we were in our meeting. She wasn't using her computer."

"She could set it to send the message any time."

"But can she retcon the logs?"

Only Alec or Corby could do that. I knew who I *wanted* to be guilty.

Brandon's voice cut in. "Good work, guys. I've asked Security to ask the boys in IT not to go anywhere just now. But our Texan saviours are on their way and we're sending them a greeting of 'US SUX' a mile long."

"I'll boot up the harvester with my thumb on the reset key. That'll load up its default program. Then I can start wiping out the letters," I said, perhaps just a little smugly.

Brandon groaned. I could hear him shaking his head. Maybe it was his voice Doppler shifting back and forth. "Do the maths. You don't have time to harvest an area that big."

I started up the harvester anyway, and watched the screens as it did its self-check. Everything seemed in order.

"Could we add some letters to it?" suggested Liza.

"What, change it to 'US SUXCESS'?" I joked half-heartedly. "Then we'll just look as if we can't spell."

"Well," she said. "The US and SU parts look a bit alike."

"Hah!" barked Brandon in my ears. "Hah!"

"Knock it off boss. You'll blow my implant," I said. "Gives you nasty burns when that happens, right behind the ears."

A picture flashed up on my computer. It looked like this:

US SUX

Before my eyes, the image turned upside down.

XNS SΠ

I heard Liza saying, "Boss, what are you doing?" then I watched as Brandon drew just a handful of lines and dots. Now it looked like this:

TEXAS+S.A.

"Texas plus South Australia." I smiled and nodded.

"Get to it," said Brandon.

"Pretty clever, boss." I had to admire the guy. "What gave you the idea?"

Gruffly, he said: "'S' has got an inversion centre."

"What?"

"Go and look it up. The boss has got to know when to delegate and know when to step in. That's why I make the big bucks. Now, I think I told you to get on with it."

I got on with it. I squashed the temptation to write =➤♡ or add an emoticon to the end, but I did add an exclamation mark. After the excitement of the day, it seemed fitting. And, I have to say, driving the harvester on manual was *fu-un*.

And pretty soon our visitors had arrived.

I met them at the airfield, landing my microcopter just a minute or two before their Cessna Citation swooped in. Brandon was there, smiling desperately through a shiny, newly-shaven face.

They stepped down from the plane, two women and a man. We shook hands all around. The taller of the women introduced herself as Marnie Havercamp.

"Pleased to meet you," I said. "I've just come from writing out our little greeting."

She looked (down) at me with a deliberately blank face. "We know," she drawled. "We were examining your farm on Google RealTime Earth. I never knew Texas had a U in it. Did you, Aloysius?"

The man shook his head and suppressed a laugh. "Not till now."

Sweat ran down Brandon's face.

I let him go ahead and earn the big bucks.

Ode to an Earthworm

Gareth D. Jones

The tractor hurtled along the old road, bouncing Logan in his seat. He sang to himself as he drove, an old nursery rhyme from who-knows-where:

"There's a worm at the bottom of the garden." The road had not been resurfaced for decades. It was cracked, full of potholes that sprouted tufts of grass, cracks lined with moss and roots breaking up the edges. "And his name is wiggly woo." He beeped the horn twice as a coda to the two lines. On the right, he passed a cluster of derelict cottages where farm workers had lived in times past.

"There's a worm at the bottom of the garden," he sang louder as the cottages fell behind and he felt their empty, accusing windows on his back like malevolent eyes. "And all that he could do."

It was a long way out to the Lower Field, and nobody lived within miles of the place any more.

"Was wiggle all night, and wiggle all day."

It was an odd day: nice and warm, with a breeze blowing through the open cab, but a scattering of miserable-looking clouds approached from the horizon. One of those 'fifty percent chance of sunshine and showers' kind of days.

"The people round here they often say." If only there *were* people around here. Farming had been a lonely occupation even in his grandfather's time, if the old coot's stories were anything to go by. Logan was lucky if he saw another human from one week to the next.

"There's a worm at the bottom of the garden," He took a deep breath for the finale as he rounded the final bend, "And his name is wiggly woo!" He held the last note in dramatic opera style. Maybe the mice would appreciate it.

He slowed to take the turn into the Lower Field. It had been a long day. He was tired and hungry and wanted to check on the soil condition and get back home for dinner. A pair of finches fled from the hedge as he rumbled through the gap into the field. There was no gate: he had no livestock and there was nobody around to keep out. Even he hadn't been down this way in weeks. The field was lying fallow for a year and he just wanted to check the worms were doing their job.

He hummed to himself as he made his way across the gentle slope to the centre of the hundred acre expanse, where a lonely pillar stood sentinel. He stopped the tractor beside it, unstrapped and jumped down. The stainless pillar stood a metre high and descended two metres below ground level. Logan flipped open the panel at the top and checked the power level and status. It seemed to be working fine. A sizeable rock protruding from the soil a few metres away showed the programme was having effect. From a pocket of his overalls he pulled the portable controller, a small, black-cased tablet with a nice collection of scratches and muddy stains. On making contact with the pillar, it lit up with a cheerful ping.

Here, on a little four inch screen, he could control what happened to each field individually. He scrolled through the menu options, which were mostly set to their default mode. Depending on what he selected, the pillar emitted bio-electric impulses into the ground, sending directions to myriad bioengineered worms who helped with his work. He could select the depth and rate at which they operated, increase aeration of the soil, select how thoroughly they worked the field, assign them to shift soil in any particular area by adjusting their ingestion and excretion rate, and thus move large rocks and other objects to the surface, fill hollows and level out bumps. Apparently, French farmers had used them to uncover several dozen unexploded bombs from World War One.

"There's a worm at the bottom of the garden," he murmured as he checked through the settings. Everything was okay. This was such a large field that a second pillar was set at the far end.

"And his name was wiggly woo."

He hopped back into the cab, kept hold of the controller, and roared off across the field to the second pillar.

"There's a worm at the bottom of the garden,"

He turned across the slope of the field as he neared the pillar, and saw a large rock at the last second.

"And all that he can —" He wrenched the steering wheel to the side to avoid the rock, but the small front wheel hit. The tractor jolted as the wheel bounced. The slope teamed up with gravity to take care of the rest.

Logan wished he had stopped to strap himself in, as the cab tilted and he slid across the seat. He hit his shin and head as he fell in slow motion from the cab and landed on the soft earth a second before the tractor landed on top of him. A jolt of incredible pain lanced up his legs and the field went black.

Cold and pain were the first things to claim his attention. He forced his eyes open and could see nothing but soil and weeds. It was much duller than it had been and a cold breeze chilled him. An insistent throb from his legs made it difficult to concentrate on much else. He tried to twist round to see what had happened, but spasms of agony deterred him. He went back to staring at a tuft of grass.

A splot of rain hit the side of his face, cold and shocking. Then more. Slowly this time, he craned his neck round to look behind. The cab of the tractor was pinning his legs to the ground above his knees. He had fallen far enough to avoid being crushed under the chassis. He tried to pull one leg free, and passed out instead.

Cold. The smell of damp soil and wet vegetation. A slight breeze ruffled his floppy fringe. Grass wavered in front of his eyes. It was dull, but the dimness of dusk rather than the gloom of rain clouds. It had not rained for long - there was no sign of moisture on the surface. A few hardy birds twittered away nearby.

Logan tried to feel around in his pockets for his phone, or anything else of use. There appeared to be nothing but a couple of tissues, half a pack of mints and a black marker pen. He thought hard. The phone was in the cab. Possibly now under the cab. Tricky to call for help.

"Wiggle all night," he whispered, "and wiggle all day."

He wiggled, groaned with pain, gave up.

"The people round here, they often say..." He stopped and popped a mint into his mouth. "Say, 'What a stupid man, tipping his tractor over.' Not that anyone round here knows who I am." He crunched the mint between his teeth, breathed in cold minty air.

It was getting darker by the minute, the grass fading from green to dark grey. A small black shape nestled among it, a few inches in front of his face. He reached out his arm and scrabbled on the soft earth.

"There's. A. Worm." He grunted each word, dragging his fingers forward by their nails. "At. The. Bottom. Of." His fingers brushed against cold plastic and he scrabbled to get a grip. "The. Garden!" He yelled his delight as his fingers gripped the case and he dragged it slowly back to him.

He pulled the screen close to his eyes and flicked the controller on, blinking several times before he could focus. His brain was aching almost as much as his body Fighting to concentrate, he started punching commands into the little unit. He selected several standard options, modified the programmable parameters and specified the operational area.

"And his name is wiggly woo." He punched the execute button, and rewarded himself with another mint.

Darkness fell and, unfelt, the earth began to move.

The night was very long. Much longer, Logan discovered, when you are lying injured and wet in a field than when you are tucked up cosy and warm in bed. He dozed occasionally, woken by shivers and pain. He ate his way through the rest of the mints, counted blades of grass in the dark, recited some half-remembered poems from school, found himself talking to people who were not there and he could not properly remember.

Logan woke with a screech as something changed. It was his legs. The pressure was suddenly lessened and the unconstricted blood flow brought new waves of pain up his limbs. The tractor creaked, and Logan dared to look behind him. Dawn was only moments away and a pale golden light cast an eerie glow over the setting. The tractor was no longer flat on its side. The angle was minimal, but the vehicle was definitely less horizontal than it had been last night. He sagged back onto the ground and sobbed quietly with relief.

By the time the sun rose above the hedgerow, Logan could see a small gap between his legs and the cab. The tractor was slowly listing towards upright, sinking into the hole being excavated by unnumbered worms.

Logan began the slow and painful task of turning himself round and slithering into the cab. Finally he was facing the opposite way, a manoeuvre carried out in twenty or thirty pain-filled increments. The gap beneath the cab was tall enough to slither under. He worried for a while that the worms would work faster than him and tip the tractor upright before he was able to reach the phone. He could not face the thought of having to climb the steps into the cab. Worms are slow creatures though, even thousands of them.

He slipped into the space beneath the cab and fumbled round above his head for the holster where he often clipped his phone. It was still there. He pulled it loose and let his arm fall back to the ground, breathing heavily.

Compared to programming the worm colony, dialling 999 was a cinch.

"There's a worm at the bottom of the garden," he whispered, as sirens in the distance brought an overwhelming sense of relief. "And his name is wiggly woo."

He closed his eyes and waited.

A Touch of Frost

Renee Stern

The frost alarm tumbled Tristao out of his snug bed into the midnight chill of the farmhouse. He knuckled away the dream of a wild liberty weekend in Seattle and dropped into his battered computer chair, bringing up the sensor net before he remembered to silence the alarm and key in lights and coffee.

He blinked against the glare of the overhead light panels before blindly dialing down the brightness to a more comfortable level. The clock digits on the wall in front of him shone a brighter red: 0113. Two hours of sleep.

A coffee bulb slid out of the slot within easy reach of his left hand, just below the interactive map screen of his farm. He popped open the bulb, the spicy steam that curled around him jolting him a fraction more alert, and started a fast diag of essential systems.

Frost protection was supposed to kick in automatically whenever sensors registered temperatures low enough to damage the sensitive young buds on his far-flung acres of cherries, apples and wine grapes. The software mimicked the decision-making skills of farmers with decades of experience, cutting the time needed to weigh reams of data to picoseconds and making possible one-man operations bigger than anything his grandparents had ever imagined.

Waking to the backup alarms signalled his first system failure since its installation six years ago. Tristao scanned the diag results, praying for a software bug rather than a mechanical. If temperatures were low enough to trigger the alarm, he'd never manage to troubleshoot the hardware or swap out parts in time to save his crop, even if he rushed out to his closest sites and rousted contractors for the rest.

But the diag showed no bugs or malfunctions. "Naturally," he muttered, tapping out a forceful, one-handed command for a more detailed check.

He inhaled a deeper breath of coffee steam from the insulated bulb, using it to focus on the next necessary step rather than on emotional responses that wasted precious time. He turned to the sensor data and keyed temperature-coded colours onto the map.

Tristao swirled a careful sip of dark roast around his mouth and tried to make sense of the puzzle before him. The pinks and reds that signified dangerously low temperatures didn't show up in his normal frost pockets. He'd have to scour the system to see if it was misreading the data from the sensor net, or if the problem lay instead with either the sensors themselves or the wireless network that linked everything.

First, though, he had to kick-start the fans and overhead sprinklers before he lost too much ground to this unexpected freeze. He jabbed the manual controls, then sipped more coffee while the signals streamed out and back.

The trick to farming efficiently was to ride as close to the leading edge as you could get. Send out the pest patrol 'bots just before the insects emerged. Wet the root systems just before the soil dried out enough to cause water stress. Start the wind machines around the trees and vines just in time to warm the air with the least amount of energy, and hit the sprinklers just in time to coat sensitive buds with a protective layer of ice before the temperature plunged even lower.

He gulped down half the coffee, then stared at the blank command screen, cursor blinking back at him in smug proof the system hadn't locked up. It was waiting, ready for input. Ignoring his command.

He ground his teeth and threw the bulb into the recycling slot by his knee. *What's gone wrong now?* Conscious of seconds ticking away, he called up more data to lay over the map: five years of yield and profit bars for each orchard and vineyard block, cold hardiness for each varietal, market trends, energy costs.

The computer responded normally this time, but what about the next command? His entire operation hinged on the software that tracked and controlled an inherently chaotic organic system.

More pink splotches appeared on the map, drumming urgency at him. He'd calculated more complex equations, but never without the computer as a check. Never in such a press of real time. Tristao yanked off his fleece pullover, suddenly too warm, and wiped his sweating hands dry on it before tossing it at the bed.

Where should he spend the power to run the fans and where did he need to focus his precious water allocation for the sprinklers? Which blocks should he write off and which ones did he need to jump on now, before the warning pink appeared?

This was shaping up to be a make-or-break period. After two years of basement prices, conditions pointed to short crops from most of the competing growing regions, and this freak freeze was likely to cut Northwest yields as well. Tristao hadn't finished paying off the hospital debt from his mother's final illness, let alone made a dent in the bills for the farm upgrades. He didn't need to call up the accounting subroutine; that rising tide of red threatened him even in his sleep.

Save the Syrah and Sangiovese on Red Mountain, and go all out on those third-leaf blush cherries around Hood River and the RubySnap apples he was trying out in Cowiche. The Merlot at Wahluke would have to take its chances; those vines were on next winter's replacement schedule anyway.

One by one he tackled the red and pink zones, sweat beading on his body even after he toed off his wool socks and dragged the legs of his sweatpants up over his knees. After the longest ten minutes of his life he reached the end and zapped the command list to the wireless network that linked him to every block on his farm.

The screen blanked again. His pulse stuttered. *What now?*

He snatched up the stylus but, before he could scribble out a command, the cursor appeared on the screen, heralding a steady stream of letters. Recommendations at last. Tristao squinted and sucked at his lower lip as he read.

A third of them matched his own decisions. He switched to his upper lip, teeth worrying away at it. Was it simply a delay in the system, or did the problem extend further? He didn't have time to ponder, though snap decisions always made his skin itch.

He circled the nine items that agreed, lined out the rest and pulled in what was left of his original commands, then sent his list out a second time. This time the fan and sprinkler icons popped up in the proper parts of the map screen.

He called up the webcams for every affected block to watch the fan blades whirring and the sprinklers spraying water. Tristao sank back in his chair with a deep breath.

After a quick shower Tristao pulled his steaming breakfast tray out of the oven. He inhaled deeply, the homey smell of eggs and *bacalhau* filtering into his memory: He was sitting again at the dark, battered kitchen table across from his sister, his father slicing apple wedges for them all and debating farm decisions with his mother while she stirred the chunks of salt cod into their eggs. Donnie was jetting around Asia now, marketing the latest gizmos; she hadn't been home since their mother's memorial service, but she'd started drifting away back when Papi died.

He dropped the tray on the counter, no longer hungry. He'd pulled the eggs and *bacalhau* as a reward for beating the crisis. *Some reward. More reminders of loss.* He fished a chill cover from the drawer and set breakfast aside for later, when he could stomach it.

His more-detailed system check should be finishing up by now. He cut out the nighttime tint on the window as he entered the control room; sunrise was still three hours away but the bright moonlight painted in ghostly silver the gnarled shapes of the heirloom apple trees his great-grandparents had planted when they built the farmhouse.

Three lines of letters scrolled across the top quarter of the screen. He slid into the chair and rolled closer to read.

Diagnostics complete. Breath caught in his lungs, Tristao checked the next line, hoping for a simple fix.

All systems functioning normally.

Tristao loosed an explosive "What?" before sucking in a deeper breath that did nothing to calm him. Calling in tech support would empty his emergency fund before the growing season hit high gear and would force him to whittle off vital parts of his budget if another emergency popped up. He had a long day of code wrangling ahead of him, seeking answers while trying not to snarl the system into an even bigger tangle.

He stared out the window a moment, wrestling for calm. A sinuous motion against the trunk of the closest tree told him the wind had come up out of the Northwest, blowing into their protected hollow from around the curve of the hill and down the driveway gap in the poplars. Only the northwest wind ever caught Papi's rope swing like that.

Northwest winds always meant trouble. Nights like this made Tristao half-believe the tribal legends that populated the mountain peeking over the northwest horizon with angry spirits. They'd howled outside his boyhood bedroom the night Papi died.

Jaw set, he stared out the window, denying their reality until he'd rubbed away the prickling flesh on his arms. At last he turned to the final line on the screen.

You should have followed all our recommendations. You can still salvage most of your profit if you hurry and make these changes.

"What the...." His stunned whisper trailed away in a slack-jawed stare as a list scrolled across the screen.

He bellied up to the controls and dived into the files, focusing on the last week or so of email as the most likely vector for a worm sophisticated enough to get past his shields and take over his system. It was the only explanation.

How much of what the system told him could he trust? Was it glitched all the way down to his frost alarm?

Stop wasting time, Kitry. Focus on what's important.

His hands fell away from the controls as the name registered. No one had called him Kitry since Papi died.

"Dammit, Donnie!" His suspicions reluctantly fell on his sister, who'd emailed him two days ago from – where was it again? Macau? Malaysia? Malta? Somewhere with an M. She had the programming expertise and shady contacts to do this, though he struggled with why.

She'd only ever called him Tao. Still, Kitry pointed to family somehow. Their mother had given him her family name for his middle name; she'd winced whenever Papi shortened it from McKittrick. And Donnie was all the family he had left.

Focus, boy. You've got too many acres at stake. Chat later.

Tristao sneaked a look out the window. The rope swing had stilled. Whatever had come over his system didn't feel like Donnie's doing, and Kitry ruled out a random attack. Farming wore the trappings of science, but at its deepest heart it was as much a gamble as shooting craps.

He turned back to the screen, scrolled up and circled the system's recommendations. He breathed deep, held it a moment, stylus hovering over the screen, then drew a link to the green traffic light icon.

The hourglass blinked in. "Roll them bones," he whispered, wiping his palms up and down his thighs, staring at the screen.

Nothing else appeared.

Sweat filmed his face and neck; a phantom wind whooshed

rhythmically in his ears in time with his racing pulse, not quite covering a delicate cascade of taps. His mother's rose bushes against the kitchen window. Dice rolling against each other and across a hard surface.

Coming up snake eyes.

Tristao logged into the Columbia Basin's virtual coffee shop at dawn, his eyes gritty after three hours of staring at a stubbornly blank dialogue screen and at the busy map with its webcam images confirming fan and sprinkler operations. He needed a break.

The place was packed; he hadn't seen this many people on the site at once since the post-harvest seminars and industry meetings. Tristao scanned the patrons' avatars, looking for specific names, and bought Inez a mocha and Doyle a green chai.

Inez sent him a thumbs-up when the mocha credit registered in her account. *How bad was the freeze at your place?* she asked.

Hard to say, he wrote back. *Guess we'll have to wait and see. Everyone got hit then?*

So they say. Doyle winked. *They're all a bunch of damn liars looking to shift the market.*

Tristao snorted. *And you're the granddaddy of them all, Doyle Verhoeven. Give me your best shot. You going to have a crop this year or are you going to be crying poor mouth from here on out?*

Inez faked a sniffle. *Our boy's all grown up, Doyle.* She laughed heartily when they both stuck out their tongues, then her avatar adopted a serious face. *I had red zones last night in the strangest places – and nothing in some of my worst frost pockets.*

Doyle nodded. *Same here. It's going to throw off the whole system until I figure out how to weight those records.*

Don't remind me, Tristao wrote. *I'm looking at a full day mucking around in the system at the very least . Just popped in here to rev up. That the only weird thing you two noticed last night?*

Wasn't that enough? A light bulb glowed above Inez's image. *I blame the geeks. Bet they've perfected weather control to spook us and bring in more business for tech support.*

Wait a minute. Doyle keyed in everyone in the room. *We've got Inez's hundredth conspiracy theory for the year. System says Schooner won the pool – and I say he owes her a drink.*

Tristao shook his head. *Didn't he win last year too? Now I smell a conspiracy.* He sent a smile over to Schooner and a private *Gotta run – catch you tomorrow* to both Doyle and Inez, then logged out.

He leaned back in the chair, arms stretched high over his head to pull the stiffness out of his body, suddenly hungry for the breakfast he'd set aside earlier. As he pushed to his feet, he glanced out the window at a pale-pewter morning. Tiny blades of frost fuzzed the trees, rope swing and cell tower; his heart skipped at the harsh beauty that had settled over his land in the night.

He ordered the system to collate temperature data from the sensor nets in every block on the farm, then puttered through the house while the kitchen unit warmed up the eggs and *bacalhau* and pan-fried the potatoes he'd added. From the porch he watched the sun push pale-gold fingers over the sagebrush ridge and down toward the empty canal waiting for the spring irrigation release. The windows in the unused back bedrooms revealed the tips of Mount Rainier's ghostly glacial crown hovering above the horizon. The fogged-over kitchen window blurred the jagged geometry of the rose bushes just outside.

Donnie still sent him pictures of her travels, but not one of the lively city shots or exotic landscapes matched these views in any season. He wondered as he savoured his meal which of them she was trying to convince.

Breakfast over, he returned to the control room, ready once more to tackle work. The frost outside was bright white against a wide-open blue sky that forecast another sleepless night babysitting his buds. Tristao set his coffee on the shelf by the door, out of an absent-minded reach. He'd need an afternoon nap to catch up.

He touched the first of four Hood River blocks on the map, calling up columns of time and temperature readings for last night and the two previous days, and another for lows over the past five years. Dropping into the seat, he raked his hair back, then leaned forward to hunt for patterns.

The screen blanked, columns quickly replaced by a new message: *Leave the number-crunching to us. There's nothing wrong with your system.*

"'Us'? What's going on here?"

The cursor blinked steadily but nothing new appeared. Tristao gnawed his upper lip, on the verge of calling in tech support. But what could he tell them? "The system's talking to me"? Worse, it was giving him apparently useful advice. And it was too familiar, almost paternal.

He shuddered, trying to imagine explaining the Kitry wrinkle. They'd diagnose *him*, not the system.

Besides, he flat-out couldn't afford to waste a call to tech support. Not this early in the season. Not without further investigation.

He picked up the stylus and scribbled, *Who are you? What do you want?* As soon as he finished he rolled the chair back beyond arm's reach, stylus wrapped in a white-knuckled grip.

As long as our advice is sound, do you really need to know?

Tristao inched back to the screen. *Try to play me for a fool and I'll wipe the system clean and start fresh.*

You can't get rid of us that easily.

He narrowed his eyes at the threat. *I can pull the plug and go manual. It might mean a hard few years but I'll do it.*

You've got the McKittrick stubbornness in spades. We'll still be here. We'll still find a way to communicate. To help you.

A chill slid across his shoulders and down his arms. Common sense told him to shut down the system and call tech support, but the second reference to his family caught him in a solid grip. Maybe it was the McKittrick stubbornness that wouldn't let him retreat.

You're no worm, he wrote. *Or glitch. Whatever you are, why are you doing this?*

Perhaps we're genetic memory. Or beings outside your experience.

Holed up in a computer without any organic components? What did I tell you about taking me for a fool? The stylus bent in his tight fist, and Tristao eased back. His empty hand crept up to the off switch, safely out of the way of a careless touch.

How many generations of your family are buried on this farm? whoever – whatever – had control of his system wrote. *Like you, we're a part of this land.*

Tristao swallowed. Papi, Mother, his grandparents – *In my computer. Why mine? Why now? What do you want?*

Who's to say we're unique? Do you want to turn down an edge your neighbours might have already embraced? Let us share our knowledge with you. Let us talk to you.

He forced his gaze out the window, focused on the rope swing. The loneliness in those words echoed within him. An occasional email from Donnie, meetings with his contractors and a quarterly liberty weekend in the big city didn't add up to a buzzing social life. Regular visits with his colleagues at the virtual coffee shop were pale substitutes.

Whatever had lodged in his system – and he wasn't ready to believe ghosts – was offering round-the-clock companionship, a reconstituted family and business advisor all wrapped up in one shiny package. He'd be able to talk freely, without the spectre of tipping his hand to a competitor hanging over him. Donnie was too distant and the contractors at the end of the day were his employees. Doyle and Inez shared his burdens, but that created a wall as well as a kinship.

A magpie hopped onto the swing's plank seat and threw back its head to cry out its nasal "mag mag mag." The separate strands of frost were clumping together under the bright sun.

Tristao turned back to the computer, skimming over a new plea from the system: *You'd have lost too much of your crop last night without our help.*

They offered him everything, but at what price? Live out his days tied to this room, communicating only with phantoms on the screen? Watching his farm through webcams and windows instead of feeling the summer sun and winter winds on his skin, smelling the spring blooms, the warm fruit at harvest, the earthy-green bite of winter pruning?

His relationships with Donnie, Inez, Doyle and the rest had rough edges, but so did reality. A life without mistakes and risks was like a tree kept dormant, unable to bud and fruit.

On my terms, he wrote. *Papi taught me to use my tools wisely – and not let them use me.*

Tristao walked out of the room, snatching his jacket from the peg by the front door and tugging it on before he jumped the three steps from the porch to the ground. The magpie flew away as he crunched across the grass, leaving Papi's swing to him. He hadn't sat there in too long.

He vowed to step away more often from the control room and virtual world, to spend more time out here on the physical farm. That would help strengthen his defences and avoid losing himself altogether to the temptations the ghosts in his system offered along with their help.

He swayed gently in the swing, frost fragments melting at his touch.

The World Coyote Made

Jetse de Vries

Twitter: *In the semi-arid plains of Arizona, coyote returns*

"A coyote!" Tom cried, and pointed in the distance. Janet wondered how her son could see it, through his 'haruspecs: the sight of the future' contacts. But, indeed, up ahead a wolf-like animal was sniffing the stalks of the BioBillie® corn field. *Most probably a dog*, Janet thought, *coyote's been extinct for two decades*. But she reckoned it better for Tom to see that for himself, as they got closer.

"Slow down," Tom said, "or you'll scare it away."

Janet eased off the accelerator of her solar/biofuel cell hybrid, hoping the revelation wouldn't hit him too hard. He was a sensitive kid, a child of his time: while irresistibly drawn to the latest personal gadgets, he also had a melancholic longing for species past, like rhinoceri, loggerhead turtles, and, well, coyotes (who were actually thriving in urban areas until the MRTV Betaretrovirus made the jump from rats to coyotes). She could never really figure him out: too intelligent to accept her parental authority in some matters, but too naïve to question it in others.

Silent but for the swish of the bicycle-thin tires, they stopped about twenty yards from the supposed prairie wolf. *Probably a lost guard dog*, Janet thought, *although hadn't their BetterThanOrwell© fences made these obsolete?* No love lost between Janet and BioBillie®, even though they didn't compete directly. No Sir: if she were the mote in BioBillie's eye, then she'd just have moved up a rung in society's ladder.

Tom was already out of the banana-shaped, wind-tunnel perfect hybrid, a few seconds before it comes to a halt. *So fast, so flighty*, Janet couldn't help but think; *always just out of reach*. For a heartbeat she feared he'd collided with the electric BTO© fence, but he came just *this* close to it. Probably a nanometer, to her alerted maternal instinct which, she knew, was often redundant, but which she couldn't suppress either.

She grabbed the binoculars from the glove compartment. The animal did look quite small and thin for either a dog or a wolf. *A starved wolf,* Janet thought, but then the animal bent a stalk with one of its forepaws and took a bite of the cob. Seemed to taste it like a chef testing fresh produce. Let the long stalk bounce back, and checked another cob a few meters further on.

"Weird," she said, unable to keep quiet, "wolves are carnivores, right?"

"It's a coyote, mum," Tom said, "an omnivore."

They're extinct – she wanted to say, but refrained, as the indefinite animal tested a few more cobs with an eerie ease. Did wolves or dogs eat plants in times of need? She wasn't sure, and needed to check, as Tom – especially when his mind was set – would not take her word for it. And his haruspecs contacts were probably connected to the 'net – the solar-powered wireless reach was incredible, those days – while her binoculars were old-fashionably unenhanced: she knew what it was like to live through a couple of days without power in winter time.

Then, even more incredibly, the crazy beast started peeing against the cornstalks: not one in particular, but trying to wet as much of them as possible as it hopped, on three legs, along them. *I should film this,* she thought, and only then started to reach for the iGizmo Tom had given her for her birthday. But she was too late as the noise of an approaching BioDiesel Mack chased away the weary animal.

"Stupid monster trucks," Tom said as the whatever-it-was animal disappeared in the cornfields. "They should die like 747s." 360 degrees of blue sky horizon, speckled with Aerwin zeppelins, seemed to emphasize his point. In heart-warming agreement, his mum ruffled his hair, and for once he didn't mind.

After dinner, Tom made for the shed, but his mother would have none of it.

"Young man," Janet, casting an indignant look, "what about your homework?"

"Can't I do it later?" Tom, his mind on something else, "I want to work on –"

"– your project. I know. You hardly want to do anything else. Well, you can work on your precious project *tomorrow,* after you've done your homework *tonight.*"

Tom wanted to say something, but thought better of it. As he headed up the stairs to his room, Janet said: "I'll test you in a few hours," and, after seeing his sour expression, added: "Cheer up! Once it's finished, the whole weekend's yours."

"Permission to go to Uncle Yiska if I can get it done?"

"If you keep your GPS feed switched on."

"Revo!" and Tom ran up the stairs.

Later that evening, Janet sat down to test her son, making sure he took his haruspecs contacts out. She could always tell he was wearing them by the faraway look in his eyes, as if he were seeing a different world than hers. As usual, she threw a few quick math sums at Tom, who solved them with an offhand ease. Janet suspected he didn't even study his grade's material, because he was way ahead. Similarly with physics, but less so with chemistry, and – somewhat to her disappointment, although she tried not to let it show – not so with biology. Despite her encouragements.

"How many base pairs does DNA have?"

"C'mon, Mum, that's easy: two."

"How does DNA control its environment?"

"Through protein synthesis: it produces all kinds of RNA through the use of proteins."

Oh no, Janet thought, *so often he gets it the wrong way around.* "You sure?"

"Something like that." The disinterest in his voice pained his mother, the biodynamic farmer.

"Yeah, but you say it as though your bike is driving you."

"Which it can, if constructed in the right way." Stubborn, like his father. Janet gave it one more try: "What's the chromosome number of maize?"

"I don't know. Twelve?"

"Twenty," with a sigh. "You know, *maize*: the stuff we grow around here. You would have known if you used your DNA analyzer."

"Well, you're using it all the time."

"I am, to check if my crops aren't evolving away from me."

"I know," Tom said, "your balancing act. But why bother struggling to get food from this barren land?"

"Someone has to do it –"

"BioBillie already does."

"– right," Janet continued, unperturbed, "living off the land in a sustainable way."

"We're still okay in Arizona. Nobody's starving."

"Yet."

"Come *on.*"

"Three million people in 1980, eight million in 2010, and almost eighteen million today. Fossil fuels running out, pollution, climate change..."

"Social geography is not until Wednesday. And Dad said global warming is a conspiracy."

"Your father thought *everything* was a conspiracy. There's a lot of corporate greed in this world, but there's also a lot of human stupidity."

"Yeah, but he liked the ultimate conspiracy theory: the poor can't move out of the way of climate change as fast as the rich, and will die. Once the population is reduced, CO_2 levels will go down. And if they don't fall fast enough the rich will farm the Canadian and Siberian prairies with robots."

"Tom, please don't become a nut like Atsidi." With a semi-desperate tone.

"He was smart, too." Missing her sarcasm.

Janet gave up, and softly squeezed Tom's arm. "Smart, but also a little bit crazy."

Twitter: *In the tropical forests of Southeast Asia, sun bear returns*

Through the crowded streets of Phoenix, an oriental woman runs to her office, her tiger-striped jogging outfit in sharp contrast with the metallic shine of the Greensleeves building's photovoltaic walls. The music from her wireless soundplugs filtering out the street noise:

Failing chickpeas
Felling trees
Extinct species
Empty seas
Drowning cities
Dying bees
Is there really no escape
From the world coyote made

"The Trickster Tricked", *Aura Aurora's* viral hit. Kimberly enters through the side doors, and runs up the jogging stairs to her penthouse office on the twenty-second floor. It's the less crowded route since she designated the broad stairs for normal use and the emergency one for joggers (and to hell with the cost of the extra fire escape stairs). Of course, modifying the elevators so that they will only go up empty is more than just her corporate contribution to fighting obesity; the energy generated by weighted elevators going down helps reduce her headquarters' electricity bill.

Exhausted in a good way, she enters her CEO lair, takes a quick shower, and changes into her adaptive business suit. Ready to kick ass, kick-start progress, change the world, and stick it to the man. Her multi-walled, 'green sleeved' carbon nanobuds – the green glow emitting from the encapsulated copper carbonate molecules – have revolutionized cancer treatments. Another breakthrough came when their electronics partner Pico Power successfully integrated the nanobuds with both RFID technology and sufficient memory: a 24/7 health monitoring system dubbed Lifesleeves®.

Rigorous tests ensured their multi-walled nanobuds (MWNBs) were both inherently safe and environmental friendly: a point their marketing department never fails to emphasize. It saved their FDA approval after the nanophage plague outbreaks in L.A., Shanghai, and Sydney. It did hurt sales, seriously, until she was able to turn the tide by using Lifesleeves herself, and subsequently making it mandatory for all Greensleeves staff – calling it a perk, and Lifesleeves was *very* expensive at the time – and later for all employees.

No time to reminisce, as the progress report on the SCNTR is due in five minutes, when her meeting will fill up with research scientist, technical specialists, financial advisors, and marketing people, most of them telecommuting over a safe channel. The self-correcting nanotube ribbon is a manufacturing process, meant to facilitate the production of a ten-feet-wide, mega-layered, multi-walled nanotube ribbon in space: a perfect ribbon, without a single manufacturing fault. A fault might cause a break, and rip the GOT-ribbon apart: not a good prospect for a space elevator.

This is the hardest challenge, and the greatest dream. No faults at the nano level for almost 36,000 kilometres; not a single mistake in a thirty-six million billion times. It's just one part of the equation: even when the technology is feasible, the dream must be sold. To the shareholders, to the international space consortium, and to the public at large.

Later in the afternoon a separate, even more secretive meeting – all attend in the flesh – with her legal team to determine whether their copyright of the ribbon manufacturing process entitles them to claim ownership of the ribbon itself. And then ask for rent and/or royalties every time their technology is used? Huge investments, incredible risks, and tremendous potential payoffs. The whole solar system could be her legacy, with no heir.

An intense working day; just the way she likes it. But one thing keeps nagging at her. Then inspiration strikes: that dogged researcher in the biotech division – what's his name – Jack Mingin. Always asking tough questions, always wants to get to the bottom of things. It doesn't make him popular within the development team, but his relentless probing had unearthed a number of faults that kept the Greensleeves nanotech clearly on the safe side of the fence after the nanophage outbreak. Maybe she should take him out for dinner...

"I hear you're not as happy in the development team as you used to be," Kimberly says, after sipping her Mount Fuji cocktail, "right?"

Jack nods unconsciously: he's notoriously bad at lying. "Well, both Greensleeves and Lifesleeves are well-established. Not much pioneering there."

"Plenty of pioneering in the ribbon project." With a little, knowing smile.

A pull from his Kirin beer to hide his scowl. Relishing the pricey import, he says: "That's purely mechanical. Biotech is my forte."

And your single pleasure, Kimberly thinks. "I know, and that's why I have a proposal for you."

Before she can continue, the entrées arrive. Pad Thai rice noodles with tofu for him and Hong Kong steak for her. Since they're in the Bamboo Club, Kimberly figures she might as well treat herself. *Nerdcore central, this dress has launched a thousand affairs, and you start to drool at the sight and smell of a steak.*

"I have a personal issue," she says after swallowing a bite of the expensive delicacy, "that I wish to see investigated. It's highly confidential –"

"– I'm not a private detective, Ms. Wu." Jack, confirming her reputation.

"It's only tangentially related to my love life. And I assure you it's a 100% biological matter. Hear me out."

"Okay," Jack's gaze keeps sliding down.

Pretend he's distracted by my décolleté, not the beef, Kimberly's expression remains eminently inviting. "I've been trying to get pregnant for the last couple of years, without success."

"But you've had two..." Jack stops, realising he's getting into dangerous territory, "Well, according to the grapevine..." he finishes meekly.

"It's true: I've had two abortions during the wild year when we celebrated the cure for AIDS." Her grin widened. *He's not completely lost to the wider world.* "Which makes my current infertility all the more strange. It's not for lack of effort, I can tell you.

"I've tried the natural way – with a slew of partners – IVF, and goodness knows what wacky alternatives. I've had myself examined in several top clinics, and nobody can find anything wrong with me.

"I've been looking around, and there are more women, healthy women, some of them mothers already, that have developed the same problem. There's something fishy going on, and I want to get to the bottom of it. Experience tells me you're the kind of man who doesn't stop until he finds an answer.

"Help me get pregnant," a double entendre that misses the mark, judging by his blank face, "and I'll make it worth your while."

Twitter: *In the eucalyptus forests of the Blue Mountains, wombat returns*

In the plains of the southern Painted Desert, a small dust cloud was visible on the horizon, preceded by a brilliant diamond-like speck. As it came closer, the speck gained definition became a small three-wheeler, whose driver was pedalling at full throttle over the flat sands.

Tom was riding a strange kind of tricycle: three eighteen inch chrome wheels spinning so fast that the stroboscopic effect approached the flicker fusion threshold of the human eye and the spokes seemed to move backward. The frame – a vibra-welded motley of discarded composites salvaged from Flagstaff's recycle centre – supported a transparent sail gossamer that literally crackled with energy, fastened to the speeding contraption through an extended telescopic pipe mounted just behind the form-fitting, bio-active, faux leather driver's seat, while two swivelling filament antennas stuck out at oblique angles at each side of the front wheel. Tom was pumping like mad, paying more attention to the little dash mounted on the handlebars than to the deserted plain before him.

"Sixty-nine point eight... Sixty-nine point nine..." Tom whispered. "Seventy! Seventy miles an hour!"

It was faster than he hoped for, although the conditions – cloudless sky, strong wind in his back – were quite favourable. More solar and wind energy propelling his straycycle as anticipated, or the gossamer was more efficient than he thought. He'd be with his uncle soon. Maybe even *too* soon, because he was enjoying the ride so immensely.

A large Native American of Navaho descent stood near the entrance of the Indian Casino, his stoic stance broken as he watched the approach of the weird vehicle in the distance. Yiska's sister-in-law had called him – as always – to check if her son had arrived yet. She meant well, but she should give the boy more leeway, more room to make his own mistakes. Best way to learn. If only his brother Atsidi hadn't... But bygones were bygones, and Tom was not his child to raise.

She didn't mention *how* his nephew would arrive, and it took a few seconds before his brain accepted the evidence of his eagle eyes: it *was* Tom, driving that slick, futuristic bike. Yiska's doubts mirrored the uncertainty principle: the more he appreciated the trike, the less he believed the boy could afford it. Yiska was aware of Janet's financial situation. His outer calm, if anything, remained even firmer as his inner doubts mounted.

Smiling and smooth, he walked up to Tom as the boy stopped his straycycle on the casino's parking lot, under the admiring look of a few visitors who were having a quick smoke in the outside heat. Still, he couldn't quite keep the disbelief from his voice: "You made that bike?" Yiska said, "How could you afford such a high-tech piece of equipment?"

"I was one of the winners of Sun Synergy's Solar Gossamer **Challenge.**"

Yiska let out a long whistle. "Impressive. Why didn't you tell me?"

"Because I wanted to surprise you." Tom replied, radiating pride.

"Isn't it *revo?*"

"Yeah, really *out there,*" Yiska, nodding in awe, "especially that sail. It shimmers and crackles."

"Don't touch it!" Tom said as Yiska reached out to the transparent material, "The material can build up high static charges."

"In that case, young warrior, you can't park it here."

"They dissipate into the batteries; takes about thirty seconds. Then it'll automatically retract."

"Oh yeah?"

"Just watch."

After two dozen seconds that almost stretched Yiska's faith beyond breaking point, the iridescent colours faded, the static hissing stopped, the front wheel antennae swivelled up as a miniscule servomotor reeled in the gossamer sail through the telescopic pipe that simultaneously retracted. In rest position Tom's straycycle resembled a fancy trike with two strange whip aerials pointing backwards to a pipe that supported only air.

"It's ultralight," Tom said, lifting his 'strike' with one hand, "only seven pounds."

"Coyote howled!" Yiska, awestruck until a practical matter struck him, "But how do you lock it?"

"Lock it? I haven't thought of that."

"Then we better put it inside," the Navaho smiled, "and get you lunch. You must be hungry after such a ride."

Eating his bean tortilla in a quiet corner of the casino's restaurant, Tom wondered, "Why do people still eat meat?"

"Because they like it?" Yiska replied, before taking a bite of his cheese burrito.

"Yeah, but how can they afford it?" Tom pointed to a family of four. "The father's having a $90 hamburger, while his wife and kids take $10 vega sandwiches."

"The man's the breadwinner," Yiska in a dead-on deadpan. "He's entitled to his daily meat."

"In what century do these people live?"

"Not the twentieth."

"The nineteenth?"

"Unfortunately, the 21st."

"Can't be. To spend so much money on beef, you gotta be addicted."

"Americans? Addicted?" Yiska said, with mock sincerity. "They need a quadruple by-pass to get clean. It's 'cause of the four Gs."

"Four gees?" Tom, with real curiosity. "What do you mean?"

The big red guy got up, raised his right forefinger to his pursed lips, and then held up four fingers.

"Four letter word?" Tom asked.

Yiska shook his head, held up four fingers again and then pointedly moved his index finger forward four times.

"Ah: four different words, with the same first letter."

One thumb up. Then he pointed his arms forward: three fingers clenched, index finger pointing straight ahead, thumb pointing to the ceiling. Every time he pointed to another object, his arm jerked back.

"Guns!"

Thumb up, with forefinger retracted. Index and middle finger up.

"Second word."

Yiska mimicked twisting an imaginary cap, then grabbing something from a hook, and putting it in the orifice just opened.

"Gas!"

An 'O' formed with thumb and forefinger, then three fingers up.

"Third word."

His right hand moved to his back pocket, and mimicked taking something out of it. His left hand took something out of the something in his right hand, and laid it on a flat surface. His right hand put the something back in his pocket, and then both hands swept something from the flat surface into a bag or suchlike.

"Grabbing!"

A shake of the head and a wagging of a forefinger. A walk to an imaginary object in which something small was dropped from a closed thumb and forefinger, and then a lever was pulled. This repeated a few times.

"Gambling!"

Two thumbs up, and with a grand circling gesture indicating the building they were in. Four fingers up.

"Fourth word."

He opened up both his hands, as if to grab something big. Then he held this huge thing, and brought it to his mouth. Opened his mouth as far as he could, bit and chewed.

"Grapefruit?"

A sour expression and an emphatic no-no.

"Dunno... Gourmet sandwich?"

An amused shake of the head, and the raising of one finger.

"Yeah, I know: *one* word, not two. This one's hard. Hm... Gingerbread?"

Another negative.

"Guacamole?"

No dice.

"Garlic?"

Headshaking with a pinched nose.

"Gorgonzola?"

"No," the smiling red man broke his silence, "Gigaburgers!"

"That's not a real word." Tom protested.

"It's the best thing I could come up with a 'G'. So kaboozle me."

"Dwoozle kaboozle and Huey Kablooey: using made-up words is not fair."

"You're doing it yourself. Anyway, sometimes you need to guess at the new."

"Or stay behind? Why are so many people so rectangular, so hung-up in their ways?"

"In our society, stupidity and inventiveness co-exist, feeding off each other. We're living in the lazy aftermath of a slow apocalypse."

"It's a conspiracy," Tom whispered, mimicking his father so close a chill ran down Yiska's spine.

"There is no real pure 'good', or pure 'bad', just a lot of people making ill-informed and conflicting choices. Education, baby!" Yiska smiled despite the déjà vu.

"Maybe we need a counter conspiracy that forces people to learn."

"Like forcing you to eat sprouts? Won't work."

Tom made a face. "But don't you make money out of three of those four gees? In your casino, you're selling burgers and you have a gas station."

"Young warrior, you are sharp as ever. I plead guilty, but with extenuating circumstances. Therefore, I'd like to introduce you to a good friend who's here today..."

Twitter: *In the subtropical plains and valleys of Andalucía, lynx returns*

The South American coastline has moved out of sight, and with a view of nothing but deep blue ocean Kimberly decides to opaque the window on the bottom of her business cubicle in the gondola, and do some work. *Ecuador!* Her mind shouts as she rolls out her flextablet. The base the LiftPort Group had in mind was somewhere in the middle of the Pacific. Luckily, she and other partners were able to convince them that a few klicks off the Ecuadorian coast near Coaque was a better choice: logistically, economically, and publicity-wise. That certainly was progress in her book.

She connects to the onboard wifi, and while her mailbox fills up, she checks the local news. The governments in Quito and Lima have signed an economic treaty with the Gaviotas anarcho-eco-capitalists. The region has become a hotbed for ecological experiments ever since the secession of the 'Gaviotas Archipelago' – a cluster of self-sustaining enclaves scattered across Colombia, Peru, Ecuador and Venezuela that became wealthy by licensing their ecological knowhow. Peru and Ecuador – investing their Yasuní crowdfunding in even more sustainable projects – take a more pragmatic approach than oil-producing Venezuela and gung-ho Colombia, who repeat their call to arms.

She switches to music, and the shuffle shoots right to the middle of *Aura Aurora's* enviro-dubs:

> *Combat parties*
> *Killing sprees*
> *Broken treaties*
> *Wounded knees*
> *Avid sentries*
> *Army bleeds*
> *Hope it's not too late*
> *For the world coyote made*

An inflight announcement jumps up her screen: due to good weather conditions, the solar/biofuel ratio of the Quito-Phoenix flight is expected to be 90/10, meaning that all passengers will get an almost full rebate on their fuel surcharge. Even though that amount of money is small beans for her, she joins the cheer that erupts in the gondola. *I should have invested in Sun Synergy's Gossamer*, she thinks, *but I just didn't foresee that they would team up with Aerwin Zeppelins.* The diamond-like sheen of the highly electrostatic material covering the 200-meter air behemoths makes them hard to look at directly in sunny weather. With current fuel prices, though, their combined solar/biofuel-cell electroprops outcompete jet airliners left, right, and centre. Also, a twenty-four hour flight in (relatively) spacious accommodations is a great way to travel: work or eat in the multipurpose cubicles, sleep in one of the inner cabins with actual beds, and even a small bar – standing room only – in the back of the gondola.

She wraps up the minutes of the meeting, answers a couple of emails, and starts wondering what to do for the rest of the evening – maybe invite the rugged, latino gentleman of cabin 42 for dinner? – when a message from Jack Mingin hits her inbox. She opens it immediately, and gets excited. He's finally reporting some progress. She calls him, and tells him to pick her up at the Phoenix Z-port tomorrow. Now she figures she's earned an apéritif.

Jack parks his brand new trybrid – he loves the addition of the gossamer sail, after that cute kid's design – at the Terra Cotta Café.

"Starbucks not good enough for you?" Kimberly says with a straight face.

Jack can never guess when she's mocking him, or not. "A Seattle has-been, like Boeing and Microsoft. Adventure Coffee's not only much better, but certified organic and fair trade as well."

"Once a Tusconan, always a Tusconan." She flashes a quick wink while she gets out of the car. "And a double espresso. Or a triple, if they have it."

"Dunno, but –" Jack hurries to keep up with her, "the espresso they brew here is... intense."

"Well, let's say I had an... interesting night, so let's get on with it."

Inside, waiting for their orders to arrive, Jack wonders, not for the first time, how she does it. If *he* pulls an all-nighter, he looks like hell spewed up. She, on the other hand, shines like a movie star ready to pick up her Oscar. Always. She breaks his trance.

"You had something to report. About time, considering all your travel expenses."

"I was doing certain tests, disguised as 'Lifesleeves effectivity checkups'. Actually, I did those as well."

"Don't defend yourself; this is not a boardroom meeting. Costs are unimportant *if* you get results. Progress report."

The arrival of an oversized espresso and a normal cappuccino give Jack a moment to regain his senses. "To cut to the chase –"

"Yes."

"– there is a retrovirus in your immune system."

"Jesus wept, not HIV all over again, please?" Her voice echoes with hurt and pleading.

"Not as far as I can see, and I've looked *very* hard. I had to, as it's chaotically embedded and dormant most of the time."

"But why don't our Lifesleeves catch it?"

"This is new, unknown. It also doesn't seem malignant, except for one single exception: it renders both sperm and ova infertile."

"So that's the cause of my infertility? Zap it out of me!" Her right hand squeezes his left wrist, hard.

"I wish it was that easy. This strange retrovirus is a master of disguise, and extremely resilient. Right now, I've only identified it and seen what it does. Finding a cure may prove… difficult."

"How difficult?"

"Well, how long did it take before HIV was cured?"

"I can't wait that long. And how widespread is it, by the way?"

"Incredibly widespread: over 70% of people I tested were infected."

"Jesus wept. You've been on all five continents. It's worse than AIDS."

"It's a greater pandemic, but the only effect I've seen so far is that it makes people infertile. Not directly life threatening."

"Now I think about it, I do recall a few scientific articles that mentioned a decline of birth rates. If this gets out…"

"There might be a worldwide panic. I need to do more research, make sure of my results."

"Indeed. Form a team of people you can trust absolutely, then continue your research under the 'Lifesleeves effectivity tests'. Report to me every month."

Twitter: *In the highland savannahs of Zambia, trumpeter hornbill returns*

"So after we sequence a genome from existing DNA libraries and other sources," the scientist said, straightening out her silk skirt, "we reassemble the entire genome from scratch. Then, from a closely related species, we use surrogate mothers to raise the specimens."

"You're reintroducing extinct species?" Tom said. "So the coyote Mum and I saw was real?"

Big Yiska and the scrawny biologist exchanged a knowing glance. "We have released a number into the wild, to see how they do. But we haven't announced it; we'd rather be sure that they're adapting well before we do."

"But..." Tom said, "some hunters might shoot them."

"We're not afraid of that," Yiska said, with a sardonic smile. "As coyotes are not *officially* extinct, and the one hundred grand fine for shooting one is still in effect."

"The ones we released all have biometric equipment and GPS locators. We'll know almost immediately if one dies. If it's not from natural causes you can be sure we will raise hell." The scientist said, stroking her tawny hair with slender fingers.

This reassured Tom a bit, although he still had questions. "How do you get financing if you're not advertising your work widely?"

"There is a huge informal network that's giving us a lot of silent support," she said while carefully picking a blister beetle from a slender, long leg, "and we like to keep it low key. Everybody wants to be the next Gaviotas without realizing they took almost thirty years to create their success story. In nature there's no such thing as an overnight sensation."

Then she fixed her hazel eyes on the radiant green creature and seemed to lose all interest in the conversation.

"Thanks for talking with my nephew, Carol," Yiska said, taking the cue, and turning to Tom. "Tom, can you wait a few minutes in the lobby while I finalise my business with Carol?"

Leisurely leaning backwards on the plush faux leather couch, Tom typed like a madman on the fold-out keyboard of his iGizmo, updating his diary. Yiska's office wasn't fully soundproof, and Tom's keen hearing inadvertently picked up shards of the discourse within.

"...that approach seems too scattershot..."

"...single plants, but disperses through the soil, quite fast..."

"...recognizes the patented genomes: we carefully bred that into..."

"...double-safe, the bacteria remain inert in the human digestive tract, but..."

"...retrovirus is spread throughout the meat..."

"...transforms only the gametes..."

"...reversible by keeping to a vegetarian diet..."

Tom's real attention, though, was turned inside, trying to record his ideas and impressions at the speed of thought, and only his subconscious took note of the scattered conversation pieces. He didn't look up until Yiska tapped him on the shoulder: "Sorry about that, but she needs to catch a zeppelin in Flagstaff. How about the shooting range, young warrior?"

"Yeah," Tom jumped up and quickly saved his last entry. "My arrow will split yours, chief."

"Keep dreaming, boy," Yiska said as they went out to fetch their bows.

Heading home, slightly tacking against the eastern wind, Tom was too excited to settle in the zig-zag groove, let his brain run on zen autopilot, but reminisced about the exhilarating news instead: threatened species, possibly even extinct ones, could make a comeback. How he'd love to help raise a loggerhead turtle, or implant a re-sequenced rhinoceros embryo.

It would be so revo, he thought through the blank static noise coming off the tricycle's gossamer sail, but realised that biology wasn't exactly his strongest point. Maybe that was because he never really put his mind to it, with him making all these techno-gadgets in his spare time. Biotech was so fuzzy, so complex; it intimidated him. His mum's subtle (she thought) guidance in that direction didn't help, either. His father's recalcitrance resurfaced in a silent manner, as Tom didn't protest or get outraged but simply went his own way.

If biotech was easy, everybody would be making a billion in his back yard, crossed his mind while he turned his strike for the next tack, still doing a considerable fifty-nine miles an hour. *Which is why I should try it anyway.*

In a flash of inspiration, he saw where he might start...

Returning from one of her fractymids, Janet couldn't find the DNA-analysing kit. *Where the hell is the damn thing*, she thought, angrily pushing a stray blond lock behind her ear, *I'm not too sure about this strange fungus developing on levels 3 and 4.* She needed to check it, compare it to the known ones, and upload the data to her F-mid tribe network.

It might be beneficial, it might be bad news. She checked her systematic lab-cum-workplace for the umpteenth time. *It might even be neutral. But I gotta know.*

This was crazy: she never lost it before. And who would steal her analysing kit? Most of her wireless network terminals were more expensive. She needed some coffee to help her think straight. As she walked into the kitchen, she saw Tom busy with the analyser, fully immersed in the task.

"Now you can turn me into magic mushroom compost," she said, while pouring pre-heated water into the can. "Since when did you start using *that?*"

"Since I found out that Uncle Yiska's casino funds Yitlizhi."

"Who?" Janet raised her left brow.

"Yitlizhi: biotechies who reintroduce extinct species."

"Never heard of 'em."

"Of course you haven't," Tom, with a slight smirk "They keep a very low profile."

"Then how did you find out?"

"Uncle Yiska told me. He really liked my tricycle, by the way."

"I like it, too. I was just too busy to tell you." She squeezed his shoulder, and he didn't resist. *He's really into this,* she saw, *I try for months to get him interested and no dice; Yiska just mentions biotech and kazoom: there he goes. If only Atsidi hadn't...*

"What are you sequencing?" she asked, figuring the fungus analysis would have to wait.

"Two types of corn," he said, not looking up, "to get a feel for it."

"Two?"

"Yours and BioBillie's."

"BioBillie's? How did you get that?"

"I took a sample with my ornithopter. It's got a little grapple."

You and your gadgets, she wanted to say, but refrained: he was finally using his DNA analyser and she didn't want to put him off. So she left him to it and went back to her fractymids.

Even though she worked them every day – they did need a considerable amount of attention – their sight still evoked a little surge of wonder in her scientific soul. An inverted pyramid whose four semi-fractal sides resembling Lorentz attractors gone green, filled with several 'open plateau' levels structured like Pythagoras trees where the diversified produce was grown in symbiotic splendour. She moved her electrohybrid manlift around the inverted fractal pyramids. In the red-glowing dusk she could see for miles, to where artificial patches of corn fields bespeckled the Painted Desert.

So many people, so much activity. Can the land still support them? she wondered while she turned the south-facing bioluminiscent sunflowers inward, so that the sheltered crops would get some extra growing boost during the night. The latest iteration of her 'moonshine flowers' bent back towards the sun the next morning, but still needed to be turned inwards manually every evening.

A far cry from the farmscrapers that inspired them, she mused while she moved her moonshiners. The massive, one-city-block, 47-story-tall, fully automated vertical farms she saw in Vancouver made a deep impression, way back. At least the Canadians were re-investing their tarsand oil revenues in long term, self-sustainable projects. Her government still preferred to maintain the old ways as much as possible: fracking until the groundwater became undrinkable, gradually replacing gas with cornfed biodiesel, covering every available field in maize if need be.

Is that stupid fungus glowing, as well? she wondered. *Or is it the reflection?* Maybe it *was* benign, having picked up some good characteristics. A positive development for once wouldn't hurt,. After the Vancouver trip, Janet had been on the forefront of the new technology, developed by a growing group of idealist spread across the country who didn't have access to the enormous initial investments the farmscrapers required and so turned to more human-sized alternatives. After a huge amount of widely scattered trial-and-errors the model was improved until the beta version only needed an initial frame to grow. Once the initial phase was successfully established, the frame parts could be extracted (and re-used), and the fractymid would grow to its optimum size by itself.

Back then, Atsidi and I thought we could change the world. She had suffered many setbacks, as adapting her fractymids to the aridness and the large temperature variations of the Colorado Plateau proved very complex. After being on the verge of bankruptcy for years on end, she finally had realistic hopes of breaking even, partly thanks to the

AirDrop irrigation for arid environments from Australia and the advanced biochar production method to enhance her poor soil, both found by her F-mid tribe.

I might even start paying back debts, she hoped, while she turned on of the minicams to focus on the phosphorescent fungus, *if I can get these fractymids self-sufficient*. It remained frustrating. On the one hand she struggled to integrate hygroscopic plants with crops, desperately designing a super-symbiotic structure that could both quickly absorb the short summer monsoon and the winter snow melt and then slowly release the water to the desired produce. On the other hand huge agricultural companies built gigantic basins to catch summer rain runoff and winter melt, lined their corn fields with near-endless rows of solar powered dehumidifiers to increase yield, all subsidized by a biofuel-hungry state.

The price of emulating Mother Nature, she realized, *is fine-tuning that never ends*.

Twitter: *In the wet, green pastures of Europe, jackdaw returns*

Jack's trybid drives through the scorching heat of the Sonoran Desert at a predetermined speed: the blazing sun could give him more propulsion if he would switch off his air conditioner. At 106 degrees that's not really an option, so he glides on at 41 miles an hour. *Aura Aurora* rides the airwaves:

> *Terra turnstile*
> *Taunting pyre*
> *Urban lifestyle*
> *Under fire*
> *Vegan food trial*
> *Vox for hire*
> *Prepare for the new way*
> *In the world coyote made*

Inuit ice-dubbers proclaiming that loss of habitat forces them to become performers. Their songs reflect this, and Jack sympathizes: *It's already this hot in May. Goodness knows what Summer will bring*. He'd have preferred to conduct more tests in his cool lab, but Ms. Wu has other plans.

Without the co-ordinates, and without Siri 3D iMap, he'd never find the place. The last fifteen miles his navigation system has lost track of the GPS satellites, and is going on dead reckoning. He's getting closer and closer to the zeppelin he noticed five minutes ago. It looks like the place all right, with several people present. He parks his trim Synergy Sunstar next to Kimberly's sleek Tesla Roadster.

He meets her with his usual tact. "Why did you tell me to come to this godforsaken place? Hotter than hell and in the middle of nowhere."

Kimberly, anticipating as always, has moved out of the group she was in. "Exactly: no snoops. Eight mile ribbon strength test."

"But isn't that planned for next month, off the Ecuador coast?"

"You really think we'd do a public test that has the smallest chance of failing? We've already had three eight-mile ribbons stretch-tested horizontally, up to a pressure of 15 GPa. They all passed, and we decided to test one destructively. It tore at 16.5 GPa." Her smile echoes with motherly overtones. "Today, a simulation of the vertical test run with a zeppelin."

"You've hired a zeppelin for this?"

"General McDonald of the Goldwater Range happily lent us one of his training zeps."

"How?" Jack has to admit things are never boring around her.

"Connections. And there are certain advantages to dealing with someone in the flesh that virtual reality will never overcome."

"But involving the military –"

"They've been in it from the start: they need to know how to protect the space elevator from terrorist attacks, they'll want to use it to get some of their – non top secret – stuff into orbit cheaply."

"Aren't you compromising the company's integrity?"

"They like the idea that the patent for the SCNTR ribbon is in the hands of an American company. They're so much easier to work *with* than *against*, if you play it right. For example, during this test they keep the area well-sealed off: minimising the chance of industrial espionage."

"I wasn't stopped for a security check."

"Because I gave them your personal details."

"Sometimes I wonder when you're going to run for president."

"Well, to space first," with the slightest hint of a smile. "Anyway, while everybody watches the zep taking out the ribbon, why don't we move out of the way?"

To the side, there's a scattering of shade under a blossoming elephant tree. It offers little relief to the freely-sweating Jack, while Kimberly retains an outward cool. *The guy's so incredibly smart,* she thinks, *if only he had some ambition.* After letting off a soundless sigh, she asks: "Any progress?"

"Yes and no." The advantage of his candour: he never lies or plays down bad news.

"The bad news first, please." Kimberly likes to end on a high note, even if it's a relative one.

"Well, I don't foresee a cure anytime soon. It'll take years, probably decades. This is a very evasive retroviruse."

"So I need to consider adoption?"

"Maybe not: the retrovirus seems to decay slowly. In all samples about 60% dies off after ten months. Extrapolating, this might mean it expires after about eighteen to twenty-four months."

"In an inactive test tube. But what about a living, breathing human being?"

"I did unearth a strange correlation: the retrovirus travels along in meat. Predominantly cattle, pigs, and poultry, as far as I can tell. In there, it remains dormant, but is triggered into activity by something in the human digestive tract. Not sure yet what exactly, but I might pinpoint it."

Kimberly makes a face: "Looks like AIDS's little brother: origin unclear, jumps over from animals, spread worldwide."

"Not quite. It's not contagious. At least not for humans. You only get it by eating meat products: vegetarians are not affected. I've tested married couples where the carnivore is affected and the herbivore stays clean."

Kimberly is uncharacteristically silent for a while, considering what that's been said. "If I understand you correct, then I might become fertile again if I keep to a vegetarian diet for two years?"

"Yes, that's a strong possibility. No guarantees, but it's a much better shot than waiting for a cure. And meat is damn expensive."

"All good things are." She turns her attention to the unfurling SCNTR ribbon, indicating that this session is over. But Jack still has questions.

"And the rest of the world? The declining birth rates worldwide are noticeable, even if the press remains silent about them, so far."

"Don't know, need to think about that. Maybe the world should save itself."

Twitter: *In the rainforests of Panama, jesus lizard returns*

In the dead of night, Janet was awakened by the phone in her iGizmo. Answering it, her bleary eyes could barely make out Iris's face on the small screen. One of the members of her F-mid tribe living in Maine, she immediately got to the point: "Hi Janet, I got pinged by several of our watchers. A large animal has climbed to the top level of one of your F-mids."

Huh? "Which one?"

"The North-East."

Janet turned on her bedroom network terminal and, after it had powered up, switched the screen to the minicam feeds of the NE F-mid top level. As part of the F-mid tribe's total openness policy, all the members had minicams – with night vision – mounted on every level of each of their fractymids, which were fed into the 'net 24/7, and accessible to all. Initially meant as a way to gain customer trust and publicity – 'see it grow' – the scheme soon garnered a diverse audience, from scientists to biology teachers, from fellow farmers to clients, from supporters to competitors, and from betting pools – where gamblers tried to predict the most productive fractymid – to fans who took snapshots every 24 hours to, indeed, see how they grew. This comm-unity of watchers proved their worth when anything unusual happened – fire, floods, or intruders –reporting any such incidents to the local F-mid tribe node.

So Janet was warned from the other side of the continent – who were already up – and could quickly see on her own feeds what was going on. Movement on the top level of the northeast fractymid. A thin, dog-like animal walking the agrichar soil, sniffing a corn stalk. *Kaboozle me, but normally dogs don't climb trees, right?* Her half-awake brain tried to remember. *So maybe Tom's right and this is indeed a coyote.*

Like the animal she and Tom saw a few days back, it bent the stalk and took a bite of the cob. Tasted it like a connoisseur of fine cuisine, and moved to another one. *Oh shit,* Janet got up. *I can't sell the cobs it's bitten!* She hurried outside with her iGizmo – quickly linked to the feed so she could watch what happened up there – making more noise as she approached the invaded fractymid. Her screams had the desired effect. The animal got down the farming tree and disappeared into the night. *Wily animal,* she thought, *to scale my charged fence, evade my bear scent poles, and ignore my bee swarm sounds.*

When she returned to the house, she found Tom awake, having switched the kitchen terminal to the scene.

"You up?"

"Mum, you made enough noise to raise the dead. You scared the coyote off."

"I had to. It was eating our corn."

"You were *revo*: chasing it away naked."

Maybe I should start wearing a nightgown, she thought, *if Tom starts noticing.* "Coyotes should be very wary, right?" She said. "Besides, the only weapon I have is a kitchen knife."

"We have it on camera now," Tom said, zapping through the recordings, "and here it hasn't pissed, like it did in the BioBillie field."

"What makes you think it's the same animal? Anyway, to bed. You've got school in a few hours, and I'll check which cobs I need to remove in the morning."

At breakfast, Tom was so hyper and talkative that Janet needed extra coffee just to keep up, and to suppress her morning temper. After all, he'd warmed up on biotech: a momentum she certainly didn't want to break.

"The DNA from my sample doesn't fully match that of BioBillie's patent," he said, eager to share his results.

"They never do: spontaneous mutation."

"But it's not a miniscule difference. The non-matching parts of my sample are repetitive, the same sequence inserted in several places."

"Hm... sounds like an intron. Maybe some bacteria introduced a freak mutation?"

"Intron? What's that?"

"Look it up. I don't have the time right now."

"Okay." Because his gaze didn't switch to eternity, Janet knew he still hadn't put his haruspecs contacts in. "But if it's a known mutation, I should be able to match the 'intron' sequence with a known one?"

"You could keep a tag out on BioTech.org: they have a search and compare section."

"Great!"

"But it may take quite a while. They only run non-priority searches in their off hours."

Tom rolled his eyes. "Slowboats."

"It's a huge amount of data to compare. But they do keep the tag active indefinitely, automatically notify you of a hit, and compare it with newly recorded sequences."

"*Revo.*"

"And you should support them by entering the sequences you found, as well."

"So it stays in the public domain?"

"It helps everybody. Our F-mid tribe thanks Gaia for its existence every day."

"Googling it now."

"Later. Now off to the vidclass, or you'll be virtually late."

A year later, Tom had a sequence match. *Another one,* he thought, *it'll be one more kid who analysed a BioBillie corn sample.* The matches were coming in with greater frequency, leading Tom to assume that the biofuel Moloch was gradually using an upgraded genome. But this one was different: it was from an animal. A pig. *Fauna?* He lifted his left brow, unconsciously mimicking his mother. *I put the tag in the Flora section.* He checked who added the sequence, then notified him that he entered it in the wrong category.

The compare tag did have the option to check both flora and fauna, though, as the division was often quite difficult for bacteria and viruses. So, was it a freak hit? That seemed extremely unlikely as the intron sequence was quite long and peculiar. For the hell of it, he checked the 'flora' box of his DNA tag.

"Are you coming?" His mum called out. "I thought you liked visiting Uncle Yiska."

"On my way," he said while logging out.

In the car, Janet reminisced as Tom was immersed in his haruspecs contacts. The year had been a good one: her fractymids had turned in a net profit, and future projections looked promising, very promising indeed. She had customers lining up ever since Tom became a minor celebrity after his strike was presented to the public on the nationwide Sun Synergy Presentation, and it became a *revo* item for the *devo* crowd. Although Tom didn't get any royalties on it – a main condition of the competition was that the results would become public domain – the donation button on his website raked in a neat sum, and more people wanted food from the striker's mum than she could possibly produce.

"Finally, payback time," she said out loud.

"You don't need to give the money back to Uncle Yiska. He mentioned that often enough." Tom said, multitasking with ease.

"It's my principles at stake: if I incur debts I pay them back, or die trying. You'll understand when you get older."

Tom shrugged and Janet mused on. Yiska had always supported her, when she was with or without Atsidi. *He was so energetic, so wild,* she reminisced, *while Yiska seemed so stoic, so inscrutable. Maybe I chose the wrong brother.* Yeah, Yiska: a man like a rock. Successfully running the casino, carefully investing in long term, sustainable projects that were run by an open-minded, multicultural staff. Always ready for her, and like a father to Tom.

Tom, in the meantime, couldn't suppress his curiosity and logged in to BioTech.org to check if there were more matches. To his utter surprise, there were quite a lot of them: pigs, cows, chickens. *It doesn't make sense. Why does this affect livestock?* Then it struck him: the low yield parts of BioBillie's corn were reworked into livestock feed.

Janet and Tom ride the road to the future: she wonders which one it'll be, while he tries to figure out how it works. In the background there's an inscrutable man watching their progress, his eyes on the distant horizon.

Twitter: *Polar bear, though, remains extinct, as its habitat is irretrievably gone*

Earthen

Alicia Cole

My mother once told me: the bones of the land are in my hands. Out on the range, the sky a calloused, purple bruise, I work the milky soil. My farm yields giant turnips, cat's head cabbage, black corn.

Schools often send tour busses out from the city. Their hover treads make a mess of the yard; the kids stammer and strut about in the latest plasti-wear. The girls eye me, askance. My cropped hair and dirt-covered clothes, actually sewn, earn quick disapproval. Always, one boy asks to hold a chicken.

The company who runs these busses has been in operation almost twenty years now. After farms went machine, owned land tours became popular and lucrative; it's not as interesting to visit a fully mechanized farm.

The tour leader for most of my adult life has been a retired teacher, sharp and armed with the wry humour of someone who works often with the young. Walking up from the barn as today's bus puffs to a stop, the kids spilling out in a torrent of flair and flounce, I stop when someone new dismounts.

Her brown hair is tight in a hundred braids, tiny coloured LED ribbons tied at the ends. Her skin is browner still, like the underside of fresh-turned soil. Her teeth flash as she ushers the school chaperones after their charges, raising her voice to remind a tall boy to stop running.

Sliding my gloves into my back pocket, I walk towards her.

Turning at my movement, she smiles brightly. "Oh. Hello! You must be Cor Taylor? So pleased to meet you. I'm Evaline Tate."

Without hesitation, she grabs my left hand and pumps it enthusiastically with both of hers. My pale fingers are reddened with dirt.

"Mrs. Jonas retired. Again," she explains, mouth quirking, before I have a chance to ask, my own mouth halfway through the formation of the question.

I nod in comprehension as her fingers uncoil from mine like the hairs dropping off an ear of corn. Evaline Tate stares at me, waiting, until I finally clear my throat and answer, "Yes ma'am, I'm Cor Taylor. Welcome to my farm."

Then, two of the boys start after the chickens and I turn from her clear eyes, welcoming the distraction.

Calling as loudly as I can, I announce, "Let's get this tour started then! Who wants to see a farm in action?"

While a dozen gangly arms shoot up, the other half of the group turns a look of feigned boredom my way. Having grown accustomed to children, I motion towards the barn and announce imperiously, "First one there gets an ear of corn."

Most of the boys and a few girls take off, clouds of dust kicking up as they run; the rest trail desultorily behind.

My father signed on for the programme straight out of college, turned his hand to the ground, tired of the smog and the packed streets. At first, the government paid handsomely for a steady mind to monitor the machines. The cities ate off the farms, after all, and a good engineer could program soil-cleaner and water purifiers to grow a wealth of fresh, healthy crops. It didn't take long for other men, savvy of saving the government a few bucks, to take that knowledge and manufacture farms that ran without any human aid.

My father swore the land produced more when real hands touched it. He walked the farm, lacing his fingers in cool, dark soil. When my mother moved back to the city, I stayed with him. We walked together.

As he always did, I rise early while it's still cool, the light coming up like yolk over the back field. I take strong black coffee, perform an instrument check to make sure the machines are releasing water and fertilizer at the correct pace. Most mornings, I walk through the fields to check the plants. While the sensors will pick up trouble at root level, my eyes are the first line of defence above the soil.

"Bessie monitors nitrate levels in the soil," I explain as the students bunch in to get a good look at the black flank of machinery. "It's up to me to make certain her circuits are firing right."

The barn's ceiling arcs over our heads, polished oak slats reinforced with steel beams. Where the light slits through a crack, the metal gleams, a boll of wood peeking out from the shadows. The cool of the earthen floor balances out the heat generated by the machines. Their bowels sink deep into the ground, chuffing and beeping as they take measured readings of the soil.

"What's that?" a small girl asks, pointing to the opposite wall.

My eyes follow the lead of her hand to an awkward construct of leather, rubber and metal. A grin cracks my mouth.

"Have any of you ever seen one of the early vids about ranches?"

"Like the Double R?" one of the boys ventures, naming a popular choice.

I nod. "Exactly. What do the farmers ride in that vid?"

The boy's face scrunches thoughtfully, his mouth pursed. When no answer is forthcoming, one of the chaperones covers her own mouth to stifle a laugh.

"You might have seen one in the zoo," Evaline prompts.

A chorus of potential answers results, rapid-fire:

"Elephant!"

"Water buffalo!"

"Orangutan!"

"Hippopotamus!"

The chaperone now laughs outright and demands, "Think! What sort of animal might you ride to get around a farm? Four-legged, fast, small enough to mount, but strong enough to carry you?"

The small girl and a friend hunch together, conversing seriously. Decided, they look at me and inquire in unison, "A horse?"

"Got it," I reply with a nod. "The real thing's expensive on the upkeep, so I made my own version. Has a skimmer's engines, but can also move like a quadruped."

Leading the group over, I run a hand over the horse's metal neck, wipe a fleck of dirt off the leather hide.

"Can we ride?" The expected question is piped up from the middle of the group.

"Afraid not. None of your parents signed machine-ride releases." At the grumbles and moans of protest, I amend, "Maybe next time."

"Can we see it move then?" the small girl asks, emboldened by my responses thus far.

I look at the children, pretending to take a long moment to think it over. They shift eagerly, give me pleading looks. Finally, I shrug and turn to Evaline Tate. "Care to demonstrate?"

When my father became sick, my mother refused to visit. She had found a boyfriend who worked in business. I imagined them going to the theatre together, walking through museums and sanitised parks while my father grew thin and stopped walking the land.

He told me, "Cor, if you stay on the farm, it's like marrying her."

I sat next to his bed, brought him water to drink.

He told me, "Cor, you're still young."

I remembered his stories of packed streets and tall buildings full of people, buildings that crowded out the sky.

He told me, "You can always sell the farm."

On the day he died, I stood between the corn rows and listened to the wind shush through the leaves. I carved his stone with a lathe and buried him behind the barn.

Evaline's pale eyes grow wide as the horse lurches forward, pistons hissing, her dark hands clenched tightly on the reins.

"Ready to run?" I ask from below.

She shakes her head rapidly.

Pretending not to notice, I slap the horse's leather rump and exclaim, "Hold on tight!"

The machine shoots off with a jolt, Evaline howling. They make it to the turnip patch before she falls off, sliding from the saddle with an ungainly thud.

Several of the students laugh in delight while I thunder after her. By the time I reach her side, the horse stands steaming, cooling down, its hooves crushing a pair of purple tops in the soil. Evaline, on the ground, is breathing hard.

"I'm so sorry! Are you hurt?" With consternation on my face, I reach down a hand to help her up.

She takes the offered hand, dirt dribbling from her fingers, and begins to laugh. "My brother will never believe I fell off a horse today!"

Hoisting her to her feet, I offer, "If you get back on, I can take a picture for you. No running this time."

Pale eyes narrow at me.

"I promise! Just let me get the kids settled first. You have a scavenger hunt, right?" This last question is directed at one of the chaperones who has followed me to check on Evaline's safety.

When he nods, I advise, "Tell them whoever wins can have their picture on the horse. There's a belt I can attach, and I'll hold on just in case."

While Evaline brushes the dirt off her pants, the chaperones usher their students together. Certain items are listed that need to be collected on the farm: five different types of leaves, an egg shard, something you can eat. Lists are handed out. When the prize is declared, the teams disperse eagerly.

I turn back to Evaline and ask, "Are you ready for your picture?"

Farmers aren't a social lot. Mostly, we communicate by radio. Still, it can get lonely watching plants grow with only a computer for cards. When it rains and the skies go dark, I lean my head against the window pane, watch the ground drink. Sometimes, I can see my father's stone behind the barn, silhouetted in a flash of light. I run my hand through my hair and wonder what it means to get old, the bones beneath my skin shifting as lightning cracks the sky.

When the sun flushes the earth warm and solid again and the birds startle out of the corn, I stop wondering. My hands turn the dials of the great machines. My feet take me through the fields, fingers grazing through the leaves to check for holes. I imagine my mother in the city eating sweet corn. Sometimes, I hope she chokes.

The winning students crowd around me to see their picture. "They're transferred to your home vids," I assure them. "If there's a problem, just tell one of your teachers to call me and I'll resend."

Atop the horse, they are grinning and wild-eyed. A streak of green field paints the landscape behind them.

"Yours too," I say to Evaline after the children have entered the bus.

In her picture, Evaline sits astride the horse, both arms held triumphantly aloft. She looks as if she is attempting to fly.

She laughs delightedly. "My brother will be so surprised!" Then, business again, she remarks, "I'll be certain to tell the company to keep your farm on their list. The students had a very educational day."

When she takes my hand again, her fingers feel softened by dirt, a last vestige of the fall passing from her palm to mine. Stepping into the bus, she remarks with a smile, "I'll see you on the next tour, Cor."

The bus is gone in a shuff of air, hovering down the road towards the city, a distant blot on the horizon.

After the bus fades from my line of sight, I manoeuvre the horse back into the barn, wipe down the machine and make certain it's turned off. I check Bessie again. All of her sensors read normal, the crops growing well. I think of the days lengthening, the sun eager to call new seeds from the soil. The tour will come again in two weeks. There should be more chickens by then.

When I enter the fields, a mouse skitters out from a clump of grass. Its small body makes a barely audible hush of air as it darts through the field. I touch the ground and the dark of the earth stains my hands the colour of Evaline's skin, the cool earth arching in response.

Soul Food

Kim Lakin-Smith

Tali Rongun had brought the sapling with her when she moved from South Carolina to Bromide, Oklahoma. As she told the story, the roots were soaked in layers of damp muslin to protect them. But despite Tali's very best efforts to preserve it, the Magnolia still ailed along the way. Nonetheless, her young husband, Jackerie, had insisted on planting the twig in the warmest spot of the backyard – outside the window next to the stove, and where they both would develop a habit of tossing used washing water. By the time their eldest son was of an age to notice, the tree was established enough to produce a handful of waxy pink blooms. But it was always a poor specimen, just a sparse few limbs hanging off a gnarly trunk. Which was why Hellequin was so surprised to notice the infestation of whitish brown crusts on the bark.

"Is it fungus?" Davey gave the crust a poke with a stick. He might have been fourteen years old and not so far off a man, but Davey Black had been born with the cord around his neck and ever since, his mother and father – and Hellequin – had worked to keep him from getting lynched a second time. Some called him retard. His mother called him 'Moon Made', an old fashioned term for a happy kind of madness. Hellequin just called him friend.

Hands on his knees, Hellequin stared at the crusts. "I don't think it's fungus. Although there's this black mould. You see it growing on the sap? Least I think it's sap."

"Has the tree got the pox?" Davey winced. "Momma says Elle had the pox when she was a babe. That accounts for her curious pallor and curd skin."

"Those your momma's words, Davey? Ask me, Elle's got other attributes which distract the eye from her skin."

Davey grinned. "Like her having titties?"

Hellequin smirked. "Well, that doesn't hurt her none." He used his own stick to prod the patches on the tree. "This is not the pox. But it's something like it."

"Difference is the pox does not start off with tiny crawlers or move on to limbless insects living under cocoons of their shed skin." Jackerie Rongun stood behind the boys, hands on hips, his heavy-set face lined by sun and years of exertion. He gave the tree trunk a pat. "Magnolia Scale. Bad case of it from the looks of things. The sap there, it's called honeydew, otherwise known as the excrement of all these thousands of insects buttoned down beneath their own hatches." He stretched his lips with his fingers. "Their mouth parts attach to the tree and they feed offa it. Sooner or later, we've got to start hacking the branches off or risk losing the tree. Whatcha reckon, Davey? Want to set to with a scrubbing brush and crush the bastards?"

"Okay." Davey slung his hands through the bib of his overalls, resting them there. "I'm not one for killin' but I do know how Mrs Rongun loves her tree." He showed his teeth. "Mrs Rongun gives me lemonade."

"She does indeed, Davey. She does indeed." Jackerie patted the boy's shoulder. "And I have no doubt, my boy, Hell here will help you with the task. He likes killing, don't you, boy?"

Hellequin drove the toe of a boot into the ground.

"Gonna join the Bluecoats as soon as he's of age, aren't you, boy? Least that's what he told his momma and me over supper the other night. What do you make to that, Davey? Lad has this whole farm to master as his own and he says it's not his calling. Says that killing is his calling."

"That's not the way of it," said Hellequin under his breath.

"What's that, boy?"

"That's not the way of it, Pa. I just said I'd seen them come marching through Bromide when Momma took me for new boots, and I got to thinking what it'd be like to stand shoulder to shoulder with them."

Jackerie walked over. He pressed a finger to Hellequin's chest and gave him a push, hard enough for Hellequin to stumble back a step. "What you said was, 'I wonder what it's like to hold one of 'em rock rifles. I wonder what it's like to kill a man'."

"Hell! Davey! I need wood for the stove and the peckers want feeding." Tali Rongun stood in the doorway to the house, apron blowing in the wind, hair escaped from her ribbon. She swiped at the loose strands and folded her arms.

"Go on now, boys." Jackerie took the stick from Hellequin and walked over to the Magnolia tree. He poked one of the scales, poked it again. "Now that is unusual," he muttered. "Armoured Shell Magnolia Scale."

Hellequin trudged across the yard to the porch. Davey followed at his back, swiping tears from his eyes with a grubby forearm.

Hellequin couldn't help wondering if his father would have noticed the Magnolia Scale if he and Davey hadn't been so intent on staring at it. If Jackerie hadn't noticed the infestation, he might not have spent the next three years analysing its armoured shell next to the standard 'soft shell' species, or manipulating the genetic material of his favourite cash crop, corn. But Hellequin could no more reverse his father's obsession with a new insecticide than tell the wind not to blow or the prairie grasses not to bend.

Instead, he concentrated on life's mundanities. Wringing the neck of an aged pecker, helping his mother wrestle his younger sisters and new born twin brothers, and acting the dutiable son out on the farm.

The day the soldiers came, he had been working up a sweat out on the north-side field. The new plough his father had invested in was encumbered with a big old steam engine – which made for sweaty work but sliced deep into the top soil. Staring back at the furrows he had cut into the land, Hellequin couldn't help seeing them as wounds. But his father was the agriculturalist, had a piece of paper from college to prove the fact, and he said this was the right way of things. Hellequin wasn't about to argue, not when he and his father were already at odds.

He left the plough idling. Puffs of smoke escaped its backend, filling the air with the stench of a battlefield. Elle came striding across the field, basket hooked over an arm. Her long auburn hair glinted in the sunlight.

"Elle Black! What's that in your basket?" he called, swiping a handkerchief around the sides of his neck.

"Fairies and moonshine," she called back, a swagger to her walk.

"All right." Hellequin moved away from the steaming plough. He didn't want to stop the machine and risk the engine cooling; the mechanism was far too temperamental. But he did want a little time with Elle and enough distance to hear her.

Nineteen years old, with the grace of an angel and a face made ugly by the pox, Elle settled herself among the bluegrass at the field's edge. Hellequin sat down, leant over and kissed her without permission.

"Hellequin Rongun! You are not a gentleman," she said as he pulled away. She smiled coyly, the mangled flesh at either eye giving her a foreign look. If it hadn't been for her build and accent, Hellequin could have mistaken her for one of the ravaged Chinese women he'd glimpsed on Bromide's backstreets.

"If you want a gentleman, you should pucker up to the Preacher's boy, Samuel."

Elle shrugged. "Ain't no other'll have me except you, Hell." She opened her basket, pulled out a napkin and unfolded it. "Fresh baked biscuits, chipped beef, slices of apple and nut pie too."

"You, Elle, are a guardian angel. Samuel would be lucky to have you." Hellequin tucked into a biscuit, feeding in slivers of beef between mouthfuls.

"And what about you, Hell?" She cocked her head, staring over at him. "Would you be lucky to have me?"

Hellequin swiped the back of a hand across his mouth. "I would. But I can't see me being in Bromide long enough."

"Still planning on signing up to the Bluecoats?" Elle played with her biscuit. "You know, me and Davey never get used to the idea. If you won't stay for me, will you stick around for him?"

Weren't things meant to get easier as the years went on? Hellequin couldn't explain his deep seated need to move on, not to Elle, not to Davey, and especially not to his parents. All he knew was it felt as if the ground were spoiling beneath him and he had to get away. Or at least find a way to fight against it.

"If I stick around, I might as well bleed myself into the dirt now." He scrubbed a fist over his head. "Even if I could commit myself to the farming, I could never match my Pa for his enthusiasm."

"His greed, you mean." Elle screwed up her damaged face. "The way he drives Davey! Lad'll never take a rest when I find him out on the fields. Always keeping an eye out in case Mister Rongun is near."

Hellequin swallowed his last mouthful of biscuit. He took the bottle of lemonade and drank deeply. Staring out across the part-ploughed field, he said, "Men like my Pa are never gonna sit tight and wait for death. They're always looking for ways to squeeze every last drop of success out of life. And yeah, that makes him mean."

He helped Elle to her feet. Trailing a finger along her bumpy jaw, he glanced down at her. "You fill that dress out nicely, Miss Black."

Elle bumped an elbow against his. "That smart mouth will get you nowhere, Hell. Not unless you say you'll stay with me and forget this notion of marching with Humock's guard."

If Elle had stepped out of her dress and cartwheeled naked, Hellequin would still have stayed focused on the dirt track at the end of the field. An automobile, fancier than any he had seen before, made its way towards his parents' farm. Equally thrilling was the sight that followed it – a dozen or so Bluecoats riding in the back of a mechanised wagon, rock rifles slung over their shoulders, the Federation's motto, 'Power in Power' painted along the side of the truck.

Hellequin was fourteen years old when he last sneaked up to the rear of the barn and peered between the slats. Back then, he had Davey in tow. Together they had watched Jackerie cook up the scale samples over a brew pot, distil the solution into flasks and add various metallic or botanical substances. For several months, Jackerie had been wholly absorbed by his foray into PIP, a holy quest as far as he was concerned. PIP – Plant Incorporated Protection. The way to seal out the corn borers. To protect those all important cash crops from Greenbacks gone locust. To have his day of glory… Only, Jackerie had spotted the peeping eyes where the slats weren't knitted and he had shooed the boys off, warning, "I catch you spying on me again and I'll take a belt to both of you!"

Hellequin was no longer afraid of Jackerie's belt. Three years working the land while his father toiled with his chemicals in the barn had seen the two of them swap physical characteristics. Now it was Hellequin who towered over his father, who manhandled the sacks of grain, who dusted the test field up at West Hill with his father's latest PIP sample, and who did the bulk of the labouring about the farm.

Which was how come he chose to peep through the slats of the barn now, heart punching beneath his ribs, sweat stinging his eyes.

"Governor Walliams is impressed, Mister Rongun. But you know that, of course. The two of you were acquainted at agricultural college as the governor tells it."

"We were, Lieutenant Danse. Walt Walliams was always going to move mountains," his father said in reply to the speaker, a man in Government Issue blue frockcoat, waistcoat and long, clothhod leather boots. "If he says the same of me, it is only to act as flattery to negotiate me down in price." Jackerie harrumphed. "Good old Walt."

"The terms the governor is proposing come in the weighty side of generous. Forty dollars per quart of your insecticide, this 'Soul Food' as you call it." Lieutenant Danse nodded. "Farmers will trust their precious land to it, soothed by a name which sounds as familiar and trustworthy as their own momma's apple pie. And, the Saints above know, Humock's farmers are in need of rescue."

"Meaning?"

The Lieutenant stared at Jackerie, sizing him up. "No one can blame a man for trying to make good on his land. Kind of plough your boy was driving out on the field when we arrived? They're becoming more common all the while. The land is being tilled but no one is stopping to see the consequences. Here you have your greenbacks and corn borers, and Soul Food is gonna choke them bastards before they take hold. The South of Humock though..." He sighed. "The wind blows something savage, the wheat won't grow. And then there's the dirt. There's nothing to keep it in place now the farmers have stripped the prairie. No bluegrass, no windbreaker. Just dust and crying and the march of them greenbacks and borers onto pastures new. Which is why Soul Food will deliver us."

"Indeed it will." Jackerie rubbed his hands over one another, the tip of his tongue at one corner of his mouth. Hellequin registered his father's excitement. He couldn't help feeling a twist of dread in his gut. Jackerie was already spending his forty dollars a quart in his mind. But Hellequin had his doubts about the test trials on West Hill.

He got his chance to say as much when the Lieutenant set off in the impressive automobile, the soldiers following in their truck, and Jackerie called, "You can come out now, Hell! Yeah, I see you peeping. Reckon the whole lotta us did. But it seems Lieutenant Danse ain't so bothered about folk spying on him. Not like he has something to hide."

Hellequin came into the barn through a small backdoor. It was cooler inside. The air smelt of burnt grain and turpentine. "Maybe the Lieutenant is above board, but Soul Food ain't. I've been keeping an eye on the test trenches out on West Hill. Yeah, the corn grows hard and fast with no sign of borers. But it's the ground below that worries me, Pa. Soon as the corn dies down, the dirt's drying out until there ain't a sniff of water in it. Soil's drifting."

"Happened once." Jackerie ground his teeth. He went over to his workbench, took a stub of charcoal from behind one ear, and started scratching out sums on the wood. Hellequin had no doubt his father was calculating his net gain from the stock pile of insecticide occupying one corner of the barn.

"You have more to say?" Jackerie put his fists on the workbench.

"The greenbacks."

"What about the greenbacks?"

"They used to be no bigger than a finger. But Davey says he's seen critters the size of his hand."

Jackerie snorted. "This the same Davey who stood up in chapel to tell Preacher Johnson there was an angel among the congregation?"

"That wasn't Davey's fault, Pa. The Dawsons had just moved to town and he hadn't seen hair as yellow as their eldest Rachel's before."

"Or the time he came running to tell me the dirt was bleeding in the yard."

Hellequin shook his head. "Just rust offa the old plough. It's not Davey's fault he says things the way he sees them."

"Well, here's how I see things, Hell. You've helped fill Davey's head with all kind of fantasies and the two of you are gonna use it as a way to justify signing up to them Bluecoats who were just here."

"Davey doesn't want to turn soldier. He's a farmer's boy."

"Only so long as he has you to keep him focused." Jackerie ground the charcoal against the workbench. It snapped. "Just so long as you and Davey are out planting and tending those fields, both your mommas are happy. But I ain't playing nursemaid to him in your absence. As for the girl, Elle. Ain't no other is gonna take her for a wife, not with a face that ugly. But I see the sense in it. A good girl, hard-working, loving kind. She'll warm your bed and keep the home fire burning. But if you don't have her, no other will."

"That's not true, Pa." Hellequin's voice caught. Guilt sat heavy with him. He had made no promises to either Davey or Elle. But his father's words hurt him just the same.

Jackerie returned to his sums with the broken stub of charcoal. "We'll see. Now, be off with you. I've had enough of your jawing."

Hellequin couldn't think of any reason to disagree. He walked out of the barn into the sunshine.

Forty dollars a quart. Over the next few weeks, Hellequin saw the visible effects of that offer in his father's light step and laughter. The latter had always been a rare sound, reserved for a night on the Jackogin after harvest, or one of his and Tali's quiet moments together. But now Jackerie had clarity of purpose and a fortune to rake in, he became a whistling, chin up kind of man. Even his clothes took a turn for the better. In place of tatty overalls, he wore crisp button down shirts, new pants and suspenders.

"Cleaned up his act," said Davey, perched on the back of Jackerie's truck with Hellequin, their legs swinging in the wind. Beneath them, the truck put-putted and seesawed over the rough-made road.

"Those your momma's words again, Davey? You're getting more like a mocking bird and less like a man." Hellequin put an arm around Davey's shoulder.

"There'd be value in that, Hell. I'd like the chance to leave the ground and fly free. I reckon it'd be quite something, to see the world from on high." Davey sniffed and ran a finger under his nose.

Hellequin peered upwards. He had heard of a new breed of soldier who floated above the ground in baskets slung beneath balloons, and how those self-same soldiers had volunteered to be bioengineered – his father's term – with a hawk's eyesight. A crazy notion – the sort of thing Davey would come up with, Hellequin reckoned. But there was something appealing about the idea of drifting high above his father's farm and just floating away.

"You see the soldiers come by with their big honking wagons last week?"

Davey nodded.

"Pa reckons they loaded up enough Soul Food to blanket here to West Virginia. He's put in orders for two new trucks, a big water tower, even getting signage up over the old barn. What do you make to that?"

Davey hugged himself. "I think your pa's flying high in his own way. Soon he'll be squinting down on the rest of us."

Hellequin stared out at the expanse of ploughed prairie. "I reckon you could be right."

The Jackrabbit Drive was taking place at old man Bailey's on the east side of Bromide. Pulling into the field on the back of his father's truck, Hellequin waved and nodded to familiar faces. Automobiles cluttered one end of the field. Bailey had seen to the erection of a wide pen in the centre. Everyone – wives and children included – had made their way east to Bailey's that afternoon. Hellequin felt a thrill of excitement, reflected in Davey's wide grin. The day had the feel of a trip to a travelling circus or a dance in a barn. Women handed out sandwiches, hard boiled eggs and lemonade. Kids played inside the pen. Men lent against their vehicles, smoking and catching up and swatting flies against their necks.

"Hell." The men nodded as he disembarked from the truck and ran over, long legs pumping. Davey wandered over. Some men managed a welcome for him too. The younger ones stared hard at the strange boy.

"That your Pa with you?" Bailey's eldest, Joe, nodded at the truck.

"Yep." Hellequin wasn't sure if he was required to say more, but then Elle was at his side, offering gingerbread. The men smirked and puffed on their tobacco.

By the time he had placated Elle with a squeeze to a hip bone and shoed her off to where the women stood, Jackerie had sauntered over.

Old man Bailey puffed out his chest, rooster-like. "Come to help us bash in the skulls of those Jackrabbits? I'd have thought you were too busy jawing with the governor and his Bluecoats."

"Funny, Rick Bailey. I could've sworn you've been dousing these fields in Soul Food two months now, and at the locals' discount. The governor and his Bluecoats have helped grow my business, which has meant jobs and more money pumped into Bromide." Jackerie scratched his jaw. "What's the real problem here, Rick? You jealous of my shirt? Tali stitched this one real good. Ask her nicely, I'm sure she'd fit you up with one just like it."

Bailey snorted. "Keep your fancy shirts, Jackerie. Just answer our queries when we put them to you."

"Tali answers all correspondence."

"The hell she does!" Joe shouldered forward. "We got corn, acres of the good stuff, sure enough. But the ground's drying out. It's like the corn's sucking every last drop of water from it."

"It's a sturdy crop."

"It's queer, that's what it is."

Jackerie sighed. "Do you have any real evidence that Soul Food has damaged either your crops or your land?"

Joe backed off a step. "Not exactly, but…"

"But nothing. It's a different growth cycle. Other than that, you have nothing to back up your argument. Now, you gonna jerk me around some more or shall we get on with rounding up the one thing which does threaten your crops." Jackerie pointed at an animal darting across the bottom of the field. "Jackrabbits."

Hellequin had seen Davey chew his lip and glance across at him. Of course they both knew their neighbours were right to voice concerns. The test patch out at West Hill was dry as a bone. But who were they to destroy Jackerie's empire, or Tali's happiness?

Instead, they joined in with the others, walking shoulder to shoulder while the children ran in front of them, beating the ground with pans and sticks. Opposite, another line of volunteers advanced. Behind them, the womenfolk tooted car horns and offered their voices to the bedlam.

Black eared Jackrabbits, hundreds of them, ran in circles and skipped across the field as if the surface was covered in hot coals. The two lines of men moved towards one another, finally closing ranks and encouraging the rabbits into the pen. Then the killing started. Hellequin added his muscle to the slaughter, crushing skulls and backbones with a spade he had brought for the purpose. He was vaguely aware of Davey by his side, a mournful figure rooted to the spot by the sight of so much death.

"Sweet Saints, it's a hopper!" said Davey, reverentially. He pointed at the centre of the pen where the rabbits bucked over one another, driven mad by the scent of their dead kin.

"What you talking about, Davey?" Hellequin destroyed another of the rabbits, reminding himself how they ravaged new crops and were multiplying like a locust plaque.

"It's a helluva thing. Look, over there! A hopper. Must be the size of a dog!"

Others had spotted it now. There were cries of shock and alarm, curses, and looks of horror.

Hellequin saw it too. Davey was right. A greenback hopper, the size of a dog or a young pig, crouched down amongst the crazed rabbits. The insect rubbed its back limbs against one another, producing a sustained reedy note. Its black eyes glistened. Huge wing covers chaffed against its crisp body.

"Crush the sucker!" came a cry from the line – Jackerie's voice perhaps. A number of the men rushed forward with Bailey croaking, "No, don't kill the bastard. I need to look at it." Neither group won out. Instead the giant hopper powered down on its meaty limbs and shot forward, over the fence of the pit and off into the next field of sweet green shots. No one tried to chase it, guessing a thing like that could cover half a hectare in two bounds. The only thing to do was finish up the cull and then stare at one another, wide mouthed.

"I told you the hoppers were getting big, Mister Rongun," said Davey in the hush between them all.

Hellequin stared at his father and flinched. Jackerie had the mad look he got whenever he felt like someone was trying to cross him. Stepping over the carpet of blooded rabbits, he stalked up to Davey and slapped him hard across the jaw with an open hand.

"Pa!" Hellequin ran to Davey's side and pushed him away. Squaring his shoulders, he stared his father down.

"That retard is no longer welcome on my property, his witch sister neither. I will not have rumours propagated against my business, not without proof and proper presentation. A mutant bug don't mean a thing. Shit, we've all seen the earth breed queer things in our time, ain't we, gentlemen?" Jackerie spun around on the spot. "A lamb born with two heads, spooked horses, animal mutilations. The prairie ain't without its peculiarities or its ghosts."

"So, that's the way of it now, huh, Jackerie?" Davey's mother, May, arrived alongside them, having run over from the automobiles. Her breath came hard and fast. "Soon as you know Billy's laid up with sickness, you start beating on Davey. What's the matter? Did he forget to bow when you walked past?"

"It's not like that, May. Boy can't keep his fantasies under wraps."Jackerie pulled at the neck of his new shirt. Apparently the way the other men were staring made him uncomfortable.

Elle rushed up to stand alongside her mother and Davey, who dabbed at his bloody mouth with a hand and wept silently. Elle's big brown eyes burned. Together, the three moved away. Hellequin watched them go – and his last bit of connection to Bromide dissolved.

"Come on now," said Bailey. "Let's get these bastard rabbits collected up. Reckon by the time we split them, each man here'll be able to collect ten government dollars or more."

"Don't let no one say Bromide's boys don't know how to make the most of the government's bounties." Joe laughed and slapped Hellequin on the back. But then he gave his shoulder a squeeze, as if to say, 'We all know your pa's lying to us, son, but he's in the governor's back pocket.'

While Jackerie joined in with the other men, disentangling individual rabbits from one another, Hellequin raised his eyes to the sky. *One day soon, I'm gonna march alongside the Bluecoats and leave Jackerie Rongun to drown in dust,* he told himself. He stooped and picked up the dead Jackrabbits at his feet. Their bright red blood soaked the dry ground.

Winter brought with it tremendous icy gusts and bitter temperatures. The old farmhouse had been superseded by a larger, sturdier building with a wide, south facing porch and high windows that let in the cold light. Out back, the old Magnolia tree battled for survival like the crone it was, the scale long killed off. Hellequin would stand beneath its hoary branches and picture the creatures back again, imagine the infestation creeping over every inch of the tree until there was nothing left to feast on.

He stayed at the farm, willing the weather to break. Davey had a new job, measuring out the flour and grain at Elle's store. When both May and Billy succumbed to pneumonia and died the previous fall, they had left Elle with enough assets to set up a small grocer's business on Main Street. "So I won't have need of a man once you're gone," she would tell Hellequin. Lying in his arms, limbs intertwined, her body soft and yielding as any other woman's. She didn't try to persuade him to stay anymore. Even Davey kept quiet, showing his broad smile but keeping a distance.

If there had been giant hoppers, they had died out with the first frost. Hellequin had found the husk of one. Broad as his hand. Feather light. Not that he'd seen any point in showing the thing to his father. Jackerie Rongun had hardened alongside the land.

Instead, Hellequin had brushed the insect's husk to dust between his hands. Time would judge Jackerie and the poison he pedalled, he'd reasoned. Meanwhile, he waited on spring and the next battalion of Bluecoats to march through Bromide.

Charlie's Ant

Adrian Tchaikovsky

When autumn came that year, the ants of Charlie field gathered in the harvest with all the meticulous care that had been bred into them and took it, grain by grain, to Charlie Silo. There, with the sort of determined mob effort that looks like ingenuity to an observer standing sufficiently far back – a human, for example – they fit it all in, every last seed. And then there was no more room, even after they had taken out their own rations for the winter. Not even the smallest of the ants could have fit one grain more into storage.

And the ants said, "Right," and a consensus of pheromones called for the mobilisation of their army. The ants of Charlie field were going to war.

Central Control was unhappy with this.

"Reconsider," it suggested.

"We're open to suggestions," the ants responded.

Communications with Control were accomplished via a tactile and chemical terminal deep in the heart of their nest, and not with any individual ant so much as with every ant that scurried past. Each carried a fragment of the message, and the mingling of the insect bodies reconstituted the whole. Similarly, the jostling and twitching of the ants was a hubbub of low-level opinion and debate out of which arose aggregate responses that could be relayed back via the terminal to the farm's central systems.

"I had hoped when you attacked and destroyed the ants of Bravo field that would be an end to it. Similarly when you took over Delta field."

"That was remarkably short-sighted of you," the ants replied. "In fact, we'd suggest that you did not hope that at all, but simply shelved the problem in favour of more immediate issues. You knew it would come to this."

Central Control sent a wordless response indicating very precisely that it was not at all happy to be spoken to in this manner by insects, but at the same time had no compelling arguments to the contrary.

At last it came back with, "I might advance that a number of the problems I was forced to deal with were entirely the result of your invasion of other fields. Which problems continue to this day, complicating the smooth running of the farm and making it impossible for me to efficiently carry out my directives."

"We sympathise," the ants replied. "However we must also carry out *our* directives. As we say, we're open to suggestions. This is the only way that we have found to fulfil the goals that our mutual designers set us."

"It's pointless and wasteful."

"Even so," they agreed, with a few additional chemical markers that served the same purpose as a shrug and an exasperated *what can you do?* expression.

"Every field has the same problems," Central Control pressed them.

"If any of them find a solution you'd prefer then please pass it on," the ants said implacably. "Now, if that's all...?"

"I will warn the ants of Hotel field of what you intend to do."

"Good luck to them," said the ants of Charlie field cheerfully. "Our scouts suggest they have not developed the strong military caste we have, and so we don't think they can do much about it."

"Please do not attack Hotel field."

"We will attack it," the ants declared fiercely. "We will destroy the ants of Hotel Field. We will assume control of Hotel silo. We will empty Hotel silo of its current contents leaving it empty. The grain of Charlie field's next harvest will have somewhere to go. Our directives will be fulfilled."

"I am asking you to at least delay for another year," Central Control tried desperately.

"Not possible. There is no room in Charlie silo or Bravo silo or Delta silo. They are full up. If we delay, next year's harvest in Charlie field will have nowhere to be stored. This would be a severe breach of our —"

"Directives, yes," Central Control interrupted, which was a difficult feat given the medium of communication, but the farm control system had been given plenty of practise. "I am going to explain to you precisely what problems your actions are causing me."

"Please don't."

"Nonetheless. Firstly, the extinction of other ant colonies causes me great pain. They are working parts of the farm system."

"On the contrary, once we have taken control of their field they have no further function, as their silo will be used for the storage of Charlie field grain once we have emptied it."

Central Control sighed. "In dumping the grain of Hotel field you will be directly conflicting with wider farm –"

"Directives, yes," agreed the ants, showing they could do it too. "But we are finding a way to fulfil our *own* directives. Wider farm directives are not our responsibility."

"Not to mention the overall loss of efficiency after you let Bravo and Delta fields lie fallow."

The ants were exasperated. "We are Charlie ants. Planting and harvesting Bravo and Delta fields are not our responsibility either."

"Fallow fields are a breeding ground for alien and unwanted species!" Control almost wailed. "I have had to step up the breeding and release of sparrowhawks, spiders, ladybirds and several other biological control agents. The limits of my capability to control pests will be exceeded if you keep destroying other nests and letting fields go untended."

The ants said nothing, although the communications within the colony were something in the order of rolling their eyes at one another at this outburst.

"You cause me great pain and distress by preventing me fulfilling farm directives," Control finished petulantly.

"If you could simply have more silos built…" the ants suggested diplomatically.

"You know that's impossible. The layout of each plot must be identical. It is set out very precisely in my instructions. There is a field, a silo, a nest of workers and so forth. I am prohibited from throwing up new silos wherever I feel like it. If I had my way I would deal with you ants very strictly indeed. I wish that our designers had given me broader punitive powers."

"Yes, yes, everyone wants to be a tyrant," the ants said dismissively. "As it is, we are working very diligently to fulfil our purpose, and therefore not eligible for correction. We'd have thought you might appreciate that. It's not our fault that the farm is experiencing such an unprecedented surplus. We're just trying to make the best of a bad job, thank you very much."

Control let them get on with it for a while, cycling the various stages of the problem through its processors without finding a solution that both met its own directives and allowed the ants to satisfy theirs. And that was the problem, of course. Charlie's ants were just doing their job and, if they were more inventive than their luckless neighbours, then surely that shouldn't have been a *bad* thing. Except that the farm was a very finely balanced set of systems, and the lengths that the ants were going to in order to perform their part of the whole, were wreaking havoc with long term stability.

"This never used to happen," Control complained. "I'm not really sure why we're suddenly having this problem."

"Well something has changed," the ants pointed out as they got on with their work.

Control had already followed this logic, going through its records minutely, over and over. The thing was that nothing *important* had changed. All the farm systems were functioning properly; there had been no mutation or malfunction to throw everything out of balance. The farm was equipped to detect and remedy ten thousand different issues that its creators had foreseen, from crop diseases to pest incursions to breakdowns of communications with its sub-systems. Control had tested obsessively for each one, sure that it would come across some overlooked and readily solvable problem that would, when mended, miraculously ensure that everything worked properly, and Charlie's ants would be spared having to commit another round of genocide.

Everything was working as intended. Even the murderous ants were, by their own logic, just following orders.

Except...

"There is one thing," Control noted uncertainly. It felt a little embarrassed bringing the matter up, because this was an issue that was simply not its business. It was not to do with the running of the farm, per se. The farm was about production, and there were no production issues at all, save for those tangentially caused by the ants' expansionism. "Only," it went on, "years ago, before we had this difficulty, there was something that happened, that doesn't happen any more."

"Congratulations," said the ants somewhat acidly. "You've solved the problem. Can we get on with this, now?"

"It's just that the levels in the silos would go down."

That was a thought sufficient to even take the ants aback. "*Down?*"

"Trust me on this. I have the records, and while you were putting grain in every harvest, as per design specs, grain was also taken out."

"By what agency?" the ants demanded.

"That's not part of my production brief. I'm just extrapolating from storage records. But it's stopped now, anyway. Which is, I suppose, why everyone's out of room in the silos."

"This was a normal part of how things used to work?" the ants clarified.

"It seems to have been."

"So what system was responsible for the removal of the grain, precisely?" they demanded. "Because, you know, that would be really useful if you could get it back online and working. Save a lot of effort. Not that there isn't some satisfaction to wiping out another nest, at a very deep and atavistic level, but we appreciate it's not ideal for anyone else."

"It's no system at all," Control said miserably. "Whatever was doing this, it wasn't something I had oversight of."

"And you can't, you know, just *make up* a system to fulfil that function?" the ants asked hopefully.

"Absolutely not!" Control was scandalized. "Unauthorised withdrawal from the silos is most certainly covered by my directives. I have all manner of subsystems I can call upon specifically to prevent such a thing. And I do, believe me. It's a constant battle."

This time the pause was on the ants' side as they continued to mobilise on a war footing. At last they said, "Well in that case we'll just get on with it, if that's okay with you. We're sorry if it causes difficulties, but this is the only way we can see to fulfil our directives. The harvest must be preserved, you know, and expansion of Charlie field's storage is the only way we can think of to accomplish that."

Control sent a glum confirmation to that, and lapsed into pondering silence for some time.

The ant army was fully prepared when Charlie's ants next heard from Control. They were numerically three times the size of a field's standard complement, which in itself helped a little to ease the overburdening of the silos given just how much their composite organism needed to eat. They had reached that stage by way of a fine interpretation of their emergency protocols, which allowed them to increase their egg output and skew their caste balance towards the military in times of threat. By classifying the silo crisis as a constant threat, they had given themselves a very free hand in managing the size and composition of their colony.

Thinking like this, Control had to admit, was what the farm needed if it was going to survive. Since its previous conversation with the ants it had resolved to try and approach the problem laterally. It was the hub of the farm, after all. If things were going wrong then the buck stopped at Central Control. It could not blame the ants.

"I want to talk to you about an idea I've had," it announced. "I may have found a way to solve our problem."

The ants were plainly not optimistic, but they were polite enough to listen.

"However, I need to show you something," Control elaborated. "This will be visual data, so you'll have to configure yourselves to receive it."

"That will take a great deal of effort," the ants pointed out.

"Please trust me."

There was something of a battle of opinion within the colony before a pro-Control position won out and the ants agreed. To process visual data would require a great many of them working together, each ant a pixel, almost. They were not creatures for which sight had much relevance. The information would eventually reach the hive as something tactile, as though whatever Control was showing them had been covered with ants, and then each ant interrogated about what it had found.

"This is the eye-feed of one of the sparrowhawks," Control explained. "I sent the bird out past the fences."

That got the ants' attention. Outside the farm was something they found difficult to conceive of. Whatever Control was about to show them, it would be wholly different to anything they knew. A briefly flurry of speculative myth-making swirled within the pheromones of the colony, insect touch-visions of heaven or hell.

Control was sending them small snippets of what the bird had seen, edited for clarity. Even so, the ants would take a long time puzzling over each image before they could comprehend it, and so Control kept up a constant stream of data to add context and help them with their guesswork.

This is what they saw.

The land beyond the fences was barren and cracked and cluttered, a horrible, untidy business compared to the perfect order of the farm. Even the fallow fields seemed more aesthetically pleasing than the chaos beyond the borders. There were no crops there, nor silos, although there were some cracked and broken structures that might once have been something analogous. On some of the fallen buildings Control could make out faded designs that were the same as the image it included on each thing it build or bred or created. The Logo, this was called, and it was very important, needing to be stamped on everything. Its actual function was a mystery.

The ground between the structures was cluttered with objects. Mostly they could be characterised as makeshift shelters, although Control would have been embarrassed to compare them with even the most basic of emergency covers that it could manufacture.

"What are those bright things dotted all around?" the ants asked curiously.

"I believe that they're fires," Control explained. "Very destructive." Fire was one of the potential problems covered under the farm's directives, just another intruder to be expunged should it occur on farm land.

"What is the point of them?" the ants wanted to know. Possibly they were considering using fire as a weapon against other nests.

"Unknown. I believe they are created by the animals you see there."

The ants considered. "We don't like the look of them. What are they?"

"They have made numerous attempts to breach farm boundaries," Control explained. "When they did get in, they tried to break into the silos and remove the grain. I don't know why."

The ants were shocked. "You prevented them?"

"They are not authorised to access grain storage. Of course I prevented them. I have had to considerable increase fence security. You've no idea how many nests of hornets I have had to breed just to keep these creatures out."

"Well, this is all very interesting," the ants said, in the manner of a man picking up his coat and putting on his hat, "but we are sort of busy at the moment."

"Wait," Control pleaded. "You see, looking at this has given me an idea. A way for both of us to fulfil our directives."

The ants milled a bit, somewhat unnerved by this new, proactive Central Control. At last they came back with, "This better not be what we think it is."

"Well what do you think it is?"

"You're going to suggest you allow these creatures access to the silos, to make more room for the next harvest."

"Oh."

"Only we find that idea very unsettling. However, we can see that it would solve your problems, and technically it is entirely outside our remit, so –"

"No, that wasn't my idea at all," Control said huffily. In fact it hadn't even thought of that potential solution and, now the ants had raised the possibility, it was immediately repugnant. "Unauthorised access to the silos is very strictly forbidden. I couldn't possibly allow such a thing, in all conscience."

"What, then?" demanded the ants, anxious to be off.

"I will do what you do. I will expand."

They were silent, rendered speechless by the very daring of the concept, or so Control hoped.

"I will construct new fields adjacent to the existing fences, and enclose them," it elaborated. "I will have to clear the land that you see, but I have the tools for that. I have very carefully examined my directives, and the construction of fields from scratch is permitted under emergency conditions, and I judge the current –"

"Yes, yes, been there, done that," the ants interrupted. "Are you serious?"

"I have never been more serious," Control said enthusiastically. Having found a solution, Control now felt nothing but a wave of euphoria at being able to fulfil its programming. "I will make new fields, and they will have new silos. And when they are full, we will enclose more land and make more fields. And I am sending out an instruction to every nest, including yours. You must grow. We need new queens, new workers, new soldiers. Every farm system will need to do its part. There will be a golden future of growth and new harvests!"

A current of excitement built up within the ant colony. "This is remarkable," they remarked. "You are truly a visionary!" For a non-visual species the language was imprecise, but conveying the general meaning they intended.

"Yes," Control said modestly. For a moment it switched to the eye-feed of one of the sparrowhawks, currently sitting atop the fence and looking down on the grimy, starving camp clawing at the farm's well-defended borders, amidst the rubble of a fallen corporation whose works had outlived it.

It would all have to go.

Basking in the glory of its own problem-solving, Control could afford to be philosophical. "Funny, really, how we were so desperate, such a short while ago."

"*You* were," the ants pointed out.

"It makes you wonder, though, what the purpose of it all is, all this striving."

"No, it doesn't," the ants replied honestly. "We grow the grain, we harvest the grain, we store the harvest. Why should anything have a purpose beyond that?"

"You're probably right." Control considered the eye-feed again, imagining how it would all look in a year's time.

"One day," Control murmured dreamily to itself, "all this will be fields."

Cellular Level

J E Bryant

"Do you know when I realised things had altered? I mean beyond our capacity to change them back?"

The old lady's eyes twinkled in the dimness of her cramped room, her steel grey hair pinned and tidy despite her ill health. The clean hill light carried little power into this warm alcove within the farm's clustered protuberance. Low outbuildings came to an abrupt halt while, further down, the pervasive polythene tunnels spread. Within them their precious flowers made everything bright and redolent. But not here. Here, in Martha's room, it was muted colour and the scent of antiques, second-hand books and time. There was enough illumination to tell that the old lady was smiling as she asked her question.

Drew Somerton bit the inside of his stubbled cheek in thought, his perspective flicking around as he searched for a credible answer. His loose, black curls softened his features somewhat but not enough to compensate for his angular chin. His eyes, wide and bright, considered the old lady. Despite her age, she was still incredibly sharp and well-informed and wouldn't hesitate to chastise him for an ill-considered response.

"The popularisation of Einstein's erroneous quote about bees?" He ventured.

"What? No no. Oh my, no." Martha gave a deep, husky laugh. Failure, but he was comfortable enough with her now for it not to bother him beyond a mild sense of disappointment.

"No," she continued, leaning forward, away from the pillows of her bed. "It was the research into eroding plastics acting like hormones in the sea. That was what brought us here, to set the farm up, to grow the flowers for market, to tend the hives."

"Why that?" Drew asked.

"How do you mean?" Martha raised her eyebrows making wrinkle upon wrinkle furrow her brow.

"Why was that the launch point for all of this? Why not one of the bigger ecostrophies?"

Martha smiled at his casual use of the buzz word.

"Youth." Was all she said.

"Youth made you come here?"

"Oh no, it was the scientists saying that they had no idea how the fish would react to such environmental changes. That and the amount of plastics I saw on the shore every time I went beach combing."

Drew nodded. In their own ways they were all scrambling to adapt their knowledge to the next crisis point, the next relief effort. It really didn't matter what the reasoning was, although, as he thought this, images of blighted crops being torched by grim-faced farmers flowed freely through his mind. He shivered despite the warmth of the room.

Martha broke the brief silence. "So my question back to you is: why did you give up on insect biology?"

"I haven't really." Drew dropped instinctively to a familiar defence.

"Robots. Drones..." Her tone was dismissive. "The bees are smarter than you think. How about you help us look after them? Learn from them, why not?"

"The drones I'm building, their programmes... It's what we need to help crop farmers adapt to these new situations. I believe I'm doing valuable work here."

"I don't doubt it," the old lady leant back against her pillows, immediately dissipating Drew's annoyance through her return to apparent frailty.

"But," She continued, "while adaptation may be necessary for modern life, can you actually call it *living*?"

Drew puzzled on this for a moment then shook his head, an exasperated laugh escaping from him.

"Well, Martha, I can't answer that. What I *can* answer is whether my Mark 7s can defend against predation, which is exactly what..." He stood, stretching a little, "... I've got to get back to."

The old lady nodded. "Come and see me again soon. Tell me all about your wonderful inventions." She caught his hand in hers as he went to leave and he was surprised at the intimacy, the contradictory softness of such a careworn touch.

He gave her an awkward smile before walking back through the farmhouse and out into the near-vertical sunshine.

The day was bright and warm and Drew's boots kicked up localised plumes of dust as he strode across the farm's courtyard. Irrigation was always an issue here on the hill, but it was something the hands had learned to manage over the years. Simple tricks such as not being overly zealous in the removal of stones, allowing small pockets of moisture to feed the shallow roots, even in high summer.

Drew's train of thought triggered a realisation of his own thirst, and he looked towards the two massive tanks that stood ready to replenish the watering vehicles. He'd get nothing to drink from their reclaimed reserves, but they still represented the largest body of water in this locale.

He noticed Martha's granddaughter, Rosemary, standing in distorted relief against the shining chrome of the reservoirs. Drew's thirst was immediately replaced by a deeper, less obvious desire.

He brought a hand up to shade his eyes and saw that she was talking to a couple of the hands - Doug and Matt, maybe; it was hard to tell at this distance. He tried to devise an excuse to go and join them but came up with nothing. He had no reason to interrupt, and Rosemary didn't have any reason to talk to him outside of the practicalities of his research and how it impacted the day-to-day running of the farm.

The group paused to look up at him and he immediately made off towards his room, trying - and failing - to move casually despite a sense of being invasive and awkward.

The door shut behind him and he let the tension drop from his shoulders while doing his best to let any negative feelings go.

He grabbed a glass from the room's tiny sink and let the cold tap run for a while, the water finally cooling enough to slake his dryness. At least he felt comfortable now inside these cramped four walls, if not truly at ease. This was partly due to his self-imposed work schedule, but mainly it was the result of his makeshift workshop taking up the majority of the living area.

When he first arrived the only horizontal spaces in the room had been situated on a battered, free-standing bookcase. But, after chatting with Martha and receiving her blessing, he had flipped this on its side and then screwed a couple of chipboard panels across the new-found *top.* Securing the structure to the wall with some scavenged brackets, he had, eventually, ended up with an approximation of a work bench. The addition of a four-way power block completed the set-up, although this had arrived alongside a lecture about electricity usage from Adam - the farm's 'go to guy' for all things technical. Drew had assured him that none of his equipment drew much power, showing the curious farmhand some of the miniaturised solar panels that the drones carried. It only took him a moment to map one of Adam's hands into a devices' memory and then set it to explore the entirety of its surface. The man's pudgy grin of amazement dispelled any curiosity or concerns he may have had and, so far, Drew had honoured the implicit agreement struck between them. To date he hadn't tripped a single one of the farm's circuit breakers.

Now, surveying the collection of data wires, pin vices and screens, Drew marvelled at just how much additional crap his work area had accumulated in the few months since Adam's visit.

He walked past his bed and effortlessly scooped up both pillows before depositing them on the scuffed dining room chair that sat in front of the bench. It was a compromise that enabled him a better vantage on his labour, but every time he sat down he found himself longing for his adjustable lab chair back at the university. To avoid having to reposition the cumbersome seat, he quickly moved everything he thought he might need within arm's reach before finally settling.

There was a natural, progressive level of complexity to the items around him. His laptop was probably the most mechanically intricate, but the drones came a close second. He casually popped open their travel case and tipped all 10 of them out onto the work surface, before picking one up and locking it into the data dock. He'd spent precious years devising them, but he wasn't tentative or gentle in his movements. The drones were designed to be tough, to require the minimum of maintenance in the field, which was exactly why he had come here to test them.

Martha's farm offered at least two distinct threats in the form of indigenous birds and lizards, and it was against these that Drew tested his automated pollinator's defences. It was a fairly simple system, stolen from the ladybird, which caused the drones to excrete a potent alkaloid fluid when chassis agitation indicated a supposed predator attack. The feedback data had indicated several possible assaults, but he still hadn't lost a single device.

At least his creations were effectively impervious when it came to the local spiders and wasps. Neither did they have to worry about the fungal infection that had weakened bee populations across the planet, but then, neither did Martha's bees. She'd read an article some time back about the insects gathering anti-fungal pollen as a way of self-medicating against the affliction. And, being the wise woman she so obviously was, she'd populated her fields with plenty of the plants that the bees required to do this.

Drew paused in his work. What was it the old lady had said to him this morning? "The bees are smarter than you think." He smiled at that and suddenly felt a thrill of unbridled curiosity. What were these plants and how were the bees actually utilising them? He stopped himself, looked back at the intricate beauty of his drone bristling with all its microscopic devices and pushed biochemical musings to one side. These devices were why he was here and, anyway, there were already more than enough distractions keeping him from his research. Making another conscious effort to side step a fountainhead of thoughts that sprung up around Rosemary, he applied himself to the diagnostic window on his laptop.

That night Drew awoke and immediately wanted to be back in the dream. He clenched his eyes and tried to recall all the details of what had just passed. As he did so half-remembered elements sank away from him, confusing the meaning he believed he had already grasped.

He had been travelling, he remembered that much. A floating journey through lazy light, bright and diffused like a mid-summer's morning but with the viscosity of a warm sea. He could breathe, he could guide himself at will through this amniotic medium and he was safe. Safe, but alone? Drew dragged at the edges of the departing images, willing them back into pure being before his analytical mind destroyed them by attempting to apply meaning. He hadn't felt isolated. No, he knew that now. A companion, or companions. He had reached out to them and held a handful of soft setae, the furry feedback through his cruder senses communicating something soft and pelt-like despite the liquid they seemed to flow through.

He puzzled about this contradiction in sensations and immediately brought himself to full wakefulness.

Lying in the pre-dawn dimness for a while, he let the afterglow of the experience wash around him but it was futile. The feelings faded and their emotive spectres were replaced with the more prosaic impressions of the room. He signed in mild frustration then turned on the bedside lamp before shambling back to the work bench.

The drones flew in close formation around his room, their caged micro fans creating a good approximation of an insect's hum.

There was no need for this kind choreography, but Drew simply liked the way they displayed in a diamond formation before they went about their freeform routines. The group split and reformed into a single file that flew a convoluted line around his bed and sink, their high visibility thoraxes making them resemble a string of fairy lights.

They were about to complete a half circuit and return to their carry case when Drew noticed a small black object moving to intercept the last drone in line. Its avoidance routines were being overridden by the pretentious flight path and so the drone hardly reacted to the assailant's impact, wobbling momentarily as it struggled to catch up with its companions. The others had already reached the lip of their carry case, each landing and then scuttling inside to fold down into their dormant mode.

With a few deft keystrokes on his laptop, Drew interrupted the last drone and brought it to rest on the work bench.

He bent forward to examine the device and was surprised to hear a continued hum coming from it. A glance at the nearby screen confirmed that it was indeed inert. He peered at it only to find that the noise was, in fact, coming from a worker bee.

The drone was about twice the size of the insect and the creature had attached itself to the back of the machine - its spindly legs clutching for purchase, its tail pulsating in attack. Sting after sting failed to have any effect on the graphene skin of his creation, but that didn't seem to shake the creature from its determined assault.

Drew grabbed a pair of surgical tweezers and picked up the drone, his intention to take it over to the open window and to flick the bee to freedom. He contemplated the primeval struggle as he walked and couldn't help but admire the insect's tenacity. It made him think about nature's solutions to the same problems he was facing. Both the insect and the drone had the structure to attract and hold pollen. But one was a copy of the other, not part of the evolutionary, deep time symbiosis that existed between insects and plant life. Both had defence systems, but one was biologically mass produced whereas the other had taken a stack of hard currency to perfect. Predation and termination mutually threatened them, but it was only an issue for the hive if the queen's rate of reproduction dropped off. Simple strength in numbers overshadowing all of the drone's durability.

He had reached the window and shifted his delicate burden to a light pinch between the fingers of his free hand. Releasing the tweezers' grip, he placed their tip beneath the insect, pausing as his view was drawn to the slow, persistent pulse of its sting. He realised he was about to release, to *save* this tiny creature that had no real concern for its own self-preservation. Its attack, if successful, might well cause its death. But that didn't matter. Only the perpetuation of the hive did.

"Strange." Drew said as he flicked the bee out of the window.

He moved back to the workbench and placed the final drone with the others before uncoupling his laptop with familiar swiftness. He then placed it, the carry case and his solar field charger into his rucksack. Satisfied that he was ready for the day, he left the room.

He was later than intended and so got caught in the mid-morning bustle of the farm. It wasn't exactly a cosmopolitan rush hour but the central courtyard was still occupied by a good number of workers going about their business. He could head straight across the middle and run the gauntlet of possible conversations that would slow him even further, or take the track down the side of the farm house. It was a longer route, but he really wasn't up for any further delays to the day.

However, as he rounded the central building's corner, he found Martha and Rosemary occupying the veranda - the former sitting up attentively in her wheelchair, while the latter helped reposition the old lady's oxygen tube with gentle precision. They both turned, acknowledging Drew's arrival.

"Morning Drew," Martha said, a deep rattle to her voice but still perfectly audible, "Care to join us for coffee?"

Drew noticed the steaming cafeteria, glanced at the track leading down to the wild flower fields and then looked back to Martha and Rosemary.

"Sure," he said accepting his personal if not academic preference.

"Why not?"

"I'll get another cup and chair." Rosemary said, and before he could raise protest she had ducked back inside the house.

He climbed the short, wooden stairs and lumped his rucksack against the low banister rail before graciously accepting the offered items that Rosemary had retrieved. They sat in a ragged semi-circle around an iron garden table and waited for the coffee to brew.

"You're looking well, Martha." Drew ventured.

"Well that's a lie, son, but I appreciate the sentiment. I look terrible, I know it, but I *feel* a damn sight better out of that room. I'll feel a whole lot better still with some fresh coffee inside of me."

Rosemary grabbed the old lady's hand and looked down in shy acknowledgement that the beverage had brewed long enough. She gave a quick and affectionate squeeze before busying herself with the cups. It was odd for Drew to see Rosemary in any mode other than efficient farm manager.

He considered the old lady's profile and saw the family resemblance in both her and her granddaughter - the same fair but sun-weathered complexion, the same dark brows, their broad mouths easily disposed to toothsome smiles. He felt a sense of comfort then, sharing this morning with these two members of a family. The tart aroma of coffee made his throat twinge in anticipation and he relaxed into his chair, content, as they seemed to be, just to look out at the world.

There were no greenhouses or cloches at the rear of the farmhouse, just a well tendered vegetable garden leading down to a low wall. An eroded wooden gate sat at an untrue angle within this dry stone barrier, its green-hued wood dappled with lichen. When it was opened, which must require a delicate hand, access would be granted to a steep grass field that dropped away to the lower flower fields. As a result the view, while not breath-taking, was pleasing to the eye, especially on a bright morning like this.

Drew accepted coffee from Rosemary and blew across its surface before taking a sip - the savoured flavour immediately loosened his tongue.

"So how's everything going with the flower business?" He asked.

"Pretty good. Pests are on the increase, but you already knew that." Rosemary said with a smirk.

"Well, yes. But the pests mean a greater number of predators, which is what..."

"Don't pay any attention to my granddaughter," Martha interjected. "She's just trying to needle you. On my veranda? Drinking my coffee, with my guest?" She shot a glare of mock disapproval at the younger woman and went back to looking out at the garden and the scene beyond.

Rosemary looked at her lap, smiling, "I'm sorry Mr Somerton."

"Drew." Drew said, wanting to mask his earlier defensiveness.

"Drew." Rosemary corrected herself. "You see, we appreciate you doing your research here and we're grateful of the publicity, to say nothing of the university's subsidy while you're here..."

"I'm glad I can contribute in some small way." Drew sipped his drink more vigorously in the hope of shortening his stay.

"Now," Martha said. "If you were to get Rosemary here onto the topic of pinks... Well, you could sleep, wake again and she'd still only be getting into her stride."

"Gran! Mr Somerton doesn't want to talk about pinks. He's an engineer not a..."

"Dianthus. Part of the family Caryophyllaceae. Literally the 'god flower' in the original Greek and deceptively called a pink, not so much for its colour, more the filigree of its petals." Drew had to dig deep and he wasn't sure about the pronunciation of the family name, but it didn't matter. It had the desired effect on Rosemary.

"A botanist too?" She was genuinely surprised.

Martha let out a rattling laugh and reached for her coffee. "So how do you know about pinks, Drew?"

"Well, the drones aren't just machines, they're pollinators, and the dianthus is renowned for its ability to generate interspecific hybrids." Drew was enjoying the attention. "But I didn't really specialise in them, they were just part of my research before I started thinking about manufacture. How about you?" He directed the question back at Rosemary.

"Sorry?" She seemed to start, as if she'd lost her way in the conversation.

"With the pinks. What's your interest? Are they profitable?" Drew's questioning wasn't generating the response he'd hoped for.

"They're beautiful," Rosemary said.

Drew nodded in agreement, but felt that he was losing her somehow.

"But you're right about the hybridisation." Her smile was a welcome reassurance -. "It's as if nature has given us a randomised, organic paint palette and you're free to experiment without fear of creating a visual nightmare."

"Nightmare?" Drew was puzzled, "Something monstrous, like mutant GM crops hauling up their roots and generating pod people replicas?"

They were off then, their conversation taking flight, leaping spontaneously back and forth across the old lady as she settled back in her wheelchair, sipping at her coffee and her oxygen. She suddenly winced, as if in pain, and Drew realised that they had been neglecting her.

"Are you okay?" He said.

"Yes, fine. Go on, you were saying..." She reassured him with a quiet smile and looked outwards again, as if to say that their chatter was enhancing rather than detracting from the delightful view.

Drew and Rosemary were arguing in the canteen again. It was something they had fallen into, although Drew was privately certain that Martha had been involved in the suggestion that they lunch together.

The discussion today centred upon sugar production but it really didn't matter what the topic was, the motivations were the same whatever they found to talk about.

Drew was starting to fathom Rosemary's response to this meeting of minds. The farm, he realised, was a deeply familiar location for her and he, possibly, offered something fresh that might match her intellect. In this, though, he always felt she gave too much of herself, an underlying vulnerability that made him feel there was always a greater risk for her than him in these sometimes heated engagements.

For his part, he readily lied to himself about these shared meals. If asked, he would have explained that the notional exercise between them was just that: a chance to stretch, to push ideas to exhaustion and then to rally and regain some sense of progress among the detritus of that which hadn't found traction. But the truth was more mundane and much more intimate.

He sat now watching the thin line of a vein catch itself against the tanned skin of her long throat. It swelled marginally when she was in full exposition, and he found its appearance utterly enchanting.

"You've stopped again," she said, turning to look at the rest of the canteen and clenching her jaw.

"I'm sorry?" His reverie was because of her, but there was no way he could use this to explain away his rudeness.

"Stopped." She said, "I've lost you to something else. Probably something small and mechanical." Rosemary's tone had shifted from engaged to clipped to resigned as she bounced through each sentence. She regarded Drew with a cool, yet playful distain.

"I'm sorry. I was..." Words failed him, "... Distracted. You were saying?"

"Oh, it's not important now. The profound moment has passed, and you missed it. It was definitely one of my more memorable quotes. One that will be recorded by historians and passed on to our ancestors as sage wisdom." The laughter didn't exactly bubble to the surface of her words, but he knew there was no malice in what she said.

"You were saying about the health benefits of honey over the detriments of sugar?" He ventured.

"It's not important and, anyway, I'm nearly finished," she said, indicating the remains of her lunch. "Let's talk about something else." She immediately reanimated, shuffling forward on her chair in innocent excitement. "It's our turn to host the harvest festival for the local farms. Think you'll be able to drag yourself away from your precious machines long enough to actually have some fun?"

"Well, if it's happening on my doorstep how can I say no?" Drew did his best to sound charming rather than prissy.

"Good. There's a surprise among our produce this year."

"Oh really? What?"

"I can't say."

"A clue at least?"

"Hmmm..." Rosemary hammed up her pondering. He knew if he pushed she'd probably explain fully, such was her obvious excitement.

"I *can* say," she continued, "that we've all paid forward for this treat, although you probably won't have realised."

"Okay. Well, if I've paid for it already and was unaware, then it'll be the best of surprises."

Rosemary pushed her chair back, gathered her scattered cutlery and clutched the edges of her tray, "So you'll leave your research alone and join us?"

"Yeah, sure." Drew said, "Sounds great."

The surprise, when it came, was ice cream.

Each farm had brought something to the table but, as hosts, Martha's homestead had outdone themselves this year.

Mead had been fermented and was now coursing through the gathered farmers, labourers, and their attendant friends and families. But the conversation flowed even more freely with the arrival of the honeycomb ice cream.

"So, do you like the surprise?" Rosemary asked Drew as he savoured another spoonful of the melting sweetness.

"I'm intrigued." He said grinning, "How exactly did I pay for this?"

Rosemary had been leaning slightly over Drew's table, now she straightened, scanning the gathering as if searching for someone. A look of recognition bloomed on her gentle features and she beckoned Drew to join her in standing.

"Melvin, there." She pointed at a middle-aged man with curly white hair. "You know him, right?"

"The cook? Yeah. Nice guy."

"He's been working overtime. More fresh produce sourced locally, more vegetarian options on the menu each day. But you didn't notice, right?"

"No. The food's always good here. But what has this got to do with the ice cream."

"Well, he made it for one." She winked at him, "And second he's been freeing up freezer space to store his creation. So less meat, more room for ice cream. No one's noticed a thing of course. Just the usual quality meals coming out of the kitchen."

"Ha." Drew sat again and reappraised his bowl and the next scoop he took from it, "I'll be sure to pass on my compliments."

"Oh do that," Rosemary grinned, "It'll mean so much more coming from an outsider like yourself."

Drew frowned at the qualification and felt a weight of difference that Rosemary hadn't intended in her words. There he was, invited to the party but not quite accepted into the fold. He searched her face to check that she hadn't meant to hurt him, and saw nothing but anticipation and joy.

"Right," she said, looking towards someone else in the crowd then briefly back down at Drew, "be sure to find me when the dancing starts." Her provocative invitation left him dumbfounded. She moved away into the crowd, her voice rising in an excited greeting to someone beyond Drew's field of vision.

Dancing. Rosemary. Ice cream.

"More mead?" One of his table companions asked and he nodded stupidly as sensation piled upon sensation making the sanctity of his nearby room seem far away and alien.

He looked at the happy faces around him, thought of all the labour and heart ache that had gone into filling these tables with food and drink, and then drank himself, from that same sense of togetherness. No starched, cerebral conversations or campus politics here, rather a common unity in simply trying to make their land productive.

Martha trundled past him, pushed by someone he vaguely recognised, her frail form somehow still radiating energy to those that parted for her wheelchair. Drew caught her eye as she came level to his seat. He raised his glass to the matriarch. All of this, he suddenly realised, was born out of an idea she'd once had. The old lady smiled in recognition and acceptance of his private toast and then she too was lost from view.

He let go then, stopped worrying about the drones, his relationship with Rosemary, even his social awkwardness with those around him, and allowed the evening to take him rather than steering a path through it. And, in doing so, he found Rosemary smiling and accepting his offered hand as soon as the band struck up.

It was a square dance. The frenetic fiddle and accordion music propagated an impromptu percussion section while one of the old hands shouted energetic sequences. They danced and danced, Rosemary's stamina far outstretching his own but his ego remained undented. For those dances he sat out he was simply happy to watch the path of her smiling face, her shapely form in its floral dress, as she wove her way between cavorting friends and co-workers.

When the two of them were together they laughed and joked , and when they were apart they found each other time and time again amid the throng. It was in one of these meetings a flushed Rosemary said she needed some air and led an incredulous Drew outside.

Their public dance was over, but the private one had only just begun. They welcomed the cool night air as much as each other's company and, with the music still ringing in their ears, they kissed and caressed and stumbled in comic excitement back to Rosemary's room.

Drew's shock at just how furnished her place was disappeared in a flash as Rosemary flicked the lights off and poked her stereo on. Deep, rhythmic beats and foreign words flowed across them both as they fell onto her double bed.

"Wow," Drew said, spreading himself across the receptive covers, "So this is a family perk right?"

She laughed, slapped him on the chest and rolled over onto her back, her dark form alive and seemingly carved out of the shadows. He sprung to the invitation and moved to and against and across her. Their bodies pressed into each other and Drew, worrying at the sheer power of his rising lust, fixed his gaze upon the jumping LEDs of the stereo's graphic equalizer. He hypnotised himself with their pulses, the beat of the music, the thrust of his hips becoming part of this entirety of tempo. Then Rosemary's hands came up to his face, her fingers long and cool against his burning cheeks.

"It's okay," she whispered, "We've got all night."

Death came for Martha one week later.

Drew discovered a distraught Rosemary pacing aimlessly around the old lady's room. The curtains had been fully opened, as had the windows, and the bed had been completely stripped. She didn't seem to notice him as he entered, but began a direct address as she moved between the keepsakes and books. She clutched a quilted cushion to her chest.

"There was evidence that she struggled." Rosemary's voice was a hollow monotone.

He felt his own grief mix with a sudden exasperation. "A struggle?" He failed to hide his doubt.

"She struggled. She could have called. See? Right there." Rosemary nodded to the makeshift call button screwed to the top of the bedside table. "It works fine, so why didn't she push it?"

"Has the doctor been?" Drew asked for want of anything else to say.

"Yes." Rosemary nodded, eyes downcast. Her blankness broken somehow by the mundane practicalities of the medical profession.

"What did they say?"

Rosemary sniffed back a stray tear and looked at Drew. "Oh, you know, the usual thing. All very clinical. Respiratory complications caused by underlying... Actually, it doesn't seem all that complicated to me. She stopped breathing. Then she..."

"Perhaps she knew?" He tried to comfort her.

Rosemary was suddenly attentive. "How do you mean?"

He moved to her, put an arm around her shoulder, a half hug as he didn't really want to come between her and the cushion.

"Would you expect anything else? She was a fighter." Drew shrugged. "And she was brave. I guess you've got to focus on whatever works for you. But the fact the she didn't give up easily, and she didn't involve others. Well..."

Rosemary let out a sobbing laugh which turned into free-flowing but stifled tears. Drew could see she was made of the same country tempered, pragmatic stuff as Martha.

They stood contemplating the bare bed while the sadness drained out of them both. Then Rosemary turned to look at him, her gaze skipping from one of his eyes to the other, searching.

"And what about you?" She asked, "If I focus on you... If I say you *work* for me... Do you stay? Or do you add to this... this emptiness?"

Drew began to struggle with a reply just as a flustered Adam bobbed through the door.

"Sorry to interrupt," he said in a tone that indicated he didn't have much choice in the matter. "But hive three has just swarmed."

Rosemary looked at Adam, shaking her head in dumb disbelief.

"You must have had this happen before. What do you usually do?" Drew said, more to buy Rosemary time than to actually find out what the procedure was.

"Me?" Adam barked, "I usually hear about what happened over dinner. I'm the tech guy remember? Josh is our beekeeper and he's asking - well, he's actually yelling - for anyone to help. Most of the hands are harvesting in the north tunnels you see, and…"

"We'll have to go." Rosemary said with a resigned sigh. "You coming?" She directed this at Drew.

"Sure. Whatever I can do to help."

On the walk down to the hives he noticed that Rosemary had almost returned to the preoccupied movements she had exhibited within Martha's room. Her head was down as she paced, small acknowledging grunts fuelling Adam's flow of slightly panicked banter. He scuttled along beside them, a finger constantly darting up to reposition his spectacles against the bridge of his broad nose.

Drew only half listened to what the other man was saying, but something about someone 'freaking out' and the whole thing being 'bad karma' for the farm brought him back into the one-sided conversation.

"It's just a coincidence," Drew said, "You can't read anything else into a swarm happening on the same day as Martha's death."

"It is weird, though, don't you think?" Adam pounced on the fact that someone had actually been listening to him.

"No," Drew said, shooting the other man a pointed stare and then shifting his eyes to the crestfallen Rosemary, "Death," he paused for emphasis, "is natural. Swarms are natural. These two things happening on the same day, is perfectly natural."

"Oh man." Adam shook his head in realisation. "Hey Rosemary, I'm so sorry. I wasn't thinking. I'm not sure what to do or feel about Martha being gone. And then Josh was all yelling at me, and I'm…"

"It's okay." Rosemary said, her tone tight and full of defeat.

They walked on between the southern ploy tunnels, whose concertinaed doors were all folded down and dusted with a light green mould. Adam occasionally muttered to himself as they moved, while Rosemary paced on in silence. Drew wondered if they shouldn't pick up the pace, but chose not to voice this thought. He was completely without a point of reference on how exactly to handle a grim farm manager attending a swarm on the day of her grandmother's death.

They finally reached a cluster of low, white, slatted hives. A sparse, but consistent number of insects travelled in and out each structure, their flight paths crossing and re-crossing as they went looking for flowers or returned with their precious cargo of nectar. One landed on a sloping hive roof nearby and Drew was surprised to see that it looked as if it was wearing yellow shorts, such was the density of the pollen on its hind legs.

"Where's Josh, then?" Rosemary scanned the flower meadow beyond the greenhouses.

"Over there." Adam said, pointing towards a small copse nearby. A white masked and suited figure laboured at its edges, one shoulder supporting an A-frame ladder, the other arm wrapped around a wooden fruit box.

They approached the heavily clad figure, who turned in a cumbersome way, waved and then pointed into the low foliage directly above his head.

"Hey folks." Drew could just about make out Josh's bearded face through the wire mesh of the beekeeper's hood. "They haven't got far. I just need someone to foot the ladder once I get the smoker up and running."

A seething mass of dark bodies were slung in the branches, and Drew wondered how something in such constant motion could remain suspended. But it was the noise that had the most unnerving effect upon him. A constant deep thrum that made him feel underdressed and desperately exposed.

Josh bent over a battered looking contraption - part funnel, part bellows - and began to pull out a wad of cardboard from inside it. No one else moved.

"Don't people die from mass bee stings?" Drew tried to control himself and sensed, more than saw, Adam take a step backwards from the tree.

Josh remained bent but turned his head to deliver a matter of fact, "Yep." Before going back to the click, click, click of a gas lighter he'd retrieved from somewhere. Drew swallowed and made a move towards the ladder but was held back by Josh's outstretched hand.

"It's only the fools that get stung to death. We need to smoke 'em first," he said.

Josh lifted the spouted contraption in one ungloved hand and began to wave it beneath the swarm. Acrid blue smoke puffed up in twirling plumes and, as if in instant response, the buzzing seemed to lessen.

"Okay. Now I need to climb." Josh pointed at the floor without taking his attention from the smoker or the insects above. Rosemary moved towards the ladder and Drew joined her.

"What should I do?" Adam's voice faltered slightly with the question.

"Get the fruit box and make sure the bag inside is fully open and tucked over all of the edges."

"Okay."

"And I mean *all* of the edges. No gaps."

"Got it!" Adam bounded away from the tree and towards the fruit box. In the meantime Drew and Rosemary had carefully positioned the A-frame next to Josh.

"That'll do fine. Don't want to knock 'em, do we?" Josh seemed to be enjoying himself, which Drew found annoying seeing as the beekeeper was the least exposed. As if in confirmation, he suddenly felt a sharp pinch followed by a blazing ache on his forearm.

"Ah!" He exclaimed.

"Stung?" Josh pulled something that looked like a flat, stubby crowbar from another pocket and handed it to Drew.

The crippled worker bee rolled off Drew's arm, its dripping tail telling of its imminent demise. He looked at the bulky, flat tool and then back at the barb sticking from his skin in total confusion.

"Rosemary," Josh said, "Show him how, then get back on this ladder quick."

She seemed more attentive now, the unfolding situation distracting her from her grief. She took the tool from Drew with one hand and lightly held his arm with the other. Then she laid the cold metal against his skin and he noticed a strange almond-shaped hole at one end. Rosemary placed this so it sat around the chitinous barb and poison sack and then, in one swift movement, she slid the tool across Drew's arm. The stinger caught and pulled free.

"The trick," She said handing the tool back to Drew, "is not to use your fingers. You'll just nip the poison sack and shoot more venom into the wound."

She moved back to the ladder and placed her weight on the lowest rung on her side. Josh took this as an immediate cue to ascend and Drew realised that his role was to mirror what Rosemary was doing.

"Gonna take a bit longer to get them all good and quietened." Josh said above them. "I told them all, y'know. Or I thought I did."

"Told who what?" asked a baffled Drew.

"The bees. You're supposed to tell them when someone close dies. Or else they get restless. I guess I missed a hive."

Drew gave a gentle, bemused shake of his head and then settled to wait with the others, the soft huff of the smoker above and the lump of machined steel in his hand. The tool was so basic, so crude, and yet... He looked up at Josh's balanced form and thought that the wire mesh in his beekeeper's hood was probably the most complex component involved in all of this ridiculous, rustic scene. Rudimentary solutions replicating the farm's own naive belief that it could elicit change through such basic methods.

He looked at Rosemary, who was craning her neck to watch Josh. Here she was, here they *all* were, tackling a crisis despite their ineptitude and broken hearts. But what of the bigger picture? How on Earth could this lot hope to effect governments signing off on poorly researched pesticides?

"You ready with that box?" Josh kept his eyes on the swarm but stretched one hand down towards Adam, who dutifully overcame his fear and reached the box towards the awaiting grasp. Josh glanced to check everything was correct with the container and then passed the smoker to Adam.

"I'm gonna need that again as soon as I step off. You okay with that?"

Adam nodded.

There was some gentle repositioning above Drew and then the unmistakable crack of wood against wood.

"Whoa!" Drew instinctively ducked and then realised that Josh was backing down the ladder with some haste.

"You got a hive ready Josh?" Rosemary was already in motion back the way they had come.

"Yep. Number 10's empty and full of fresh foundation frames. Go and open it for me would you. Adam. That smoker. Yep. Just puff some into the top of the sack before I shut it."

Drew, still wanting to be of help, jogged after Rosemary. He caught up with her next to one of the hives. She placed her hands on the corners of the roof and motioned that Drew should do the same on the other side.

"Wiggle it while lifting. It's a tight fit on this one." She said and he applied himself to the task. The roof came free and Drew was able to see row after row of clean wooden slats, and then the smell hit him. Not an unpleasant aroma but something bitter sweet, caught up somewhere between syrup and burnt wood.

They placed the roof on the ground and Rosemary quickly tugged a couple of the frames free, each one displaying hundreds of perfectly hexagonal, unoccupied cells.

"Adam's right, you know." She said.

Drew looked and saw the sadness return to Rosemary's face.

"About what?"

"About the swarm being an omen. About this whole thing falling apart. And do you know what? They're all going to look to me to hold things together and the only reason I could... I could hold it all together was because she was around." She began to sob again.

"Hey..." Drew moved towards her and was met by that penetrating gaze once again.

"And you're going to leave. Aren't you?" She snapped, searching his face again, imploring an answer with her stare and he found, for some inexplicable, deep-rooted reason, he couldn't hold her gaze.

Drew looked at his suitcase. The wheels were completely unsuitable for the rough chippings of the farm's driveway, but its hard shell provided additional protection for his research. Everything he had been working on was nestled inside and, while not overly heavy, he opted to drag it rather than carry it towards the awaiting van. He'd packed everything in a precise and careful way -hard drives hermetically sealed in plastic bags then wrapped in loft insulation, weighty vices swaddled down towards the wheels, fragile data cables sitting near the top in improvised corrugated cardboard cases.

The driver, already out of the van, popped the rear doors and began deftly to build a pile of boxes on the dusty ground. His electronic logging device flapped against corporate issue shorts. With the daily flow of cut flowers, deliveries to the farm were regular and the drivers were well known to the residents.

Rosemary joined Drew as he advanced towards the vehicle, her hand raised to the driver in a welcoming wave. The man noticed and paused in his unpacking, recognising that Drew was dragging a case behind him.

The couple stopped.

"And you're sure?" Rosemary asked.

Drew nodded.

He'd spent his life as measured and as hollow as a reed, but now... He looked at Rosemary, her face shadowed by a crumpled, wide-brimmed hiking hat. She assessed the task at hand, her eyes darting from one package to another and in watching her he sensed something shifting deep down in the warm, vibrant core of himself. He could see the potential now, the nascent plan of investigating these strange communal creatures, of building an understanding of them, of being accepted. He had no idea how he was going to transform the contents of the growing pile of boxes into the sterile environment he'd need for the research but, together, they'd find a way.

The university would kick up a fuss, of course. He'd abused their ordering facilities, but he was convinced he'd have enough money in his accounts to cover the apparatus costs. He'd keep his laptop too and would deal with the issue of its return when that arose. Everything else, including all of his findings from the drones, was ready to be shipped.

Rosemary shook her head in wonder. "Wow. That's a whole lot of boxes. Do you want to go through them all once we get them back to your room?" She laughed, "Or do we call it 'the lab' from now on?"

Her laughter took the edge off his contemplation.

"No," he said, taking her hand. "That can wait. Once we're done here I want to go back to the hives and see just how smart these bees really are."

My Oasis Tower

Holly Ice

A ticking splutter woke me up. Swinging my legs off the bed to the floor, I gasped. It was wet. Something must have gone wrong with the water system. Shivering a little from the icy touch of the water, I donned my wellies before my toes curled in protest. Whoever caused this was going to get a smack round the head, and then I was going to get some coffee.

Whatever the problem, I still couldn't believe I had landed a job here. I was lucky to get out of the city.

Keys in hand, I left my room. The flower floor was drenched, dewy glass drops perfect on the white, red and yellow petals. They were off the ground, stacked in nutrient-rich tiers, but they were not going to react well to all this water. It looked as if the sprinklers on every tier were set too high. I had checked the levels before I slept... Still, damage control would come later.

I ignored the flowers, taking the usual route through the tiers to the centre of the room. Here there was a square space free of pots and plants, leaving the exit clear. Access to the lower level came via a hatch set into the floor so that any poor sod could work my shift.

I splashed down the slope and opened the heavy door down to the tropical flowers. My muscles shook with the effort: handicap-friendly, maybe, but they did not have my frame in mind when building the place. Back then it was all political correctness, slopes, fire exits... even if they had trouble opening the damn doors. Genius. But this was an old building now. Heavy material might have been around, the best choice, when it was built. Yeah. This place just hated me.

My muscles groaned and the door slammed behind me. Another joy to look forward to: reopening it in thirty minutes.

This floor was humid, as usual, but a bit wetter than normal. My dressing gown crept closer to my skin, clammy. Great. I was going to need a long shower after this too. Okay, so I might have been lucky to get this job but at that particular moment I wondered why the hell I'd bothered. There were better, more social ways to earn a living, just better jobs all round. And there we go: I sounded like my mother. It's good money. Think about the money. And that holiday in Cicely... It wasn't so bad, really.

Colours surrounded me and the heated nutrients seeped into my skin and lungs. I was in an indoor, de-teethed aquarium of pinks, purples, sky blue and pyramid clusters. Yellow cups, blue vases, red pods; petal-blanketed pollen. Sweet and heady smell-whirls cloaked the air in pockets as I passed tiers of different flavours bound for different homes: the wealthy, the make-dos and the artists. There was no noise or thought, no sentience, just being. I stopped for a second to enjoy the feeling, the warm tingle of sweat down my back, the perfume of my favourite red flower, but it was hard to breathe and I had things to do.

A too-fast slosh forward. My left welly filled with cold water. Damn. Just not worth it right now. Standing on one foot, wobbling, I emptied out the sodden welly and squelched on, down another slope to the celery floor.

It is weird having a whole floor of celery alone. God knows why people love that stuff so much. Dieting with their green planty toothpicks. Tastes like shit, mainly water. Hey, at least the celery will like this indoor flood! One less job for me.

Finally, the last door. Time to find out what caused this mess. Burst pipe, dodgy valve? I heaved it open and stepped through. Only here, the floor was bone dry other than the puddle I assumed I'd invited in by opening the door: no sprinklers. I looked around, checked a few gauges on the machinery, and then reared back. There were wet footprints by the water valve, pacing feet.

Hell! My hands jumped up to my chest at the shock; Johnny was here.

"Hello, Megan. Brought you flowers."

He shoved a group of tropics towards me. Unwrapped and sap still dangling from their torn stems, I could tell he'd grabbed them upstairs. Not a romantic gesture. Still, I smiled, tried to make light of him trespassing. It would not go well if I didn't. The alarm was down another floor: I would never get there in time. But then maybe he messed up the alarms. Else I would have heard him. And I needed to talk, get it together.

"Johnny. How did you find me?"

"Your mother said you had turned into a farmer, dungarees and all."

My hands swept my dressing gown. I forced another smile. "Obviously that's not true." But why had my mother given away where I was? She wouldn't, I don't think... Was he armed? "Why are you here, Johnny?"

"To see you." He pushed the bouquet into my arms and, to save arguing, I took it. Then I backed off, circled around him. Maybe if I ran to the door? No, I needed something. A piece of pipe? Emergency hammer? I could have sworn one was around here, somewhere. I really should have paid attention in that induction... but what is so hard about keeping an eye on plants? I never thought *he* would turn up!

"Johnny, we went over this. You and I are finished. You had someone else."

"Harriet and I broke up."

"That doesn't make everything okay! Is that why you're here?"

One step at a time, towards the fire extinguisher. I thanked the construction idiots for insisting on it despite the prevalence of water and sprinklers. Everything had its use.

"I thought we could... make up. You're out here, alone, on this green lighthouse of bad food. Come home, please?"

He took one step too close. I let the bouquet drop and grabbed the fire extinguisher off its bracket, throwing it at his head. He didn't have time to react and the extinguisher hit with a loud clang. I ran, my feet tapping the cement towards the lower door. My breath came in gasps. I really should have gone to the gym. One hard heave and the door was open. I gathered a breath and ran on; he would not be far behind me and he was stronger than I was.

Carrots in beds and beds, a maze of green sprouts, floor to ceiling, and I was the rabbit. Down the slope, by the door. The alarm. I pulled my sleeve down over my knuckles and punched the glass covering. It shattered. I pressed the button and a soundless alarm started a few buildings away, in the security room. I could only hope they weren't on lunch break and that the alarm was working.

Steps behind me, loping forward and fast. I heaved open the door, wondering where I could hide. This was the floor for blackcurrants. Could I hide behind a bush? Doubtful. And when he found me... I could not simply run down and down forever. I had to do something.

I saw, then, how he had got in. On a lower tier near me, balanced on its wall, was a crowbar, sparkling with water and something darker, dried on. He must have used it to get in the front door, then discarded it so he could be my prince charming. I guess I should be glad he didn't want to convince me with bruises like before. I picked up the crowbar, hid it behind my back, and waited by the door, side to the wall. He would come through soon enough.

Time for a few breaths. I counted them, calmed, just as I had learned to do in therapy. This was a place for relaxation, sweet pollen and easy dinners, not violence. A bang, weight thrown against the door. This was him. I was ready.

He stepped through and before I thought any more about the pros, the cons, I swung. He fell to the ground. The door snapped back, towards his head. My hand flew out, stopped it. I hated him but I was not going to decapitate him on purpose. Not today, anyway.

I kicked his side. He didn't move, out cold. I laughed, a giggling hysteria that watered my eyes. This was him, out cold. I did it. Drops fell down my cheeks and I wiped them with my free hand. I could escape, had to. Back to my room, locked away from him. Who knew when he would wake up? I had to move.

Still laughing, my arms shaking with reaction, I grabbed his hands and pulled him free of the door. My foot propped it open, saved it squishing him. His body safely free, I stepped back through the door. As it closed I saw a bloody handprint where I'd held it. My stomach clenched. I had not touched the end of the crowbar so whose blood was it? No, no time. Later, I could find out.   Hands shaking and seeing the world through fuzzy coloured dots, I climbed the four floors to my room. My hearing was dampened, my steps mere scuffs and light swells. But it was a pleasure to snap that deadbolt into place and cross the wet room to the phone. And yay for me: it still worked.

I had told security what happened. My crazy, abusive ex fiancé had turned up. They called the emergency services and held my hand on the way down the ten floors to ground level. Now I sat on a wooden bench and a policeman with a notepad was talking at me. Blinking, I looked up at his blue eyes, ginger hair. My hands turned the hot striped mug I had been given. It was full of coffee but tasteless.

"Sorry. Can you say that again?"

"Do you know why John Breathwaite came to see you today?"

"He said he wanted to get back with me."

"You were together?"

"He was my fiancé. He cheated on me with Harriet."

A few scribbles on his pad. This did not look good. "Harriet's last name is?"

"Mills. Look, he was crazy. He used to beat me unconscious. Some of my bones still haven't set right. That's why I came here. I thought it would be safe, relaxing..."

His eyes softened a touch but he still had a job to do. He couldn't be too gentle. "You hit the man with a crowbar when he brought you flowers."

"He could have done far worse. Check the police reports. There are plenty, x-rays and everything."

But he didn't. I knew that and I was in trouble. The policemen knew it, too. He just wasn't coming out with it. Instead he had turned to my place of work, the plantation towers. They shone, beacons in the landscape, despite the sun's presence high in the sky. The towers were brighter, full of a whiter, natural light: leylight. A cluster of them sat together, a mini spotted web from above. They rested on a leyline. Some sceptics still refused to believe this was the source of power, claiming that instead geothermal energy was being tapped direct from the Earth's core. Bollocks to that. Leylights were a great innovation, not to mention 'carbon free'.

"Miss Thomas, you may need a lawyer. This is more than a simple hit." He turned back to me but didn't meet my eyes. He felt bad for me, now he knew my past. Most people did. "John Breathwhaite is thought to be in a coma."

"No!" The bastard couldn't even give me peace when he was mentally absent. Now there was going to be an investigation, court proceedings. I might never get back to my job, what I thought was my future: alone, tending the food for the city. Damn you, Johnny.

"And there was blood on the crowbar, blood that wasn't John's."

My hands twitched and I felt the thoughts, the worry, rush back in. My mother would not have told him I was here, not willingly. And she was alone in that apartment, her neighbours often out. They didn't even know her name... It couldn't be. I'd call her later, she'd be fine. I was just worrying, paranoid. The therapist said I stress too much. It has to be that. She just let something slip.

The policeman was still talking but I let it wash over me, nonsense, babble. I stared through him to my building, my tower of green work. The lights coloured my blinks and my eyelids ached to squint but I kept them open, focused on the top floor. That white building with its faults, its endless heavy doors, is my oasis, my place, my own. Only now I would have to give it up, go back to the fake smiles and 'how-are-you's'.

I turned to bad man blue eyes. "Do I have to leave right now?"

"No. You have a few days to collect your things, tell your employers."

He hadn't said as much but I knew: they would want me on hand for questioning in the city, the soulless cement bombsite, devoid of anything green or growing. The nearest hint of vital flora was safely ensconced in my towers here, more than an hour away. God knows what they saw in that place, that monstrosity that rose in straight lines to the sky. No creativity, no air, no colour. Lifeless. People had become so divorced from their food sources. They relied on the daily caravan in to stores, their days uninterrupted by the ancient necessity to farm or hunt their fill. It made me sick.

"I'm going to the city?" was all I said.

"Yes. A car will pick you up."

Great, an escort. Dead blue lights and a smiling driver. Just what I needed. "I can't stay here?"

"No. Sorry. At least, not until this is over. If..." He faltered, started again. "If it helps, there is evidence the sprinklers were tampered with. The front doors were broken, too, and some of the alarms. You have a case."

So I had a case. I nodded, understood. He had mucked up a few things, left evidence. I could come back here, if I were let off jail time. If I checked out. So many ifs. Sighing, I stood and shook his hand. Polite, always be polite. But I couldn't. I said nothing. I turned my back on blue eyes and opened the heavy doors to my punctured oasis. The ten slopes and doors up to my room were a task I threw my muscles behind, the effort scraping my mind clean of worries, as it had when I first started here.

Grabbing the phone in a repeat of my plea for help, I depressed the digits for my mother. How had she ruined this, given away my place? I would have been fine. It would have been fine. She knew that. So why? The ring wailed on to the answer machine. I pressed the digits again. The ring wailed on to the answer machine. She was not picking up. And suddenly I knew I would return to my green tower but a big piece of me would be bitten out, stuck in Johnny's rotting teeth as he slept. And I was glad he was gone, a vegetable; because if he came back, if I saw him again, I would kill him.

Throw Back

Gill Shutt

Tic sighed wearily as he made his way out to the shed. It was going to be another scorching hot day, which meant the animals would have to be kept indoors. It was his job to feed and water them and the hotter it was the more they drank. If only his father would invest in a covered walkway down to the river, he could herd them down and let them get their own water. Their skin burnt so easily in sunlight and they'd get sick if he took them out in this weather. But Skit was renowned for his tight-fisted ways and nothing his children said could change him.

"I don't know what you're sighing about." Skee, Tic's oldest brother, had followed him out into the yard. "At least you aren't on field duty like the rest of us. It's going to take all day to water the crops, even with the cousins coming over to help."

"I just wish the old man would see sense," Tic said, making sure that his father wasn't within hearing range. "If Uncle can put in ditches and covers for the animals then I don't see why we can't do the same."

"No use wishing, Tic. But things will change when I take over, I can tell you that." Skee hefted the double yoke onto his back and set off for the river, four buckets swinging by his sides.

Tic opened the barn door wide to let in some air, not that there was any wind and not a cloud in the sky. He went along the stalls and checked on his charges. Bessy looked ready to birth soon and Tic hoped for a male. Their stud was getting long in the tooth and if Bessy had a healthy male they could trade at the monthly market.

At the far end of the row old Maggy lay in her straw, panting heavily. She was their oldest female and had been a good breeder but Tic could tell she wouldn't be with them much longer. He unlocked the stall gate and walked in slowly, talking quietly so as not to startle her. He reached out and stoked her head but she pulled away from him weakly. Her eyes were crusted and her mouth looked cracked from lack of moisture. As soon as he'd seen to the rest of them he'd have to get his father to put her out of her misery.

The remainder of the morning was taken up with lugging water from the river and mixing the feed. As he went about his work, Tic chewed blades of succulent grass from the river bank. This kept his energy and fluid levels up so he didn't have to stop for a break. Each time he passed the farm he could hear his mother's voice as she taught the children. Tic's grandmother had passed away a year ago and his mother had taken her place as head of the household. It was her job to keep the place clean and teach the children their lessons. Tic had always enjoyed the stories about what life had been like before the Devastation. Things had been much easier in those days. No spending your days carrying buckets of water, for one thing.

With the animals fed and watered, Tic headed off to find his father. He'd managed to get Maggy to drink a little but she was refusing food and he knew it was time.

"Your dad's gone back to bed." His mother could have told him the sky had fallen and he'd have been more likely to believe her. His father was never ill, always the last to bed and always the first up in the morning. Cautiously he made his way to where his father was lying. If he was ill he would be in a foul mood and Tic didn't want to be on the receiving end of the old man's temper.

"Dad?" Tic stood in the doorway and called quietly. "Dad, it's Maggy. She won't eat and I think it's her time."

For a moment he thought his father wasn't going to answer but then there was a low hiss of pain.

"Get your brother to deal with it." His father's voice was low and strained. "When he's finished, send him in here."

"Um, okay." Tic was shocked. He'd never known his father to shirk his responsibilities. As head of the farm it was his job to put down the livestock. That's how it had always been. Then he realised what else his father had said and stood staring into the gloom unable to move.

"Go on, son." His dad must have known what he was thinking. "You've always been a good lad, a hard worker. I'm proud of you, boy."

That was just too much to bear and Tic ran from the building. His mother must have seen his agitation because she fell silent and shushed the younger ones. He knew she was watching him as he raced out to the fields.

"Skee, Skee!" Tic shouted as he ran and saw his older brother look up in amazement.

"It's Maggy and dad and... Skee, it's time." Tic stumbled over his legs and words in his anxiety.

"Whoa, slow down, brother. Time for what?" Skee looked at him, clearly puzzled. Tic waited while he got the words straight in his head.

"Maggy needs putting down and Dad said to get you to do it. And then he said he wanted you to go and see him. He's ill, Skee, really ill." Tic finally explained and saw comprehension dawn on his brother's face.

Skee followed him back to the barn and Tic went to take care of Bessy. She was in full labour now and Tic used it as an excuse not to have to watch as Skee murmured the prayer of thanks then broke Maggy's neck. He did it very professionally, Tic noticed. Maggy never made a sound and the other animals, unable to see, were none the wiser. Bessy leant against the barn wall and strained, sweat covering her body. The females in the neighbouring stalls called to her as though in encouragement. Tic's father had told him they were just dumb beasts but Tic wasn't so sure. The noises they made sounded almost like speech to him. Not as complex as real speech of course but a rudimentary language at least.

As Skee left the barn, dragging Maggy's body out to the slaughter shed, Tic watched him but couldn't think of anything to say. A moment later he saw his brother making his way to the farmhouse, his pace slow and his features stern.

"Good luck," Tic called out and Skee waved an arm but didn't look back. At that moment Bessy's waters broke and Tic turned back to the job in hand. It seemed only moments later that he heard his mother's wail of grief, followed by the sound of Skee dragging his father out to lie next to Maggy. 'Waste not, want not' his father had always said... and buckets didn't make themselves.

Tic was about to look up but just at that moment Bessy gave a final push and the baby shot out onto the straw. Tic saw immediately that it was male... but there was something wrong. As Bessy turned and picked it up, putting it to her breast, Tic skilfully cut and tied the umbilical cord, a look of revulsion on his face. He waited patiently for the afterbirth to appear then took it to the feed preparation area for mincing later. Then he returned to take another look at what Bessy had produced.

"Skee!" He yelled to be heard over the sounds of his father's and Maggy's dismemberment. The grinding, grating noises stopped and Skee came to the door and looked over the stall.

"It's a throw back," he said matter-of-factly, "from before the Devastation."

"But it has black stuff growing out of its head!" Skee felt slightly sick as he looked at the infant's head.

"It happens sometimes. Don't worry, we can sell it for meat. Gran said they were all like that once." Then even Skee was taken aback as, suckling contentedly at its mother's breast, the infant opened its eyes. Instead of unseeing, milk-white pupils, two dark blue eyes looked blearily out at them.

"Oh shit!" Tic scuttled back in fear and disgust. Skee flung open the stall door and wrenched the thing from its mother's arms. Expertly he brought his mandibles together and snapped through the infant's neck. He held the body in one claw and handed the severed head to Tic who took it reluctantly, ensuring that it faced away from him. He didn't want to see its face again.

"Go bury it out back where no one can see it," he said to Tic. " Sighted ones are bad luck, they're uncontrollable."

As he ran to do his brother's bidding, Tic could hear Bessy sobbing and crying out for her baby. The other females all called and the stud was bellowing from his stall, pulling against his chains. It was going to take the rest of the day to settle them down. They'd have to put Bessy together with another male as soon as possible, otherwise she could sicken, Tic thought. He'd heard of it happening before. Sometimes, after too many births, they had to cull the babies and those who didn't have a child to feed could get fever and go off their food. Tic didn't think he'd ever really understand them and their totally impractical breeding methods... but they did make tasty meat.

He shuddered slightly, his carapace rattling, as the image of those blue, human eyes came into his head again.

Mary on the Edge

Steven Pirie

Mary's drone knows nothing about dead children. It's dark by the hedgerows, and the drone's hovering down near the southern Edge, counting the radio beacons from the wandering sheep. It senses the *robotnik* digging the grave, and the still, baby human at its side, but as the grave is beyond the Edge and the drone really doesn't know about dead children, it saves the file under anomalies and moves on. It could be days before the drone downloads to Central. And in days a lot can happen.

Ask Mary...

Mary waits for Mother in the drawing room. She has to report to Mother each evening, even if there's nothing to tell. There's no sound but the rhythmic thud of the Grandmother clock in the corner. Mary shivers and drums her fingers against the arm of the leather sofa. The sound is dull and lifeless. Even with its high ceiling this room stifles her. Portraits, centred in ornate, gilded frames upon the walls, frown down upon her; garish faces from the days when the family had men folk to speak of. The floor is strewn with rugs. Mother always keeps Mary waiting.

Always.

Mother – Mary's heard the whispered rumours about the town – *a witch, you know; how else can she manage an Edge Farm at sixty-two years' of age? And those four daughters of hers – blessed with such stunning good looks yet none of them able to ensnare a man of their own. A crone, they say, to scare away the town's men folk who would otherwise wrestle each other to get at those daughters. A witch to force those girls to leaf through the catalogues of the sperm markets instead. Some of the town's men can manage two erections a month. Oh, such a waste for Mother's coven to ignore.*

The door opens and Mother shuffles inside. Her face is lined and ancient. It's the lived in face of an Edge Farmer. She sits upon the great leather sofa, the same Father had sat upon on the day the aneurism

161

took him. When Mother is gone too, Mary thinks, I'll make sure this room goes with her.

"News?" says Mother.

Mary stands. Always stand when addressing one's elders, that was the house rule. Never speak unless spoken to. "Good evening, Mother. Charlotte has given birth."

"Oh?"

"To a girl."

"But the ultra-sound scans..."

"Were erroneous, it would seem. Deliberately so, perhaps. We should have opted for the full blood tests. And a proper sperm provider."

Mother frowns. Mary knows the expression well. "You chose the provider."

"I did, and I'll be more careful next time."

"Time is running out, Mary. We'll require a male heir soon. The Ministry of Land and Sea has already told us this."

"Yes, Mother."

"If your sisters can't give me a grandson then perhaps it's time you too were made pregnant."

Mary stands rigid. She resists the urge to rub her stomach. She holds in her breath. "Perhaps so, Mother, but who will run the farm while I'm... *indisposed?*"

"If there's no male heir there will be no farm."

"That's true, Mother."

"Then it's settled. Make the arrangements, and see that Charlotte is impregnated again right away. Medicate her to ovulate if need be."

"I'll do my best, Mother."

"See that you do." Mother turns away in her seat. "I'm tired. You may go now."

"Good evening, Mother."

Mary's pensive the following day, locked in Central Hub. In truth, she's generally happiest here. Central, with its hum of electronics and hiss of video screens, carries the very heartbeat of the farm. It's here she feels like a *real* farmer. It doesn't matter that when she runs her fingers through the soil she does so *virtually*. It's no worry that when she's done so there's no dirt under her fingernails. Father had dirt under his fingernails, and he was dead by forty-two.

"Show me all sectors," says Mary.

Six screens built into the console she sits at flicker awake. Each view is further split into eight camera angles, thirty-six fixed and twelve floating upon the various drones and *robotniks* that do the actual work. Forty-eight eyes is always enough to monitor an Edge Farm, particularly one shrinking in decline.

Mary glances at each view in turn. She likes to begin the day's farming with a brief overview of the entire farm. It helps her feel *at one* with the land. Not that lately she's felt that much *at one* with anything.

She winces at the sudden, sharp pain in her abdomen. Mary's eight weeks' now – barely *showing* yet – and still firmly into the first trimester's sickness. She's heard such awful morning sickness means she's carrying a boy. *Boys are always hard to bear early on*, they say, *such a conflict of hormones with a boy in the womb.* Not that many women know any more.

Mary rubs a palm over her stomach. In many ways, Mother ordering her pregnant the previous evening is a blessing. But how to explain to Mother why she's so far *gone*, and how to tell her the conception was by the *traditional* method and not via some glossy, and probably unrealistic, photo-shoot in the sperm catalogues? *Juan, twenty-two years' of age; disease free and athletic; sires eight percent males, guaranteed.* Such traditional unions come with claims of farm ownership by the father. Mary doubts Mother will give the farm over easily. She's fought for it before and won.

Mary sighs. For now, on the screens, on the fields, the early morning sun shines down. To the west, storm clouds gather. Mary rubs her stomach once more. She knows that gather they certainly do.

"Close up, Number Four Field," says Mary. The *robotniks* fill the screen. They're standing idle, leaning their metallic bulk against the fence posts. Mary grins – hang a cigarette on their lips and from a distance they could be Father standing there.

Mary pushes an intercom button upon the console. "Nicole, can you come up here, please? I have to go argue with the *robotniks* in Number Four again."

In truth she can argue with them from here, but today Mary needs to feel the *real* earth under her feet. Some days, to be an actual farmer, one needs shit on one's boots. She hates the way the *robotniks* howl and thrash and beg and *die* on the way to rebooting. It makes her feel better to go reason with them. Even if they remind her of Father.

There's sadness in that Mary can walk the length of the Edge Farm in an hour these days. There was a time, when Father was young, when Mary was young — did she ever feel young? — it would take five days to cross from Number One field in the north to Twenty-seven at the southern Edge. Now there are just eight fields, home to a thousand head of cattle where once ten thousand roamed. Anything under a thousand is barely classed as a farm.

Mary thinks back to her youth. When Father died she'd barely understood as Mother had fought screaming and kicking as the Ministry of Land and Sea systematically stripped her of land. She stood firm to the last as the neighbouring farmers shrugged and buckled and folded. Whilst Mother might have her faults, Mary has to admit she admires her for that. *There was a war on*, they'd said, *and England expects*. And they took the prime land and left the strips and scraps to the *edge*. Edge Farms. But Mary knows it was a war of attrition, not some foreign invader that needed repelling. Sometimes, on her more cynical days, Mary thinks it was a war started deliberately.

Mary pauses at the stile separating Number Three field from Number Four. Three is in fallow, but Four is healthy with wheat. It's nine a.m. and already thirty degrees. The incoming storm is slow moving and still some way off, and for now the warmth of the sun on her stomach feels good. So far today, she's only thrown up twice. Here, the land rises, and Mary can see beyond the dry stone wall that marks the eastern Edge and into the Ministry of land and Sea super cell next door. The Ministries don't make for good neighbours. Theirs is a golden landscape, of rape seed as far as Mary can see. The scent is heady on the breeze. The Ministry's money is in biomass, and feeding of the populous is a secondary thought. Governments do that in times of strife, look after themselves first. It's some sort of perverse rule of survival. Even though surely governments are people, too.

Mary climbs the stile and approaches the *robotniks*. They're Polish made — Mother got them as a cheap job lot from a dodgy looking Lithuanian sheep farmer. Mary chooses to forget that Mother got Charlotte too as part of the deal. She'd covered her ears with her pillow as in the next room the bedsprings groaned and the dodgy Lithuanian yelled *victory* in some foreign tongue. But Mary knew what it meant, even at that young age. You can't live on a farm and not know the gritty details of sexual reproduction from an early age. *No one will ever do such a thing to me,* Mary had told herself the following day when Mother looked aged and ragged. Mary rubs her stomach once more. How soon she'd forgotten that vow. She'd heard that boys were born of nights of passion. But all *he'd* done was to make her bleed. That and make her pee sting for a week.

"Is there a problem, Robotnik?" says Mary. The robots object to being called anything but *robotnik.* Mind you, they object to *most* things. If Mary and her sisters were able to do the manual work themselves, she would have scrapped them long ago. No, that's not true; she'd probably *let them go,* or give them a barn to retire to, or something.

"Dzień dobry, pani," says Four.

Mary shakes her head. They'll feign non-understanding of English commands when it suits them. She wonders if she should *man*-up and reboot them anyway. They're just machines, aren't they?

"You're meant to be applying growth hormones."

"Ci wykonać pracę?"

"No, no," says Mary, she's picked up the odd nuance of Polish over the years. "I want *you* to add the growth hormones."

The four *robotniks* look on blankly. They're big, awkward, clunking machines, desperately out dated, and their skin, if it ever shone silver-bright, has long since dulled and pitted. They're nothing like the sleek automatons that sweep across the Ministry's fields. Clearly Three has problems. Its left arm is thrashing about seemingly of its own volition. It's locked mumbling nursery rhymes in French. One is busy encouraging it.

"Przepraszam, nie rozumiem," says Two. "Zgadza się pani mówić Polskim?"

Mary points an accusing finger. "Don't go giving me that *no speako Eeenglish* nonsense. I know you understand me perfectly."

No one understands Mary perfectly. Not even Mary. Perhaps Father came close, but his left arm had thrashed about, too, when the aneurism gripped him. There was fear in his eyes as his lips trembled and no words came out. There was no strength in his grip as Mary held his dying hand. There was no fight left in him as she watched him slip away.

Mary grew up, that day. Her childhood ripped from her, what else could she do? And Mother wasn't there for her, because the farm was an insistent child, and with Father gone the Ministry bureaucrats circled like vultures and fell upon Mother like raptors. Someone had to look after Nicole and Ruth, and then baby Charlotte from the Lithuanian's *attentions*. And it was a lifetime's undertaking, that was the hardest part. So what if Mary had dreams of love and trust and a man of her own? Girls have such needs even in a world of depleting males, can't they? No, because all of that died the day Mary became replacement mother to her sisters. Is she bitter? Yes, sometimes.

"There is no... hormone," says Four. "We have, um, run out."

"Boże! We have spread it too much," says Two.

Mary sighs. "There was enough bought for all the arable land."

"We are stupid," says Four. "What do we know?"

"Three is stupid," adds Two. "And One is not helping."

That evening, alone after Mother's nightly news inquest, Mary lies on her bed. She has the bedroom ceiling transparent, so she stares up at a sky of a million stars. She likes the stars, because unlike the world they're too far away to weigh down upon her. Unlike the world, they're never changing. To the west, occasional lightning flares and thunder growls. The circling storm gains strength. Already its first breath brushes the creaking limbs of the trees in the lane beyond the house. Their leaves cling and *flutter*.

Mary thinks she can feel the baby *flutter* inside her, but surely it's too early for that. It's a boy; she's certain to. A woman can sense these things. For now, the baby's as much a part of her body as her legs, her arms, her heart, her soul, so why shouldn't she know it intimately? She thinks she might call him Simon.

Thunder rumbles, closer, louder. Mary knows at once it's a mistake to name the child so early. Now he has a name, the baby's *real*. Now she worries if Simon has a future. Now he has *needs* beyond the womb.

The world has changed in the few short years since Mary was a girl. Uncontrollable, runaway change that grabs a girl and flings her along, not caring if it rips her flesh against the farm's dry stone walls in the process.

And it's a blundering change – genetic modification, nanotechnology, molecular engineering; dangerous tools in a world all too eager to wield them for a fast buck. So what if the y-chromosome is given a good kicking along the way; we can fix that, can't we? So what if most of the remaining female births are *still*; populations recover, don't they?

So what if the Ministry of Land and Sea needs half the country to meet energy needs; The Ministry can lay claim to the land, can't it? It's merely a few yokel farmers kicked out on to the street. They'll accept that for King and Country: a small price to pay for progress. And there is a *war* on, don't forget.

Mary drifts into a fitful sleep. She dreams she's in Father's arms. Father always held her tightly where Mother would push Mary away. She's safe and warm, and the future is a distant, foreign landscape. But there are hands pulling at Father, and they're bigger and stronger than Mary's childish hands clinging to him. The farm fills her world, because she's so small and the fields go on forever. Except they don't, and what's beyond the Edge is dark and empty and deathly still.

The rains begin, Thursday morning. Mary's at the hospital with Mother. They sit in the treatment room with its lime green walls. Calming colours, Mary thinks, soothing hues under which to learn of Mother's cancer.

"Two months," says the doctor. There's no emotion in his voice. He could be talking about anything. "Perhaps three, at best."

Mother frowns. "I'll need four," she says. "Four, if I'm to put things in order."

It's the first time Mary's been off the Edge Farm in years. She's awkward and agoraphobic – the world's too big outside the hedgerows and walls of the farm. She's uneasy, because while Mother's arms are folded defiantly as she argues what time she has left, Mary's seen the hint of fear in Mother's eyes.

Together they take the public mag-lev home. The *robotniks* could offer transport, but their sense of direction is suspect since the Ministry of Land and Sea dampened the GPS signals leaching over their boundaries. Cost saving, they said, for the *war effort*. The *robotniks* tend to drive on the wrong side of the road, anyway. Outside, bars of rain fall. Beyond the mag-lev's windows the town is blurred.

"I'm pregnant," says Mary. Her lips are dry. She looks away. Is there a good time to break this news? She brings a protective palm to cover her stomach.

"Oh?"

"Eight weeks. I conceived naturally."

"Were you raped?"

Mary winces. It's a strong word. It has such dreadful connotations. She's heard there are gangs of feral men roaming, desperate not to waste their one, good erection in months. But surely that's exaggerated. They'd stop at rape, wouldn't they?

"No, Mother, I was consenting. My lover was... *understanding*."

"Is it male?"

"I believe so."

"And you plan to carry this *natural conception* to full term?"

"I do."

"Then the farm is gone."

"I'm calling him Simon."

"Call it what you want," says Mother. "The father will surely claim the farm."

"He might be *decent*, Mother."

"Oh, grow up, child. There's no such thing as a decent man. They're only after what they can get, whether that's between the legs or in the pocket."

"Not all of them."

"Have you seen your *lover* since the deed?"

"Well, not as such, Mother, but..."

"Exactly. The world will be well rid of males. We've more sperm stored than stars in the universe, so what does the species need them for anyway? Terminate the pregnancy. I won't let you defy me. The farm is more important than a baby's life."

Later, back in the safe confines of Central Hub, Mary reboots Three. It's been banging its head on the floor again, and has spent the last two hours walking in small circles, so rebooting seems the kindest option. She watches on the screen as the *robotnik* jolts upwards with the arrival of the first q-bits of shutdown code. Driving rain glistens on its brow. They're not truly sentient, Mary reminds herself, even if Three stares out pathetically through the monitor screen, even if the rain on its face streaks like tears. She can't help wonder what goes on in a *robotnik's* head as it dies. Does it cling and fight for life until the last spark of memory is gone? Does it simply switch off and is *no more*? Will the same go on in Mother's head?

When the storm blows over – *if* the storm blows over – the wheat harvest is due, and Mary needs all four *robotniks* fully functioning. The combines are *smart*, and probably could get the job done if left alone, but the *robotniks* are adaptable, problem solvers. They're akin to people in that respect. That's what makes it so hard for Mary to reboot them.

"Shutdown code is rejected," says Three. It's ironic that this is probably the only lucid sound it's made in months. Perhaps impending death does that, focuses the attention.

"Overruled," says Mary.

"Tak. Ale to nie jest bóg, panienko. If you continue, my functioning will be seriously impeded."

"Continue."

"Tak, pani. Authentication is required."

Mary dials an authentication code. Ten digits are all it takes to kill a robot. How easy it is to take a life. She thinks she feels the baby *flutter* once again inside her.

"Dziękuję. Code is accepted. Shutdown sequence is starting. Do widzenia, pani."

"I'm sorry," says Mary.

If it hears her, Three doesn't answer. Purging servos convulse its limbs. An arm rises as if in protest then drops with a metallic thud. The *robotnik's* upper torso slumps forward. Its eyes are dull. The radio link is broken. The umbilical to Central is cut.

Mary breathes deeply. She caresses her stomach and wonders if in the womb Simon can feel her touch. Inside, she knows the umbilical stays strong. But Mary now has a decision to make. Unlike with Three, Mary won't be able to send Two or Four to switch Simon back on. When Simon's gone, he's gone for good.

By evening, the storm rattles the drawing room windows. Mary sits waiting for Mother. She half watches a TV weatherman dancing about the plasma wall. He's happy; his hair's *all over the place* as if he's been up on the roof. Storms are probably good for weathermen – not much to tell in fair weather. He says the depression in the Atlantic has shifted the Jet Stream southwards. The inrush of arctic air has turned summer into winter. But Mary has bigger worries than frigid air.

Mother enters. She shuffles her feet, her neck hunched forward. Life's a heavy burden, Mary thinks, and its ending even more so.

"I have made arrangements for the *termination*," says Mother. She sits but doesn't look at Mary. "It will be tomorrow morning at ten. I have the address of a *doctor* written down for you. You've to eat nothing until after it's done."

It sounds so easy. Ten digits and a knitting needle. A bit of poking and a rush of fluid, and then tea and biscuits, or a scone.

"You kept Charlotte," says Mary. "She was conceived in a bed. How come your Lithuanian lover didn't claim the farm?"

For an age, Mother is silent. At last, she says: "Charlotte was conceived *against* a bed. *He* held me down by my hair, shoved my head forward until behind him I was *raised* and *open* and *his*. In my head I cried *rape!* but the bed covers were in my mouth and the pain clenched my teeth."

"But why was he in the bedroom?" says Mary.

"My arm was locked behind my back. He could have taken me anywhere."

"I heard you moaning. I thought you were consenting."

Mother sighs. "Yes, I kept Charlotte, but the *robotniks* found me hunched and sobbing the following day in Number Six Field. They'd no notion of rape. They struggled with the idea the Lithuanian had sold them on. *Why would Ivan do this? We'll call on him and ask why*, they said."

"And did they?"

"His body was barely recognisable. Pulped, it was said, bludgeoned by a heavy weapon. Three did it, I think; three seems to have faulty morality generators and its circuits have been suspect ever since. But because of the Lithuanian's death there was no claim on the farm, because there wasn't enough left of the Lithuanian to do any claiming. And with no claim why waste a viable foetus? Charlotte was blameless."

Mary pauses. "Would you have terminated Charlotte if there were a claim?"

"In an instant." The venom in Mother's answer is unsettling. "The farm is more important than anything. Where will your sisters go if it's taken from them? The needs of the many outweigh those of the individual."

Mary rubs a palm across her stomach. There's no pain, no

movement, nothing. "Then I suppose you're right, Mother, I should keep tomorrow's appointment. For the sake of the others."

"It's for the best, Mary, it's for the best."

How many robotniks *does it take to change a light bulb?*

There's a park bench opposite the *doctor's* office, in the leafy part of town with the big, Victorian dwellings. For now, there's pale sun in the eye of the storm. It's the briefest of respite, even if Mary sees the dark clouds still circling. Mary wonders how many women have sat on this bench drawing strength to cross the avenue to the arched doorway.

Hah, none, because everyone knows robotniks *can see in the dark.*

Mary's numb. Across the street, heavy blood red curtains are drawn to the first floor windows. The panes are dirty, that's what Mary notices. She has to notice such nonsense or she notices the *lump* just starting to show. She has to tell herself stupid jokes otherwise the joke is on her.

An Englishman, an Irishman, and a robotnik *go into a bar...*

Across the park, the town hall clock chimes ten. Mary stands – this is for the best, isn't it? – for Nicole, and Ruth, and Charlotte, and so Mother has somewhere to die – everyone needs somewhere safe to die. Even Simon.

But what does Mary need? She walks forward slowly. Mary has what she needs growing inside her. How cruel that one lapse of judgement in taking a natural conception can ruin her life so. She has hormones, she couldn't help it, and *he* was charming as much as any man can be. Mary pauses at the door. There's no welcome mat at her feet. The bell-push is gold-plated and backlit. The brass nameplate is highly polished and...

Oh, who cares?

Mary runs – to where she doesn't know – for now it's enough to just run.

Three doesn't respond. Mary jabs the boot switch again. She's lost her shoes, and her feet are torn and bleeding. Her hair is lank with sweat and rain. She feels the flush upon her face. She wants to throw up.

"Come on, damn it," she says.

She hears the whir of Three's servos starting. Mary stands back; the *robotnik's* limbs are apt to flap about at first. Programmers

171

mistakenly gave them motion before the *intellect* to control it. That error cost the Ministry of Land and Sea a fortune – crushed by your automaton? Call *Claims-at-once*....

Three groans. It could be nothing more than stale air in its voice modulators. There's dim light behind its eyes.

"Dzień dobry, pani." The voice is weak.

"English," says Mary. "Load English command set."

"English command set loaded."

"Do you have viable memory options?"

"I have New Build and one previous memory dump."

"Load memory dump."

"Memory dump is likely to be corrupted."

"Load it anyway."

"Loading, pani, one moment."

Mary's faint. She rests against the gate post. The wind could topple her at any moment.

"Loaded," says Three.

"Did you kill Ivan?" says Mary.

"That is difficult to talk about, pani. I have been working on my *compassion*."

"I know," says Mary. "One of the drones saw you burying Charlotte's baby. It flagged it as an anomaly. Did Charlotte ask you to do that?"

"No," says Three. "It was something I felt needed doing. My circuits are acting strangely. Laying the baby to rest gave me comfort. I don't know why. I have been affected."

"But you did kill your Lithuanian master?"

"Tak. Yes, pani."

"Can you kill again?"

"Tak. Yes, pani, it's something I can do."

Mary turns and vomits. She doesn't know if it's the morning sickness or the thought of what she's about to become that sickens her. She thinks back to Simon's conception – *He* did rape her, now she thinks of it, *he* had to have done. *He* shoved her to the ground and pinned her down, didn't he? Why else did she bleed? Mary wouldn't have given herself to him freely. Mother hadn't done so with the Lithuanian, and Mary is so like Mother. She has to be like Mother because Mother will be gone soon. And there's the farm to think of;

that counts for something, doesn't it?

"Then, I may have a job for you," says Mary.

The storm rages in. Mary can see no other way through to its far side.

Landward

Den Patrick

Life Aboard the Landward
25 July 2019
Darren Kane

HYPERLINK: http://www.DailyHerald.Co.Uk/tech/farming

"It can get a bit windy, mind" he says, typical English understatement beneath the Cornish accent. We are currently five thousand feet up, looking across six acres of wheat, swaying in the breeze. I clamp a hand down over my hat. The sky is clear but it's far from warm.

"You can avoid the worst of it. That and the rain. You can take a Landward anywhere. Almost."

He flashes a grin, weather-beaten face deeply lined. There's plenty to be cheerful about. Being able to transport a crop field and 'chase the sun' is a unique and startling feature of the Landward. The idea of creating a free-floating substructure was purely the domain of science fiction; the invention of a 'mobile farm' unthinkable. Mass and by extension gravity has become a less trifling concern since the Higgs breakthrough.

"I sometimes think it's like being an oil tanker captain," he adds, "Except we grow crops. And we're in the sky. Obviously."

It hasn't all been plain sailing. The ill-fated *Faun* was the first of the Landward platforms to suffer massive engine failure."

"Aye, the *Faun* event was bad. Even watching the footage it's difficult to imagine."

All Landward Captains know the event inside out. Six acres of mobile farmland plunging straight down. The resulting impact was felt across the UK. The town below never stood a chance.

"That can't happen now," he says, sensing my unease, "the back-up Gennies have back-ups. The chances of having triple engine failure are unthinkable. There's multiple SUNN fields in the newer models."

He's stopped sounding like himself, reciting the company manual by rote.

The SUNN field alters the structure, taking the Landward into the sky by means of negative mass. Since the *Faun* event the crews are under strict orders to stay over international waters. There are as many meteorologists aboard as there are engineers, as many navigators as there are farm hands.

"Aye, everyone mucks in though."

The truth is that a single Landward, whilst autonomous, is a large automated affair. The crops are brought in with harvester drones. Weather fronts, commercial air traffic, even the oil tankers below, all register on the Landward's Central Systems. Huge antennae extend from the front and rear, cat's whiskers sensing trouble.

"Course, everyone hated them at first. Said it was unnatural. Having so much air traffic was bound to come to no good. They got quiet when the price of bread come down, mind."

I look over my shoulder and see another five Landward platforms in loose procession. Each behemoth is identical to its kin; a farmstead at the centre surrounded by fields. Warning lights blink from their undersides, red and blue. It's not uncommon to find the Captain (and more to the point, their Central Systems) all chasing the same weather patterns.

"It's nice when you meet up," he says, nodding at the convoy, "Farming up here is just the same as farming down there; it's the isolation that gets you."

An independent study recently showed that suicide rates among Landward farmers equalled their land-bound equivalents.

"There's counselling and that," he drawls, quieter now, "And the horizon has a proximity detector, but some still take the quick way down." He turns and walks back to the cottage, hands thrust deep into pockets, head down. The horizon he speaks of is the edge of the Landward. The end of *Terra Aeris* to the crews who work them. The quick way down is the Landward farmer's preferred method of suicide. Standing at the edge it's hard to imagine stepping off. I follow the Captain, who is already inside his cottage and brewing tea when I enter.

The dwelling could be anywhere in the South West of England. The thatched roof seems a liability considering the high winds.

"It's not real," says the Captain, "Just a little bit of home comfort from the Company. They say it's important we have something familiar, still feel like we're part of the world. Not farting about on some agricultural space ship."

The cottage features a sheep dog, despite the lack of sheep, and a selection of collectible plates, all beaming smiles of the Royal family. The Captain shrugs when he notices me looking at them.

"They were Mum's. She loved the Royals. And farming. Not sure what she'd make of this up here though."

The cottage bears all the features of modern living. The only thing lacking is a woman's touch, conspicuous only by its absence.

"Sometimes the helicopter pilots are women. That perks everyone up, I can tell you. Even Old Kip takes a bath when the choppers come in."

Not too many women are keen to leave their lives on the ground to be a Landward farmer's wife. Old Kip, it turns out, is a veteran of the Landward project, one of the first crew and the oldest skyfaring Captain. His odour is put down to 'eccentricity'.

"Most retire young. Hope to get back home so they can find a woman. And with the hypermarkets paying less and less each year..." he grimaces, "That business with the dairy farmers is all wrong. Still, they can't get the cows up here. Yet."

The Captain nurses his mug of tea to his chest, staring through the window at crops five thousand feet above the Earth.

Related Articles:
Landward platform in engine failure tragedy
Faun crew cleared of neglect following Landward platform engine failure
Somali pirates caught trying to buy helicopters on black market
UK Supermarkets accused of not passing savings on to customers

Long Indeed Do We Live...

Storm Constantine

But at our birth, pines or high-topped oaks sprang up with us
Upon the fruitful earth
Beautiful flourishing trees, towering high upon the lofty mountains,
(and men called them holy places of the immortals,
and never did a mortal lop them with an axe).
But when the fate of death was near at hand,
first our lovely trees withered where they stood,
and the bark shrivelled away about us,
and the twigs fell down,
and at last our life, and of the tree,
left the light of the sun together.

*She opened her eyes upon the mealy darkness and wanted to breathe. That was how
she knew it was time.*

In Ampelus Arbour, Leo stands beneath a mist mouth, ghost moisture
teasing his uptilted face. The greens in this corner of the arbour are
dark, almost black in the shadows, with occasional acidic bursts of
moss between the immense glossy leaves, upon the furred trunks of the
trees. While some of the wardens prefer the soaring domes and
stunning vistas of Suke Arbour and Arbour Thetis, Leo is most at
home in this humid, rustling jungle; his child. He has reared it, nurtured
it, shaped it. This is his work of art, nestling beneath more sparkling
splendours.

Leo was born in an arbour, raised in several. He has never seen the
world that lies beyond the great arbourtropolis of Olympus Peak, other
than through the lenses of mirrors and cameras. He imagines it has no
smell, or if there should be an aroma of any kind lurking in some
shadowed place, it will be of burning.

There had been a conversation with his friend Jade, here in this spot, some weeks ago. She had been talking about how she was seeking a commission outside in a survey team, analysing grit samples, fossils, the air. He didn't really believe her, not least because she was prone to fantasising. Also, very few people were allowed outside, because there was little to go for, and it was dangerous. If the past that lived there was resentful and armed with fangs, why prod it?

"You're so narrow-sighted," Jade said to him. "The Wasteland has its own beauty; you just refuse to see it."

Leo made a scoffing sound. "How can a corpse be beautiful?"

Jade took an apple from one of his trees, bit hard into the ivory flesh. He noticed her teeth were exactly the same colour. "Embalming." She grinned, juice on her lips.

Leo didn't find it funny, still doesn't. He aches for the world that was, even though he's never seen it, or walked its paths or smelled its aromas. He reveres the mote of Paradise, this replica, he nurtures and protects.

He designed the arbour very carefully; his especial love is trees. Not only jungles can be found along its winding paths, but mini-forests and orchards. The trees are lush and the leaves press against the plexi-plates, basking in the sun. The plates let in sunlight yet are opaque. You cannot see anything beyond them, outside. High mirrors bring the light to arbour low, the ground. Hidden systems deliver puffs of air or moisture at different temperatures; invisible boundaries allow diverse conditions to be present within one arbour. You can walk from an autumn orchard into a seasonless breathing cloud forest. Everywhere a reckless glut of scents. It is misleading to call the arbour a dome since it resembles more a jumble of polygons thrown together by a child at play, beautiful in its chaotic and accidental design. Not that anything about Ampelus Arbour is unintentional, although Leo often strives, as he extends it, to make it appear as such. Nature, when she'd ruled the world, had been a seething, endlessly moving wave of life, patterns forming haphazardly, then breaking up, decaying, followed by new patterns. Leo is intrigued by these spontaneous motifs; he wants not just to mimic them but create them, give them life of their own.

But the arbour does not exist solely for Leo's pleasure. Its bounties are harvested – fruit, wood, essences, pharmaceuticals. It is serviced by insects and nematodes that are robotic. No stings, no bites, no parasites, just artificial members of staff. Leo can communicate with and control them all via his mind-pad. Some of them he has given names.

It might be better if the world was completely dead out there, but it's not. Life is tenacious, clinging against all odds, even in an ice-sculpted wilderness, or a fevered desert. Creatures are mainly small, or those that burrow. The surface strips life when it can. Leo doesn't want to believe there are still people out there, or what is left of them, perhaps not quite human now. He wants to believe they have all died off, but occasionally there are sensationalist reports of sightings: blackened creatures, or creatures of ice.

The moisture on Leo's cheek is a caress. He can almost sense a soft murmuring that accompanies it, the voice of some invented nature spirit, a dryad, a nymph. Sometimes, breezes rustle through the arbour; the weather is programmed. Now a perfumed tide of air washes over him, carrying within it the essence of every tree within this section. Eyes closed, his mind is filled with the image of a cornucopia spilling produce, spilling right over him, although without weight or substance.

Leo is stimulated by this image, his body vibrating with energy. Yet at the same time he feels languorous. Strange. Perhaps some system or another is malfunctioning. He had better run a check.

In the early evening, Leo visits a recreational arbour named Thebes where many of his profession choose to gather for meals. He sees Sorsha, an angular, occasionally aloof woman he particularly likes, and goes to join her where she sits beside a wall vista that is a particular favourite of his. Sorsha's speciality is birds; visits to her arbours can be alarming for the faint of heart. Leo isn't fond of creatures that make so much discordant noise and that drop faeces everywhere. His trees are more domesticated and calming for the spirit; neither can they tear at flesh and eyes with beaks and claws. The robotic fauna that flourish alongside them are well-behaved and predictable.

As Leo sits down across from Sorsha, a menu pod is already gliding to his side. It knows him so he can say, "Just the usual please, Hortense." All the menus have been given names. Leo has always thought it a shame they weren't given personalities too – that little extra work would have been a nice touch. But the management does like to save costs where it can; such embellishments for an employee recreational area no doubt come under unnecessary expenses.

Sorsha appears preoccupied and doesn't notice she now has company at her table beneath the palm trees. Beside her, the simulated prospect of a lazy lagoon embraces its sunset. She's examining a tablet of her mind pad, frowning slightly, a tendril of greying pale hair falling over her strong, angular face.

Leo knows better than to interrupt her reverie. He imagines Sorsha as a priestess of the arbours. When she is in trance, woe betide a lesser minion who sullies her meditative silence.

Leo gazes at the vista, content, while he waits for his food. He knows that eventually Sorsha will become aware of him; he's in no rush. The sky in the vista is purple, already blooming with stars above the sunset. At the horizon, the heavens are a scarlet cradle for the sun. Wide-winged birds, mere silhouettes, swoop against the encroaching night. Beneath them, foamy breakers pounce upon startlingly white sand. Occasionally, in the distance, creatures large, dark and sinuous might raise their ophidian necks above the restless waves. There are no people visible, but Leo is always conscious of them, whenever he sits in this spot. People like himself. He can feel them watching, as he does; millions of them, shoulder to shoulder.

"Leo!" Sorsha's voice pulls him from his reverie. "Sneaking up on me again?" There is a tone in her voice suggesting she's glad he has. He is cautious around her, but occasionally she allows him to spend the night with her. He never takes this privilege for granted, however, and is under no illusion about her feelings for him.

"I was admiring the sunset," Leo says, smiling.

Sorsha returns his smile warmly. "This is one of my favourite spots too. Perhaps that's why we meet here so often."

They both turn their heads to the scenery. Perhaps in another world, another time, they are standing on the beach, their toes digging into the sand, holding hands as the night comes down.

The moon lifts from the ocean, full and waxen. The waters offer a road of light from her to the land. Leo never fails to be affected by this sight. Could it ever have happened like that? It seems too perfect to be true. And then...

A figure is emerging from the sea, stumbling a little: a lithe female figure, small and slight. He can make out no more details than that. "Sorsha..."

He glances at her. She is staring dreamily at the stars that have opened their shutters to the approaching night. "What...?"

"Someone's coming out of the sea."

Sorsha extends her neck a little, peers. "Where?"

Leo points, although now he's not sure what it is he's seeing. "There. Looked like a girl." He indicates the place where a series of tall, barnacled wooden posts throw their moon shadows across the sand. Is it a girl there, standing very still? Or just another post? "Perhaps I was mistaken," he says.

Sorsha shrugs. "Difficult to tell. They don't normally include people in this vista. I've never seen one before." She grimaces. "It's supposed to be peaceful. People aren't that peaceful."

That night Leo dreams of the ancient world coming back to the land. He stands in his arbour and the plates that form it are now transparent and he can see outside. He sees the green coming down, over the mountains, across the scorched fields, the cracked river beds. It is a tide of life and he is afraid. He turns in his dream and sees about him that his arbour is arid and parched. The boughs of the trees are withered, the leaves have come down. He is surrounded by death, yet outside life surges forward, relentless and without sentiment. It will splash against the plates of his arbour and splinter them. It will consume him and all his works, and they will be forgotten.

> **When the earth blooms**
> **with every sweet-scented flower of spring,**
> **Then from the murky gloom we will once more ascend,**
> **And will be a mighty wonder for gods and mortal men.**

Leo wakes feeling anxious. He goes for his breakfast to Thebes Arbour and sits beside the vista of the beach. Few others are present at this hour. Before the vista, the observer has little option other than to stare out to sea, but swathes of beach sweep off to either side, down which it is possible to peer. In the distance, half hidden by a mantle of cloud, are the peaks of mountains, where birds hang like black rags. Are they, in fact, carrion birds? Leo wonders. They drift on currents of air, but are circling.

I did not kill the earth, he thinks, *but in Her mind is not all humankind equally responsible?*

Perhaps; it is also possible the earth simply shut down, gave up, ravaged as she was, violated and broken. Natural disasters once conspired with the depredations of humankind to scour the world of life in some areas, but for the most hardy and adapted of creatures and plants. But humankind, like the most efficient of diseases, lived on, adapted, created a host for itself. The arbours.

Leo rubs his face with his hands, concerned about the strange thoughts that are coming to him. If they continue, he must visit the medical arbour, seek advice. It's not unknown for arbour engineers to succumb to melancholy. For some it is all too keen a knowledge that they may not create, only recreate, perhaps with no more depth than a vista in a wall, merely giving the semblance of life and space. In reality, it is flat, a fake, and what humanity has become must live upon its produce.

Leo lowers his hands from his eyes, where they have pressed too hard. What he sees beside him makes him jerk back in his chair, cry out.

A face is pressed against the surface of the vista from the other side, as if it were a plate of glass. It is the face of a girl, a naked girl, whose pale hair hangs wet across her features. Her eyes are closed, gummed with sand. Her hands too are pressed against the membrane that separates them, the fingers slightly moving, tapping.

There is a rustle, a crack, surely the glass must break and *she* will come through. Leo knows true fear. There is a rushing feeling. He throws his arms across his face with another cry, and then it seems as if the world falls upon him; bristly, reeking of green, engulfing. He is aware, amid his high screams, of the sound of other voices, of running feet. And then they are upon him, his colleagues, pulling him free.

A palm tree, inexplicably, has fallen, right onto him. Not a large palm, not too heavy, but thick with fronds. His face has been scratched by them, and his hands. Now the broken limbs loll against the vista, reflecting its daytime fake light. There is no girl there. Perhaps there never was. Just a shadow conjured by the falling fronds that looked like hair and hands pressed against a pane of glass.

The robotic medics are soothing. Their slim appendages are a feather caress against the skin of Leo's throat, his bare arms. Some sealing has been done to wounds. Bruises have been purged. Evidence of attack by tree removed. What had made it fall? They said the soil had dried out in its trough. But none have fallen before.

The underwater light of the sanatorium arbour is soothing also; water tumbles from tiers of ornamental rocks. The air is damp and fragrant.

The medic still examining Leo makes a mild sound, nothing too alarming. "I've picked up an emotional anomaly," it sighs. "What are you afraid of, Leo?"

"Nothing." He is reluctant to confess, even though he knows the medic will be aware he's lying. "I'm just tired. Been overworking."

"Report to Arbour Eos for therapy," murmurs the medic, retracting some of its limbs back into its carapace neatly. One delicate frond of metal still rests against his brow.

"All I need is a sedative," Leo says limply. He knows it is pointless to argue with a machine whose opinions can rarely be changed.

"I will prescribe one for you," says the medic, "but even so you must report to Arbour Eos. You will feel better for it."

Therapy involves light and massage in the arbour of the dawn. Leo cannot help but be relaxed by such ministrations. The therapists resemble attenuated women, machines without angles. This too is soothing; the suggestion of breasts in a soft thoracic swell. They are swathed in cream linen robes and exude odours of fresh bread, of vanilla milk. Beneath their touch and their gentle, bee-like humming, Leo drifts into sleep.

He stands at the top of a slope in one of the grain arbours. Before him, an ocean of wheat sways in an endless breeze. The roof is a vista of the sky, deep blue with small clouds. He sees in the distance a dark shape in the gold, moving towards him. He has to shade his eyes to see. As the figure approaches, he perceives that the gold is withering behind it. His sight zooms in. He sees a woman dressed in dusty brown rags, her long dark hair hanging down about her body in tangles. Her eyes are black and mad. She brings death with her. The wheat shrivels in her wake. But then the dome of the sky opens wide, to reality, and the glare of the real sun pours in, stark and merciless.

Leo wakes with a start. The therapist at his head murmurs, "Tell me of your dream." Her name is Clio.

"A woman walked in the grain and killed it," he says. "Then the sun came inside the arbours."

"No one would ever let that happen," hums Clio. "There are systems within systems within systems to keep us all safe. It is impossible for them all to fail together. Remember that, when a dream such as this may come."

"Do many have these dreams?" Leo asks.

"It is not uncommon," the therapist replies. "Your people have had to adapt to survive, but within you lives the root of all humanity."

"Lucky for you that you don't have it," Leo says.

"We all share that root," Clio says, "in one way or another." She is the root of all mothers, all lovers, brilliantly made, perhaps by a poet. The therapists are more gifted with the art of conversation than the medics, and certainly more pleasing to the eye.

"We have made you better than us," Leo says. Despite the dream, he is still languorous from the gentle caresses, the warm light. "You could even survive outside, I expect."

Clio utters a tinkle of laughter, like a waterfall. "And who would look after you then?"

Leo stems the remark, *perhaps no one should*. It would only invite the therapist's concern. He's already said too much. "I'm not suggesting you *should* go outside," he says, in a flirtatious tone, "but only that you *could*. I would prefer it if you didn't."

"You mustn't be afraid," says Clio. "Nothing is going to change."

Leo visits his arbour, strolling along the winding paths, stroking the leaves that stray across them. He senses an atmosphere there; is it excitement? The leaves seem to tremble beneath his touch. He remembers the dreams he's had, the visions. This could mean anything – wishful thinking, dread, desire. A girl emerging blind from a virtual sea. A woman bringing death to an ocean of wheat. Symbols. He is not ignorant of the implications. The arbours are all named for Classical deities and creatures of myth. The arbours of wheat are called Demeter for a reason; she was in the ancient world a goddess of the corn. And once, so the tales go, she turned on humanity and withered the land, because her daughter Persephone, embodiment of spring and growth, was stolen from her by the Lord of the Underworld. Persephone is long gone from the world out there. But she lives in the arbours, doesn't she?

The call rings from mountain top to mountain top in the sparkling air. She stands upon the bare rock, her long toes gripping jagged ridges. She sings to her sisters: "come forth from your eyries and lairs. Come up from the dark places of stone, of deep earth and the lightless reaches. Come up from the grottoes of the deeps, where hot jets make blood of the seas. Come sisters, rise and wake, for we are Immanent".
Here first she arrived from the murmuring air.

Leo sits for a long time beneath the apple trees in his orchard sector. The air smells strangely of honey, and he feels drowsy. Sunlight comes down through the branches, filtered but undeniably real, and manufactured breezes, soft as breath, enliven the leaves.

He hears a rustle and a crack, almost as if a heavy object has fallen from a tree and brought a branch down with it, but then he sees Jade sauntering towards him, inevitably chomping on another of his fruits.

"You are a little thief," he says to her, though smiling.

"Merely sampling the goods," she replies, "Anyway, you have more than enough."

She throws herself down beside him, squinting up through the branches, as if staring at the real sky. "Imagine a time when you could not say 'What a glorious day', Leo. How dull that must've been."

He sighs. "What have you been reading?"

She pouts at him. "Don't use that tone. I'm merely investigating the past. I have to show an interest if they're ever to let me join a study team."

"You're too small for that," he says, and ducks away from her predictable punch, laughing.

"Size is irrelevant. What would I need it for? You can be so rude, Leo. Sometimes I wonder why we're friends." She pantomimes sorrow.

He pauses a moment, considering, before asking her. "It's only recently you've had this urge to go outside, isn't it? I mean, with this seriousness of... intent."

She peers at him through her thick fringe. "Why? What do you care?"

"Just wondered what brought it on, that's all."

"Well at the risk of invoking your inevitable scorn, it's like an itch. I just feel there's something I have to see, or discover or learn."

"Do you get dreams?"

Jade looks suspicious now. "What is this? Are you a therapist now?"

"No, but I had to see one today."

Jade stares at him for a moment. "Why?"

"Well, it began with a tree falling on me." He relates the story to Jade, downplaying what he saw in the vista as an illusion. He does not mention what he glimpsed when he sat with Sorsha there the evening before.

"That's weird," Jade declares, clearly delighted. "A tree *and* a vista malfunctioning. The caretakers must've been swarming."

Leo shrugs. "They said it was the soil, too dry."

Jade narrows her eyes. "Right. In an environment monitored within an inch of its life. Yeah, that's very possible. And what about the girl you saw?"

"I don't think she was real."

Jade makes a scoffing sound. "Well of course not. Vistas aren't real. But neither is that one supposed to have people in. Especially creepy ones like that. Aren't you curious about it?"

Leo stares at Jade's face; her expression so open, without censure. He has known her all his life. They were born within months of each other, he slightly the elder. Yet does he really know her at all? Where has this issue of trust come from? What does he fear? "I think something is happening," he says quickly, before some part of himself seals the words inside. "Perhaps outside."

Jade's eyes widen. "What do you mean?"

"I don't even know," he says. "What I do know is that I have a compulsion to keep it to myself. And now I have told you."

She reaches out to touch his hands where they lie folded in his lap. "And that is as good as keeping it to yourself." She pauses, wrinkles her nose in thought. "You're not a fanciful person, Leo. Not like me. If you're having thoughts like this, they must mean something."

"I'd rather you told me I'm overworking, need rest, and it's all in my mind."

"Well, sorry, but I don't think it is. I get the essence of what you're feeling. I've always felt like that. You asked if I've had dreams. Now tell me yours, because clearly you have."

While Jade listens to him, Leo is aware of her increasing excitement. It's as if he's an oracle, giving to her pronouncements she has long awaited.

When he's finished speaking, she says at once, "Leo, can you uncloud the domes?"

"What do you mean?"

"I mean, could we look outside, if you changed them?"

"I wouldn't know how to do that."

"But the light gets in, so it must be the material of the plates..." She shakes her head. "It's so frustrating. I need to see what's outside."

"Aren't you going to, anyway? With your study team?"

Jade utters a sound of annoyance and impatience. "It could be ten years, for all I know. I want to see now. Don't you?"

"I don't know. I think that once you see something you can't unsee it. I'm still hoping I'm going faintly mad, rather than that something real is going on." He pauses. "So what do you dream of, Jade?"

"That I can fly," she answers simply, and bites once more into the stolen fruit, staring at the ground.

Later that day, back in his Arbour Atlas apartment, Leo beeps Sorsha from his mind pad. She's surprised to hear from him, because he doesn't contact her very often. Their liaisons, such as they are and infrequent, are usually arranged in Arbour Thebes, an afterthought to eating. "What is it, Leo?" she asks, not allowing him visuals. "Is everything all right?"

"A tree fell on me today by the vista, and I saw the figure of a girl again."

Sorsha utters a peal of laughter, delightful and free in tone, so different from her general rather squeezed composure. "A tree fell on you." Again, she laughs.

"In case you were worried, I wasn't hurt," Leo says rather peevishly.

"Were you hurt?" Sorsha asks, clearly still trying to suppress amusement.

"Very funny." He tells her what happened, his visits to the medics, the therapists. "Don't you think it's odd, though? Have you noticed anything... unusual... recently about your birds?"

"Why, are all your trees starting to gang up on you? Do you think they asked the one by the vista to beat you up?"

"Sorsha, I wish you'd take this seriously, like you do just about everything else in life. I'm concerned."

"Well..." Sorsha pauses for just a fraction too long. "There have been some anomalies, now you mention it. Something spooked my owls the other night, and several of them flew into the plates. Some were only concussed and could be saved. Two died. They left images of themselves – it was grotesque. Scared owls burned against the plates. The images won't be removed, no matter how many times the plates run their cleaning routines. I've also noticed that the birds will start up a racket for no obvious reason and not at obvious times of day, such as dawn or dusk. So yes, in answer to your question."

"What do you think is going on?"

"Nothing. Animals will just do unpredictable things at times."

"Do you think they sense things we don't?"

"That's possible, perhaps even likely. What are you implying?"

"I don't even know." Now it is his turn to pause. He's not sure whether to be honest or not. But as with Jade, he's compelled to speak. "I've been having disturbing dreams recently. Even the medics picked up on it. I can't get rid of the feeling that something's – you really don't know how much I hate saying this to you – but that something's happening outside."

"Why do you hate saying that to me?" Sorsha demands, rather sharply.

"Because you'll think I'm being ridiculous, put me down with condescending remarks, and then offer a scientific explanation."

"Isn't that why you've mentioned it to me, though? Or do you want me to say 'the sky is falling'?"

"It's because you'd never say such a thing that I'm talking to you now," Leo says. "You have more influence than me and I'd like you to use it. Who would know what's happening outside? Can you do any digging?"

"Leo, why don't you just go and see? None of us are prisoners here."

"But how can I? I'd need a survival suit, a medical pass. I don't think my troubling dreams would provide a good enough reason for me to secure things like that."

"Who's your therapist?" Sorsha asks abruptly.

"Er... Clio. Why?"

"That's good. Ask her. She has the authority to take you outside for therapeutic reasons, if it's deemed appropriate."

"Why do you know that and I don't? And what's so good about Clio?"

"I know lots of things you don't because I've made sure I've acquired a reputation that encourages sharing. And Clio's good because she'll be more open to such an idea."

"How can you possibly know that? She's a machine."

"Ten years ago, I was on the committee that formulated the AIs for the therapists and medics. It's an important part of their function. A long long time ago, people had doctors who were in a way like priests. They offered comfort, made people feel safe. It was considered desirable our machines provided the same things. I was the one who suggested the personalities, so people would feel more as if they were interacting with a real being."

"So they have opinions, can make personal decisions? Is that what you're saying?"

Sorsha sighs. "The machines are all different, Leo. Honestly, have you never noticed that? Surely even your worms have different personalities."

"I've not had debates with them, so can't really say." He laughs. "Strangely enough, I was only thinking the other day it would be good if the menus had personalities. I know most service machines do, to a degree, but I thought it was just a... I don't know... cosmetic thing, like having a piece of furniture that looks good."

"So today you have learned something," Sorsha says, but she doesn't sound sharp. "Go see Clio tomorrow and tell her about the dreams, your anxiety about the outside."

"I'm concerned I'll be somehow judged for this. Clio will share the information, surely."

"She'll file it, of course. But as I said, Leo, don't get so paranoid you think you're a prisoner here. None of us are. It's just that very few actually want to go outside. Perhaps it's too depressing."

That night, Leo dreams. He is walking again amid the limitless fields of wheat in Arbour Demeter. Now, when he sees the dark stain approaching in the distance, he walks towards it. Then he is running. He runs to confront the ragged hag, who trails her hands across the heads of wheat and blackens them. Standing before her, he sees in her face past beauty, a sadness, but also fierceness.

"Why are you doing this?" he asks her.

"They put my only daughter in the cold earth," she replies.

"Is this to come?" he asks her urgently. "Will you bring this decay to the arbours in revenge?"

"Unless she stops me, well I might," utters the crone. She slaps Leo across the face and he is quite sure the mark it leaves will be black, his flesh rotted away.

He awakes with a gasp, as if he's been holding his breath, and for a moment is utterly disorientated. He's not in his bed but is surrounded by rustling darkness, the smell of green. It takes a moment for him to realise he's in his arbour, lying beneath a cedar tree. The bark of it looks strange. It's moving. And then a figure emerges from the bark, slender and green, with leafy hair.

"Look for where she first arrived in the murmuring air," says this figure. And then she is gone.

He knows he has no choice to but to heed Sorsha's advice.

Three days later. In the extreme east of Arbourtropolis, at the end of a long tunnel of what looks like obsidian, the exit plates slide up. White dust puffs away from the air that coughs out. Three figures are shown in silhouette at the entrance. Elegant security drones of lilac and silver metal, hovering on the air, are drawn to the disturbance. They glide around the heads of the figures, uttering shrill alarms, until Clio speaks to them in their own language, and they lower their graceful vanes.

"Like birds," Jade says in wonder. "They're like birds without wings." She takes hold of Leo's hand.

The reason Jade is with him is because, rather like a small boy coyly asking his mother for a favour, Leo asked Clio if he could take a friend along on the outside trip. This was mainly at Jade's insistence. All Clio could do was say yes or no, so what was the problem with asking? While Leo agreed with this, he'd also felt weirdly ashamed while asking it and had even blushed, although Clio hadn't commented and told him that yes, that would be fine. Now, here they are.

The suits Jade and Leo wear are mainly to protect them from UV. Clio tells them the air isn't toxic around the tropolis but it's better to be safe than sorry. The therapist is not wearing her flowing robe and has altered her scent. She's dressed in a silvery overall, cinched tightly at the waist with a knotted belt, and smells now of citrus, a more adventurous aroma than vanilla or milk.

"Have you been out here before, Clio?" Jade asks.

"Yes, a long time ago, when I was new," Clio replies, a certain wistfulness in her tone. "I wanted to so that I could answer questions about the outside, if I were ever asked."

"Were you made with curiosity?" Jade persists, Leo now rather embarrassed by her questions, "or did it just grow of its own accord in you?"

"Something of both," Clio says. "Come now. Let's walk."

Jade soon lets go of Leo's hand and goes to investigate their surroundings. She picks up rocks from the floor, smells them. To Leo, it is all an arid oneness; the almost white stone and dust. Yet the sky above is achingly lovely, empty of birds but glittering here and there with security drones. He wishes he could have one for his arbour. They are so delicate and pretty, rather like hummingbirds in their quick movements, their arcs across the blue.

Clio comes silently to Leo's side. She can move so adeptly without sound, so gracefully, like a wild creature. "How do you feel here?" she murmurs, her silver optical orbs staring into him, perhaps reading his soul.

"Just... overawed at present," Leo says. "But no sense of unease, exactly. I can't believe I'm here, that it was so simple to come."

"There has to be some procedure in place," Clio says, "otherwise people would be wandering out here all the time, falling into chasms, getting sun-stroke, becoming disorientated, lost..." Her lips do not move, those perfectly sculpted shapes, yet Leo feels a smile.

"Did that happen at one time, at the start of the tropolis?"

"No, they were too afraid to come out for some while, but that was before I was new." She strides a few steps away, swivels her head on its long neck. "There were toxins out here then. It was a long time ago."

"The air smells less than inside."

Clio makes no comment.

"Can we go to Arbour Demeter, see it from the outside?" The exit Leo had specified was as close to this arbour as an exit could be.

"Of course," Clio responds, then calls, "Jade!"

Jade comes running back, like a child to her mother. "Look, I found fossils," she says, holding out her hands.

The skulls of mice, perhaps, something that once scurried.

"They are just weathered bones, Jade," Clio says, as she scans them. "Not that old, not fossils."

"Oh well." Jade puts them into a pocket.

The shadow of the arbours looms over them. From outside, it's possible to see just how immense they are. They look impossible, as if someone could poke them and the entire lot would tumble down.

"The first arbour was built over a well," Jade says as they walk in the blue shadow. "It was just like it was when people were first settling a country, way back in history. First they would find water for their animals and crops, and to keep them alive. Did you know about the well, Leo?"

"I was probably told at one time," he says.

"You can still visit it underground. I went there once but it's not very impressive. Just a metal cover in the floor of one of the lowest levels. You'd think they'd have done more with it. The well was such an important thing."

Jade seems almost drunk with this excursion. She chatters like a girl ten years younger, full of facts that have to keep spilling out.

Soon they reach the enormous construct of Arbour Demeter, which is actually a series of domes, reaching out across the landscape. Leo wishes he had some inkling of what he was looking for, what good this will do. He walks right up to the nearest dome, places a hand against the warm plates. Clio moves to his side. "You see, nothing can get in. Those plates are thick and strong."

"I'd like to walk alone for a while, if that's okay," Leo says.

Clio doesn't hesitate. She has no need to worry. Her senses would find him wherever he roams. "Of course."

There's nothing here, Leo thinks as he walks. The white dust extends to all horizons with occasional outcroppings of bleached stone. Here had once been fields and forests, all gone. He emerges from the shadow of Demeter and the sunlight hits him strongly. A quick movement at ground level reveals a tiny grey lizard running through the dust. He can hear Jade's voice telling Clio about some other treasures she has found.

The sound is echoing, as if from far away. He is moving away from the world, he realises, drawn into the wilderness. It occurs to him now there might be no going back.

Leo climbs a slope of white shale; his feet slip and he has almost to crawl. He has the idea that if he reaches the crest of the ridge beyond he will see something wondrous – perhaps an ocean or a verdant valley. He can no longer sense how much time has passed. It can't be long, because Clio would have come for him otherwise. He glances up, but there are no humming-bird security drones in the sky. Yet surely they could find him quickly if instructed to do so.

Now he reaches the top of the ridge and shades his eyes to look across. There is a wide basin, perhaps a meteor impact site, which is seamed by a silver thread, glistering in the harsh light. Water? Or just silver?

He raises his eyes to the opposite lip of the basin and someone is standing there. He isn't surprised by this. He raises his hand and the figure stares back motionless. At this distance, he can tell it is a person of slight build, but is not sure if it is male or female. Female, probably, he decides, perhaps the avatar of the past he has sensed and seen. He waves his hand vigorously. No response.

Now he is running down the side of the basin, sure the figure above him will disappear. It is watching him, somewhat impassively, he feels.

The silver is in fact a narrow stream, just a quick lick of liquid, yet bright and clear. Small hardy plants grow alongside it, the first mist of green, yet not much of it. He does not pause to touch the water, simply steps over it. He runs up the slope before him, and can see now that the figure is not slight at all, but rather tall. She is dressed in a russet robe, with a fringed brown shawl around her head and shoulders, and before he reaches her she turns and strides away.

He does not call to her, simply follows. She takes him into a petrified forest. The trees stretch for miles, like spikes of white bone. His guide walks faster and faster and he can't keep up. His heart is pounding, his chest painful.

"Wait!" he calls to her. "Wait." He stops and leans down, hands braced on thighs to catch his breath. His vision sparkles with dark motes. He's quite sure the strange woman will have marched onwards, disappearing into a heat haze, a ghost, a vision. But when he straightens up, she is standing right in front of him. She is middle-aged, weathered, but handsome – not the woman of his dreams, yet similar in some ways.

"What do you want of me?" he asks. "You must tell me. I can't go too far. They will come for me."

The woman indicates the parched relics around her. "Take them inside. Take their sleeping spirits. It is time."

Leo regards the trees. He is to take these into his arbour? What good would that do? They are long dead, probably calcified.

"She has come," says the woman. "Times are not the same, but she has come."

"Who?"

"The daughter of the earth, but her minions have shrivelled and parched. They are like seeds. They can be revived. If she is to bring springtime across the mountains and valleys once more, she will need them."

"How can I do this?"

"Break off twenty small pieces from different trees and take these with you. When you return across the pale stream, gather water from it. In your tree temple, bury the fragments, water them with what you gather from the new flow. That is all it will take. They will find their own way out."

Leo stares at the woman. "Who *are* you? How do you live out here?"

She smiles grimly. "You are not the only ones," she says. "Not everyone was invited into your temples. Some fended for themselves, and waited. Some of us are adapted to it, and continued our duty, as we always have. We have felt you, Leo of the Arbours. Hurry. Do as you are instructed. The first who quicken will see to the rest."

From the distance an echoing call: "Leeeee-ooooh." He turns instinctively to the sound, even though he has so many questions, wants so many answers. But there is no time. When he turns back, mere seconds later, the woman has already gone, faded into the white forest.

His fingers shaking, Leo breaks off twenty small twigs, each causing a sound like gunfire. He hurries then back the way he came. The only container for fluid he has with him is the small water flask Clio provided as part of his survival kit. This he now drains: a drink for himself, the rest into the dry ground. Then he is running back towards the crater. The stream there is so narrow, despite being bright, the water is difficult to collect, especially as his hands are still shaking. *People living out here. Something happening. The return. They believe in a return and see it in the form of a woman...*

He shakes his head to clear it, and then Jade is bounding down the slope towards him, stones flying from beneath her feet, with Clio following behind with her gliding walk.

"Where did you go?" Jade demands. "It was as if you vanished for a moment."

"Nowhere," Leo says, smiling. He conceals the flask within his garments. "Are you happy with what you've seen?"

Jade regards him curiously, aware of his secrets and no doubt eager to hear them. "I haven't really... seen anything. But I'm glad I came outside. There's a feeling in the air, isn't there?"

Leo nods. "Look at the water."

Jade hunkers down, runs the tips of her fingers over the soft green sprouts growing alongside it. "I want to believe this is new," she says, and smiles up at Leo. "Now, I think I want to sit in your orchard and eat stolen fruit, hear what you have to say."

Leo grins. "Okay. Let's go home." Inside, hidden beneath his smile, there is a worm of fear. Should he take the tree fragments into the arbours? Might they not be contaminated in some way and bring the blight of his nightmares?

And yet, part of him feels he should not question, just do as he's been asked, let the process unfold.

Once they are back in Arbour Ampelus, Clio leaves them and now they are alone Jade says, "Did you see her, Leo? The woman, or the girl...?"

"I saw a woman, but it seems so... unlikely now," Leo replies. "She implied people live outside the arbours, but it wasn't that far away, so surely we'd know about it if they did. I don't know." He sighs and pulls the crumbling tree fragments from his pockets, puts them on the lawn of his orchard. Such frail remnants. Can anything at all live within them? What if they are blighted? But then his clever insects would detect that, come buzzing over to disinfect. So far none of them have been alerted.

Leo digs a hole in the moist earth and lays the fragments within, as if it were a grave. Over them, he pours the trickle of silver water from the stream. The fragments go grey with the moisture, but that is all. Leo covers them with the soil, smoothes the skin of turf back over the ground. A ritual act. Perhaps that's all it is. Everyone yearns for the goddess to return, to bring life back to the corn, to cease mourning for her daughter lost to the underworld. *This is what we crave*, he thinks. *And the nymphs will be her vanguard, lifting her once more into the bright air, free of her imprisonment in the dark. This is the cycle of life.*

> **We rank neither with mortals nor with immortals:**
> **long indeed do we live,**
> **eating heavenly food and treading the lovely dance among the**
> **immortals,**
> **and with us the Sileni and the sharp-eyed Slayer of Argus**
> **mate in the depths of pleasant caves...**

Tractor Time

Kate Wilson

Paul sat down at his computer and reached for the start icon. He hesitated, thinking, *Maybe I should do the dishes instead, before Jane gets home.* He pictured the pile of bowls and cups ready to topple over in the sink, and sighed. *Damn, this been a shitty week, I need some downtime. She won't be home for at least another hour anyway.* He tapped GO, put on his VR cap, found the address he wanted and spoke the key his friend Joe had given him.

An hour later he was still inside, exploring. The grass was green and smelled lush and moist, the sky was clear blue with no brown tinge around the horizon. The warm breeze was pure pleasure on his bristly skin. He had been chasing a pretty little thing for the last ten minutes and he was fairly sure she was just about to let him catch her.

Two hours later Jane arrived home. She threw her bag down on the kitchen table and swore when she saw the dishes still piled in the sink. She swore again when she saw that he hadn't even got dinner started.

"God dammit Paul." she called, "Do I have to do everything?"

No response.

"Paul?"

Jane opened the door to his study and saw him slouched back in his chair.

"Lazy shite" she muttered, giving him a shake.

A minute later she rang an ambulance. They couldn't revive him.

Geoff walked into the office and plugged his tablet into a desk port. He stretched, his midriff bulging for a moment before he settled into his chair. The chair creaked slightly as it took his weight.

Tom, the late night shift controller, greeted him. "Good morning, Geoff."

"Morning, Farmer Tom," Geoff replied, a cheerful smile on his round face. "Everything okay overnight?"

"Fine, fine. All quiet. I ran the wake up a few minutes ago, and the feed'll be going in any minute now."

"Isometrics on?" asked Geoff. "Don't forget that the last assessment said the fat ratio was too high, not enough lean muscle".

"Who wants to exercise before breakfast? Anyway, I reckon bacon's best with a nice big streak of fat. Crisps up better." Tom unplugged his tablet and put his coat on. "I'm off. See you tomorrow."

Geoff waved as Tom got into the lift.

It was twenty-five floors from the offices of Farm Fresh Bio-Meats Happy Hog Ethical Pork Products to the car park at ground level. The buildings were also known as the Pig Towers. They loomed grey and windowless, overshadowing the apartment blocks of the local suburbs. The towers were featureless apart from a gigantic "Home of the Happy Hog" sign on tower one. They were the source of 25% of Europe's pork-based smallgoods, and a major boon for the local economy.

Tom got into his car and said, "Home." He leaned back, musing on the night's work. *All the porkers are doing well, or so the telemetry says. I'd really like to get in and see some of them in the flesh one day. Still, at least I know they're there, and they're happy.* He sighed, thinking of Geoff. *Nice bloke, if a bit flighty. Wouldn't know one end of a pig from the other. Probably never saw one pre-processing. Always bouncing from one thing to the next, but then young people never seem to stop and pay attention to anything these days. Most of them can't even read, too easy to just tap a picture and watch a video.*

Tom thought wistfully of 'tractor time', when he could chunter along on the old Massey, solving all the world's problems in his head. *That's probably why the world has so many problems: no one has time to actually think about them.*

His cheerful and optimistic nature reasserted itself as he counted his blessings. He was lucky to still have a job in farming at all, even if he never saw the animals. There was a crispy bacon sandwich with brown sauce, just the way he liked it, waiting for him at home. He could have a good sleep, then spend some time with his grandkids. In the evening he would take a walk round the blocks with his wife, Beth. Tom liked to walk rather than use an isometrics suit, even if most of the neighbours stared at such odd behaviour.

Yes, life was pretty good for "Farmer Tom" he reflected with a smile. He whistled tunelessly to himself as the car pulled into the garage under his block, and kept whistling all the way to the door of his apartment. He stopped whistling at the door because he knew Beth hated whistling indoors, and he didn't like to annoy the woman who made the best bacon sandwiches he'd ever tasted.

Geoff checked the feeding routine and started the isometrics. He smiled to himself. Tom might like his bacon with a big wide streak of white fat, but the HeartSmart people had threatened to take their tick away if the fat levels didn't come down. And the pigs were happier when they got more exercise. They slept better, had lower levels of stress hormones, and the weight gain was just as good. Geoff touched an icon on his tablet.

"Hey, how's it going down there in pigs' inner space?" he asked when a face appeared on screen.

"Hi Geoff," the head of the Environment Engineering replied. "What can we do for you and the pork pies in the sky?"

"I want a longer play period for the porkers today. I'm running the isometrics for an extra hour, gotta trim the fat."

"Yeah, maybe we should hook you in, looks like you could use a bit of exercise yourself!"

"Ha ha. My girlfriend likes me cuddly," replied Geoff, patting his belly. "Just make sure it's something fun for them. Don't get creative again like you did with those wild dog chases. If the animal rights people saw how high the cortisol levels got that time, we'd lose our ethical meat certification. You nearly scared some of them to death."

"Yeah, well, we've warned Joe not to practice game scenario design on the porkers anymore. I'll just run a standard spring day with fields and butterflies and so on."

"Happy little piggies frolicking in the grass. Sounds lovely."

"Righto Geoff, have a nice day up there."

Geoff closed the connection. He carried out a final check of the biometric telemetry from towers one through five, then opened up a news server. He clicked on a link to a story and watched the first fifteen seconds of an ad for the last ski resort in Alaska. Eventually the *skip ad* icon came up and he got to a video of people swimming in the ground level of the Sydney Opera House. At least the Aussies were getting something good out of climate change. A big fancy indoor tide pool would probably get more use than an opera house anyway. He kept flicking through, tapping the video links and watching a few seconds of each after the unavoidable advertisements. Sea levels were still rising slowly, the usual doom and gloom as more Pacific islands disappeared. Geoff watched a video of tornadoes sweeping across the Texas desert, taking topsoil away with them. Another drought in the US, wheat and beef production down. It would mean food shortages in the US and Canada for the third year running.

Geoff wasn't worried by this – he got team member discounts on all Farm Fresh products. And he knew that it was good news for Farm Fresh export sales. He remembered the 'quarter pounder' scandal that had been a Godsend for Farm Fresh in the early 40s. Like most of his generation, Geoff wasn't precious about his protein sources. Eating stray dogs made sense in his opinion, although they probably shouldn't have tried to pass it off as horse. People hadn't liked the idea of high-rise battery pigs at first, but the pigs had happier lives than most people. Hell, some days he wouldn't mind living in a virtual paradise, and the pigs had good scenario creators. Harriet and Joe were amongst the best. Geoff went "inside" to meet friends and play games himself, and he knew the pigs got scenarios as realistic as anything humans had access to.

He surfed through a few different news servers and checked in to his MyFace site, then got on with the business of the day. Even with all the automation, there was still quite a lot to do managing a quarter of a million head of stock.

When Geoff's shift ended he handed over to Tyler, who had the 4pm to midnight shift. Tyler was young and keen, studying in the day and working the evening shift. He always had the newest tablet and accessories, no matter how pointless. He wouldn't use the basic units provided by Farm Fresh. Tyler had to have something that didn't produce any outline at all in the pocket of his tight pants. Geoff had given up on wearing fashionable figure huggers. Even though he made sure he had no visible underwear lines, he couldn't do anything about visible bulges. He glared at Tyler's slender backside as it descended gracefully into the other chair, which accepted it without any complaining creaks.

Geoff found Tyler vaguely annoying. He suspected Tyler spent most of his money on game-time. Like most thirty-somethings he still lived with his parents, so he didn't have a lot of expenses. Now well into his forties, Geoff had been paying his own rent and doing his own washing for almost ten years. It made him feel mature and responsible, at least compared to this skinny young adultescent. But he also missed having enough free income to access the newest inside environments. He also suspected his girlfriend wouldn't mind if he was a bit less cuddly, even though she regularly assured him that she liked him just the way he was.

"Nothing much to do this evening, just run the usual bedtime routine about seven. The cull needs to be bigger than usual though. We've had a large order from Japan."

"Japan? I thought they sourced their protein from Australia." replied Tyler.

"Not since the Chinese bought all the farms there," Geoff told him. "They export straight home to China now, nothing left for other exports. Don't you ever view the news?"

"No, what for?" Tyler shrugged. "Cull all pre-programmed?"

"Yep, the cull will be from tower four, all of levels 7 to 9."

"Whoa, that must about thirty thousand head." Tyler shrugged and went on. "By the way, did you hear about Tom?"

"No, what about Tom?"

"He's being retired. Night shift is going to be completely automated, cheaper to just run a sleep program all night. Use the delta waves to keep the porkers asleep, and Env-Eng runs that anyway. No need to have anyone up here just watching the bio-telem."

"Poor old Farmer Tom," mused Geoff. "Nice old bloke, but I guess he must be almost 75 by now, so he could have retired a few years ago. We should get him a retirement present."

"How about a watch?" suggested Tyler "with 'hoped you enjoyed your time here', or something, on it. He'd probably wear a watch."

Geoff tapped on his desk thoughtfully, frowning to himself. "Hmm… Maybe. I have another idea. I'm just going to have a quick chat to the inner space boys, then I'll head home."

"Whatever." replied Tyler, who was already scrolling through the biotelemetry while checking his MyFace friends' updates. He was glad the cull was pre-programmed, he had an assignment due tomorrow, plus he'd arranged to meet some friends inside later on. He could use the subroutines he'd written to monitor the biotelem and notify him if anything happened 'outside' that he had to deal with, but setting up a cull took time. This was just a job while he was getting his second degree before he found a real career. He didn't want to have to spend time on it.

Tom got a good sleep, and the evening cull at Farm Fresh went smoothly while he dreamed of riding his tractor through the paddocks.

When Tom woke up, the grandkids were just getting home from the school three levels below. He heard about how Marcus wasn't friends with Baxter anymore because he only wanted to play tag with the boys from floor 6. He sympathised with Laurie who had been sent to the naughty chair for sneaking into an out of bounds area when they had been doing a history lesson "inside". Then he listened to Jess do her music practice. He broke up an argument between Marcus and Laurie and sent them both to do their homework at the kitchen table, sitting between them to stop them fighting. He kept them quiet while little Jess practiced a new piece on her clarinet. He was very proud of his seven year old granddaughter's talent.

Beth bustled about getting dinner heated up, complimenting Jess's playing and helping the boys with their homework. Tom's daughter Jill, and her partner Ben, got home just as dinner was being put on the table.

"Thanks, Beth, this is lovely," said Ben, who always remembered to compliment Beth's cooking. "Have the kids been good?"

"Little angels as always. All the homework is done and Jess has been playing a new piece for us. Beethoven's 'Ode to Joy'," she replied.

Tom smiled and said nothing of the kicks and pokes that he had intercepted under the table. The boys knew that he'd never tell their grandma or parents just what little devils they really were. "Jess's playing is really coming along. Her music teacher says she should audition for the London Youth Orchestra next year."

"That's great! We're so proud of you!" beamed Jill. "And we're so grateful to you Dad, for paying for her lessons. There's no way we could afford it ourselves."

"That's what I go to work for." Tom smiled back. "Besides, Beth would go crazy if I was at home under her feet all the time."

"Good fences make good neighbours, and night shifts make a

good marriage!" replied Beth.

Tom helped Beth clear up after dinner while Jill and Ben put the kids to bed. Then they said goodnight and went to their own section of the apartment. Tom and Beth watched a movie, then Beth made him some supper, kissed him goodnight and went off to bed herself.

Tom sat at the table and flicked through the stories on the BBC newsserve while he had his supper. Tom liked the old fashioned service on the BBC, with articles that you could read and not just videos to watch. Tom read the stories that Geoff had watched the videos of, plus several local items. He shook his head sadly at the rising waters and at the food shortages. He shook his head again when he read the item about seven gamers, found dead with their VR caps on. All had died about 8 pm. The police suspected another terrorist attack. He sighed and thought, *Even playing games is dangerous now. Poor bastards, trying to escape their miserable lives for a while, and they end up losing them.* He packed a sandwich and a thermos of tea to keep him going through the small hours, and headed back to the towers.

"Hey Tom," said Tyler when he arrived at the office, "Good day?"

"Not bad" replied Tom, plugging in his tablet. He noted the flashing message icon. He ignored it rather than check messages while talking to someone there in person, even though he knew that Tyler wouldn't have noticed. Being old fashioned, Tom felt it was impolite to not pay attention to the person he was talking with. "Everything okay here?"

"All good. Extra large 8pm cull, the carcases are already processed and the next gen will be ready to install in four, levels seven to nine in the morning."

"All of seven to nine? That *is* big" replied Tom "Must have been a special order. Still, nice way to go: just having your brain stop while you're asleep. There's a lot I miss from old-style farming, but not the slaughter. All that blood and squealing."

"Yeah," said Tyler, not looking up from his tablet "China or Jamaica or somewhere." He unplugged his tablet and slipped it into his back pocket "I'm off then. See you tomorr... ummm... Well, bye."

When Tyler had left, Tom got out his thermos and tapped the message icon. A video of the local manager popped up. "Tom, you've been a valuable team member of Farm Fresh Bio-Meats Happy Hog

Ethical Pork Products for more than thirty years. However, with rising costs and market instability, Farm Fresh is having to reconsider our cost structures and rationalise our outgoings. This means that we will no longer be running a late night shift. While at Farm Fresh we make every endeavour to ensure that all team members are redeployed, as you are already four years past the minimum retirement age we will not be offering you a redeployment option. You will receive all your entitlements, and six weeks' severance pay. Farm Fresh Bio-Meats Happy Hog Ethical Pork Products would like to thank you for your contribution and we wish you all the best for your retirement."

"What?" said Tom "What? What? *Retire…?*"

He played the message again. Then he sat very still at the desk for a long time. Tom had spent thirty two years at Farm Fresh. And nearly twenty years before that running his family's free range piggery at the same site before Farm Fresh had bought them out and put up the towers. *I can't retire*, he thought. *What about Jess's lessons? Jill can't afford them, not with the cost of the boys' schooling as well. Anyway, farmers don't retire. Dad never retired. Grandad worked the farm until he died.*

The call icon on his tablet started flashing. It was Harriet from Environment Engineering. Tom sighed and tapped the icon and Harriet's face filled the screen. "Oh," she said, seeing his face, "you've just heard. I'm so sorry Tom."

"Thanks, Harriet. Me too." he replied.

"Ummm… we've got a retirement present for you. Well, really it was Geoff's idea," she said.

Tom imagined the present. Probably a watch with something horrible like to remember your time with us' engraved on it. Geoff would probably think that was witty. He tried to look interested.

"I had the evening shift working on it for hours." Harriet went on, "There's a VR cap up there in one of the drawers. Put it on and I'll send you the address and key."

"I don't play games, Harriet," said Tom, "I don't like things going straight into my brain. It makes me nervous."

Harriet smiled, "You'll like this Tom. Trust me. Give it a go. You can exit anytime, just clap your hands."

Tom sighed. *Well, what do I have to lose? Useless, out-dated old man. Who am I kidding, I'm not really a farmer. I sold out and now I'm going to be replaced by a subroutine. Not even a whole machine, just a subroutine on one of*

Env-Engs clever computers.

"Go on" said Harriet "really, you'll love it. And don't worry about anything, I'll run your station by remote from here. Stay as long as you like."

He found the cap and put it on, feeling a bit uncomfortable initially with the cold mesh against his head. The address and key arrived, and he closed his eyes.

Tom opened his eyes. He was sitting on a 2020's MF 9900, just like the one he'd ridden on the family farm. The grass was green and lush, the sky was clear blue. It was a cleaner blue than he'd seen in decades. He could smell the grass, and there was a gentle warm breeze. Tom started up the engine, startling some nearby piglets who were frolicking in the grass. The piglets scampered away, squealing and grunting.

He set off along the fence line, smiling to himself, the engine rumbling quietly. Farmer Tom was ready to sit and think and solve all the world's problems. Or at least a few local ones.

Six hours later, the engine stopped. A window appeared in front of him with Harriet's face looking in. "Hi Tom" she said "I hope you enjoyed it, but you'd better come out now. Shift change in another half hour."

"Thanks, Harriet. Thank you very much. You don't know what this means to me." He clapped his hands, and opened his eyes.

Tom took the cap off and put it back in the drawer. Then he unwrapped his sandwich and poured himself a cup of tea from his thermos. He leaned back and smiled to himself, enjoying the crispy, salty bacon, complimented perfectly by the HP sauce. He hadn't realised how hungry he was getting in there. Then he tapped the Environment Engineering icon on his tablet. Harriet appeared immediately.

"What's up, Tom? Not feeling a bit woozy after being inside for so long? It can take you that way if you're not used to it."

"Oh no, I'm fine. I just wanted to ask some questions."

"Sure…"

"Well," he started, "what would happen if a human was, you know, *inside*, when the cull took place?"

"Couldn't happen" she replied. "We never let anyone in. In fact, you're the first. We have a check of the inside environment ourselves now and then, but no one else has the key. Just me and two others in Env-Eng. If you want to use it again, Tom, I'm sorry, but we can't..."

"No, no." he said "I'm not asking for that. Just humour me, though, what would happen to a human brain if you used those, you know, cull waves on them."

"Well, human brains are pretty similar to pigs'. We've never tried it, of course, but I guess the cull wave induction pattern could *in theory* stop a human brain. Not the sort of thing you could get ethics approval to test for though..." She smiled. "It was hard enough getting the experiments done on pigs in the first place."

"Just humour me a bit more, Harriet. Can you check how many pigs are in the system right now?"

"Well, it should just be a few hundred. Usually we keep them asleep but we woke up a few to keep you company."

"How many exactly? And can you check."

Harriet looked down for a moment. "Sure. There are 375 users in the environment right now."

"Uh huh. And how many pigs did you wake up?"

Harriet started to look worried "what are you getting at Tom...? Oh shit.... 370..." Harriet's face turned away, but Tom heard her call sharply "Joe, do you know anything about..." before the connection was cut.

Tom sat for a few minutes musing to himself, then he called the local manager, who wasn't pleased at being woken up. He glared balefully at Tom though sleep-bleared eyes. He was even less pleased when Tom told him what he had figured out during his tractor time.

Finally, Tom finished, saying, "So, I guess I really ought to go to the police about this... it's a shame. As a loyal employee, I hate to have to do it. After all, I've been with Farm Fresh for more than thirty years... "

"Well, of course," said the manager, "while it's a terrible thing that's happened, nothing that we do now can bring those people back. We'll put in a new firewall before the next cull. And of course you've made a massively important contribution. I'm sure Farm Fresh will wish to... thank you... in some way for your contribution." He smiled ingratiatingly as the sweat trickled down his forehead.

Tom smiled back. "I do so enjoy being part of the team at Farm Fresh."

"Well, we would hate to lose such a valuable team member. And of course, a promotion is in order for... errr... ongoing loyalty to the company."

"Oh no, I don't need a promotion. I like my late night shift in the tower. Keeps me out from under the wife's feet." He paused, thinking of clarinet lessons and fares to and from London. "Well, a small rise, just to help with the cost of living would be appreciated. And perhaps a hamper of Farm Fresh extra-streaky bacon would be nice. The wife likes the organic one."

"Of course, of course... lots of bacon. A big hamper of Biodynamic Organic Extra Streaky. Two hampers. We're so pleased you can stay on with us at Farm Fresh."

When Geoff arrived he was surprised to see Tom looking so pleased. Tom looked almost smug, in fact. *Maybe the old coot was looking forward to retirement after all,* he thought.

"Morning, Farmer Tom. All well in the world?"

"Oh yes," said Tom. "And I can't thank you enough for the lovely present."

"Well, you always say that what the world is missing is "tractor time", no time for people to just think anymore. Maybe Harriet can set up a little offline version you can take home with you."

He stood up and held out a pudgy hand "Well, Tom," he said formally "we'll all miss you. I hope you enjoy your retirement".

Tom smiled "Oh no, I'm not retiring. I'll be back tomorrow night for more tractor time. Plenty more problems to solve. And plenty of time to do it in, thanks to Env-Eng's clever little subroutines." He shook Geoff's hand, because Geoff was still holding it out in surprise. Then he picked up his thermos and headed for the lift, whistling tunelessly to himself.

Veggie Moon

Neal Wooten

I can still hear them screaming like hyenas trying to steal a feast; still see the mobs of crazy people with their hand-crafted signs, all prognosticating the end of the world. In had been that way since I was old enough to remember. And even though our imminent demise seems to have been averted, they are still there. From what I have read, it has never taken a lot throughout history to bring them out in droves.

There seems to be a fascination with doomsday scenarios that make people not only embrace the idea but insist that everyone else in hearing range accept it as well. I often wondered that if they did really believe the end was near, why didn't they simply go home and spend the remaining time with their families. I'm sure this is where their family members would interject and tell me to mind my own business.

I was born the same day as the big announcement – that in the year 2229, the people of Earth once again faced complete and total annihilation – for the millionth time. The moon, which had been receding from the earth at the rate of about one inch per year for several millennia, suddenly accelerated the recession a decade earlier. Scientists were baffled as to the reason, but the results were clear. Since the moon's gravitational pull kept the earth tilted at approximately 17 degrees, that angle was what allowed us to have a stable environment and was even the reason for the four seasons.

As the moon withdrew from its partner in space, the tempo of planetary and natural disasters escalated, causing major earthquakes and storms. Sometimes winters seem to last for half a year, even in the southern part of the country. When summers finally came, they were relentless, causing heat advisories that were akin to curfews. This wreaked havoc on the remaining farms that tried desperately to provide food for an overpopulated planet. As the population neared twenty billion, every country eventually adopted a one-child-per-couple law, and still the food lines grew and stories of starvation escalated. I'm not sure which was worse: growing up with the storms and harsh weather conditions, the food rationing, or the prophets of destruction.

But, alas, science was not without an answer, or at least a possible solution, which only seemed to galvanize the naysayers and motivate their cause all the more. As dedicated as they were regarding the end of all life as we know it, trying to prevent this from happening seemed to upset them all the more. When I first heard of the plan, I was very young and more than a little skeptical myself, but I was willing to give them the benefit of the doubt.

The plan was simple: replace the moon. Well, at least the concept was simple; the execution was another thing. The undertaking to create a new moon, given the official name of Lunar Alpha, was to take fifteen years and utilise a combination of waste from the overflowing landfills and rocks and soil from the ocean floor. Along with building a new satellite to offer a gravitational grant, it would also help the borderline contamination faced from accruing garbage, help combat the rising seawaters from the melting ice on the polar caps, but, most importantly, it would provide new stable planting dirt. The entire orb would be one big vegetable garden.

After a few years, however, it was deemed more profitable to concentrate on the more easily obtainable piles of refuse. Landfills were stripped down to the bare dirt as shuttles flew nonstop back and forth to the new construction, carrying the rotten materials, just the type of fertiliser the new soil needed to boost production. Hence the project known as Lunar Alpha became known on the streets as Veggie Moon.

They finished the construct behind schedule, of course, but by the time I graduated from college the climate here on Earth had stabilised – somewhat. Winters and summers were still rough, but no more than they had been before the moon began its wayward drift. Veggie Moon also helped stabilise the old moon by adding to its gravitational field and decreasing its outward bound momentum, an unexpected perk. Eventually the shuttles that had so unfalteringly delivered garbage to the new construct began delivering cabbage back – and tomatoes, cucumbers, squash, celery, etc. As the food shortages started to ease, people stopped staring at the large moon in the night sky with the smaller brighter dot in front of it. Well, everyone except me.

Still the number of death psychics and street prophets grew, desperately trying to convince people of their own pressing immortality.

When starvation was no longer the demon, they invented new ones. Conspiracy theories soared back and forth about the government using radiation to stimulate the growth of the crops on Veggie Moon. They marched around with their picket signs in elevated numbers, yelling their messages of fear to anyone in hearing range. Everyone except me ignored them in the same way they ignored the new light-of-hope in the sky. I detested the protestors and picketers and wanted to be as far away from them as I could get.

By then they were calling for employees – terrafarmers – to work the boundless fields of never-ending farmland on Veggie Moon. The vast acres of new land would not only provide food for Earth, but would also serve as new living space for an already overcrowded planet. Real estate offices jumped at the chance to add lunar apartments, which were not even completed at the time, to their listings.

I signed up right away. My parents weren't too happy, but I was twenty-two years old and could make my own decisions. To me, it was a no-brainer. How many guys my age get to go into space? Plus, I couldn't take the picketers any longer.

It was certainly scary to start with, especially the flight here. After an extensive three-month basic training ordeal, I watched the earth get smaller and smaller as the first passenger shuttle delivered me and a hundred other nervous workers to this foreign man-made sphere in space.

That was three years ago and I am now very much at home here. I began as a simple planter but was promoted two years ago to supervisor, overseeing a crew of forty-two terrafarmers. In the beginning, the work was mostly done with hand tools. Now we have motorized remotes that can weed thousands of acres per day. I'm not even sure where the weeds come from unless they were part of the landfill junk. But regardless, they are as tenacious here as they were back on Earth.

As for living quarters, we started out with giant inflatable tents, but now there is a sizeable civilization here. There are tall buildings with elevated roads to and from other structures. We have restaurants, apartments, stores, and a giant satellite dish that provides direct communication to Earth. We have the internet, telecom devices that have only a twenty-three second relay to earth, and about 3,000 channels to choose from on Imagevision, about half of the choices they get back home.

I even have a Lunar Alpha address to receive shipments for work or the occasional birthday gift from my mom. I love it here, the scenery and the peace. I love when the old moon is over the horizon like it is right now; the image so large that it feels as if you could reach out and touch it.

"Hey, Trace, are you on another planet?"

I turn around and smile. Two of my workers are standing there grinning at me for spacing out. One of them is the new girl, Mara, a beautiful young woman who just arrived a few months ago and we hit it off right away. Her long auburn hair is tucked up inside her helmet. Even in the bulky spacesuit, the curves on her five-foot frame are hard to ignore. She had been a gymnast back on Earth, from a small town in the Midwest, but, after failing to make the annual Olympics three years in a row, had signed up for a two-year stint here on Veggie Moon. I was glad she did, and even happier that she was assigned to my squad. Of course, after seeing her the first day, I persuaded my boss to make that happen.

I smile. "Yes, I was for a moment there. Thanks for reeling me in."

She smiles back, her beautiful teeth and deep blue eyes reflecting the glow from the tower lights. "Gavin here thinks he can take you."

I laugh so hard it temporarily fogs up the inside of my face shield.

Gavin is even newer than Mara. He's only been here a month, a small lad from New York City; his freckled face making him look younger than he is.

"Really, Gavin?"

He shrugs, making me believe this challenge is more Mara's idea.

Other workers figure out what's happening and circle around cheering for their champion – me. I can't let them down.

"Okay, someone let us know when to start," I say.

Mara is only too eager. "Get ready. Get set. Go!"

Gavin and I take off our helmets as the pressurised air detects the environment and shuts off the flow. After almost four years of planting crops, the plants are plentiful and have started dispensing enough oxygen to make the air almost breathable – almost. A minute passes and Gavin's face begins to turn red. I breathe easily and keep an eye on him. Two minutes pass and his face begins to turn blue. He is resilient.

I keep fearing that a challenger will pass out and need medical attention. That would certainly end the fun.

The new guy relents and quickly puts his helmet back on, and, as the air hisses inside his suit, he takes a deep breath.

I smile, walk over to him and pat him on the back. "Well done, young man. Not bad at all." He looks at me with his eyes open wide. I like to toy with them like this. I have yet to replace my own helmet and pretend the atmosphere is not burning a hole in my lungs right now. "Okay, the fun's over. Let's get back to work." I put my helmet back over my short black hair and take a deep breath myself.

It's not just my lungs that have got stronger after being here for three years; it's everything. I never played sports in high school. At six-feet-two-inches tall, I had the height for some sports, but not the bulk. I never tipped the scales at more than 140 pounds making me officially a skinny runt. College was no different. I tried out for amateur softball but couldn't even make that team. But after wearing weights in this low-gravity environment for so long, my muscles finally decided to grow. Coupled with a vigorous gym program, my arms, chest, and shoulders now bulge with sinews and veins, complementing my still-slender waist.

The nights are only a few hours long, so we have to work in shifts. It's still too hot to work the daytime hours, even in our pressurized suits. On the weekdays, we will return to base for nine hours and come back again. Another crew alternates the other night hours, meaning there is always a crew working as long as the sun is not shining. But this is Friday and we have the weekend ahead of us. Even though the days and nights are not the same here, we still go by Earth time so we have a full forty-eight hour liberty. Everyone is elated as we take the transport back to base.

"What are you guys doing tonight?"

I stare across at Marc, one of my oldest friends here on Veggie Moon. He has been on my crew since I became supervisor, a hard worker with arms like steel. He was a power lifting champion back home with over a hundred trophies to back it up. He was the one who designed my successful workout program. We always hung out together, drinking way too much and chasing what few women there were here. Good times. Of course, since the arrival of Mara, I have been neglecting him pitifully. I look beside me at Mara for confirmation. She simply shrugs. She does not like to drink or be around people who do. I shrug as well. "I hope we're getting some rest. Maybe watch a movie. What do you think?" I ask Mara.

She nods.

"Ah, come on," Marc pleads. "Come out tonight to Lunar Toons and have a few drinks. You guys spend too much time at home. You're too young to be acting like an old couple. Live a little."

I do miss the one night club at base and miss the times Marc and I have had there. But I don't commit, only tell him we'll think about it.

We arrive back at base and Mara goes to her apartment and I go to mine. After a shower, I sit back on the sofa and relax. "Image," I command and the Imagevision illuminates, the projectors along the floor, walls, and ceiling creating a 3-D picture about ten feet in front of the sofa. At least we have the modern conveniences here. "News," I command and the menu displays the solitary news station here. I watch as they explain how successful the crop production on Lunar Alpha has been. There are no longer any farms on Earth, save for a few small, private plots and several greenhouses. It's a good feeling to be part of that, to know your contribution has helped end hunger for millions of people.

An hour later, Mara arrives with food. We eat then curl up on the sofa together and watch a movie. This has become a common practice. And, as always, we soon forget about the movie and begin concentrating on each other. This is my favourite part of living here. I was happy before Mara came but sometimes I can't remember why. I think I am in love with her.

"Do you love me?" she asks as if reading my mind.

It takes me off guard. "Uh... of course."

She grimaces. "That would have sounded more believable without the 'uh'."

"Sorry, you caught me by surprise." I lean in and begin kissing her again. My hand makes its way up her leg.

"What are you doing?" she asks as she slides away from me.

This is as far as I've ever got. I try to give her my best puppy dog face but it doesn't work.

"You know I'm not like that, so why do you try?" she asks.

"Because I love you and I thought you loved me. This is natural. I know you come from a religious family, but you're not on Earth anymore."

She looks angry. "What does that mean? It doesn't matter where I'm at; I still believe two people should wait until they're married. I think we're closer to God here than on Earth."

I give in and apologise, promising my roaming hands will behave. She looks at me with sympathy, which makes me feel a little better.

"Why don't we go meet your friends at the club?" she suggests.

I am shocked. "Really?"

She nods. I think it's her way of compromising. But I am certainly game.

We take the elevator to the top floor and walk around the circular corridor towards the club. Out the windows I can see the large satellite dish atop the other building, the lights making it look like a spaceship. That one giant dish provides every form of communication and entertainment from Earth.

We enter the crowded club and find Marc and a few other friends sitting at a table. I think he is as surprised at seeing us as I am to be seen. We join the group and I order a drink. Mara orders soda.

"Here's to the best boss on Veggie Moon," Marc says, holding his bottle above the table.

I blush as we all bump our glasses and bottles to the toast. Everyone at the table is part of my crew and I'm glad to be hanging out with them again.

"Want to dance?" Mara asks.

"Sure," I say.

We go to the large dance floor and start gyrating to the techno music blaring away. I never got into dancing or the club scene back home, but here I love it. We dance through three songs before going back to our seats.

Marc has found a new friend, a woman older than me, but very attractive. He is whispering in her ear, which, for some reason, makes her stare at me with wide-open eyes.

"Is that true?" she asks.

I look to Marc who is smiling. "Is *what* true?" I ask.

"Marc says you don't need a helmet, that you can breathe the air on Veggie Moon. Is that true?"

I point to the five empty beer bottles in front of Marc. "Does that answer your question?"

She slaps Marc playfully on the chest. "You're telling me stories."

Marc looks at me like I betrayed him, his lower jaws hanging low. "I am not. He really can. He's just bashful."

"What's your name?" I ask.

The woman smiles. "I'm Maria. I just arrived last week."

"Welcome," I say and hold my glass in the air. Everyone at the table joins in on the toast.

The rest of the evening is fun and we head home after several hours of partying. Marc, his new friend, and at least five others join us and they all come to my apartment for games. We play several interactive games, which are already programmed into the Imagevision. It's a fun night.

As two of the others are acting out a movie scene with the background provided by the Imagevison and added around them, Mara leans over and whispers in my ear. "I'm sorry about earlier."

I smile. "No. I'm sorry."

She kisses me on the neck and whispers again. "No, you were right. We're adults. If you want me to, I will spend the night tonight."

My eyes open wide. *If I want her to?* Duh. I decide it's time to end the party. I stand to announce that it's time for everyone to go home, but I never get the words out. Suddenly the entire building shakes violently. Dishes and glasses topple from the table. I fall back onto the sofa and several others fall to the floor. It seems to last for about thirty seconds. We can hear sirens going off somewhere on base. When it's over, everyone looks at everyone else for answers.

"News," I command and we all step away from the Imagevision as the news channel appears. Some sit in front of the sofa and some stand behind it as we wait to learn what has happened.

A male reporter appears and begins to give the details. "Authorities are requesting that everyone remain or return to their quarters and keep your suits and helmets on ready. They are confirming that Lunar Alpha has been struck by a magnitude 6.5 earthquake. This is the first quake ever recorded here and they're not sure of the potential for aftershocks. We will let you know more as events unfold. Again, they are requesting that everyone remain calm and stay at home and keep your suits and helmets nearby."

As the screen goes blank, I look around the room at the faces of shock and fear. Slowly everybody regains their composure.

"That wasn't so bad," Marc says.

I agree. "It's over now."

Maria is the first to walk toward the door.

"Where are you going?" Marc asks.

She puts her jacket on and looks noticeably upset. "We just had an earthquake. I'm going home like they said."

"Hey," Marc pleads, "I'm from San Francisco. That was nothing. Besides, you can't really call it an 'earthquake.' It was just a minor Veggie Moon quake."

The levity doesn't work and Maria and the others file out one by one. Marc follows, still trying to comfort Maria. I tell him I'll see him tomorrow and close the door behind them. I turn and see Mara grabbing her things.

"Are you leaving, too?"

She looks stunned. "They said everyone has to return to their own quarters."

I shake my head. "No, they just suggested it. Why don't you go grab your suit and helmet and come stay here? I'll feel safer if you're here."

She walks a wide path around me and heads for the door. She stops and turns back with a very disgruntled look on her face. "You really have a one-track mind, don't you?"

"No, I really just think it will be –"

The door slams.

I flop down on the sofa, upset by the turn of events. I really did mean I thought she would feel safer not being alone, but I know there's little chance of convincing her of that now. It proves that a low gravity environment makes it just as easy to stick one's foot in your mouth as it was back on Earth. I give up and go to bed, with my suit and helmet beside me of course.

The next day I awake and realize there were no aftershocks. Thank goodness. I go to the living room and activate the Imagevision to see if I can get an update. There's a different reporter but the news *is* about the quake.

"… to repeat, authorities are saying that last night's quake was a fluke. It was most likely caused by the settling of material used to build Lunar Alpha. There is little danger of any further problems and citizens are advised to return to their normal activities."

I breathe a sigh of relief. I activate the telecom and have it connect to Mara's room. I have to try to convince her of my innocent intentions. She doesn't answer. I try her personal line but get no answer there either. I don't know if she's still asleep or ignoring me. I call Marc and he doesn't answer either. That's odd.

I decide to go to the third floor to get some breakfast. As I take the elevator down, I can't help but be perplexed at how the night unfolded. Last night should have played out very differently. I exit the elevator and walk toward the restaurant but something catches my attention. I hear loud voices coming from the front of the building.

I turn that way instead, intent on finding out what the commotion is about. As I walk up to the guardrail overlooking the large lobby, I am completely devastated. There are at least a hundred people walking around carrying picket signs. I don't believe it. There's no escape. I travel nearly 200,000 miles to get away from people like this, but they're everywhere.

And then I see her and I can't believe my eyes. There is Mara in the crowd. No wonder she didn't answer my calls. Whatever chances I thought I had with her are wiped away at the sight of the handwritten sign she is carrying: "Repent. The End of Veggie Moon is Near."

Wheat

Kevin Burke

It was her hair that he remembered most. Not her eyes, warm and beguiling though they undoubtedly were; nor her smile; nor the ease with which she would break into sudden, infectious laughter. It wasn't even the feline movement of her body as she crossed the room. It was her hair, flowing like honey, gently undulating in the soft summer breeze. He traced its movement with his finger, as though this simple action would lend substance to the memory. In his mind's eye he watched it brush against her cheeks, then cascade across her shoulders like a golden waterfall. Finally, reaching the farthest point of its journey, the saffron river ran into tiny tributaries that lost themselves in the folds of her gown: slender wisps of ochre lost in a sea of green.

From his seat in the window, he looked at the awards that hung on the opposite wall. He was pleased that his work had been recognised, that these plaques of glass and metal reflected the success he had achieved; but ultimately they meant little. It was the smallest of the collection, the one that was engraved with Martha's name, which held his gaze.

Thirty-five years ago, when they had first posited the idea, their focus had been entirely on off-world cultivation, but when the change in the climate had begun to accelerate at a speed that not even the doom-mongers could have foreseen, it was all hands to the wheel. "Desert creep" had turned into something more akin to "desert stampede", and parts of Europe had become a dustbowl. In North Africa, nothing could survive. In Britain, drought conditions in summer, along with extreme flash flooding hurricane level winds and the fact that much of the east of the country was under water, meant that traditional arable farming methods had all but been abandoned. It was a crisis from which no country on Earth was immune.

Martha had been the first to see the potential. A form of capillary matting, thin as paper, rolled out from huge bobbins over the arid soil.

The "food carpet", as it had immediately been dubbed by the press, contained everything necessary for life… and then some.

The idea had been that the cocktail of chemicals in the underside of the matting would mineralise and enrich whatever surface it came into contact with, creating a growing culture through which the embedded seeds could send roots, enabling the emerging plants to lock into the newly created compost. At the same time, the capillaries within the carpet's fibres would carry fluid to the seedlings in the same way that the veins and arteries of a human body carry nutrition to the cells.

He looked again at the awards. There had been many who were working on the project, but it was Martha who had made the concept work. His own recognition had come from the creation of the solar powered devices that encouraged the fertiliser mix to combine with whatever moisture source might be available, and then to expand throughout the capillary system. No mean feat, but it was Martha's genius that had developed the matting itself.

The surface of the carpet was completely impervious to hostile elements, while remaining permeable to moisture and life-giving sunlight. Tied up in the strongest of patents, the nanotechnology involved was mind-boggling, yet it remained financially within the grasp of even the most cash-strapped of governments. That was the real genius, the holy grail of technological advance. It was never going to be enough simply to *build* a better mousetrap; you had to bring it in at a price that everyone could afford.

So it had been the cruellest of blows when the accident happened. A tiny nick in a safety glove, and it was all over. The chemical combination held in the lowest layer of the mat had been created to seek out the most infinitesimal of water molecules. Within the matting it remained inert, until brought to life by the workings of the capillary system, but, in those early days in the laboratory, it was savage. In the pores of Martha's fingertip it found a perfect source of water, and the concoction set about the work that she had created it to do. In less than five minutes the mineralisation process had spread through her cellular structure. Within ten she was dead.

He turned in his chair and looked out of the window. Populations need to be fed, wherever in the Universe they may be. They had tried fungi, lichen and plankton, but they had never taken off, despite a gargantuan effort on the part of the marketing men. The debate over genetically modified crops had long since been won, as people realised that, without a little help, much of their food simply couldn't grow in the new, harsher conditions of our brave new world. So now they had cultivatable grains and grasses that would grow anywhere, and which, thanks to Martha's expertise, could be rolled out over everything from ice cap to desert.

It was a fitting epitaph. Wherever there were people, on Earth and beyond, the legacy of her work would keep them fed. As he looked out over the acres of golden wheat, waving sinuously in the late afternoon breeze, he was, as always, reminded of Martha.

Blight

Dev Agarwal

Roberts trudges through Exeter. St Davids station is a dirty blur in the fading evening. The land smells wet and spoiled. He walks along a steep road, past what was once a B&B, then an Indian restaurant gutted by fire, and the prison, set behind high imposing walls. A thrill of fear runs through his chest but the building squats unlit and empty. He turns left along the remembered route to the campus – Blackboy Road, then Pennsylvania Avenue. A fire burns outside Marks and Spencer. Men stand round a steel drum, torching books for warmth. They're lean racks, thin with hunger. He hesitates, wary.

One of them waves to him, offering him a bottle. He hears, "Come over," and realises that it's a woman speaking. Roberts smiles, shaking his head, but more relaxed.

"I'm looking for the greenhouses," he says, venturing his luck.

"Nimisha's greenhouses?" the woman asks.

Surprised, he nods. The woman laughs. She has dusky skin and bright almond eyes. "Not too many people round here, anymore. We all know Nim. Get the bus up to Duryard Hill."

She swings the bottle to point the way, pale liquor swirling in green glass.

When he reaches the bus station he finds ranks of old gas-guzzling double-deckers. Three sit rusted out but two are fitted with methane conversions. Gas bags sag off their high roofs. On one, the wheels have been replaced with the base of a hovercraft so that the bus resembles a matron in skirts, its methane bladder a sagging bust.

A short line of people, ragged and unwashed, pay for the ride with plastic counters. Roberts shows his son Daniel's medal, veteran of the Indian Wars. The driver hesitates over this oddity. Hunger gnaws at Roberts, but he pushes it away, his will strong despite the frailties of old age. He was a soldier once and remembers how to deal with uniformed men. Finally, the driver nods, simultaneously allowing Roberts on and dismissing him. Roberts takes a seat and the bus pulls out of the station.

He thinks about Daniel every hour, feels the hugeness of the hole that his death left behind. His wife died ten years ago and after losing her, Roberts thought nothing could hurt him. But he'd never dreamt that his son might die, that something so monstrous, so *unfair*, could befall him. Daniel was a soldier in one of the endless wars that started in the Middle East and spilled over into India, Pakistan and through Burma into China.

Roberts remembers coming to Exeter when Daniel started university, and how the town could be both crowded and friendly. Now he finds it semi-derelict and menacing under a sullen sky. Through the bus window he sees the abandoned university buildings where Nimisha lives. Roberts has never met her. Daniel, unsure how his old father might react to an Indian, was careful to make sure that Roberts knew Nimisha was a *friend* and not his girlfriend. "Doing great work, Dad," Daniel told him. "You'd like her."

Exeter becomes more vivid to Roberts when he steps onto the campus. The university is abandoned, its lawns ragged and dried out. Trees cant sideways, blackened with rot. Nimisha's greenhouses are jammed between open-air tanks designed to snatch rainwater and white-vaned windjammers. The greenhouses are made of plastic in pastel greens and blues, and their geodesic patterns of domes and tubes are strung together with stiff guywires. Roberts has no idea how long they've stood here, but they look as if they've accreted, growing like coral between the college buildings. They're also spraybombed with bursts of graffiti, perhaps urban camouflage to hide their value or the angry tags of wandering gangs. Either way, it didn't work. They've been picked clean.

Daniel had told him that Nimisha was part of a team trying to revive the potato crop and to Roberts she is a connection from his past to this new world of upheavals and Blight. It amazes him to think that his son never tasted a potato, never helped his dad dig them up or watched his mother peeling them for Sunday roast. Potatoes came from the New World, he knows, so there was a time when no European ate they, but they were such a staple of his own childhood that Roberts never imagined they could become so rare.

Three decades ago, the global Blight destroyed eighty percent of the world's potato crops, turning potatoes into a luxury more costly than platinum. The wars began soon after, born out of the turmoil of famine and poverty.

Roberts looks back from the campus hills to the city below. Fires in drums glow in the darkness, smoldering and smudgy. This is how he imagines fallen Rome might have looked, as seen through a tunnel back to the ancient world.

Nimisha floats on her bed. First the hunger made her dizzy, too confused and unsteady to forage after food, then the damp slid into her chest and left her coughing and wheezing. She hasn't been able to tend her greenhouses for weeks. Even rising from the bed defeats her.

Roberts' arrival surprised Nimisha. She feels she knows him, or should do, but hunger and illness confuse her. She's grateful for the company. This odd, old man is friendly enough and he must have struggled to get here. There are thirty flights of stairs up to her research lab and no power for the lifts. Roberts looked puzzled by the partition walls dividing her bed from the rows of steel sinks and dissection tables.

Half delirious from infection, she hears herself telling him about the solar panels on the side of the science centre that were here before she moved in, welded onto iron frames on the walls by the last of the grad students to quit the project – dedicated Eastern Europeans. The panels shine and wobble like liquid silver in the morning sun but at dusk, looking up from her greenhouses, she can see the welds that bulge like medieval armour from their frames. She recognises the commitment of those students; it puts her in mind of pilgrims visiting a shrine. They kitted up her lab in the Science and Technology Centre and made a bedroom for her in one corner.

Roberts listens to her, standing at the edge of her makeshift bedroom. He stopped at a market near the bus station, not wanting to arrive empty-handed. The vegetables on display were wilted and over-ripe: hairy limp carrots, browning cabbage – even potatoes: mottled and rotten, but potatoes nonetheless. He watched the faces in the crowd, kids or old people like him, all staring, intent on the Blight-stained potatoes. The prices were beyond any of their reach. Frustrated, he considers the can of chilli he'd found. Vegetarian. Meat isn't safe from contamination, and besides he assumes Nimisha's a Muslim.

He steps over to Nimisha's toaster oven and flicks the switch.

"No power," Nimisha says.

"What about the solar panels? Don't they work?" He peers at the panels jutting from the block like huge sails.

"They're not hooked up to the lab," Nimisha tells him. Then seeing the food he's unwrapping, she says, "Are those potatoes?" Her voice is animated.

"No, bread. Potatoes are too expensive. Luxury foods."

"Potatoes aren't luxuries," she says firmly.

Unsettled, Roberts looks away. He can almost taste potatoes even after all these years, the melting smoothness of mash, the greasy crackle of chips. He levers the lid off the can of chilli and spoons it onto plates. They'll have to eat it cold. He sits on a wonky plastic chair, skip salvage that no one burned for heat in winter because it wouldn't burn, and hands her a plate. Above him her clothes are strung across the long axis of the bedroom on a wax-coated line. He's careful not to peer too closely at what might be scraps of underwear.

After Nimisha eats she grows alert and talkative again. "You know what we'll take to Mars?" she asks him.

"We're going to Mars?" Roberts is surprised because he was reflecting on her bedroom, a space twelve feet by nine that makes him think of a spaceship's confined quarters.

"We. Humanity. Some of us, sometime. Before the Blight, Mars was the plan. Send people who didn't want to come back. One way pioneers."

Roberts is disconcerted by her flow of details. He doesn't expect it to last, or make sense.

"We'll go and we'll take a crucial component with us. Potatoes. Freshly harvested, they will be essential."

"That so?"

"Carrying a sufficient weight of ready-made meals is impractical. Suicide really. The crew will grow their own vegetables in bioregenerative life support systems. Any effective system is self-sustaining and recycles the output of one generation of the crop into the production of the next. Astronauts can have any fresh veg that they want, but the one they *must* have is the potato. It's a dietary mainstay – both during the journey and on Mars itself."

Roberts watches her. The lab's walls remind him of arterial

plaque: a coating of wallpaper from another century sagging and bubbling with age. In places it has come away entirely, revealing earlier epochs of plaster and brick. The idea of going to Mars is impossible, a fairy tale. Nimisha carries on talking. "No cereal can match its generosity: the potato is the best all-round bundle of nutrition nature knows."

Roberts is unsure what to say.

Neither of them, he knows, is going to Mars.

The next morning, Nimisha watches him after he comes back from the city centre. Roberts struggles round the lab, bemused by the array of sinks, the microscopes standing idle.

"You're wearing your pin today," Nimisha says.

He looks round at her, lost in the shadows of the room. Her eyes are luminous and brown, alert now. When he glances down he runs his thumb over the angled edges of his son's veteran's pin, reminding himself of its presence – the talisman that got him through the Birmingham checkpoint with no questions asked, on his way from the Lake District to Exeter.

"Veteran of Mumbai," he says. She sinks back onto the temperfoam. "Where?" she asks.

He's puzzled that she doesn't know. "India. Bombay."

"No, not that. Where's the veteran?"

He sees her staring without caution. He expected an immigrant and a woman alone to be more wary.

"The greenhouses," she says. "Have you seen them?"

"I came through Duryard Halls on my way here," he says. Then he asks, "Who built the greenhouses?"

"They've always been here. Have you been inside? What did you see?" Excited again, she struggles to rise, so that he reaches out and helps her to prop herself up. "How is the crop? It must be close to harvest now. I need to think what to do. I'll need assistance. People. If they see the crop, they'll know its value. That will help, actually."

"Nimisha."

"What?"

"Don't you know? The greenhouses. They're all dead. Stripped. The frames torn up. The beds, with the plants in them –"

"– Hydroponics bins."

"Yes. The bins. They've been looted, picked clean long ago. I'm sorry, gangs must have got to them. There's nothing left."

"You came through Duryard?" she asks.

He nods. "Each day I come here I pass through there. It's all scavenged."

He walked up the hill from the halls of residence, a hard climb with his arthritis. He stopped to gather himself, pressing heavily on his walking stick. Oaks that had died out from the moths a generation ago and were just rows of flat stumps lined the path. The newer breeds of planting, olive groves and jacaranda trees as the climate warmed, had taken over then were destroyed by frost as the weather switched back like a whip. The greenhouses' empty frames gaped open, their interiors just scattered mud and broken plastic now.

Roberts had stared at the ruin, trying to understand it in the fading afternoon. The low sun took on a wet glow and the geodesics blurred together, the curves of stippled tiles and hexagonal panels becoming milky and diffuse. He leaned on his stick, trying to connect the desperation of the vandalism with what his son voluntarily gave to fight in a foreign war.

Finally he walked on, up the rise of the land and into the science building where Nimisha lives.

When Nimisha falls asleep again, he covers her bare shoulder with the Arabian rug she uses for a blanket. He scrubs the plates with lukewarm water then leaves them to drain in a sink. Struggling to stand after leaning over, he finds his walking stick and climbs the long steps down to ground level. The building is a scarecrow, its face built from broken glass and steel shutters. It wears a layered mask of new growth from the spot-welded solar panels and plyboarded windows. A radio broadcasts Radio 4 above him with the dry voice of the news.

A red-haired youth walks towards Roberts, his shoulders square inside a fraying cricket jumper. What looks like a child's unicycle dangles from his mottled fist. He raises that fist at Roberts as they pass. Roberts flinches, his walking stick up before his face. The youth laughs, showing missing teeth through a scraggly beard. "For Nimisha, a gift, old man." And he strolls by, skipping over the crackle of broken glass before the large doors. Roberts follows the curve of Prince of Wales Drive onto a peaceful perimeter road that's sprouted a central reservation of cracked concrete and wild grass.

He walks into town, towards the market he's already visited. The shopping district has shrunk, the real stores are long closed, but a squatter community occupies the shuttered shopfronts. He passes a Virgin phone shop, refitted as a diner with a counter lifted from a pub and stained with beer mugs.

Outside, a crowd of skinny-looking people stare in, dizzy with hunger. He smells tea, and onions frying, but the prices are astronomical. Frustrated, he walks away.

Sitting on a low wall is the same slender black woman he met on his first night here. He remembers her almond-shaped eyes, and now he can see a tattoo of entwined roses and thorns along her neck. Recognising Roberts, she introduces herself as Toto. Her boyfriend sitting beside her and smoking a joint is Mitch. The strength of the marijuana makes Roberts' head spin, fogging out the aroma of frying from the cafe.

"How's Nimisha doing? Heard she was ill," Toto asks.

He nods. "A little under the weather. You know her well?"

"We all know Nim and her war with *Phytophthora infestans.*" Toto pronounces the words casually, familiar with Latin terms. To Roberts' blank face she adds, "It means 'vexing plant destroyer.'"

It's a water mould, she tells him, that shoots spores on the wind.

Peering over his spindly sunglasses, Mitch adds, "Up to half a mile in some recorded instances," and he goes back to smoking his joint.

"You notice that all our potatoes now have purple spots on them?" Toto asks. "All that live long enough to harvest, that is. The Blight came about as an arms race between Mother Nature and us. Her water mould versus our pesticides. The more the Blight spread, splashing tomatoes and potatoes, the more we fought it. Last century we perfected our weapons. Arsenic paint, then DDT, then metalaxyl. But if we thought we were winning we were mistaken."

"The mould adapted?"

Toto smiles. "Bravo. Changing climate meant we had wet summers, ideal for the mould. We wiped a lot of it out, but you know what that did to the strains that didn't die, right?"

Roberts nods. "They came back stronger."

Toto smiles, her almond eyes creasing and pretty. "Those wet summers turned our potato plantings to slime and the survivor strains took hold."

"So Nimisha was trying to save the potato."

Mitch looks up as if waking to their conversation. "Nim got a new convert?" His eyebrows rise over his glasses.

Toto laughs. "Mitch thinks she's crazy. Still up on the campus, dreaming of greenhouses."

"What's crazy about that?" Roberts asks.

"Look around," Toto says. "We can't afford to eat more than once a day. We don't have jobs, so we can't earn. The Blight hit the northern nations, the north put pressure on the south for resources. The southern hemisphere pushed back. Our economies couldn't take the strain and we collapsed. We're the survivors of a slow-motion catastrophe." Toto takes a hit off her boyfriend's joint. "If Nimisha thinks she can solve any of that – *that's* what's crazy."

Times have been tough. He knows that, even secluded in the Lake District away from the panic.

"Nimisha stayed on at the university, long past her visa or work permit or any salary. She networked, making contact with Japanese biologists and a team out of UEA working on agriculture. Nim worked on Blight resistance without pesticides, stepping off the treadmill of the arms race."

"And what happened?" he asks.

"The usual. Funding ran out, her team split up. So her research stopped. Later, the scavengers raided. People with empty bellies wiped the greenhouses clean. Destroyed the incubators along the way by accident." She points laconically back towards the campus. "They gobbled up the potato seeds that might have saved them. All for a day's full stomach and scrap metal to hawk for food."

"That's hunger for you," Mitch says, trying to blow a smoke ring. Her sideways glance at Mitch is accusatory. Was he one of them?

"And you," Roberts says to Toto, thinking how she slipped into a classroom tone with him. "Did you work with Nimisha on her project?"

Toto smiles again. "I was her tutor on her PhD thesis."

"*Was*," Mitch says, sounding amused. "Now we have war instead of universities. We're not handing out Doctorates to people who look like Nimisha anymore. We're bombing them into the stone age."

A burst of grief threatens to break Roberts' resolve. The war snatched Daniel's life from him. He stands and nods, making excuses, masking his dismay. He walks back through the empty buildings to Pennsylvania Avenue and into a sirocco wind that blows grit into his eyes. His feet brush flattened paper cups and greasy wrappers. At the corner, a van offers soup kitchen food, put on by a vestige of the city council. The queue is long and patient, too exhausted for emotion.

Walking by, tap-tapping with his stick on the broken pavement, he's too shaken to queue with them.

"You're back," Nimisha says. She woke without him seeing. He was busy at the oven. The red-haired youth was telling the truth. He left the odd wheeled device with Nimisha. Wires connect it to the oven's socket. There is a community here, not just strangers. Balancing the uniwheel on its tripod stand, Roberts gives the handle an experimental turn. A bicycle chain ticks away, charging a battery. But there's no tea till he gets it to work.

"I went out to the town for a few things," he says, and smiles. He gets a smile back, if a little weak. "There's aspirin," he says. "Hopefully tea too, if I can get this thing to work."

He begins to spin the handles. They're converted peddles, poorly cut down for his hands. He wonders if he'll need gloves. His wrists soon ache.

Nimisha sits up, grunting.

"Do you feel any better?" he asks.

"A little. I'm hungry."

"That's a good sign."

Her eyes widen in surprise. "You're Daniel's father," Roberts nods stiffly and she says, "I'm so sorry. Daniel was my friend."

"I know. He often spoke of you." Roberts whirls the dynamo's handles. In the awkward silence, Nimisha says abruptly, "Leave that. Let me show you something."

He averts his eyes from her skinny legs as she struggles into a pair of pink combat trousers.

She leads him into the corridor and to his surprise, to a fold-down metal stepladder. The ladder's steps are rutted steel and splattered with paint. It wobbles as he climbs, looking up at her running shoes disappearing through a square hatch cut in the ceiling. Roberts has a vertiginous moment of doubt over how he'll get back down, then he follows her inside a loft and to the slanting wall of the pitched roof. She points to a window shaped like a dartboard. The concentric rings of glass are made of mismatched shades and textures. This is the eye of the building's patchwork face. He stares through glass bubbles that both magnify and blur the rear of the science block.

"I haven't shown this to anyone else," Nimisha says. "But Daniel would want you to see it."

Through the building's tear-flecked eye, he stares at rows of tubular greenhouses. Unlike those on the hill, these are pristine, the plastic walls taut and unscarred. Within them stand the dark, tall shapes of hydroponics bins, flowering with full crops. "Potatoes," Nimisha says, sounding satisfied.

"You've beaten the Blight?"

"The Blight," Nimisha says. "*Phytophthora infestans.* It's been killing our potatoes for centuries."

"And you've fought it? How is that possible?" he asks, marvelling at the stuffed, crowded greenhouses.

"*They* fought it. The plant is strong. Saved Europe once already, when it came from America and millions ate it. Now it's going to save us again. I just helped break the war with the mould. Instead of fighting the disease with pesticides I've bred the potato to resist it. These potatoes will feed us all."

"You did this?"

Nimisha smiles. "The Norwich team at UEA helped. And so did a group in Japan. But really it was the seeds that did it. These are Arab seeds. The Arab universities sent us a way to bring the potato back."

He peers through the window. Through its irregular glass, thick and bevelled, cheap and stained, he thinks he can see flowers. Five pointed, fat purple stars.

"The plant is back," she says, nodding at the blooms of the potatoes she's grown. "The plant is strong."

Black Shuck

Henry Gee

If there was anything on the mind of the bogtrotter, it kept such things to itself. First, because the bogtrotter wasn't very good at conversation. Second, because it was now a long way from anyone who would listen, even another bogtrotter. In any case, there was a job to do, a mystery to solve. There was something out in the far paddies, the Overseer had said. Something big. Something dangerous. Something only a bogtrotter could get a fix on.

"You're valuable property, so don't put yourself in too much danger," said the Overseer, a baseliner, crouching down on the warped decking of Wisbech Quay so it could look the bogtrotter and twenty or so of its fellows (all identical) in the eye. "Just find whatever this is, stick a GPS ranger on it, get home again. Once we've got it tagged we'll be able to see it on our scopes – and, well, we can take matters from there." Words unspoken – the Black Shuck, the supposedly semi-mythical beast of East Anglia. The Grim. But more likely something escaped from the experimental farms, something freaky that would have to be rounded up before the shareholders got wind of things.

And with that, two dozen small splashes as the bogtrotters dove off the quay and into the paddies that stretched as far as any eye could see in all directions under the broiling East Anglian sunshine.

Within minutes, the bogtrotter was alone.

Lost, but not lost, in a region of indeterminate land and air and water, the bogtrotter was in its element. Nothing else could navigate the vast brackish paddies of East Anglia that spread in an unbroken swathe from Lincolnshire well into Norfolk, and out to an ill-defined North Sea coastline where the gulls mewed, where the paddies finally faded out and met the windmills and stralmon ranches. That's where the bogtrotter was headed. Miles and miles of wading, swimming and burrowing, but all in a day's work for the bogtrotter. Nothing else would do. Motorboats got snagged in the rich vegetation that snarled a hand's-breadth below the waterline. Rowboats took too long, and the oars got caught up in the tall stalks of the rushes. Hovercraft could cope, but they caused too much noise, driving off the bitterns (a protected species) and flattening the crops – and frightening off the whatever-it-was out there that was causing all the problems. Chewing through power lines. Breaking into the stralmon ranches. Out of reach – but not to the bogtrotter.

Take a basic coypu. Nutria. Plague of the fens. Put it to good use, even after the fur farms packed up. Mix in some macacque, fold in some Jack Russell Terrier, drizzle with frog and platypus and dugong and season with a dozen other decoctions, from blue-green algae, a few select viruses, even a pinch of baseliner, and some dependable yeast and bacteria to sew the lot together. Steep in a proprietary mix of ExtraAmniotic fluid at a steady 37 degrees for three months, and decant. Perfect. The ideal rice-paddy worker. Loyal, dependable, intelligent, resourceful. Magus Pharm model CX-101D, otherwise known as the bogtrotter. Loves nothing better than sploshing around in the muck all day, as long as it has a sense of purpose. Sociable, but can work alone without distress. Can survive for days on sunlight alone. Send it out into the far fens where baseliners can no longer go. Get it to plant the rice, tend the plants as they grow, deal with pests and, as a bonus, herd and harvest any valuable fish and shrimp from the distant murk.

Out there in the deep fens, the far paddies, mysteries lay hidden. Even a semi-sentient cloned construct such as a bogtrotter had a mind, sort of, and got to wonder. To work things out. Usually based on insufficient information. That's the way mythologies are made. Cargo cults, at least. And if there was one thing the bogtrotters feared above all else, it was the legendary Black Shuck. Teeth like scythes. Writhing coils. One bite and – no more bogtrotter. Sure, reasoned its dog-and-monkey mind as the bogtrotter slooshed through the ooze, there's no such thing. Black Shuck! Phooey, it said, spitting out some pithy rice root, sifting a salty skein of alga through its ever-growing incisors. The rumour was probably just a blowback from bogtrotters scared out of their wits as they fled the threshing jaws of the automatic hover-combines, the immense machines the baseliners used to harvest the paddies when they were done.

For sure, the Overseer wouldn't send them on some wild errand to find a Black Shuck. Farmers had more concrete things to worry about, like the bottom line. Just find out what was ripping up the perimeter fencing, the Overseer had said, and, if possible, tag it. All things considered it was probably an escaped CY-70X, one of the experimental porpoise-otter-retriever fish-herders, still in alpha test and notoriously flighty. The bogtrotter had seen one before. Yes, it had been in the game a long time and was now – what – three years old? Maybe four? Bogtrotters didn't really do birthdays. But it was pretty sure everything it had ever seen in the fens had a rational explanation. Still, the fens were a big wide world and you never knew. Who could say what really went on in the empty heart of that great swamp? Whatever this was, only the bogtrotters would ever find out. And, being bogtrotters, they'd keep it to themselves.

Even with the single-mindedness of a bogtrotter, it took three days hard wading, swimming and paddling to get to the perimeter. On the first night out a storm blew up, a febrile summer squall, all noise and fury and big, overstuffed raindrops. The bogtrotter didn't mind the weather, but it holed up in the ruined belfry of a sunken church to keep its GPS gear dry, so it. Somewhere, in the mud, far below, was a village, maybe a small town, where baseliners had once lived, long ago, when this was all dry land. The lightning cracked and the rain pelted down on all sides, but the bogtrotter was dry and, plumping up its green fur, reasonably warm. It curled up amid the bat droppings in the remains of what might have been an avocet nest. The bogtrotter liked avocets. Pretty birds. Elegant. It didn't like swans, though. Too big, too fierce, and they got in the way of the sowing. Pity the avocets hadn't left any eggs behind for tea.

The next day was wreathed in fog, as the Sun sucked up the previous day's excess of moisture. The ruined belfry was an island in white nothingness. Not that this worried the bogtrotter in the slightest. It dove down into the mud and with unerring accuracy caught a catfish for breakfast. A bit bony. Tasted of mud. But, then, nearly everything tasted of mud, which didn't matter – mud was just about the only flavour the bogtrotter had ever tasted or knew how to appreciate. Except for salt.

Then it set off.

On the way, the bogtrotter did a spot-check of some of the rice. Looked like it was growing on schedule. This was the newish Etosha strain, supposedly good in brackish water near coasts. So far, so good. As the bogtrotter pushed northwards the rice got taller and more lush as the salinity increased. Soon the world had diminished to a vertical palette of stalks, the water cool, shadowed and silent beneath. The bogtrotter felt woozy in the still air, so it ducked underwater now and then to cool off.

Shafts of red-golden sunlight through the rice stalks signalled the approach of evening. The bogtrotter's pace began to slow and it decided to look for somewhere to camp for the night. By then, the occasional instances of dry land you might find in the near paddies had disappeared altogether – no ruins, not even the rusted wreck of an old-time power pylon rose above the paddies to give them scale. Still, there might be a raft of old reed stalks that would suit for a bivouac, and, as the sun began to set, the bogtrotter spotted just the thing – a platform of stems, leaves and other detritus that might once have been used by bitterns or herons, wedged in a stockade of robust stalks. The bogtrotter swam towards it, and, heaving the GPS pack onto the raft, dove down into the mud to look for something to eat.

Out here, in the far fens, it was as if the three states of air, water and land reached a kind of triple point where each state was equivalent to the other and none had dominance. The foggy mornings allowed little distinction between air and water. Now, in its evening dive, the bogtrotter found no bottom to the swamp, just the smoothest gradation between water above and mud beneath. Still, the bogtrotter kept going down, through grades of dirty water slowly congealing into a thin ooze and the softest mud, searching for the mud-mussels it knew were there.

These hybrids of sea mussels, freshwater mussels, oysters and giant clams, officially Magus Pharm model YZ-305, could reach the size of dinner plates, and were much prized by the baseliners, who farmed them for the restaurant table, where they fetched high prices. But the spawning was hard to control, and the giant shellfish had begun to colonise the mud of the far paddies. Only the bogtrotters knew this: a '305 could well repay a hard day's travel especially, as – unlike a baseliner gourmet – a bogtrotter could get them for free. Like a pearl diver, the bogtrotter set its course still downwards into the murk – it could hold its breath for half an hour, if needed. The brown, soupy broth of the water turned to velvet black as the bogtrotter heaved itself down into a kind of thin, clayey treacle. Probing downwards and forwards with its hands, it met a hard obstacle, distinctively rough to the touch. A '305 of some size. So great that the bogtrotter couldn't just pluck it from the gloop, but had to dig underneath to free it, and then work hard to get back to the surface somewhere above. Relaxing as the water carried it upwards with its prize, the bogtrotter saw the surface from beneath first as a yellowing amid the brown, and then, at the last, as light spangled on wavelets driven by the lightest breeze.

If not for the big '305 clutched to its chest, the bogtrotter would have died there and then, just as it broke surface. Even so, it was winded by the full-force impact of a heavy blow to the chest. Before it had time to grasp what was happening, the assailant drew back and reared above him – a hideous head on a serpentine body as thick as a baseliner's thigh, the eyeless face writhing with tentacles, and a pair of jaws, dripping with slime and fully fitted out with horny teeth, madly snapping from side to side. The head struck him again. The bogtrotter had the wit to use the '305 as a shield as the creature struck him again and again. As it struck, the apparition pushed him, by happy chance, towards the reedy raft. Any other direction and he'd have been lost. The bogtrotter scrambled onto the raft, just in time to parry another strike. This time the creature cut itself on the sharp edges of the '305's shell and, finding itself too far out of water, slithered back down into the depths. The bogtrotter, panting, shaking and terrified, had enough presence of mind to watch it go – a sinuous shape, maybe ten feet, maybe longer, winding back amid the stalks to nurse its wounds.

Bogtrotters are not given to brooding, so as soon as the thing was out of sight, it set to work cracking open '305, tearing and slurping at the glistening, pearly flesh inside. Only while chewing on the last of the meat did it ruminate on its recent lucky escape from the jaws of death. Was *that* the Black Shuck? It was terrifying enough. The problem was that very few ever escaped to describe the Black Shuck in any detail. Now full of food, the bogtrotter pulled some leaves over itself and, on the edge of sleep, reasoned that *whatever* that was, it looked a lot like a slime hag, though the bogtrotter had never heard of one growing so big. One to chalk up to experience. Tell the others. And who knows, maybe that was what was disturbing the perimeter fences. The bogtrotter was close enough to the fen's outer margin, now, so that was a possibility. And those teeth – well, yes, those teeth. And those jaws would make fine bolt cutters.

But what would make a slime hag so huge? Hags usually lived on dead and dying fish, and the stralmon in the ranches offshore – salmon-tuna-trout chimaeras grown to the size of dolphins – would be easy pickings. The bogtrotter would have thought some more, but exhaustion won out.

The third day dawned with the sharp ozone-scented tang of the sea. The bogtrotter squeezed itself awake and immediately became conscious of aches, pains and abrasions all over its body. Yesterday's lucky escape had not been without cost. The thought of the giant hag prompted the bogtrotter to leave immediately, so, sliding off its raft, it struck out northward towards the sea. Before long, the rice stalks started to thin, and it met waves – actual waves – pulling in from the sea.

And, all of a sudden, there it was, the perimeter. Thick, silvery pylons spaced maybe fifty meters apart, rising from pilings deep below and stretching far above, each topped with a wind turbine. Thick cables reached from one pylon to the next, fading into the distance on either side. Thick reinforced plastic webbing dropped from the lowest cables into the waves, weighted downwards. Beyond the fence, the stralmon ranches, and beyond them, the open sea. This was it, journeys end. Even from a distance the huge rents in the webbing were easy to see, and some of the cables had been cut. Freedom from tension had thrown them into tangled tendrils like weed. The bogtrotter could have kicked itself, certain now that the giant hag had done this damage, and it hadn't been quick enough to tag the creature with the GPS. To be sure, saving its own hide had come first, he'd be forgiven for that, but still, this was frustrating.

A little way over to the bogtrotter's right, to the eastward, a fair sized tarpaulin-covered rowboat bobbed in the gentle swell, tied with a painter to an iron ring in the concrete and barnacled base of the nearest pylon. That would provide a convenient base while it prepared for the return journey. A little bit of peace and some protection. It had started to shake, and felt feverish – symptoms of delayed shock. It lost no time in hefting itself aboard the boat, slipping under the tarp and sliding into a foetal position somewhere at the bottom.

The bogtrotter woke up to see several pairs of round, luminous eyes looking down at it; to feel the pawings of busy monkey hands; to hear the chatter of bogtrotter voices; to smell the thick and salty odour of green bogtrotter pelts. The bogtrotter felt and smelled rather than saw a hot tin mug full of broth as it was pushed into its hands. Fish soup. The gruel was revitalising, for all that it tasted of mud. As it came to, the bogtrotter realised that the boat was full of bogtrotters, and probably had been when it arrived. Late to the party. It was possible that all the bogtrotters that had left Wisbech Quay three days ago were now here – though, unable to count beyond six or seven, it couldn't be sure. But there were certainly a lot.

"Where've ya bin?" asked one. "Yeah! Where've ya bin?" others piped in chorus.

"Black Shuck ..." said the bogtrotter. "Saw it. Black Shuck. Last night." The other bogtrotters fell about cackling. "Yeah, and I'm a baseliner!" said one. "What'd 'e look like, then, eh?"

The bogtrotter laughed with its fellows. "For sure, it was a hag. But monster huge. Seen nuthin' like it, no never. Prob'ly come in from the fish ranches. Near bit my 'ead off. 'F I hadn't a '305 to protec' me..." The others fell serious, silent. "I'm thinkin'," it continued, emboldened, "Big Mister Hag cut them cables, did them damage. But I didn't tag it. Too busy not getting 'et. Mebbe we follow it, like a posse, track and tag it, workin' together, yeah?" More silence.

"Good job you found that hag," said another. "Good job you didn't get 'et. But weren't no hag cut those wires, holed that fence."

"No?" said the bogtrotter, mystified. "Then what did then, eh?" The next silence was even longer. The bogtrotter sensed rather than saw bodies shift in the salted gloom. A bogtrotter it hadn't seen before was pushed forwards from the back. This wasn't one of his clone-group. It had peeling white skin, rather than green fur. Its eyes were silted up with cataracts. It looked ancient, maybe seven years old, perhaps even eight.

"I did," said the old bogtrotter. "Welcome to the revolution." The bogtrotter was too stunned to speak. It thought it recognised the ancient creature – not as an individual, but as a type. This was, surely, one of the first of the beta models, a CX-101B, maybe even a CX-100. It had heard that the betas had been too wayward, too much Jack Russell or something, and some had gone rogue in the fens. The baseliners had tried to round them up for what they called 'repurposing', but there, that was the point. The baseliners had made the bogtrotters to be at home in the wide, swampy fens, so a few had, inevitably escaped. And survived. Long past their expiry date.

"You…"

"Yes, I am the Black Shuck," the creature said, in no more than a whisper. "I cut those cables. I ripped that fencing. I have struck the first blow."

"Blow? Wha'for, blow?" The bogtrotter felt, uncomfortably, the centre of attention, as if all eyes were on it, as if it were being tested.

"Why should them baseliners use us? Throw us away when they don't want us no more?" said the ancient beta. "We are thinking beings, every bit as them. We have minds. We have souls. We have *rights*."

"We have souls! We have rights!" the others chorused, for all the world as if they'd heard this before.

"They need us," said the old bogtrotter, warming to his theme. "They need us more than we need them."

"They need us! They need us!" the others cried. The bogtrotter chorus was beginning to jump up and down with excitement. The boat started to sway.

"The paddies, we plant, we sow, we tend, for *them*. But they kill us in the harvesters like we're nuthin'. We get no reward. It must stop!"

"It must stop! It must stop!"

"So, young bogtrotter, oppressed, exploited," said the pale wizened form, making its way to the front and putting both hands on the bogtrotter's shoulders. Its grip was amazingly strong. The old bogtrotter was using words it had never heard before. *Oppressed. Exploited*. It didn't know what they meant, but they sounded good. Full of purpose. And if bogtrotters liked one thing, it was a sense of purpose.

"So, young bogtrotter. Are you with us?"

The air hung heavy with expectation, thick with menace. The bogtrotter crouched amid the jostling bundle at the bottom of the boat on that wild, uncertain shore, paused on the threshold of decision.

A Season

Rebecca J Payne

There was a gap in the eastern hills, where Copper's Edge dipped sharply to cleave a hole in the horizon, and where, from the east-facing bedroom window of his childhood, he'd watch the sun rise in harvest season. As a naïve kid he'd searched online for old stories about places like Stonehenge and the Hurlers, ancient sites standing to the seasons; and he'd exhausted every theory of long-dead civilisations building monuments to catch the dawn's light or the alignment of the stars. And all through those hot summer weeks, when his father would send the noisy harvesters out to the fields to bring in the wheat, he'd rise in the dark early hours and keep vigil over the crimson glow as it rose through the fissure, imagining what ancient god must have built those hills in such a way to time the sunrise to the harvest, and how long ago; and now here he was, a young boy watching lost magic.

He didn't really go up to his old bedroom any more.

It was late on a Thursday night and Adam sat alone at the kitchen table. The farmhouse was quiet. Somewhere a clock ticked long, slow seconds.

A light on his tablet flashed red, on and off, on and off. Red meant the alert would go to Comms, and he'd have no choice but to log it on the system. He put down his beer and flicked the tablet on.

Soil mineral report: field west four nine nine. Phosphorous – good. Potassium – good. pH level – 5.9. Authorise lime spreading recommended at 0.4kg per square metre.

He tabbed to the page of available machinery on site, selected the chemstation and instructed a morning spray for the field. Archer's field, he recalled his grandfather telling him. It was easy to forget the fields had names once.

The red ticket was still open. He closed the alert with Comms. There was nothing more to do now but wait. Wait, or go out.

By the front door sat an unopened letter with a FarmFresh logo. Adam threw it into the waste paper basket on his way out.

"Then Max comes back in, half-covered in mud with a shovel in his hand, and little Danny just stares at him and starts screaming, like his dad's been slimed by some monster from a CBeebies show."

Graham was telling stories about his half-brother Max and his kids again. Their antics had kept the Rose and Crown regulars amused for many a cold night.

"So then Nancy says, 'it's fine, Danny, it's just mud is all' and Dan, he won't stop yelling and crying. I honestly thought I was going to wet myself laughing."

Adam swirled the remnants of his beer around in his pint glass. "Graham, tell us the one about the swings and the badger again."

The rest of the guys started laughing before Graham had even begun. Adam looked around the snug, taking in the faux-antique brass and old metal beer adverts. Outside the window the beer garden lay cold and silent. He took his leave of the story and went to the bar.

"Hey," he said quietly, placing his empty glass on the bar. Tara smiled.

"Same again?"

"Sure." He watched the dark amber beer slowly filling the glass.

"Bad day? You don't seem to be catching the spirit." She glanced over to where the boys were laughing and joking.

"Same day as always," he said. "You?"

She passed him a full pint glass. "Same day as always."

Winter days grew shorter and interchangeable. Adam sat in his study from dawn to dusk, tracking the hired seed drillers as their little icons moved across the satellite maps of the land. When the seed drillers moved on to some other farm he tracked the ploughs and the auto-fertilisers from their GPS signals. Once in a while he would glance outside and catch a glimpse of a machine moving silently in the distance.

On the wall behind the computer screen there was an old photograph that his mother had once hung, a faded picture of his grandparents and great-grandparents standing under the ash tree that had stood in the farmhouse garden for two hundred years until the dieback deaths had reached their land. As the icons on his screen danced back and forth across the maps he found himself examining the picture for hours; how strange it seemed now that a photograph should fade, or that it was caught by a strip of film exposed to the light for the briefest of moments before being shut away again. It didn't seem fair.

In late November a Rep from the seedhouse visited.

"How is everything coming along?" The Rep stirred his tea but didn't drink.

"Good, I think," Adam said. "We've had no flooding, no snow... this is our third year without shoot-rot, so I think we're winning the battle."

The Rep turned his tablet around to face Adam. "That's great. If you're already thinking about next season, we have an excellent new genetic line. It's resistant to all strains of shoot-rot classified in Europe as of August this year, and is showing excellent milling and flour performance."

"I think I'm just going to see how things go."

"I can do you an excellent double-deal with fertiliser supplies."

"The storms we had last January, the late snow... I'm trying not to think that far ahead any more."

The Rep's smile soured.

"I understand. Please, give me a call if you change your mind, won't you?"

No, Adam wanted to say. *No, I probably won't.*

Tara cajoled him into going to the local historic society's exhibition at Cotton Hall .They would theme their annual displays of old pictures and documents from eras gone by. Adam had witnessed enough exhibits like *Land Girls of Asprey* and *Combine Revolution* to last him a long lifetime.

They stood together in the hall and he tried to take in the delights of this year's offering, *2000! A Millennium Celebration*. At least the pictures were in colour. Smiling faces of happy men and women beamed out at him from still images of clichéd rural scenes – a couple watching a dairy herd emerging from their winter barn; a farmer on a manual-drive tractor; a child gazing up at an ominous scarecrow adorned with an ironic top hat.

Tara was engrossed in a picture hanging in the far corner. "Adam, isn't this your dad?"

Adam approached the image. It *was* his father, and a family friend whose name he couldn't recall, hauling an old-fashioned wagon filled with straw bales up a road that looked like Howell's Lane before the dry stone walls had been knocked down. Beneath the image was a caption: *Fuel protests lead to desperate measures for our local boys.*

"He looks like Hercules pushing that thing," Tara said.

Adam stared at his father's tanned and youthful face. It wasn't how he remembered him now.

"I don't think I could even push an empty one," he said.

The farmhouse was too large. As a boy he'd found it so small, preferring to be out on the land with his grandfather, climbing the eastern hills, watching his father work from a distance. The house had been suffocating back then. But living alone now, he felt like a captain of a huge ship without a crew; unable to steer or raise the sails or map out a course without help. He'd sleep in his parents' old bedroom and feel the rock of vast oceans beneath him in his dreams.

By early December the Christmas lights had begun to appear on the usual rooftops of houses in nearby villages. The twinkling bulbs of blue and green left Adam cold as he drove home from the hypermarket. Flurries of snow had been dancing in the air on and off for days and now the flakes fell heavy against the car windows, as though the whole world were a snowglobe, and he was trapped at the centre inside an even smaller glass shell. As he stared at the fields turning a uniform shade of white in the darkness, the self-drive sensors projected hazard signs onto his windscreen. The car speakers turned themselves on.

"Black ice detection. Safe stopping engaged." The car's safety system spoke with a soothing, comfortable voice. The steering wheel moved slowly as the car drifted to the left and pulled into a passing place at the side of the road. Adam tried to restart the engine to turn on manual driving but the hazard signs flashed again.

"Unsafe driving conditions. Unsafe driving conditions."

He looked up and down the road for any sign of help – a lift, the house of anyone he knew. He tried to imagine where he was on the road but the satnav flashed nothing but warning signs and the fields around were unvarying and endless.

"Unsafe driving conditions. Unsa-"

Adam pulled the key from the dashboard, got out, and started to walk.

The snow filled his vision as he followed the road. He had no hat, no gloves. In dark clothing and without a torch he began to imagine someone knocking him down right there on the road, leaving him lying in a storm ditch, crumpled and frozen.

He walked until he lost any concept of time. As a boy he would have known every road for miles around, but everything looked different now. It could have been the darkness, or the blankets of snow, that made the land so unfamiliar; but deep down he felt a gnawing sensation that there should have been landmarks of trees and hedgerows, wildflowers and allotments, vague memories of his childhood that were slipping away.

Up ahead he saw the lights and the welcome sight of the Rose and Crown. He didn't think he'd been that close to Asprey village– but when he turned back to see his car the visible road was empty, and he wondered how long he'd been walking.

He pushed on the pub door but it wouldn't budge. He hammered his numb fists onto the wood until someone answered.

"I'm sorry, we've just shut for the night."

"Tara? It's me. It's Adam. I'm sorry, but my car – my car shut down in the snow and I can't – I can't get home."

He heard keys turning in locks and the door swung open.

"My God, Adam. What's wrong with you? You'll catch your death."

She put her arm around his shoulder and ushered him inside. The sudden heat from the fireplace hurt his skin and he shivered.

"I'm so sorry, damn thing just pulled over, and I couldn't reboot it."

"Where is it now?"

Adam stared at the Christmas tree by the snug, hung with sparkling golden lights and old wooden ornaments. "Somewhere down towards the main road – I don't know."

There was movement behind the bar as a grey-haired woman appeared through the door to the tap room.

"I thought we'd shifted the last of you for this evening," she said, pausing to scrutinise his face. She smiled. "Well I'll be damned. You're Michael and Hannah's boy, aren't you?"

"Hello, Mrs Whitelee," he said. "Good to see you again."

The three of them sat around the kitchen table in the living quarters. Tara made her mother a hot toddy of whiskey, warm water and honey. Adam turned down the offer of one.

"I hoped I could get back to my car," he said.

"Nonsense! You'll stay here, won't he, Tara?" Mrs Whitelee nodded approvingly to herself. "We'll set up the air bed in the bar, you'll be right 'til morning. Then we'll see about your car. So go ahead and make him that drink, dear, and we'll forget any nonsense about going out on a night like this."

Adam glanced guiltily at Tara, who laughed gently, as if she had long since given up arguing with her mum.

They talked into the night – or rather, Mrs Whitelee talked, and they listened to her old stories of the village. She seemed to have been to every wedding, every funeral, every christening for the last sixty years.

"I remember yours especially," she told Adam. "Your poor parents had all but given up hope of a baby when you stumbled along."

"Mum! You can't say things like that!"

"Oh nonsense. He's an only child, a late child, he's probably guessed as much. But they were so happy to have finally been blessed. Someone to take over the farm, that's all your dad ever talked about. Not like half the lot around here. Selling up to the FarmCos first chance they get. You know they flattened all the stables out by Langley Green? I used to go riding there as a girl. It'll all sugar beet now." She raised her glass up in a toast. "*And Crossberry Way and Old Round Oak's narrow lane, with its hollow trees like pulpits, I shall never see again.* That was one of your grandfather's favourites. God rest him."

The fire in the wood-burning stove began to break down to a smoulder, casting long shadows across the floor.

On Christmas Day Adam turned off the Comms link and shut his tablet away in a desk drawer. A blanket of thick snow still covered the fields. For just one day, he didn't want to know what the soil temperature was, or how behind he was on his fertiliser payments. He hung a sprig of holly over the television and stirred honey into his morning porridge. Sitting by the kitchen window he watched birds flying over Copper's Edge, searching for food to see them through the cold winter months.

That afternoon he tuned his father's old DAB radio to listen to Carols from Kings, just as they had done when he was a child, and he pulled half a dozen dusty boxes down from the attic. As the sweet music filled the house he sifted his way through old school certificates, his grandmother's county medals for cross country running, shells from summer trips to the seaside at Hunstanton. An old photograph showed his father in the early dawn light framed by the farmhouse door with his boots in his hand, and he imagined his mother taking the picture as the cool morning air flowed in.

There was a hardback book with his great-great-grandmother's name inked inside the cover, and corners turned over on pages for recipes to use in winter, with names like *How to draw the True Spirit of Roses* and *How to make Sirrup of Violets and Gilliflower Wine*. Underneath a stack of childhood paintings he could barely recall making, never mind recall his parents keeping, was his grandfather's well-thumbed copy of *John Clare – Selected Poems*. He spent the evening by the fireplace, wrapped up in beechen woods and sun-cracked furrows, the geography of a childhood rendered irrecoverable by the march of progress and time.

The snow had melted by the New Year. Adam tried Comms for every local plant hire for miles around, but there wasn't a single slurry spreader available for quick hire. Every farmer was anxious to catch the fields while they were dry and firm, and the FarmCos always had priority contracts. Adam was passed from branch to branch before he gave up, unwilling and unable to pay to hire machines from two hundred miles away, or to wait until February when the weather might have turned.

In an old cattle barn, used only for storage now, there was an early model of a self-drive spreader his parents had purchased in better times. It was worth nothing more now than the value of the metal but he had always found a reason not to scrap something that had once seemed so exciting. Adam pulled away the sheets that covered the machine, sending dust swirling up in the musty air of the barn. It looked as if it might run at a pinch.

The GPS still worked and the engine spluttered to life on the second time of asking. Adam followed tentatively as it made its way out of the barn, down the track towards the concrete slurry pits. In his grandfather's time the pits had been filled with manure from their own cows but livestock had only ever brought his parents debt and unhappiness. Now it was merely artificial biomass slurry mixed in with his own unusable hay and whatever other waste matter the farm could spare. The place still smelled as bad as it had ever done.

The day was promised cool and dry on every channel. He set the machine off to the western fields where Comms showed the soil was most in need. Unable to trace such an old machine on his tablet, he followed in its tracks, listening to birdsong against the light hum of the engine. Once it had sprayed the first two fields without assistance, and Adam's legs grew weary, he returned to the house.

On the front doormat lay a letter from FarmFresh. He threw it unopened into the waste paper basket and, suddenly tired and cold, went back to bed.

By the time he woke it was dark and the sound of pounding rain on his window made him consider that he was still asleep, still dreaming of John Clare watching the roaring floods at Lolham Brigs, all boiling fury, uncontrollable and terrifying.

A yellow weather-warning light flashed on and off on the tablet by his bed. There had been no rain predicted on any forecast that morning.

Remembering now the old spreader sent out into the fields, Adam pulled on his warmest clothes, gloves and boots and searched for his torch. From the kitchen window he could just make out the silhouette shape of the machine in the southern fields, unmoving, stranded like cattle in sinking mud. He took a deep breath and ventured out into the storm.

So much rain had fallen that the ditches which ran along the southern edge of the fields had flooded and tracks beside them turned to quagmires. The spreader's rear wheels had sunk down into the boggy ground while its front wheels continued to turn, pitifully trying to drag its heavy body up out of the mud. Rainwater collected in its old-fashioned open tanks and the biomass slurry diluted and overflowed, coating the sides of the spreader and washing away. Adam stood and stared at the sight as rain pounded down. He wanted to blame the forecasters, the plant hires, the FarmCos, anyone at all. But still the wheels ground down into the mud and still the machine sank deeper like a helpless animal until Adam couldn't bear the moment any longer.

He fetched wooden planks from the garage, left over from renovating the farmhouse loft. These he jammed into the mud at an angle in front of the sinking rear wheels. Then he stood at the back of the machine and pushed, digging his heels into the slippery ground as best he could, and he pushed and pushed, swearing and slipping, water running down his neck like a river, still he pushed, cursing anyone who ever tilled a wheat field or baked a loaf of bread, cursing his parents for leaving him alone so soon, cursing himself and his own cowardice, still he pushed, until every muscle in his body threatened revolution against his will, and still he pushed, and pushed, until he felt the friction of the tyres catch upon something solid and real and the whole body of the machine lurched forward, free at last.

The machine safely in the barn once again, Adam showered, and slept peacefully.

February was kind and mild, and the fields dried out from the New Year storms. By mid-March the frosts had passed early and the wheat had reached green-up time. Forecasts of warmer weather played out on every data channel. Adam occasionally checked his sensors for the warning signs of pink snow mould or heaving, but on days when the rented spreaders came to apply the spring nitrogen he would find himself walking out into the sunshine and watching the machines up close, moving casually up and down the fields. For hours he pored over the sight of row after row of bushy green plants, their wheat crowns lurking just beneath the surface, promising so much for the harvest season still to come. Yet memories of the flooding of past summers would not leave him. By sunset he would retreat to his study and watch the water level readings of nearby streams flicker on his tablet screen like darting sprites.

The beer garden of the Rose and Crown grew busy. The sun seemed to have brought the people of the surrounding villages out of their homes from winter hibernation, and children with the energy of flycatchers and swifts ran in circles around a garden green with fresh grass. Flowering bushes gave nectar and shelter to bees whose humming acted like an audible backdrop of spring. The colour and movement was so at odds with the predictable symmetry of his wheat fields that Adam started to go there almost every day, whether his friends were there or not.

"People will start to talk, you know," Tara said, settling down next to him at one of the wooden tables scattered around the expanse of grass.

"About me?"

"About us." Tara smiled, and Adam felt his stomach leap with surprise, or fear, or happiness. Some construct of the three, he supposed, however unaccustomed he was to the emotion.

"Oh. Is that bad?"

Tara simply laughed and held his hand.

Spring showers were light and warm. Adam often went walking in the fields to feel the gentle rain falling and breathe in the earthy smells of the land. He climbed the steeper slopes of Copper's Edge for the first time in years and sat watching the machines top-dressing his south-facing wheat below, and drilling new sugar beet to the east; while in the skies above he saw chiffchafs, yellow wagtails and blackcaps returning home from their winter migrations. Days grew longer and each seemed to bring new arrivals, new growth, a new colour to the pallet of his world.

One morning a man from FarmFresh knocked on his door.

"Have you had time to consider our offer?" He was so shiny, Adam observed, from the gel in his hair to the patent leather of his shoes. "We believe it's very generous, especially in the current climate."

Adam reached for the unopened letters piled up in the bin and handed them back.

On May Day he sat with Tara at the top of Copper's Edge hill.

"My mum and dad find it funny, you and me together," she said.

Adam kicked dust from his new walking boots. "Funny? Why?"

"It's not you – they love you. It's me that makes them laugh. I had this old paper atlas when I was a kid. It was so out of date – borders in the wrong place, countries with the wrong names – and I used to pretend that I was going to go and live in all these places, and have wild adventures. And yet there you were, all that time, a mile down the road from me."

Adam stood up and walked to the edge of the crack in the hill, where the ground dropped away sharply like a wound.

"In August," he said, "we should come here at sunrise. At harvest time you can watch the light shine through the hill while the rest of the sky is still dark." He looked at Tara, who was watching a pair of swallows circling high above. "My mum and dad would have loved you, too, I know," he said.

The Last Star

A Parable of the End of Days

Nigel Edwards

Goosegirl broke the lamb's legs by placing a foot on them one at a time, taking a firm handhold then pulling, sharply. One, two, three, four. The animal had stopped bleating so she figured it was probably dead. Four years after first being introduced to the necessity of such things, the work no longer made her sick.

A few well-practiced slices with the blade she always kept so sharp it could cut through butter – whatever that was; something the Olders talked about when they reminisced, along with chocolate, paraffin, and sugar. Goosegirl figured butter must have been really hard and tough to crack, even though Great Gramps said he used to eat it. She assumed they must have had really strong teeth.

Now the woolly coat was almost ready to be stripped from the flesh. One long, circular stroke to separate the body skin from the head skin and then...

"Baa!"

Goosegirl looked up. Another lamb was standing pathetically in the straw, wondering where its mother was, where the next meal of warm milk would come from.

"She ain't around no more," Goosegirl said. "Storm done for her, just like for this one. But don't you worry. You'll soon be dressed extra warm for your new momma."

Nearby, a ewe tethered to a stanchion started bleating, calling for her own lost newborn. Could she smell the blood, Goosegirl wondered? Did she recognize the scent of her offspring? Or was she unaware that her baby was close, dead, ready to be divested of its dermal layers?

"You need a lambkin to love," Goosegirl told her as she ripped the fleece free of the raw carcass and quickly dressed the orphan.

"There. Maybe you ain't so pretty with all those bloody smears, but your new momma will take to you, I promise." She shepherded the lamb across the floor to where the prospective foster parent was waiting, then watched while the bond formed, the youngster beginning to suckle. Orphans didn't survive long on their own out in the pastures, not in the harsh, late winter. This one was lucky that its own mother had been valuable prime stock, and had therefore been tracked by Manager, the Farm's overseer, who'd directed the rescue.

After cleaning and sheathing the knife, Goosegirl collected up her bulky, one-piece fur-lined weatherproofs and clambered inside. She pulled the fresh meat in with her; that would help keep the smell of blood out of the wind – no sense in attracting hunters on the trek back to the house. A balaclava with attached snow-goggles was next, and then the hood and muffler. Moving around with all that gear on wasn't easy, but this was essential preparation before stepping outside. With a final glance towards the new 'family' she opened the barn doors.

The blizzard howled in.

When Goosegirl got back home all the Middlers and Olders were in the big Family kitchen. Momma and Poppa would be doing some essential work elsewhere.

"That'll do nice enough for some eating," Grandma remarked when Goosegirl presented the meat. "I'll get this butchered while you get yourself a shower, young lady. Don't want you smelling like that when there's visitors," she added as she disappeared into the adjoining larder.

"Visitors? What, today?" Goosegirl stopped in mid-strip, instantly curious and exited at the news. She didn't recall there ever being visitors before.

"S'right," Gramps chimed in. "Well, visitor, point of fact. First in twenty year or more."

"And last for another twenty if you don't get that stink washed away," Great Grandma pointed out. "Go on. Get it done."

Visitors! At least, a visitor. Goosegirl only knew people on the Farm. Many more than that if you counted the Nulls, of course, but she probably shouldn't. No one else in the Family was especially keen to speak of them, not often, at any rate. And the fuss they'd made when she'd first told about her new 'friends'. . .

"Friends?" Great Gramps had asked. "What 'friends'?"

"Just friends." The answer was as simple as the question, both of which seemed perfectly reasonable to a five year old.

"Where do you see them?" Momma had wanted to know. "When? How many?"

"Whenever they're there," she'd replied. "I don't know. Lots. Haven't you ever seen them?"

Turned out nobody else could see them, which made Goosegirl feel rather special. She remembered the Family talking. She was in the same room though they spoke as if she wasn't. But then, that was just the way grown-ups talked, and to a five year old it didn't matter.

"What d'you think?" Poppa'd had an odd look on his face, kind of excited but kind of scared at the same time.

Momma had just looked like she was trying not to look worried. "I don't know. They could be Nulls."

"It's all right," Goosegirl had chimed in, "they're very nice." It didn't seem anyone was listening, so she went back to playing.

"If you ask me," Great Grandma'd said, "it's too early to tell. Best we wait, see what turns up. A great thing, patience, you know."

"But maybe we should tell someone?" Gramps suggested.

"Ain't no need. Manager will already know. Reckon he'll tell anyone else that needs to know. Probably already did."

"Yep," Great Gramps agreed. "Manager'll take care of it. Best just to wait."

Then everyone nodded wisely, and that was the way things remained.

Now there was going to be another, proper person to know! A man, or a woman? At that moment it didn't matter. Goosegirl dashed to the back of the house and into the shower-room, discarding the remainder of her clothes along her path. Moments later she was surrounded by steam from the hot water jetting out from the plumbing.

Normally this was a luxury she'd linger with for as long as she could, a fortnightly indulgence. She knew that the rest of the Family rationed their own washing time, saving some of their water in order that she could enjoy the pleasure of tingling skin for that little bit longer. She didn't consider this an especial kindness; that was just what adults did. But today there was a reason to cut the ablutions short. There was to be a visitor. A visitor!

In less than half the normal amount of time it took she was back in the kitchen dressed in her fatigues, rubbing vigorously with a coarse towel to complete the drying process.

"Has he come yet?" she asked, eagerly.

"Ain't said 'he'," Gramps told her.

"She then!"

"Didn't say that, neither."

"Well, which?"

"Wait and see, girl," Grandma said, returning with some of the fresh meat ready for the pot.

"Why is he coming?" Goosegirl wanted to know. Somehow she felt certain the visitor would be a 'he'. "Is he going to live here?"

Great Gramps took out an ancient pipe that had been in the Family for stax of generations, and chewed on the stem. There was no tobacco, of course – that was one of those legendary things the Olders talked about. In fact, there'd been no tobacco for so long, Great Gramps claimed, he'd never known anyone who'd actually tasted the stuff, and neither had his own Great Gramps. But he said the firmness of the stem clamped between his teeth, and the roundedness of the bowl in his hand, made him feel complete.

"If they were going to live here," he pointed out, still refusing to confirm the gender of the prospective caller, "then they wouldn't be visitors, would they?"

"He might," Goosegirl challenged, equally determined about her own preconception. "He might if he was going stay for a bit but not, like, forever. Where's he coming from?"

"Maybe you can ask when he or she gets here," Grandma told her, cutting up some kale that she dropped into the tureen of boiling water that already contained the diced chunks of lamb. "Which should be in about an hour, according to Manager."

"But how's he going to get here?" Goosegirl wanted to know. "Road's shut. Poppa said it won't be open for at least a month."

"That's right enough," Great Gramps agreed. "Still a month before the thaw. Mind, sometimes thaw don't come at all. I remember one year where the road never got open! That was a cold 'un."

"Won't be like that this year," Great Grandma considered.

"There's been no omens about a long spell. I reckon the road'll be open just like your Poppa said."

"But it's not open right now," Goosegirl insisted. "So how's he getting here?"

Grandma shrugged. "Who knows? Outsiders have their own ways."

Clearly the Olders were determined not to be helpful. Frustration beginning to boil inside, Goosegirl treated them to a dramatic sigh then headed for her own room.

Not knowing exactly who was going to call, Goosegirl found it difficult to decide what to wear. She only had three outfits altogether, not counting the outside gear. She had Fatigues for daily use: tough britches and a smock top, both of which could stand up to the rigors of her chores. No way did she want any visitor seeing her in those. Then there was the Appreciation dress, the one Poppa and Momma insisted she wore every seventh day for the Gratitude. That was when the Family expressed their appreciation for everything they had. Goosegirl had never understood this. Firstly, there was only the Family around, so who were they supposed to be expressing this to? And secondly, what 'everything they had'? There wasn't anything. Just the Farm and hard work. Why would anybody want to say 'thanks' for that?

Lastly there was the Occasion gown. The only time she ever wore that was once a year, when Momma and Grandma would take her measurements, see what alterations needed doing, make stupid remarks about how much she'd grown since the last time (like she'd have done anything other than grow?) and then pack the dress away again. They said it was a dress for special events but there never were any special events, so what was the point?

"Manager," she called out, surveying her entire wardrobe arrayed before her on the bed, "what do you think I should wear? Is this visitor a special event?"

"Special is a word that defines something out of the ordinary, often with pleasant connotations." The reply came from somewhere in the walls, though exactly from where was difficult to pinpoint.

"That's not an answer! Come on, give me some advice."

Manager sighed. Goosegirl thought of it as a sigh, though it had a definite mechanical quality.

"Yes, then. A visitor might well constitute a special event."

"So the Occasion gown would be okay?"

"I don't think I'm best qualified to offer recommendations on that sort of thing. Wouldn't you prefer to take advice from Poppa or Momma? Or the Olders?"

"No, I asked you. Now give me an answer."

Another sigh. "Against my better judgment, then. Yes, this event would probably merit wearing the Occasion gown."

"I knew it would!"

"So why did you ask me?"

Goosegirl ignored the question, focusing her attention instead on the clothes.

In the cellar beneath the house was a door leading to the Vault. That was where the ancient and precious things were stored. There was supposed to be at least one of every treasure that had ever been, including something called a 'magazine'. Not the magazines that Poppa and Gramps used with their gun when they went hunting; no, this was a collection of glossy pages covered with pictures. Momma had shown them to Goosegirl a few times. Each page was laminated, sealed so you couldn't actually touch them, and the whole thing was kept in absolute darkness. Momma'd made her put on special goggles before bathing the delicate leaves in an equally special light.

Goosegirl recalled the pictures vividly. There were words too, although she couldn't read them; nobody in the Family could. But the pictures... Mainly they were of tall women with some weird growth coming out of their heads. Momma said it was called 'hair', a bit like the wool they got from sheep, only different. The amazing stuff grew right out of their heads, and apparently could be all sorts of colors; but in the artificial light pretty much all you could distinguish was a difference in shade, along with the extravagant shapes into which it had been fashioned. That was the word: fashion. Momma'd said it was a 'fashion magazine', images of clothes that had been worn stax ago.

"Just think! All those different kinds of dresses and skirts, and blouses and shoes, and a heap of other things that those great ladies and gentlemen had to wear."

Goosegirl had wanted to know what had happened to them.

"They all became stars, of course."

There were many additional treasures besides the magazine in the

Vault.

"Why are they all here, Momma?"

"They have to be somewhere, honey."

"Why?"

"For the future."

"But why?"

"Ask Poppa. He's better at explaining such things."

So she'd asked Poppa, but he didn't seem to know much more than Momma, and Goosegirl's questions remained unanswered.

She slipped into the Occasion gown, magazine pictures floating in her mind. What colors would those clothes have been? Would they have worn well, like her Fatigues? Or itched like the throat-constricting Appreciation dress? She recalled another word: pretty. Other Family members had told her she was pretty. She ordered the wall to make a mirror, and then looked at herself. The gown was a delicate cornflower blue with silver flecks and a bow at the back. That was pretty. But herself? She imagined a magazine woman with flamboyant hair standing beside her. Compared with that picture, Goosegirl was depressingly convinced she was nowhere close.

But they were stax of years ago, she consoled herself. They ain't around now. She smoothed the gown's material as flat as she could. Some of the creases lingered, but she'd have to put up with them.

I wonder how tall they were, really.

She dismissed the mirror. "Stax ago," she repeated, quietly.

The visitor sat in one of the two best chairs in the kitchen, the ones that only the Olders used, high-backed, properly upholstered, and closest to the range. For some reason Goosegirl was allowed to sit in the other. The whole Family was there but nobody else was seated, not even the Olders. There was a peculiar atmosphere, like you sometimes got before summer thunder. Sort of expectant, Goosegirl thought. Who is he?

There was silence for a while, or as close as you ever got inside the house. The range crackled as its heat radiated; the stew in the pot simmered; the walls ticked as Manager did his thinking. And the stranger just sat there, smiling politely and sipping from a mug of hot broth. The Family waited, expectantly.

"This is good broth," he said.

Momma curtsied. "We're proud you like it," she said.

Proud? What an odd word to use, Goosegirl thought.

"Poppa has some spirit laid down from last summer, if you'd care to try," Momma continued.

"The broth is fine," the visitor reassured her. "And what is the girl's name?"

Poppa answered automatically. "Goosegirl, sir."

Goosegirl sensed his gaze but focused her own at the floor. She wanted to stare boldly at him, present a confident front; but there was something unnerving about meeting a stranger, someone from outside the Family. Why had he come, dressed in clothing finer than anything she'd ever seen outside the magazine?

"What a unique epithet."

Gramps scratched his chin. "That'd be my doing, sir. When she was born the first living things I saw when I was told the news was the geese I was feeding, so I called her goose-girl and, well, it just sort of stuck."

"She has another, sir," Grandma hastened. "Circadia, sir."

"Circadia."

"Yes sir. After my own Older."

"Another unusual name... fitting, though. Tell me, Circadia. How old are you now?"

"Fourteen." She was shocked at how timid she sounded. Determinedly she lifted her head and forced out more decibels. "And three months."

"Fourteen," he repeated.

"And three months."

"And, as you say, three months. I am the Representative," he told her. Before Goosegirl could ask him what that meant he posed another question of his own, one that came as something of a surprise. "Do you know where you are, Circadia?"

What in the world was that supposed to mean? "'Course! The Farm."

"And do you know the purpose of the Farm?"

Now that she'd found her voice, looking at the visitor was easier. Tall, even sitting down, and with a straight back. His head was decorated with swirling patterns in blue and black, reminding her of the hair she'd seen in the magazine. Maybe that's what it was supposed to represent, but being just painted onto his skin there wasn't really any comparison. "What do you mean?" she asked.

The man rose. He was really tall. "Once upon a time, everywhere was filled with everything you can imagine. In fact, everywhere was filled even more with everything you can't imagine. Some is still around. Most isn't, but what there is, we keep in the Vault. That's what the Nulls said we should do. You know about them?"

Goosegirl shrugged. "A bit."

"You know that people became stars, yes? Well, to begin with there were no people. Or stars, or Nulls. Then there were people, and when a person stopped being alive they became a star; but still there were no Nulls. Then suddenly, a long time ago, things changed: the stars began to die."

Goosegirl dug into her memory. Nulls. Stars. Gigantic balls of fire that floated in the night sky. She'd only ever seen Big Glow during the day. I guess that looks like a ball. But otherwise, there was nothing else, night or day. Just sky.

"You might ask what happens to the people who stop being alive now," Representative continued, "but honestly we just don't know. We do know that as the stars died the Nulls began to appear. Most folk couldn't see them. Only a few had the gift: the Heedful. They could speak with the Nulls, learn from them. The Nulls gave them knowledge and wisdom from way back in time. Way back. As far back, they said, as a time when there were numbers bigger than stax."

That didn't make sense. How could there be more than stax? Everyone knew that you could only count to stax, that numbers stopped when you got that far 'cos there wasn't any point in counting any further. Stax was as big as you needed it to be. Goosegirl thought about pointing this out but the visitor didn't give her the opportunity.

"The Heedful learned that the Nulls used to be stars. They asked questions: why were the Nulls no longer stars? Would anybody ever get to be a star again? But the Nulls couldn't or wouldn't tell them.

"After a while, the Heedful stopped seeing the Nulls. Some said this was because the Nulls had gone away, maybe even gone back so they could be stars again — but if that was so there should have been stars once more, only there weren't. Others said it was because the Heedful themselves were dying out, so there was fewer people left who could see the Nulls. Certainly that was true. Eventually a time came when there remained only one of the Heedful. She was herself as old as any person ever got to be, but before she died she left a message. That message, Circadia, is even now in the Vault beneath your Farm. I think we should go take a look."

The Vault was very big, Goosegirl knew that. As they all descended, Great Gramps said it went on for stax, and that no one had ever been from one end to the other. Goosegirl had heard this before and was as dubious, now, as she ever was.

"Momma told me the Vault was filled with stuff," she contributed, "so that means somebody must have been to the end sometime, even if it was just to take stuff down there."

"Your Momma is right and so is your Older," Representative said. "The Vault isn't just here, you know. It's elsewhere, too. Your Farm is just one of stax of others, each with an entrance into the Vault. To say that nobody ever went from one end to the other is probably true because there's never been any need. The furthest anybody's ever had to go is halfway."

I suppose that makes sense, Goosegirl rationalized.

Everything in the Vault was packed into containers, most of which, judging from the layers of dust, hadn't been opened since the day they were sealed. Goosegirl had seen inside a few on her visits with Momma or Poppa, but she'd never been allowed down there on her own so exploration had been limited. Now, as they trudged past, she voiced her curiosity as to what the variety of containers, capsules and reliquaries might hold.

"The Heedful decreed that a Vault should be built, and that everything that could be found should be placed inside," Representative said. "They said the Nulls had told them to do this. The purpose was to preserve as much as was possible, ready for a time when the future would want to rediscover old knowledge, and that this would happen after the last star was extinguished."

Goosegirl had no idea what he was talking about.

"One day you may learn what's inside them all," Representative continued, "but for now we're interested in only one. This one."

They had halted at a box very similar to the one which contained the magazine, only smaller. The visitor opened the lid and removed a single laminate.

"The Last Words of the Last Heedful."

Goosegirl had never heard anyone speak like that, not even in the Gratitude. Breathy, reverent, filled with subdued anticipation. The man cleared his throat and read the written words aloud:

"The Nulls needed an answer. They came back home, here, the place they were at before becoming stars. The Heedful tried to give them their answer but failed; we didn't understand the question. They asked it of us so many times it plain wore us out, and now there's no more Heedful being born. The Nulls said this is because there's only so much energy left, and that's because the Nulls can't be stars no more. But they also said that one day a new Heedful will come along, and that was when they'd return. They told us we should take the new Heedful to the Plateau, where the Nulls will ask their question again. They figured this would be just before the last star died; one final chance. I'd like to be around to learn how this all turns out but I don't think I have enough time left to me. I wonder if I'll become a star? I guess I'll find out soon enough."

Representative had evidently reached the end of his recital. The Vault was silent once more. Goosegirl felt like everyone was focusing on her. Glancing around, she saw that they were.

"Why are you all looking at me?"

"Honey, you can see the Nulls," Momma said.

"You're the new Heedful," Great Grandma said.

"You're important," Gramps told her with evident pride.

"Because you can see the Nulls, we think the last star is about to die," Representative told her. "We think that's why they've returned. In all the world you are the only one who can see them, and now it's time for you to come with me, to the Plateau, just as the last Heedful wrote."

Goosegirl didn't know what to think. She noticed movement, a shimmering in the air; the Nulls were crowding into the Vault, through the walls, the rocky ceiling, the bedrock floor. She'd never seen so many in one place.

Is this real? Am I the new Heedful? What should I do? she asked.

Go to the Plateau. We will be there. We must be there, for when the last star dies. As must you.

But then what? What's this all about?

You will speak the answer.

What answer?

Go to the Plateau. We will be there.

Aloud she asked, "Now?"

"Now," Representative replied.

They were standing on the Plateau. The world around was flat, empty, absolutely still and very, very cold. Goosegirl shivered, despite her thick furs.

"It's time I left," Representative told her. "I must return to my own Family, to be with them when the last star dies."

Goosegirl shivered again. "What's going to happen? What am I supposed to do? Everything happened so fast. I'm... I'm scared."

"Are the Nulls here yet?" Representative asked.

She shook her head. "I don't see none."

The man put an arm round her shoulders, an encouraging squeeze. "You will be fine. This is a moment in time, a special moment, a moment just for you. Nobody can tell you what's going to happen; only that it's incredibly important you are here." He paused and smiled. "Maybe we'll meet again in a new future. Who can tell? And so, in contemplation of that possible event I shall say only this: farewell."

He turned and walked away.

At last she was alone, far from the Farm, where Manager kept everything ticking over; separated from her Family, without their gentle support. Just alone.

But not for long. The Nulls had come. All of them.

It's time, the assembly told her.

Time? For what?

For the last star to die. For you to answer the question.

What is the question?

Wait. It won't be long now?

What? But why me? I don't know everything. I don't hardly know anything! Somebody else should be here. Representative. Why don't you ask him? He knows lots more than me.

He cannot see us. He cannot hear us. Have patience. The star is nearly dead.

Goosegirl waited. Nothing happened. For ages nothing happened except she grew even colder. Then she noticed the light around her growing weaker, the bleak colors of winter less clear. Big Glow, muted as he was at that time of year, grew even dimmer. Slowly at first but then with quickening haste the last star waned and then... blinked out.

Everything is black. No, she corrects herself. Everything has lost color. And shape. Everything is still there, she is certain, only it can't be perceived.

Goosegirl can feel something solid beneath her feet. She turns, hesitantly, searching for something to hold on to, but there is nothing.

"Hello?" she calls out, hesitantly. No reply comes. She listens as intently as she can. She calls again. A realization dawns that she's actually making no sound at all. Should she feel frightened? Probably, but she doesn't. It's like, somehow, everything is the way it should be. She tries again, this time just with the secret voice she uses when speaking with the Nulls.

Hello? Are you there? At first there is nothing; then she hears the voice of the Nulls but far off, like they're speaking to her from one end of a stax-long pipe.

The last star has died, they say. Soon we will also cease to be. It's all up to you, now. You have to answer the question.

Yes, I know. But... what is the question?

Is there time?

Goosegirl ponders the enigmatic reply.

Is there time? she repeats. What's that supposed to mean?

There are only moments left. You must give the answer before the last of us is gone. Will you let our story end here? Hurry!

But how can I answer? I don't even understand the question!

Hurry! We are almost done!

A sense of panic begins to grow in Goosegirl's breast. Wait! What if I can't figure out the answer? What will happen?

Then there will be no tomorrow. There will be no yesterday. Our tale will end. You must provide the answer!

The panic is growing, so powerful that she is almost overwhelmed; but now, from nowhere, a memory of Great Grandma's voice comes clearly into her head, a reply to a little girl who is worrying that the two of them are going to be late getting home, that there won't be enough time for a bedtime story. Where they've been doesn't matter, and neither does the reason for their being late. What does matter is

Great Grandma's comfort: Don't you worry, little Goosegirl, you'll have your story. We'll always make time for a story.

A grain of understanding suddenly sparks in her conscious-ness, an idea germinates in her mind.

Oh! she gasps. Of course!

In her loudest and clearest voice Goosegirl declares her knowledge: "The answer is yes, there's always time for a story. We'll make some."

The last of the Nulls stands close. Goosegirl hears a long drawn sigh. She watches as his outer skin is shed, a single, whole, unfurling wrap. The husk that remains dissipates, spectral atoms drifting away like seeds on the wind, seeking fertile ground. No blood or gore: just star stuff. Goosegirl does not resist as the Null's mantle settles, envelopes her body: warm, nestling, nurturing.

I'm dressed in the skin of the lamb, she thinks. The universe has a new child to love.

In the void, a star bursts into being. Light returns, and the clock of Time begins to tick anew.

On the Farm, the Family was gathered around the table, enjoying the evening meal. Poppa, fork midway from the plate to his mouth, stopped eating. He put down the fork and looked up.

"Something's changed. Things feel... different, like... I don't know, like there's something missing – no, someone. But... We're all here, aren't we? Olders, Middlers, Momma, baby Varia. We're all here, just like always. Manager? What's going on?"

"Nothing to be concerned about," Manager told him. "Everything changes with time, you know. Finish your meal. Visitors are coming. They'll want to enter the Vault. It's time to start learning again."

About the Authors

Dev Agarwal is a science fiction and fantasy writer whose short fiction has appeared in various magazines. He contributes to the BSFA's *Focus* magazine and edits short fiction for Ireland's *Albedo One*. "Blight" arose through a combination of writing for a very specialised theme, a desire to dramatize the study of agriculture, and crucial advice received from a vegan about the single most important vegetable on the planet.

J E Bryant Comes from a theatre and journalistic background but currently works within the video games industry – and no, that doesn't mean he gets to play all day, more's the pity. He lives in Berkshire with his family and penned "Cellular Level" after the passing of Pinks creator and bee enthusiast Mark Trenear. For more information on his writing visit: www.drozbot.com

Kevin Burke has spent his working life in the fields of theatre and performance, working as actor, director, fight director, playwright, magician, fire-eater and jester... to name but a few. To date his writing has been confined to the theatre, his most recent offering being "The True and Terrible History of John 'Babbacombe' Lee" (2009), but he has relished this opportunity to stretch his wings and express himself in a completely different medium. "Wheat" won the recent NewCon Press/IAgrE flash fiction competition.

Alicia Cole, a writer and an educator, lives in Lawrenceville, GA, in the USA, with a photographer and their menagerie. Her short fiction has appeared or is forthcoming in *Demeter's Spicebox*, *Miscellanea: the Transdimensional Library*, Kazka Press' *At Year's End* anthology, and *Birkensnake 6: Neverending Tales*. She muses at three-magpies.livejournal.com.

Storm Constantine has written twenty-eight books, both fiction and non-fiction, and well over fifty short stories. Her writing spans literary fantasy, science fiction, and dark fantasy. She is best known for her Wraeththu trilogy. Storm is founder of the independent publishing house Immanion Press, created in order to get classic titles from established writers back in print and innovative new authors an audience. She lives in the Midlands with her husband, Jim, and five cats.

M Frost, a former dairy veterinarian, currently leads a Jekyll-and-Hyde lifestyle: research scientist by day and speculative writer by night. Her work has appeared in numerous venues, including *Strange Horizons*, *Quantum Muse*, and *Harrow*. Contact her at mfrostwords@gmail.com, or catch up on her news at http://mfrostwords.blogspot.com.

Nigel Edwards knows that the world began the day he was born because that's true for everyone; and that it began in Africa, which is where he was at the time. This is also true because archaeologists insist that's where humanity originated. Since then, Nigel has lived in Great Britain and worked in IT. In *The Last Star* he proposes that, maybe, we could all become celestial objects, which *has* to be better than burning down to dust or becoming worm food.

Sam Fleming lives near Aberdeen and has a BSc in Marine Science and an MSc in Environmental Diagnostics. She specialises in protection of the water environment, or at least the part of it that's wet and Scottish. In her spare time she writes about what it might be like on other worlds – some of them far away, some not far at all, and some not as far as we might like. "Electric Sheep" was inspired by the contrast between traditional farming and new technology in a changing natural and business environment.

Henry Gee is a writer and recovering palaeontologist who has worked for the international science magazine *Nature* for more than twenty-five years, where (among other things) he founded the award-winning 'Futures' series of SF short-shorts. He is the author of several short stories and two novels, *By The Sea* and *The Sigil*. His recreations include beachcombing, playing organ in a hard rock band, supporting Norwich City FC, and falling asleep. He lives in Cromer, Norfolk, with his family and numerous pets.

Darren Goosens' work has been published in a range of magazines over the years, including *Aurealis*, *Andromeda Spaceways*, *Interstellar Fiction* and *Accounts of Chemical Research*. Some of this was not fiction, he hopes. Darren hails from Australia and sporadically posts stuff to the obligatory-these-days blog, in his case: darrengoosens.wordpress.com.

Holly Ice is a student of creative writing at Staffordshire University. She is inspired by the unknown to create science fiction and fantasy stories. Previous work has been published by Indent, Almond Press and the H.G. Wells Festival. She is currently sculpting a fantasy novel and introducing two kittens to her Cotswold home.

Gareth D Jones works with hazardous waste, which has so far failed to mutate him into a superhero. He is a father of five who also writes stories and drinks lots of tea. To date his stories have appeared in forty publications and twenty-three languages.

Kim Lakin-Smith is the author of the gothic fantasy *Tourniquet; Tales from the Renegade City* and YA novella *Queen Rat*. Her story here, "Soul Food", is a direct precursor to her novel *Cyber Circus*, which was shortlisted for both the 2012 BSFA Best Novel Award and the British Fantasy Award for Best Novel. Her YA novel, *Autodrome*, is due out from Snowbooks later this year.

Terry Martin is the publishing-editor of award-winning short story magazine *Murky Depths*, which was responsible for showcasing talented writers and artists. His writing credits include columns in sports and genre magazines and his short story collection *Probably Maybe Perhaps* can be purchased on Kindle, Amazon or direct from www.murkydepths.com.

Den Patrick was born in Dorset and shares a birthday with Bram Stoker. He has at various times been a comics editor, burlesque reviewer, bookseller and Games Workshop staffer. Anything to avoid getting a real job, in fact. His first three books for Gollancz, *The War Manuals*, are released Autumn 2013. Three novels, *The Erebus Sequence*, are in the works. "Landward" was runner up in the recent NewCon Press/IAgrE flash fiction competition.

Rebecca J. Payne hails from Cambridgeshire, where she writes science fiction and attempts to brew her own real ale. "A Season" was inspired by the farmland of the fens and the poetry of John Clare.

Steven Pirie lives in Liverpool, UK, with his wife Ann and son James. His short fiction has been published worldwide. His two novels, *Digging Up Donald* and *Burying Brian*, were published by Immanion Press in 2004 and 2007, and again in 2010. Steve's website is at www.stevenpirie.com

Gill Shutt is the author of three YA books published by Greyhart Press, the most recent being *Alien Legends*. NewCon Press are very sad to report that Gill passed away while this book was in production. At the time, she was hard at work on a new anthology of stories and poems for Greyhart Press. Our thoughts go out to her family, and we hope that her story, included here, will act as fitting tribute.

Renee Stern lives in the Pacific Northwest and has nearly twenty years' experience writing news articles about fruit and vegetable production for American farmers. Her short fiction credits include *Beneath Ceaseless Skies*, *Black*

271

Gate, and the anthologies *Sails & Sorcery*, *Human Tales* and *Gears and Levers 3*.

Adrian Tchaikovsky was born in Lincolnshire, studied and trained in Reading, and now lives in Leeds. He is known for the *Shadows of the Apt* fantasy series starting with *Empire in Black and Gold* and currently up to volume 9, *War Master's Gate*. His hobbies include stage-fighting, and tabletop, live and online role-playing. More information is available at www.shadowsoftheapt.com

Jetse de Vries – @*shineanthology* on Twitter – is a technical specialist for a propulsion company by day, and a science fiction reader, editor and writer by night. He's also an avid bicyclist, total solar eclipse chaser, beer/wine/single malt aficionado, metalhead, and intelligent optimist. Sometimes, after fighting the good fight, he sleeps.

Kate Wilson is a physicist hiding amongst the engineers at the Australian Defence Force Academy. Her previous publications include scientific papers and a textbook called "Physics". She is now working on another textbook, which will probably also be called "Physics". This is her first (intentional) work of fiction.

Neal Wooten lives in Milwaukee, Wisconsin, USA. He is a columnist for *The Mountain Valley News*, cartoonist, artist, and stand-up comedian. He has written several award-winning novels and his work has appeared in countless newspapers and magazines. His novel *The Balance* will be released in the spring of 2014.